Bratva Beauty

Sabine Barclay

OLIVERHEBERBOOKS

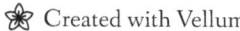

You can't please all the people all the time. At best, you can please some people some of the time. That means beauty truly is in the eye of the beholder.

Happy reading,
Sabine

Subscribe to Sabine's Newsletter

Subscribe to Sabine's bimonthly newsletter to receive exclusive insider perks.

Have you read *The Syndicate Wars*? This FREE origin story novella is available to all new subscribers to Sabine's monthly newsletter. Subscribe on her website.

The Ivankov Brotherhood

Do you also enjoy steamy Historical Romance? Discover Sabine's books written as Celeste Barclay.

Chapter One

Pasha

"Holy shit. I got pounded like a drunk college girl. I feel like I took that last one up the ass."

Who the hell is that? There may be three women approaching me, but only one of them has my attention. I'm supposed to be checking my tanks, not ogling a surfer. But fuck, she's hot. Fuck my tanks and gear. Where's she going?

"Nothing's gotten me this wet in months."

That isn't what I was expecting her to say, either. Raunchy sense of humor. I like it. Why do I want her to look at me so much? Because she's fucking hot.

"Pasha, you done?"

"What?"

I didn't even notice my brother walking over. I never don't notice things, especially people approaching me. Then again, I did notice her.

"Your tanks? Are you done? I'm headed to strip out of my

1

wetsuit and rinse off. Misha and Sergei are already at the showers."

"Yeah."

I heft my scuba gear and take it over to the cart where my brother and friends already put theirs. I watch this mystery woman stick her board in the sand next to her friends' and walk toward the very showers where Sergei and Misha are already stripping out of their wetsuits.

Damn. That ass. The things I'd do to it.

"Planning how to get that blonde's number?"

"Huh?" I glance at Anton. "No. Not that one."

"Really? I don't believe you. You're staring at her."

"Not her."

I walk away, ignoring my brother as though I'm in a trance. As I approach the hotel's outdoor showers, I lock eyes with Misha and jerk my head to the left. His brow furrows, but he moves down a shower. It leaves the one next to my dream girl open. She turns toward me just as I step onto the tiles. I reach back and unzip my wetsuit, peeling it down my arms like a striptease. I have her attention. Good.

Wait. Not good. She just turned to look at her friends. I glance down at myself, but there isn't anything wrong. It's not like my dick is hanging out. Shit. Did she notice that fast how hard I am?

"Pasha, catch."

I nearly don't look at Sergei fast enough as a bottle of shampoo sails toward me. I snatch it before it hits the woman. She must have sensed me and twirls around. The motion moves her bikini top dangerously close to her nipple. She tugs it back into place, much to my disappointment. I smile, and I get one in return. It crinkles the skin around her almond-shaped eyes, which are so dark, they're nearly black. They're only slightly lighter than her thick, black hair. Her bottom front two teeth are ever so slightly crooked, but it's her ruby red lips I'm more interested in. Women buy lipstick to match that color. There's no way she just surfed and came out of the water with lipstick in place. That's natural.

"Hi."

My voice practically cracks like a teenager. Her smile falters as she glances toward her friends, who're watching us.

"Hi."

She shifts away, allowing me to see past her. My eyes dart to her friends, and I dip my chin, but my attention is once again riveted to her. I need to look away before I freak her out. I pour shampoo onto my hand and pass the bottle to Anton. I scrub my hair, then lean back to wash the soap from me. I scrub my face, then wipe my eyes before opening them. I glance sideways and find all three women staring. But they're not just looking at me.

The four of us—Anton, Sergei, Misha, and I—are used to the stares. We're all six-and-a-half feet tall or thereabouts, and we're covered in tats. There are few people outside our world who would know what they mean, but we have several matching ones. The eight-point stars on Sergei's and Anton's upper right chests stand out the most on them, and they should. Anyone who knows the bratva would recognize their senior positions. Not everyone merits the marking.

My Madonna and child tat covers all of my left pec and half my ribs. It symbolizes my undying loyalty to my family and the Ivankov Bratva. My dark-haired beauty is looking at it. The other women are feasting on Anton, Misha, and Sergei. Anton and I share the same chestnut-brown hair and dark brown eyes we inherited from our father. Sergei and Misha have blond hair and blue eyes like their mother. We're all cut like bodybuilders. I know Misha's enjoying the attention, but Sergei and Anton couldn't care less.

"They like what they see."

Misha chuckles as he speaks Russian. I watch, and none of the women appear to understand.

"Stay away from the one next to me."

I look at my friend, the warning clear in my tone and my eyes. He shrugs.

"I figured you'd be vying for the blonde."

My brother said the same thing. Sure, she's beautiful. But in the same way plenty of beauty queens are attractive. There's nothing unique about her. It makes her unmemorable to me. I know why both Anton and Misha assumed she's the one I'm into. I don't date, and I rarely hook up now that I'm in my late-twenties. That ended after college. But she's the type of girl I used to go for. She's what I knew people expected me to go for —thin and aware of her good looks. People joke that I'm the pretty one in our family, the one who makes women melt. Maybe.

However, that assumption irks these days. I don't appreciate how superficial everyone thinks I am. I'm not the college jock thinking only with my dick. I grew up. Well, at least until I saw the beauty standing next to me. I'm definitely thinking with my dick right now.

"No. You want her? Go ahead and try."

"Maybe. The one next to you? Really?"

I narrow my eyes at Misha, my teeth clenched.

"She's pretty, but I just didn't think that's who you'd be into. She's not your type."

"When's the last time I went out with anyone for you to know what my type is? I don't approach women. They approach me. Doesn't mean they're my type."

I know my tone is getting testy. I turn off the shower and realize the women have already walked away. What the fuck? How am I so damn distracted thinking about her that I keep missing what's happening around me? That's the best way to get killed.

"I'm getting a drink."

I grab my board shorts from the cart, duck into the bathroom and change, before taking the wetsuit back to our stuff. I already spotted my mystery woman at the swim-up bar. The others can follow me if they want or not. I dive in across from the bar and swim underwater until I come up near the women. I know Misha followed me, and he appears at the stool next to the one I pick. It's two down from my fantasy.

"Sergei and Anton are going back to their room."

Misha's still speaking Russian, but he's looking around and whispering. We checked in as two sets of brothers, each with a room. But that's not the sleeping arrangement. I nod as the bartender walks over to the women. I listen to them order before the guy comes over to Misha and me.

"Vodka neat, and the Asian woman's drink is on my tab. Room 1026."

"Same. The vodka part."

The bartender nods and turns to make the women's drinks first. He walks over with their fruity beverages and places them in front of them.

"The gentleman over there bought yours, miss."

It's the brown-haired friend who leans forward and smiles coyly. I hadn't really noticed her, but she's as attractive as the blonde in the same sort of All-American kind of way. I flash a quick, and hopefully uninviting, smile. Anton and Misha assume I want the blonde. The brunette assumes I want her. Why the fuck can't anyone tell who I'm drooling over? Fuck this.

I slide over to the stool next to my fantasy and lean against the bar so I can look at her.

"I'm Pavel."

I rarely go by my given name, but it is how I introduce myself. I prefer Pasha because in English, Pavel and grovel are too similar. It was pointed out to me a few months after I moved to America. The guy's nose was never straight again.

"Hi."

She looks up at me, and I cock an eyebrow, waiting for her to introduce herself. Instead, she looks at her friends.

"I'm Tiffany."

Of course the blonde is.

"I'm Sarah."

I nod to the brunette again. I can tell Misha's watching and trying not to laugh. He knows how annoyed I'm getting. No one else can tell. No one else knows what I'm thinking or feeling unless I let them. But my family reads me like an open book. We're all the same. Anton, Misha, Sergei, and me. Throw in our cousins, Maksim, Aleksei, Nikolai, and Bogdan, and we look like an NFL first string determined to win the Super Bowl. Brooding is how my mother describes us.

"What's your name?"

I keep my voice soft and wait for my nameless beauty to answer. She looks a bit surprised.

"I'm Sumiko."

"Are you Japanese? You sound American."

We're in Anguilla. She could be from anywhere in the world.

"Yes. Sort of."

"Sort of?"

Now I'm intrigued.

"Japanese-Brazilian."

Is that why her ass is so juicy?

"Which half is which?"

She knows I'm checking her out. My eyes are roving over

her tits, belly, and thick thighs I want wrapped around my waist. The dirty things I would do with her.

"Both halves are Japanese, but my parents grew up in Brazil. I grew up in America."

"Your great-grandparents left after World War Two."

It's not a question, but it surprises her. She nods. We do plenty of business in Latin America, so I know my history. It pays to know who we're dealing with when we're running drugs and guns.

"You sound Russian, but you speak English like a native."

"I came to America when I was twelve. I speak Russian every day with my family, but I believe I grew up American. I go by Pasha."

As American as a Russian living in a Russian community and being part of the Russian mafia can be.

"Cool."

She doesn't seem to know what else to say. She's gone shy, which doesn't match the outgoing woman I saw walking out of the water or how she was with her friends a few minutes ago.

"If I'm intruding—"

"You're not. Thanks for the drink."

It's the brunette talking. She's resting her elbows on the bar and squeezing her tits together. There's no polite way to answer that. I turn to the bartender.

"Put the other two ladies on my tab, too." I look at Sumiko, whose drink is almost gone. She's been sipping it any chance she gets. "Would you like another? It's on me like the first one."

Her eyes widen as they meet mine. She glances down at her glass. She shifts on her stool, and my hand darts out to her lower back. I press against it, worried she's going to fall off. The moment I touch her, I'm done for. It's the softest skin I've ever felt. It's slick from the water and sunblock. I should let go, but I

7

can't. She doesn't shift away from me, so I take that as a good sign.

Her friends sit back, and I think they both got the message I'm only interested in Sumiko. It still annoys me that they assume they can get my attention when I'm pretty damn sure I've already made my interest clear. I don't think either Tiffany or Sarah realizes how insulting that is to Sumiko, and I get the feeling it's not the first time it's happened. Even Sumiko's body language said she assumed I was interested in one of them.

"Have you been here long?"

I want to keep the conversation going. If I don't, then I have no reason to linger, no reason to keep touching her. Well, I really don't have a reason to keep my hand on her back, but I want to.

"A week. We leave tomorrow."

"Same."

If we've both been here for a week, how haven't I noticed her? Before half an hour ago, I was always aware of everyone around me. It's the key to survival in my life. I glance at Misha. He gets my message. He wades over to Tiffany and Sarah and strikes up a conversation with them.

"Have you been surfing long?"

She perks up and smiles.

"Practically since I could walk. I grew up on a surfboard."

"Really?"

"Yeah. I'm from SoCal."

She sees my confusion and chuckles.

"Southern California. I lived ten miles from the beach. I was on my high school surf team and was on the water twice a day when I could be. Do you surf?"

"A little. Nothing like that. I was a diver in high school and college. Now I scuba and skin dive whenever I can. I live in New York, so not nearly as often as I want. Neither the

Hudson nor the Flushing River are anything you want your skin to touch."

"I know."

She offers nothing more than that.

"Sumiko, we gotta get going if we're going to make it to dinner on time."

"All right, Sarah. Let me finish my drink. I'll be ready on time."

"You can take it with you."

I force myself not to shoot her friend a dirty look. Sumiko sighs, but she lifts her glass in cheers to me. I clink my now empty glass against hers. We didn't even have time for her to accept my offer for a second drink. She slides off the stool, forcing me to finally move my hand.

"Thank you."

I watch her wade over to the steps, and I can't take my eyes off the way her bikini bottom sticks to her ass. I know she catches me watching as she looks back while peeling the material from her skin.

"There are six-hundred-thousand lakes in Siberia for you to take a dip in, and I don't think any of them are cold enough. You're lucky you didn't scare her off."

Misha cocks an eyebrow and glances below the water's surface. I look down. Sure as shit, my hard on is way too obvious. I turn back to the bar and order another vodka. My guess is I can be ready way faster than them. My dinner plans just changed to wherever they're going.

Chapter Two

Sumiko

"You have an admirer, Sumiko."

Tiffany nudges me in the elevator as we go up to our rooms.

"You should have given him your room number."

"I'm not fucking a guy I met ten minutes ago, Sarah."

But that is the reason we each have our own room. In case we meet someone and want to hook up, that is. I have never seen a hotter man than the one who just bought my daiquiri. He's fucking gorgeous. I noticed him as I walked past while he was kneeling in the sand. He was hot from a glance. I nearly jumped out of my skin when I turned and found him standing next to me at the showers. When he peeled off his wetsuit, I wanted to lick every inch of him. The way he did it...Is he a stripper? Because if he were, I would have climbed that pole.

"Maybe you'll see him again."

I shrug as I look at Sarah.

"Don't you want to?"

"So I can hook up with the hottest man I've ever seen for one night, Tiffany, then spend the rest of my life wishing I'd gotten more than just that. I'd rather not know what I'd be missing."

"Better to have loved and lost than to never have loved at all."

Tiffany nudges me again as the elevator doors open. He didn't even tell me his last name. I didn't tell him mine. I get vacation hook ups are no strings attached, but I usually know the guy's full name before I fuck him. But then again, there's an air of excitement to the semi-anonymity. I don't know that I really want to give him my last name. He's a stranger, after all. Since we both live in NYC, I don't need a stalker or some shit. Though...if it were him...

Whatever. I'm not the type that men stalk. I'm a fucking accountant. I'm an introvert. I can't wait to take my contacts out as soon as I get home from work and put my glasses on. Men who look like Pasha have no need to stalk women. They probably line up and wait for him.

"I'll be ready in thirty."

And that means forty-five when it comes from Tiffany. I have time to check emails and make sure I'm not falling too far behind on work.

"Give me your phone, Sumiko."

"What? Why?"

Tiffany sticks out her hand.

"Because you're going to work. We know you."

"I take fifteen minutes to get ready. What else am I supposed to do?"

"Watch TV or something."

Sarah plucks it from my hand, and I don't fight her. It's not worth it when they're on the same side. We go into our rooms, and I'm ready in twenty minutes. I know I have at least thirty before either of them will be done, since I'm pretty sure neither is in a rush. I could have stayed at the bar with Pasha, had another round, and still be ready before them. I call Sarah on the room phone and let her know that I'll wait for them in the lobby.

If I lie down to wait, I'll fall asleep. I'm not much of a drinker, so I'm not raiding the minibar. I'd rather people watch. I make sure I have my room key, my wallet, and my ChapStick in my clutch before I head downstairs.

It's like he's wearing a honing device. I spot Pasha immediately. He's standing with the guy from the pool bar. He's in a short sleeve navy shirt that hugs every muscle that was on display earlier. His dark beige pants are snug over an ass I could bounce a dime off. His black loafers look freshly polished. His dark hair is combed back and still wet. In a word, he's delicious.

I spotted him. What if he spots me? Do I go over there?

While I try to decide, two more guys that I recognize from the outside showers join them. The two blond guys look like twins. Pasha and the other dark-haired guy are practically mirror images of each other. The four of them standing together are like a fucking runway show waiting to happen. They're all smoking hot, but only Pasha keeps my attention.

When they turn toward the door, our eyes lock. He says something to the others before he walks toward me. My feet are moving me forward, but I have no idea what I'm going to say.

"Hi."

His voice rumbles as he keeps it low, as though we're sharing a secret. It's like a vibration that shoots straight to my pussy. I could tell myself earlier that it was the pool water that made me wet, but that's a lie. There's nothing to blame but him for how my panties are now drenched.

"Hi. I didn't realize how much you look alike earlier. The

guy with the brown hair has to be your brother. Are you twins?"

He chuckles.

"No. Anton is four years older than me. I'll have to tell him you asked. I tease him he's well preserved." He grows serious for a moment, then grins. "Unless I'm the one who looks prematurely old."

"None of you look old. Are the blond guys twins? They could be."

"No." He shakes his head, and a strand of hair falls over his forehead. God, how I want to brush it back. He runs his fingers through it and puts it back in place. Damn. "Misha is a year younger than me. Sergei is the same age as Anton."

"Are you all related?"

I can't believe I'm asking so many questions. When did I become a Chatty Kathy?

"Sort of. My uncle on my dad's side married their mom's sister."

What does the rest of that family look like? They might not be related by blood, but they're still connected. Are all the men that hot? Lucky wives and girlfriends.

"Have you known your friends long?"

It's his turn to ask questions.

"Yeah. Since college. We were all accounting majors, so we kept running into each other in class. We finally started hanging out after like the third or fourth one, and we've been thick as thieves ever since."

"That's nice that you remained close. Girls' trip?"

"Yeah. Tiffany's moving back home because her mom's sick. They live a few towns over from where I grew up, so I'll see her when I go back to visit my parents. But it's not likely Sarah will see her unless we plan more trips."

"Back to see your parents? You don't still live in SoCal?"

I laugh when he says that. It's as though he's trying the abbreviation on for size and isn't sure if he likes it.

"No. I live in New York too."

That's as much as I'm willing to admit to a stranger. He smiles, and I wait for him to say something about us living in the same city, but he doesn't. Maybe he isn't that interested after all. Maybe he's just friendly. Maybe I'm making an ass of myself.

"I don't want to make you keep your family waiting."

Is that disappointment in his eyes? It was so fast that it was like he let me see it for a flash, but now I don't know what he's thinking or feeling.

"I hope to see you around, Sumiko. Maybe you'll let me buy you that second drink."

"Thank you for that. I didn't realize—"

"I know. I wish it had been clear from the start."

"I—"

"Sumiko!"

Sarah has the worst timing. I turn toward my friends. She hands me my phone back and smiles up at Pasha. Did she just bat her eyelashes? What the fuck? It makes me retreat when I'm certain Pasha's going to turn his attention to her. She looks even better than she did at the pool. I'm unprepared for Pasha to lean forward, place his hand on my waist, and whisper in my ear.

"I'm only interested in you."

He steps back and turns around. I watch him in stunned silence as he joins his family. He looks back at me before he walks through the hotel doors.

"What'd he say?"

Tiffany's practically demanding to know.

"He said he's only interested in me."

I say it in a daze as I watch him disappear.

The nightclub is way too crowded with tourists from all over the world. I can only recognize half of the languages I hear. I'm working my way to the bar, and I'm wondering if we should just leave. We had a great dinner at a local fish restaurant, and I'm the one who suggested coming here, but now it doesn't seem like such a great idea.

Tiffany and Sarah snagged a table to stand at, and I'm the one practically elbowing my way forward. I have to stand sideways once I get to the bar as I squeeze between two guys who look at my tits, then turn away. When I'm finally able to turn and face the bar, a hard body presses against my back, and a hand goes to my waist. I stiffen.

"Another daiquiri, *malyshka?*"

I know that voice. I relax as I look over my shoulder. I didn't expect Pasha to still have his face beside my ear. Our lips are practically touching, and he's looking at them like he wishes for more than a taste. Our eyes meet, and I lift my chin. His hand slides around to rest on my belly. I suck it in.

"Don't hide from me, *malyshka*. I know what I want."

Pasha's other hand travels around my waist to rest on my belly, too. I exhale, but I'm uncomfortable. That is until I feel his cock against my ass.

"You didn't answer me."

I'm still looking at him. Each time he speaks, his mouth practically brushes mine. His breath is warm and mint flavored. There's an air of command when he talks, and it's thrilling.

"Yes, please."

"I'm only taking my eyes off you long enough to watch him make your drink."

"Watch him?"

"Yes. If I couldn't see what he's doing, I would suggest you get something out of a can or a bottle."

Pasha signals the bartender and orders my drink. I order two Stellas for my friends. We don't talk until he walks away.

"You think he'd spike it?"

"You're a beautiful woman in a full club in a foreign country."

"What does that mean?"

He glances at me, surprised by my question. I don't think he's sure if I'm serious.

"It means that there's probably a hundred guys in here wishing they were standing where I am, and at least half of them would drug you to fuck you."

His hold on me tightens, and it's possessive. But as my back presses against his broad chest, it feels protective, too.

"I was going to order three beers in bottles for that reason."

"Then why were you so surprised by what I said?"

"Because I don't think it has anything to do with looks so much as being a tourist."

The bartender places the drink in front of me. I reach for my purse, but Pasha shakes his head.

"Add eight vodkas."

I look to my left and spot the three other guys with Pasha. He releases one arm, so he can hand two drinks each to his brother and friends. They clink their glasses and exhale before taking the shot, seeming to savor it for a minute before swallowing. They down the first, then immediately down the second. None of them seem fazed in the least. I would be gagging.

"I've been drinking since I was eight. That was like two sips of water, *malyshka*."

That's the third time he's said that. It sounds like a term of endearment. He's still got one arm around me, and I can still feel how hard he is. I sip my drink as I watch them, but now that they're done, Pasha grabs the two bottles of beer. He lets go of me long enough to put money on the bar. I grab my drink as he slides his hand into mine. I look down before my gaze meets his.

He leads me back to the table, and it's clear he already knew where my friends were waiting. Their surprise is obvious. I look around, but Anton, Sergei, and Misha—those were their names, right?—didn't follow us. I notice them already on the dance floor. All three move with ease, as though someone trained them as dancers.

"Our mothers thought making us take ballroom dancing as children was a good idea. I'm surprised they didn't sign us up for the Bolshoi Ballet."

"I can't picture you in tights."

"That's why I'm grateful they didn't. Will you dance with me?"

I look at Tiffany and Sarah, who are watching us. I put my drink on the table and nod. His hand is still in mine as he maneuvers us through the crowd. Once we find a spot, he draws me against him, and I can feel him all over again.

"I can't help myself, *malyshka*."

I press my hips forward as we grind together.

"Then don't."

We look at each other for a moment before he lowers his head, and I lean in. Our lips meet, and everything falls away. The music suddenly seems distant. I no longer hear hundreds of voices trying to scream over each other. All I feel is his body pressed against mine, his hands resting at the top of my ass. I smell his woodsy cologne and taste a combination of mint and vodka. It's intoxicating. I hear his groan as my hand slides down to his ass. I can't believe what I'm doing in public. I've danced with plenty of guys, even grinded with them, but never have I grabbed a guy's ass in public.

He slides his thigh between mine, and I'm practically ready to come.

"The things I want to do to you, *malyshka.*"

Chapter Three

Pasha

She feels even better than I imagined. Did I insist we follow the women here? Yes. Is it completely stalkerish? Absolutely. Am I in tortured bliss with my thigh rubbing her pussy? One hundred percent.

I didn't have a choice about where we had dinner because we had business to conduct. We're on vacation, but that doesn't mean work completely disappears. Once Sumiko wasn't within reach, I came to my senses. I couldn't bail on dinner. A Jamaican grower eager to trade with us was willing to fly in. While we are bratva first and foremost, all of us have private business ventures. My cousins, Maks, Aleks, Niko, and Bogdan, are equal owners of Kutsenko Partners.

Misha and I are co-owners of Bear Imports. Not an extremely original name for two Russians, but only Anton and I are also Kutsenkos. We prefer not to have our family names branded on everything. We're a bit more discreet since our legal enterprises toe the line a lot more than our cousins' businesses do. We import pot and sell it where it's legal. It's made us both independently wealthy.

Sergei and Anton own a private security company that employs forensic hackers. Theirs is so buried in shell companies that no one can trace it back to them. It's best for everyone if no one knows the extent of their IT skills.

Once dinner was over, we decided to check out the nightlife. Do the other three know I was hoping to spot Sumiko? I didn't have to say a word. I got lucky and spied them leaving a restaurant across the street from ours. I followed Sumiko, and the others followed me.

Now I'm kissing her, and I want to strip her naked and taste her. All of her.

"I could do that all night."

I have to speak close to her ear to be sure she hears me. She reaches back and pushes one of my hands to cup her ass. She nods.

"I wouldn't stop you."

I squeeze, and I watch for when she flinches. I'll know when to stop and ease my hold. The moment doesn't come, and I'm gripping her ass tightly enough to hurt. Her chest is rising and falling faster, and her pupils are dilated. She dives in for a kiss that I let her start, but I cup her nape and hold her head in place. She stills as I take the lead, then she melts against me.

"Do you like that?"

She nods.

"I need to hear you, Sumiko."

"Yes."

Our eyes lock, and there's clarity in hers once more. My hand slides around to cup her jaw as my thumb sweeps over her cheekbone.

"Are you giving up control so I can take it? Is that what you want?"

"Yes, Pasha."

"I will not do anything you don't want, *malyshka*."

"I know. You've called me that five times. What does it mean?"

I wondered when she would ask. We'll see how much control she's willing to give up.

"Baby girl."

Her nostrils flare as she sucks in a breath.

"Is—is that a common Russian endearment?"

"No." At least not outside my family. I've heard Maks, Niko, and Bogdan call their wives that.

"Is it a common one for you?"

She's trying to figure out whether she's special.

"I've never called another woman that. Only you, *malyshka*."

"Why?"

I can't hear her, but I can read her lips. Lips I want to be kissing again.

"I don't know." I answer honestly. "It just feels right."

She nods. She's not sure what to make of this. I don't push the issue. I've already eased my hold on her, but as I swoop in for another kiss, both of my hands grip her firmly again to press her against my cock. The harder I hold on to her, the wilder her kiss becomes. I'm going to fucking jizz in my pants if I don't slow down.

"Do you like a little pain with your pleasure?"

"Yes."

"Can you guess how much I want to bare your ass and lay my hand across it before I spend all night fucking you?"

Her hand slides between us to cup my cock.

"I think I can guess."

She rubs her hand over me until I have to grab her wrist to keep from coming. We're kissing again, and I'm struggling not to drag her into the nearest restroom and fuck her. I will not do that. She deserves better than some disgusting public bath-room. But I want her enough that I'm tempted to drag her around back and fuck her against the wall. We continue to dance through three more songs, kissing most of the time. She's running her fingers through my hair as I nibble at her neck.

As she continues to ride my thigh as we move together, I can feel her miniskirt has hiked so far up her leg that she's about to flash everyone. A surge of possessiveness rushes through me, and I tug down it. She looks up at me in confusion before she reaches back to see how much of her is exposed.

"Shit."

She mutters as she pulls away and straightens her clothes. Her halter top has a plunging neckline, so she adjusts that. It would be so easy to brush the material aside and see her tits. I wonder what color her nipples are. I wonder what they'll taste like. I have every intention of finding out.

"Hey. We're ready to head back."

I look over her shoulder as Tiffany comes to stand behind her and taps her back. Sumiko lets go of me and turns toward her friend and nods. She glances back at me, and I see the regret. She doesn't want to leave yet, but neither is she sure she should stay.

"We'll walk you back. The three of you shouldn't be out this late alone."

"Alone? There's three of us."

Tiffany smirks until she sees I'm not smiling. Sumiko looks up at me again and nods. Something has shifted in her since her friend walked over. I don't know if she doesn't want our night to end, or if it's Tiffany. I get the feeling it's both.

"Misha, let's go. Get our brothers."

Misha's dancing with a girl a few feet away. He lets go of her with a wink and steps back. She looks around, baffled by what's happening. He says something I can't hear, then walks over to me.

"Meet us by the door. We're going to walk the girls back."

Misha nods and winds his way through the crowd to find Anton and Sergei, who have probably found a corner of their own somewhere. Tiffany and Sarah are drunk. They must have gotten more rounds while Sumiko and I danced. I realize it as I watch them walk toward the door. As we step outside, Sarah reaches down to her shoes.

"No. Sarah, you can't walk barefoot here. You're going to step on something and give yourself hepatitis."

Sumiko grabs her friend's hand and shakes her head. Sarah looks up, her eyes glazed. Making sure Sumiko and her friends get back to the hotel safely is one thing. Babysitting her drunk ass friend is another. Thankfully, Misha, Sergei, and Anton step out of the club a moment later.

"Where did you two go?"

Tiffany's looking at Anton and Sergei. Her expression says everything. She wouldn't mind a threesome with her in the middle. That shit will never happen. Never mind that neither has ever been with a woman. Neither has been with anyone other than each other. They opt to ignore Tiffany and fall into formation. Anton leads with the three women between me and Misha. Sergei is behind us. People move aside, not just because the sidewalk is narrow, but because we look like bodyguards surrounding famous clients. People aren't sure who we are, but all four of us are bodyguards at home.

When your cousins are the *pakhan* and the Elite Group of your bratva, then you become a bodyguard. Anton and Sergei have the senior most positions that aren't part of the Elite leadership. Misha and I guard Maks's twin infants, and we take turns guarding Niko's wife, Anastasia. Sergei guards Maks's wife, Laura, and Anton is usually with Bogdan's wife, Christina.

"You're rather intimidating."

Sumiko whispers as she looks up at me. I have my arm wrapped around her waist, and I draw her closer.

"Good. That's the goal."

"I think you're scaring Tiffany and Sarah."

"Am I scaring you?"

Sumiko shakes her head, and I repeat myself.

"Good. That's the goal."

We walk the five blocks back to the hotel, mostly in silence. Misha has to help Sarah stay upright for most of the walk, but Tiffany merely weaves a little. I can see my brother's profile, and he's hardly impressed. I glance back at Sergei a few times, and he grins. None of us would have let them walk back alone, but he knows I'm doing this for Sumiko's sake more than anything else.

"I'll go with them."

Misha speaks to me in Russian when we get to the hotel. I know he means he'll go with Sergei and Anton. I feel badly and shake my head. While they spend most nights together, they have to be careful every single one. I don't want to interrupt their time together on vacation. Traveling is the only time when they can usually justify sharing a room, since everyone believes they're best friends. They are and have been since we were all kids. It only became more in high school.

The elevator pings and opens on the seventh floor. Sumiko darts a glance at my relatives before she looks at me.

"Do you want to come?"

My wolfish grin makes her blush. I don't bother looking at anyone else as I follow her out of the elevator. I watch Tiffany and Sarah each head to a door before I stop behind Sumiko at a third one. I'm glad she has her own room. Once the door closes behind me, I snag her arm, spin her around, and pin her against the door.

"Tell me what you do and don't want. We stop when you say so."

"I want you."

"To do what, *malyshka?* Tell me, and I'll grant whatever wish you have tonight."

I watch her bite her lip, and I can't stop myself from prying it loose with my thumb, then replacing her teeth with mine. I nip and tug as her arms come around my neck. I push her skirt up to her waist and run my hands over the outside and inside of her thighs. I can feel the sticky moisture that coats the inside of her thighs. Then my hands are on her ass. Her smooth, bare ass. Finally.

"Fuck, Sumiko. I've been wanting to do this since you walked past me on the sand."

I step back and spin her around before dropping to my knee. I smatter kisses over each globe, kneading the flesh and squeezing until I see my fingerprints. I drag my teeth along her left cheek, and she pushes her hips back. I flick my tongue into the top of the division between each half. I wait to see what she does. She reaches back and presses against the back of my head. I snag her hand and pin it to her lower back. The other joins it, surprising me. When she crosses her wrists, I know all I need to. I bring my hand down on her right cheek, enjoying the sound and how the flesh bounces. I squeeze as hard as I did in the club. She pushes back into my hand. I alternate spanking her with squeezing. I keep gliding my teeth along her ass and flicking her crack with my tongue.

"Pasha."

She's begging. But for what?

"You have to tell me, *malyshka.*"

"More. Something. Anything. Just more."

"Do you want my fingers in you?"

"Yes."

It's a breathy answer, and it makes my cock twitch. I thrust two fingers into her, and she tightens her muscles around them, locking them inside her pussy.

"Do you want my tongue in you?"

"Yes."

That was a definite moan. I nudge her legs apart. My free hand stops smacking her and pulls her hips back until I can get my mouth on her clit. I lick and suck until I feel her trembling and getting close. I draw back, and she whimpers.

I stand and sweep her into my arms, making her squeak.

"You don't have to—"

"I want you in my arms."

I carry her to the armchair near the window and sit, arranging her to straddle me. I pull the pieces of material covering her tits out of the way. Her light brown nipples are hard, pointing straight at me. They're begging to be sucked, and I'm happy to oblige. As I go back and forth between them, I return my fingers to her cunt and work her as she rides them. My thumb rubs her clit until I feel her pussy tightening again. I pull back again.

"Pasha, please. I need to come."

"Then ask, *malyshka*. I think you know that."

Her eyes widen as she sits back onto my knees. My hands rest lightly on her thighs. When our gazes lock, she asks the question I expected.

"Are you a Dom?"

Chapter Four

Sumiko

"No, I'm not a Dom. But I like to be in control."

"Isn't that what a Dom does? Dominant."

"Yes. In and out of the bedroom. I am not interested in both."

"Only during sex."

"Yes. I spanked you, and it didn't seem to surprise you."

"Everything about you says you're in control of what's going on. You held me against you at the bar before you knew I would accept you. You assumed I would. You're rough, but I don't fear you hurting me if I gave you complete control."

"I would never intentionally hurt you, Sumiko. That's why I need to know what you do and don't want."

"But you also want me to beg, so you are in control."

"Ask at this point."

He waggles his eyebrows and winks. Fuck. He can do whatever the hell he wants. Pasha is a kind of hot that makes movie stars famous. There are millions of people in NYC and

27

billions in the world, but there are only a handful of men like Pasha. He and I do not exist on the same plane. It's not like hot guys don't approach me. I do more than fine. There are plenty of men—hot, ugly, and in between—who like women leaning toward plus-sized. My last boyfriend had a similar broodiness to Pasha and was just as ripped. But there is a quality to Pasha that only stresses how perfect his features are. His brother is practically his twin, but I don't have any reaction to Anton. Misha and Sergei are as hot as Anton, but they do nothing for me either.

"*Malyshka,* if you're not down with that, if you want strictly vanilla, then that's what we do."

"May I come, sir?"

I'm not prepared for him to surge out of the chair and carry me to the bed. He practically tosses me onto it and follows me down, but he doesn't press any of his weight on me. He's careful. I'm not dainty. I probably weigh closer to what Pasha does than either of my friends, even if I don't have an eighth of his muscle. He won't squash me, but I can tell he's aware of his strength and will always watch for my limits.

"I'm going to make you come all night, baby girl."

He reaches beneath me and unzips my skirt before tugging it down my legs. He grabs my thong and pulls that down, too.

"Take your top off. Push your tits together."

"Yes, sir."

He growls. He fucking growls as he shifts down the bed. He slides his shoulders beneath my thighs, kissing the inside of each before he attacks my pussy. He devours me. I'm glad I waxed before this trip. I did it for the sake of my bikinis, but I appreciate it more now. He eats me out like he hadn't had dinner tonight. When my fingers go into his hair and try to press his head closer, he snags my wrist and presses it against the mattress. He reaches his other hand up and tweaks my nipple. He pinches, then twists, and I come. Hard.

"Pasha!"

My back arches off the bed as my neck strains with my head tilted back. My fingers claw the bedding as he continues to suck my clit. Just when I think I'm going to come down from that intense high, his fingers thrust into me again. He finds my g-spot, and I'm writhing as I come again. It's almost too much, and I consider wiggling away from him. He knows. He can tell. He grips my hip and holds me in place. My thighs tighten around him as my hips rise to press against his mouth and fingers.

When my second orgasm subsides, he kisses the inside of my thighs again. He seems to like them despite them being my least favorite body part. He kisses the creases where my legs and hip meet before kissing my soft belly. He spends so much time there that I grow self-conscious.

"I know what I like, Sumiko. If you want me to stop because I make you uncomfortable, then I will. But I've never been this hard in my life. I want to taste and savor every part of you."

"How'd you know?"

"Because you're tense, and it's not the same as when you're coming."

He shifts, so he's hovering over me again. He licks the fingers that were inside me before resting on both forearms. His kisses are feather soft on my cheeks, the corners of my mouth, my temples. They're affectionate, and I'm completely unprepared for it. They're seductive as hell, but they're gentle, too.

"You keep asking what I want. What do you want, sir?"

His brow wrinkles.

"I don't think I like that as much as I did a moment ago."

"What don't you like? Me calling you sir?"

"Yes. It doesn't..."

"Fit right now?"

That's how I feel, at least. It doesn't seem right when he's not being as dominant.

"Yes."

"Pasha, what do you want?"

"To watch you come all night. To know I'm making you come."

"That's very altruistic. But it doesn't tell me if you want me to suck you off."

I can't believe I just said that. I am not that blunt with strangers. Then again, I usually am not naked and beneath a stranger in a hotel room. What the fuck am I doing? I don't do one-night stands, even on vacation. But the hell I'm turning down an opportunity with an Adonis like Pasha. Especially not now that I know what he can do with his tongue.

"I'm pretty certain you know I would want that."

I look down between us. That I'm naked, and he's fully clothed, doesn't escape me. He's been pleasuring me since the moment we walked in here. Actually, he's been doing it since the moment we stepped onto the dance floor. He hasn't tried to get me to do anything for or to him. I don't think I've ever been with a guy who's purely given. Even my last boyfriend, who could have been a porn star for how good he was in bed, was generous with his attention, but I always knew he expected me to reciprocate. I don't get that expectation from Pasha.

"I want to have sex with you, but I don't do one-night stands."

I can't believe I just said that. I didn't lie. I thought I could make an exception because I'm really horny for him, but I'll break my own heart if I have sex with him, and it's as amazing as I bet it would be. I'll be miserable wishing I could see him again after this.

"Then we stick with what we've done so far."

"You don't want to spend all night finger fucking me and eating me out."

I shoot him a look that says I know he can't be serious.

"I know exactly what I want, *malyshka*. I will gladly spend all night between your thighs with my tongue in your pussy. Do not argue with me, or I will give you a real spanking."

"But I'm sure—"

I squeak again as he pulls back and brings me with him. I'm unprepared to find myself going over his lap.

"I warned you. Do you consent?"

"To a spanking?"

"Yes. It's one thing to do it while we're fucking. But this is a different type of control, Sumiko. You know that. I won't lay a hand on you as a punishment if you don't consent."

"I consent, sir."

It seems like the right time again for that title. It must be because his hand rains down five stinging slaps across my ass. I don't know how his hand can cover so much of it since it's not exactly small. Both hands squeeze my ass after the last smack.

"Fuck, your ass is perfect. I'm partial to your tits, too."

"Are you always an ass man?"

"No."

"Tits?"

Pasha eases me to sit up and positions me on his lap. His fingers tunnel into my hair as he kisses me.

"I don't do hook ups. I haven't in years. I'm not one or the other."

"Wait—are you—with someone? Involved? Like—fuck. Do you have a girlfriend or a wife?"

"Shh. No. I don't have either. I haven't dated anyone in a long time. And I'm over doing random hookups."

"A fuck buddy?"

He laughs, and it's that rumble again.

"There are women I see occasionally that I've been with off and on for years. But I don't make late night booty calls if that's what you're wondering. We contact each other when the mood strikes. Do you have a boyfriend? A husband?"

"I wouldn't be naked, on your lap if I had either."

"Good."

"Do you not want me to touch you?"

The thought suddenly crosses my mind, and I see his shock as soon as I say it.

"Of course I want you to touch me. I practically came in the club when you rubbed my cock."

"You're still completely dressed, and you haven't said that you want anything."

He puts me on my feet and stands.

"If you help me undress, it'll go faster."

He starts unbuttoning his shirt as I loosen his belt, then unbutton and unzip his pants. I kicked my shoes off just before he sat in the armchair. He bends down and pulls off his socks as he steps out of his shoes, then his pants. My eyes sweep over him. Every chiseled inch. Tats cover his arms and shoulders. It's the same with his chest and back. I noticed them earlier, but I didn't pay close attention. The details on all of them are intricate and clean. He has a fortune in ink on him.

Normally, I'm not into tats. But my last boyfriend had plenty, so I've gotten used to them. Part of me wishes Pasha had none. It seems wrong to mar such perfection. But they add to his aura of hot and dangerous. That's what I realized was part of it. The way people moved out of his way as we walked back to the hotel. They did it for the other three guys, too. There's an air of danger, of constrained strength, waiting to burst free. It's so counter to how gentle he was with me a few minutes ago.

I lower myself to my knees and place my hands at the small

of my back, my wrists overlapping. I keep my gaze down as I wait for him. His cock is even with my mouth, and I'm forcing myself not to lick him. It's so tempting. I don't mind blow jobs. They're definitely not a favorite, but I think I'm pretty good at them. I want to feel him against my tongue.

"Stroke me, *malyshka*."

It's a quiet command that I don't mistake for a request. My right hand wraps around him.

"Can I lick you, sir?"

"Fuck, yes. Whatever you want, Sumiko. Fuck. That feels good."

He looks down and watches me as I run my tongue along the length of his cock before taking him in my mouth. I bob my head as I work him. He's too long for me to take all of him. Even when I relax and let him slide along my throat, it's too much. It's like trying to swallow a Coke bottle. He has length and girth. I'm reconsidering my no sex decision.

"Get up."

I shake my head and suck harder. His hand fists my hair and tugs. His other hand rests at the base of my throat. He pulls free and lifts me onto the bed. He presses me to lie down as he strokes himself. We watch as his cum splatters my chest and belly. I cry out as his free hand slaps my pussy before three fingers enter me. He finger bangs me as his thumb works my clit. I'm over stimulated within seconds.

"If you come without permission, I will spank you again and edge you all night."

"Please, may I come?"

"No."

It's another growl. I'm shaking and trying to push myself away from his hand.

"Sir, I can't not come if you keep touching me."

"I know."

"Are you trying to make me fail? You can edge me regardless. Please, just let me come."

"Come."

That's all it takes for me to erupt. He can do whatever he wants with me tonight. He's like a drug that only takes one hit to become addicted. What am I going to do when my stash runs out?

Chapter Five

Pasha

Shooting my load across Sumiko's tits and belly was entirely territorial. Possessive. It's like I'm marking her as mine. She's not. And rationally, I know that. But never have I felt this about a woman. About anything. With a brother and four cousins, plus Sergei and Misha, I've never been possessive of my belongings. We've always shared without reservation, and I've never minded that. Even with women I dated in college or girls in high school, I wasn't possessive. To where some doubted how I felt about them. They were right to do so. The depths of my feelings were always shallow because I knew I couldn't bring them into my world.

"Come with me."

I reach out my hand and draw Sumiko off the bed and lead her into the bathroom. I turn on the shower and wait for it to warm as I kiss her neck and jaw. I can't get enough of touching her. When the water's ready, we step in together. I grab the bar of soap and lather it between my hands. I run it and my hands over her chest and belly, washing away the evidence of my desire. Even though nothing of mine brands her anymore, the mere fact that I'm the one washing her, doing something so intimate, feeds this unexpected possessiveness. My hands travel over her shoulders and back until they're back where they belong.

Our bodies press together, the soap making them slick. Her hands explore everything she can reach until they return to my ass, just like in the club. I'm hard again, and her pussy is so close. The temptation makes my balls ache.

"What do you want next, baby girl?"

I see her hesitation. Her mind is warring between what she wants and what she believes is right. I lift her, and she wraps her legs around my waist. I press her against the wall and rock my cock between us.

"If you want me inside you, put me there. If you want me there but not bareback, then we get out of the shower. If you don't want either of those, then my mouth gets another feast."

"I want you inside me. It aches like a fucking burn to know what you feel like, but I don't have random sex. I'm so—"

"Do not finish that sentence. There is nothing to be sorry for, Sumiko. If that's your limit, then that's your limit. I won't coerce you or force you."

"I just don't want it..."

"Don't want what? For it to be one time and the best sex of our lives, then never get it again?"

"Something like that."

"You're wise because I don't know that I could live with only one memory."

It's the truth. I want to fuck her into next week, but part of me doesn't want to regret taking a bite of the sweetest fruit, never to taste it again. That would be worse than any torture I've inflicted on someone.

I move her along my cock, pressing against her clit with each thrust. I hold her with one arm under her ass as my free hand lifts her right tit with its perky nipple to my mouth. I flick and tease it until she's covering my hand and offering it to me.

"Please, sir. Suck it."

I wrap my mouth around her nipple and tug as I suck. I switch arms that hold her and tweak the other nipple. I pinch until it must hurt. It only makes her move faster as she squeezes her thighs to ride my dick, that wants to be inside her more than anything.

"You're going to make me come again, *malyshka*. Then I will just have to wash you off all over again."

"Yes...I want to make you come...I want your cum on me again."

I set a rough pace, even though we're not actually having sex. We're moving together, and I'm working her clit until she screams. I hope everyone on this fucking floor hears and knows someone's getting a good fucking. I erupt as we both look down to watch my cum shoot onto our bellies. She rests her head against my shoulder, breathless. I continue to support her with one arm as I hurry to run the soap over us. She rounds her back enough to let my hand between us and then for the water to rinse us clean.

"You're really strong."

My brow furrows. Doesn't my build make that obvious?

"I mean, you're holding me with one arm again. I'm not exactly made of air."

"You're made just right. And I hadn't thought about it."

I hadn't.

I grab a towel that I drape over her back until I step out of the shower. I lower her to the floor and rub her dry before I quickly run the towel over me, too. I fling it over the towel rack and lead her back toward the bed.

"Slide in, baby girl."

We go back and forth for hours, pleasuring each other until neither of us can last. It's nearly four in the morning before I wrap my arms around her and press her cheek against my chest. I'm not a monk, but I haven't had sex in months. I can't remember the last time I fell asleep with a woman curled next to me. The women I see usually fall asleep on their own side of the bed, or one of us is going home before we fall asleep. Sumiko could be Goldilocks. She feels just right.

When I woke up, I worried it would be awkward with Sumiko. She was still asleep when I opened my eyes. It took me a moment to realize where I was since I'm so unused to sharing a bed. I laid there and enjoyed the peacefulness. A wave of affection rolled over me for at least the tenth time since meeting her. I never thought I was affectionate by nature. I mean, I am with Maks's twins, but who doesn't love kissing babies and making them giggle? Even mafiosos can have a soft spot for kids. But the women I dated in college complained I wasn't affectionate enough, not in private or public. It was usually what broke us up. What they believed—rightly—was indifference.

But it wasn't uncomfortable when she stretched and looked up at me. Just the opposite. I rolled her onto her back, and we went another two rounds of her giving me a hand job and me fingering her. When I could no longer delay, I dragged myself out of bed and got dressed. She reached for a t-shirt on the dresser, but I tossed it onto the bed. I didn't want her dressed when we said our final goodbye. I looked back when I got to the door, soaking in every memory.

Now I'm getting off the plane in New York, and I'm back to reality. We landed at JFK rather than the private airfield we prefer. Foul weather forced us to reroute to a larger runway. The upside is we don't have to enter the terminal. It's raining, and we have to make a dash for the SUVs waiting for us, but there's no crowd or baggage claim to deal with. A customs official already came on board. Even if we had anything to declare, we wouldn't. It's never the type of Duty Free most people bring back.

I look out the rear passenger SUV window as a plane taxis to the gate. It makes me wonder if Sumiko has arrived yet. She said she and her friends were leaving today. I looked for them in the lobby as we left, but I didn't see her. It tempted me to bribe the front desk clerk to give me her contact info, but that's too much. Especially when I can have Anton or Sergei look it up. Sergei heads our intelligence branch. They're known as the two spies, the *sovietnik* and the *obshchak*. Anton, as the *obshchak,* is our head enforcer. He plans and carries out any of our major operations. He's a strategic genius and can track anyone, and Sergei can hack anything. Between the two, no one out maneuvers us.

"Thinking about your lovely lady?"

I look over at Misha, and I want to wipe the shit-eating grin from his face. He's right, obviously. But I don't need it pointed out.

"Yeah. All I know is she lives here in the city. I didn't want to scare her off by asking where. But I want to know. I want to find her."

"You said you didn't have sex. Was everything else really that good?"

I glare at him now. I returned to my hotel room to find Misha already packed and ready. He didn't ask, but I knew he was curious. I told him we hooked up but didn't have sex. He knows better than to ask for anything specific. I don't want to divulge anything else more personal.

"Yeah. I don't know. There's something about her. It's not just looks. There's something about her personality that intrigues me. She can be assertive when she wants something, but she wanted things the same way I did."

I give him a pointed look. She let me know she wanted to submit. I spanked her a few more times after we got out of the shower, and she begged for more.

"But she's also got a tendency toward being shy when she's unsure of the situation."

"Not a whole lot of time for talking?"

"No. And like I said, I didn't want to scare her off by seeming too nosey."

"If you don't know her last name, and you don't know what she does, and you don't know where she lives, then what're you going to do?"

"I don't know. She mentioned she majored in accounting."

"Speaking of accounting, we need to interview new ones. Niko texted me this morning. They tracked the missing money back to Andre. I told them he'd been skimming. Unless you want the job, Pasha."

I look at Sergei as he fills us in. Vacation's over, and we haven't even left the airport. Reality bites. We like to keep our bratva business within our bratva community, but for our legit businesses, we look for Russian companies that can use the opportunities for rich clients. No one ever guesses what the men in my family studied in college. Most don't believe any of us went to college. Maks and Aleks couldn't because they were already entrenched and rising within the ranks. But the rest of us did.

Anton and Sergei went to UPenn on athletic scholarships and studied computer science. Niko and Bogdan went to NYU and studied finance. Misha went to Fordham and got a degree in entrepreneurship. I went to Columbia and majored in accounting. I knew I had that in common with Sumiko, but I didn't think either of us wanted to discuss anything work related. My role in the Support Group under Anton usually keeps me away from an adding machine, but I'm a CPA. When I'm not guarding members of my family or supervising our criminal activities, I handle the numbers for our imports and exports that could get us all locked up for life. There's some intricate bookkeeping needed when you handle millions of dollars of product coming from all parts of the world and going to people who won't think twice about a bullet between your eyes if you're off by a penny.

"I don't have time to handle the legitimate businesses, and I don't want to draw attention to myself. I don't need people knowing I'm an accountant, or they might guess I know more about our illegal businesses than I want them to. I can manage things until we find someone, but this isn't permanent."

"You did the interviews the last time. Will you do them again?"

"You trust me to pick someone, Anton? Look at what the last guy did."

"Salvatore got to him."

The Italian don, Salvatore Mancinelli, is a pain in the fucking ass. We're on decent terms with him one moment, and then it all goes to shit the next. But things have been pretty quiet with him for the last three months. None of us are over what his nephews did to Niko's wife, Anastasia. We're still gunning for blood, so it surprises me that Salvatore is poking into our businesses right now.

"Doesn't Christina want to handle it? Andre did the accounting for the construction division. She heads it."

Bogdan's wife, Christina, worked for the city planner before Kutsenko Partners poached her. She trained as an architect and has a master's in construction management. She's cut expenses in half and doubled the speed of building completion. I know she's impressed everyone.

"She asked for you, Pasha. She trusts you to know what to ask and what to look for. She'll be there, but she wants you to lead."

Sergei hands me his phone, and I read the text thread. He'll handle the background check for anyone we consider. I don't know how he found his way into the FBI and DOJ records, but he can find a speck of dirt on anyone if it exists.

"Is tomorrow soon enough?"

"Need a nap?"

"Shut up, Anton. Yes, I do."

"I'll ask."

I watch Sergei type another text. A moment later, he nods. I go back to looking out the window as we approach my building in Manhattan. I don't own a penthouse like Maks, Bogdan, Niko, or Aleks. But I do more than good enough. I have a top floor, three thousand square foot loft in one of the most desirable buildings in town.

"Anton, are you guarding Christina tomorrow? I'm going to text her and see if someone's coming to her or if we're going to them." My brother nods. "I'll let you know what time. I'll meet you at their place."

I could walk to the penthouse Bogdan owns, but he and Christina are rarely there. They prefer their house in Queens near my aunt. Maks and Laura have a place around the corner, and it's near the house Niko and Anastasia bought a few months ago. We all left Queens as soon as we could afford to leave our parents' homes, and nearly half of us have moved back. Anton and Sergei will always keep their places in Manhattan. It works for them. But who knows about Misha, Aleks, and me? We're the only bachelors left.

With only a couple hours of sleep last night, I'm ready to

crash. I make a beeline for my bedroom and drop my luggage before stripping off my clothes. As I step into the shower, I look over my shoulder at the mirror. I can see the red marks from Sumiko's nails. I left love bites where no one but she will see them. I normally hate women trying to mark me, and I rarely care enough to mark them. But I wanted to leave her something to remember me by, and I'm glad she did the same.

It's barely been twelve hours since I left her hotel room, and I'm already missing the feel of her pressed against me, the taste of her skin, and the whimpers she makes when she needs to come. I didn't need a hard on the entire flight, so I made myself think about anything else. But I'm alone finally, and I've got a cockstand that could pitch a fucking tent. I close my eyes, and I can see her clearly as I stroke myself. It's a good thing I'm alone because I finish in an embarrassingly record time.

How hard can it be to find a Japanese-Brazilian American accountant from SoCal in a city of eight-and-a-half million people?

Chapter Six

Sumiko

It's raining. A wonderful welcome home to New York after the perfect weather in the Caribbean. The water is splashing the tiny window next to me as I squint through it. As we approach the gate, I watch the stairs unfold and lower on a private jet. I press my nose to the plastic window as I try to see past the raindrops.

I know that walk already. The confidence. The determination. I know that chestnut hair I spent all night touching. I can't see the tattoos clearly from such a distance, but I know what's on the bare arms I can see.

I reach back and tap Sarah's arm before I move out of the way and point.

"They're getting off a private jet. How fucking rich are they?"

Anyone could tell from their clothes, their shoes, and their watches that Pasha and his friends are wealthy. There's an aura of money that surrounds them that only rich people have. But I never imagined they were private jet kind of rich. Somehow, I don't think it's rented either.

I lean forward again and watch Pasha climb into a black SUV that's just pulled up to meet them. Misha, then Sergei, then Anton follow him. A car service on the tarmac. I don't even begin to know how someone arranges that kind of luxury. Then the SUV is gone, and the jet is taxiing away to wherever it's going. A private hangar or something. I doubt it's parking between the 747s.

"Hey. Earth to Sumiko. Come on."

I look over and notice it's almost our turn to get out of our seats. I gather my stuff and shove it back into my hand luggage. I thank the guy who gets my wheely bag out of the overhead bin. I'm the only one of the three of us who packed light. How much space do you need when you spend seven days in a bikini? My friends like options. I like not going to baggage claim. When we get down the escalator, we say our goodbyes. I'm headed to Harlem while Sarah and Tiffany are going to Staten Island. The light luggage makes it easy to take the subway. No chauffeured, tinted window car service for me.

I hop in the shower after having something quick to eat. As I run the loofa over me, I notice the hickeys Pasha left on my breasts and belly. I think about each one and how they got there. If I weren't in the shower, I'd be in a hot sweat by now. Fuck. I didn't even have sex with him, and I'm ruined for any other guy. The things he can do with his tongue. He'd be an Olympic gold medalist if it were a sport. It doesn't take my vibrator long to get me off once I'm in bed. I'm out for the night, and the sun hasn't even set.

I know that voice. It's been whispering in my head for the past week. This isn't the time or the place for me to run into Pasha. Not while I'm on a date with someone else. Fuck my life.

I agreed to this date because Sarah's been swearing up and down that this guy from her office is perfect. I've met him a couple times at work events, but I was never super impressed. I said yes, more to get her off my case than anything else. I know she thinks she's helping distract me from Pasha, but I've been comparing the poor guy for the last thirty minutes, and he's falling short in every way.

I look in Pasha's direction in time to see Anton point to me. He waves, and Pasha spins around in his chair. He's out of his seat before I take my next step. He weaves around the tables as I continue to follow the hostess to my table. With my date. Fuck me.

"Sumiko."

"Pasha."

We stare at each other for a moment before we both snap back to reality. I glance at my date, who is looking between us. He appears annoyed, but he's been that way since he picked me up. I've been trying to figure out how to Uber home instead of being stuck with him in the car again. Unless something drastically changes, we have not hit it off. Especially not now that I'm standing in front of Pasha.

"I'm Steven Wagman."

My date thrusts his hand forward and nearly pushes me out of the way. Pasha narrows his eyes before he looks down at Steven's outstretched hand. He takes it, and I can tell Steven is trying not to wince.

"Pavel Kutsenko. Nice to meet you. Sumiko, it's nice to see you again."

Kutsenko. The name sounds familiar, but I can't place it.

"Funny running into you here."

I flash him a smile before I wave to Anton. I don't know who the other man is sitting at the table, but he looks remarkably like Anton and Pasha.

"That's our cousin, Aleksei."

"Cousin? You could be triplets."

Steven speaks just as I'm about to excuse us. I want to extract us from this awkward situation, but Steven seems to want to make small talk. It's obvious we're on a date. My dress, my makeup, the restaurant. Pasha is watching me, but I can't tell what he's thinking. I have no reason to, but I feel guilty. Like I've been caught betraying him. I never imagined I would see him again.

"Yeah. Strong family resemblance."

I look back at the table and notice Pasha's cousin has brilliant blue eyes, but they're almost chilling. They're the same as Misha's and Sergei's.

"How does your cousin look so much like you and Anton, but just like Sergei and Misha, too?"

I blurt out the question and wish I could suck it back in. Now I'm the one keeping the conversation going.

"Strong family genetics. Aleks is often confused for Maks, Niko, or Bogdan."

I nod and realize the hostess is still standing near us. Shit. I forgot about her. She looks seriously peeved.

"Sorry." I offer a smile before I turn back to Pasha. "It was nice seeing you again."

"You, too."

He steps back, and Steven and I continue to follow the hostess. She seats us at a table where I have a clear view of the back of Pasha's head. Anton watches me, and now Aleks is too. I try to focus on the menu and not make my interest any more obvious to Steven.

"Who was that?"

"I met him and his brother on vacation last week."

"Ah. Vacay hook up."

"No."

He was so much more than that, even if that's all he was.

"Isn't that why you and Sarah went on that vacation? A little foreign fling? That's what you do on a girls' trip, right?"

I frown. Gross.

"No. Neither Sarah nor I had a fling. We surfed a lot. Our friend, Tiffany, was there with us too."

Sure. We got separate rooms in case we wanted a fling. Sure. I brought Pasha back to mine and hooked up with him. But there's something in Steven's tone that grates. He's looking at me differently than when he picked me up. It's more speculative. Does he think he's getting lucky tonight? He'll be lucky if I don't order an Uber and slip out the back door. Maybe he isn't a bad guy, but the vibe is off. What was Sarah thinking?

"Do you like to travel to exotic locales?"

"Yes. I enjoy traveling, and I've been all over the Caribbean. What about you?"

"Thailand, Cambodia, Myanmar, and India are favorites. Japan's cool too. And Mexico's close. I wonder if your friend knows good places to visit in Russia."

He can't be serious. I cannot—he cannot mean what I think he does. Those are all top sex trafficking and forced prostitution countries. Is he saying he travels to pay for sex?

"You're Japanese-Brazilian. What's Brazil like? Nude beaches and Carnival are all I know about it. Gisele Bündchen is Brazilian. Do most women look like her?"

"No."

He can tell I'm at least part Japanese. Does he not realize I look nothing like the supermodel? Most women look nothing like supermodels.

"Is Carnival like Mardi Gras?"

"Yes. They celebrate the same thing."

"No. I mean, with the beads and everything. Do women flash for them?"

"I've never been to Brazil during Carnival. My parents are both Japanese but born and raised in Brazil. I was born here."

"Oh."

He sounds disappointed. Did he think I have some feather costume hiding in my closet at home with six-inch heels and fishnets?

"Where are you from?"

Let's see if we can steer the conversation away from me and the lands of freaky-deaky.

"Rhode Island."

"I've been to Providence and Newport I liked both."

"Yeah. I'm not from the rich parts."

Okay then. Just making an observation. Jeez.

"What type of accounting do you do?"

"The boring kind. Have you ever been to Asia?"

"I've been to Japan many times."

He leans forward as he puts his menu down.

"Where are the hot spots to go?"

Are we back to this? He finds out I went on a vacation with two friends, and now all he wants to talk about are places known for sex. I glance over at Pasha and notice he's watching me. He shifted his chair, so he could see without making it too obvious. But our eyes meet. He raises his brow. I want to shake my head, but I can't.

"I'm going to wash my hands. Just water for me when the waitress comes. Excuse me."

I grab my purse and make a beeline for the restrooms. The door's barely closed behind me before it opens again. I see Pasha in the mirror. He glances toward the stalls. All the doors are open, so he reaches behind him and flicks the lock. I turn around, and his hands are in my hair, and he presses his lips to mine. He backs me up until I bump into the sink. He hoists me onto the counter and slips his hand up my skirt.

"You're wet, *malyshka*. Enjoying your date?"

"No. Not in the least. You know you did this."

He pulls his hand free and licks his fingers.

"Mmm. Dessert before my main course."

I'd like to be his main course. I'd be his appetizers and desserts too if I could.

He's sliding his fingers into me, and I moan. I noticed the other night that he loved it when I did that. He's working me harder and faster with each sound. He still likes it.

"Baby girl, you're hotter than I remembered. And I remember everything from the moment I saw you until the moment I left your room."

"You've been thinking of me?"

"Driving myself crazy thinking about you.

"Me too...Uh, Pasha...Please, sir. May I come?"

"Yes, *malyshka*."

He squats and pushes my legs back. His tongue flicks my clit before he latches onto it and sucks. I explode. I grip the counter as my pussy spasms. I squeeze my eyes shut to keep from screaming. I moan as my orgasm draws out. The moment I come back down to Earth, I hop off the counter and reach for his zipper.

"You don't have to."

"I know I don't, Pasha. All the more reason I want to."

"Not tonight, *malyshka*. I let the need to touch you get the better of me. I was going to wait in the hallway and ask you on a date. I followed an impulse, and I'm glad I did. But I didn't come in here to fuck you."

"A date?"

"Yeah. Hopefully, a way better one than the one you're on now."

"I said I wanted to wash my hands. I came in here to hide for a moment. I was going to go back out there and tell him I got a call and need to leave. I was going to have an Uber on the way."

"No Uber. I have a driver who can take you wherever you want to go. I'd go with you, but we're waiting for a client to join us. I can't leave."

"Thank you."

"I'll walk you out if you want."

"No. He's—" I sigh. "He'll assume we're fucking. He already asked if I hooked up with you. He works with Sarah. Walking out is going to be bad enough. I can't look like I'm leaving with someone else."

"He asked that?"

I watch Pasha stiffen as he looks at the door through the mirror. That aura of danger just amplified and ripples in the air.

"He wondered if my friends and I had vacation flings."

"What else did he say, Sumiko?"

His tone tells me I better not prevaricate. But I'm sorta scared for Steven if I tell Pasha the truth. He's not the type of man who'll laugh off Steven's questions. He'll see them as an insult.

"Sumiko, what did he say?"

"He mentioned some places he likes to travel, and he asked about Brazil."

"You're being evasive."

Damn. I thought I was downplaying it. His hand tunnels into my hair and holds my head in place. His eyes pierce me, and I can't look away. It's like he's captivated me, and I'm ready to confess all my innermost thoughts. When he tugs, it's not enough to hurt, but it reminds me he's back in control.

"He said he likes Thailand, Myanmar, Japan, and Cambodia. He asked about Carnival in Brazil. He wondered if you might know some good places in Russia."

"Motherfucker."

I barely hear Pasha, but I know what he said. He's pissed. I can't tell from his tone or even his expression. It's not even the way he's holding me. I can just sense it. I don't think anyone else could tell just from looking at him.

"I'm already leaving, Pasha. It's not a big deal."

"Yes, it is. He insulted you enough that you're leaving before you even ordered. Come with me. I'm walking you to the car."

"Pa—"

The look he shoots me tells me I can argue until I'm blue in the face, but it won't do me any good. Rather than feeling controlled, it excites me. It's like having a knight in shining armor ride in on his pure white steed. He's coming to my defense, and it lifts a weight off me I'd felt settling there ever since Steven picked me up.

He leads me out of the bathroom and to the table where Steven's waiting. He's clearly confused since Pasha is holding my hand.

"I thought you said you didn't hook up."

"We didn't."

Pasha surprises me, but at least it matches what I said.

"Sumiko told me what you asked. Your date is over. Do not call or text her. You don't tell a woman you like to vacation in countries known for sex crimes. I can guess why you asked about Carnival. And let me be very clear to you about Russian destinations. The only place I will suggest is a gulag in Siberia. Just because I'm Russian doesn't mean I know of any brothels."

He doesn't wait for Steven to respond. He leads me to the door and out to a waiting town car.

"Stefan will take you wherever you want."

"Thank you, Pasha."

"I'd still like that date, *malyshka*."

I bite my lip, and I see the heat flare in his eyes. He pulls my lip free and presses a soft kiss to them. I hand him my phone, and he puts his number in it. When he hands it back to me, I shoot him a quick text, so he has mine.

The driver opens the rear passenger door for me, and I give him my address in Harlem. I go up on my toes and give Pasha a quick peck before I climb into the car. He stands on the sidewalk until the car turns, and we can't see each other anymore.

Holy hell. I got his number. Better yet, he has mine. Nothing's going to come of it, most likely. But at least he offered his number first. What the fuck am I going to tell Sarah?

Chapter Seven

Pasha

It's taking all my restraint not to go back to Steven and bash his face in. But I said what I needed to, and now he looks like he's ready to piss himself. Good. He sees me heading back to my table, and I watch him scurry to the door. Run, little rat.

"What was that all about?"

Aleks raises an eyebrow before taking a sip of vodka. No shots tonight. No need to look too stereotypical. It makes people wonder just what kind of Russians we are. The less people wonder, the better.

"That was Sumiko."

"I know. But why'd you just drag her out of here? And why does her date look like he's going to cry?"

"He asked her if we hooked up. That's none of his fucking business. Then he mentioned places he likes to vacation. They're all known for sex trafficking. Then, as though that wasn't enough, he asked if she thought I'd might have some recommendations in Russia."

"Fucking-a. Not every Russian runs a whorehouse."

Aleks rolls his eyes. He and his brothers may own a slew of strip clubs in New York and New Jersey, but their rules are strict. They never recruit. The dancers come to them. If there's even a hint of more than a legal lap dance, the dancer is out on her ass, and they ban the customer for life. Our mothers faced enough danger while our fathers were in the KGB and Podolskaya bratva. We would never enter that underworld after what our parents sacrificed to keep our mothers safe. My aunt Galina, Aleks's mom, is easily one of the world's most beautiful women. No lie. She and Uncle Kirill had four children in four years to keep the bratva away from her in Moscow. None of us would spit in our parents' eyes by going near sex trafficking. They'd kill us.

"Anyway, she ducked into the bathroom to give herself a chance to pretend to get a call. She wanted to leave, so I sent her with Stefan. He'll see her home safely."

"You could have gone. Aleks and I can handle meeting with Pablo."

"It's fine. I got her number, and she said she'd go out with me."

"A date? Hasn't it been like three years since your last real date?"

"Something like that. I didn't know you were keeping track, Anton."

My brother shrugs. It's actually been closer to four or five. I don't remember the last time I picked a woman up from her place, took her to dinner and a movie, and then took her home. It's been months since the last time I saw Julie or Kate. They're both dating guys, and I'm not looking for anyone else to see casually.

"I'm starving. When the hell's Pablo getting here?"

"You're always starving, Anton."

Aleks is one to talk. He eats the most out of all his brothers, and he can eat me under the table. How he's ever hungry is beyond me. I had lunch with him at his place today. He had a foot-long sandwich, about three pounds of fruits and vegetables, and half a sleeve of cookies. We're not nineteen anymore, but even at thirty, he can eat like he is.

"He's here."

We stand as Pablo Diaz, heir to the Colombian Cartel in NYC, stops at our table. His bodyguards blend in along with ours. If people know what to look for, they're easy to spot. But a couple are at the bar, there's one at each door, and a few are at tables around the restaurant.

"Why'd you call me here?"

"Always a pleasure to see you, Pablo."

Aleks raises his glass to our nemesis.

"Since you don't seem interested in breaking bread with us, I want to know why the fuck Juan is back in town."

Aleks sounds casual, but Pablo shifts in his seat and looks around.

"Where the hell did you see my *manito*?"

Pablo barely contains the anger in his voice when he asks about his little brother.

"Maks heard he's back. You better pray Laura doesn't. You and your *tío* promised he would never be back in this time zone. Why the fuck is he?"

Anton and I listen as Aleks and Pablo talk. Tonight, we're just silent reminders that no Kutsenko stands alone.

"I didn't know he was. *Pinche pendejo.*" Fucking asshole.

"That's not a nice way to talk about family."

"He stopped being family when he crossed Laurita. She was like our sister. *Tío* Enrique definitely does not know. He's going to lose his shit if you're right."

"What about you? What happens when your *pequeño*

hermano comes knocking at your door, begging your forgiveness?"

"He won't be coming to my door."

The certainty in Pablo's voice makes me watch him more closely. None of us know for sure, but we've all suspected for a long time that Pablo is his family's chief torturer. I think it's a role his uncle and father forced him into, not one he ever wanted. I've known him since we were teens. He's not the same as he was then, and it's not just the regular weight of responsibility and maturity that has changed him.

"Could he be trying to get his old job back?"

Pablo snorts as he looks at Aleks.

"He's in no position to pass the physical. One look at him, and he's disqualified from ever being a cop again."

"What'd you do to him?"

I can't help but ask.

"That's family business. Maks wanted him gone, and I made sure he was. If he's back, then he'd do well to hide from Enrique and me. My *papi* is home again, and he knows what happened. He's been trying to reconcile with Laura's parents. We will never go back to Sunday dinners, but they're still my parents' next-door neighbors. They've lived next to each other for twenty-five years. My father might see him one last time, but he'll tell him to go. My father doesn't want to see one son kill the other. That's the only outcome if I see him."

Nothing about Pablo makes me think he's bluffing. I know Pablo can't read Aleks's expression, but Anton and I can. The Ivankov bratva beat unintentional reactions to anything out of us as kids. It was part of our bratva initiation. But Anton and I understand Aleks as well as we understand ourselves. Aleks believes Pablo.

"I'll keep that in mind when I talk to Maks. But like I said before, you better hope Laura doesn't find out. She will tell

Maks to do what he originally wanted. She won't give Juan another chance. He'll be dead before you get your turn. Maks won't keep this from Laura once he knows for certain either way. If your brother is back, the clock is ticking."

"Aleks, I get it. You don't have to say what I already know. I'll make some inquiries, and I'll let Maks know what I find out. But if he's back, he's with *gringo amigos*. He's not near any of us. No one affiliated with the Cartel will risk protecting him. Everyone knows."

Pablo arches an eyebrow. Everyone knows there's a bounty on Juan's head, and there's likely several hits authorized. Watching Pablo, no one would know that he's talking about his own brother. No matter what Anton did, I could never imagine sanctioning his death. I could never do it or be responsible for it. Never. Maybe Pablo hides his feelings better than I think. But I suspect he just doesn't have any anymore.

"If that's all..."

"It is. Thank you for meeting with us."

Aleks stands and offers his hand to Pablo. Anton, then I shake it before Pablo leaves.

"What do you make of that?"

Anton keeps his voice low as we speak in Russian.

"I think he genuinely hates his brother. From what Laura's told me, Juan was a real shit to him while they were growing up because he was bigger than Pablo for years. Laura was closer to Juan since they're the same age, but I know she misses her friendship with Pablo. I think he does too. If Juan isn't back, we may never know what Enrique ordered Pablo to do. But I think Pablo will never forgive Juan for betraying Laura and risking her life. I think he's already chosen her over Juan. Enrique certainly has. She and her sister are like his nieces. Hell, he has their initials tatted on his arm, along with Pablo's and Juan's. They're old school. Women and children are off limits. Juan violated that cardinal rule, and as far as they're concerned, he went against their own family."

"Then we can consider him dead if he's dumb enough to be back in the city. If the Cartel doesn't do it, we will."

Anton's mouth twitches as he shakes his head at my comment. I can hear him thinking, *poor bastard.*

"If we don't do it, Laura will."

My cousin-in-law may be a mom now and look innocent, but she's proven she's a badass. A year and a half living in Russia before she met Maks taught her plenty. She's also loyal as the day is long and protective of Maks and her children like a mama tiger. She won't hesitate if Juan is back to threaten any of us. I almost feel sorry for the poor bastard if Laura's the one to find him.

Me: Goodnight, malyshka. Sweet dreams.

I don't expect a response even if I'm hoping for one. I put my phone on the bedside table, forcing myself not to stare at the screen. When it pings a minute later, I tell myself it must be someone else.

Sumiko: Goodnight sir.

Me: No sweet dreams for me?

Sumiko: Lol. Sweet dreams sir.

Me: So formal. Though I do like hearing you call me that.

Sumiko: I know you do.

Me: And?

Sumiko: I might like calling you that. A little.

Me: A little. Lol. I can think of something that's big.

Sumiko: Should I guess?

Me: You can.

Sumiko: Is it something guys send pics of?

Me: Some guys might.

I push back the covers and jog into the kitchen. I pull open the fridge and grab the sandwich I saved for tomorrow. I unwrap it and tap on my camera. I shoot a photo and send it to her.

Sumiko: A sandwich???

Me: It's big isn't it?

Sumiko sends me the face palm emoji and a smiley face.

Sumiko: Yes it is. Is that what your sweet dreams will be about?

Me: Hardly. There's this gorgeous woman I met on a white sandy beach. She calls me sir and likes to be spanked. I'll be dreaming about her again.

Sumiko: Again?

Me: Mhmm. Daydream. Night dream. I wonder if she thinks about me.

Sumiko: That must be rhetorical.

Me: Have dinner with me tomorrow night and find out.

There's a pause. She'd been firing off responses as fast as she could type them. What happened? Did I scare her off? I thought she agreed to a date. Did I ask too soon?

I feel like I'm fifteen and trying to ask a girl out for the first time. I kept getting tongue-tied every time I tried to talk to Angela Spellman. I couldn't get my Russian and English straight. I feel that way all over again.

A screenshot of an address comes in with a photo of a restaurant. Then there's a link underneath.

Sumiko: Have you ever had Brazilian BBQ?

Me: I don't think so.

Sumiko: If you're willing to try this place is amazing.

Me: Tomorrow?

Sumiko: Yeah. How about seven?

Me: I can pick you up or I can send a driver.

Sumiko: I can walk from my place.

Me: In case you need to make a quick exit?

Sumiko: I don't think that's going to be a problem. Goodnight Pasha. Sweet dreams.

Me: Goodnight malyshka. They've been the sweetest since you've been in them. Sleep well baby girl.

She sends me the sleepy emoji twice. There doesn't seem to be anything else for me to say, so I send the same one back to her twice. I plug my phone in and put it back on the bedside table. I roll over and look at the empty spot next to me. I've looked at the same spot and thought the same thing every night since I came home. I just want to fall asleep again with Sumiko in my arms.

My dreams might be filled with us having sex, but when I look at that pillow, I just want to hold her. And just as often as I dream about making love to her or fucking her, I picture us doing normal couple things, like going for walks, making breakfast together, me picking her up from work. I desire her without a doubt. But there's something about her I need to discover. I see hints of it, and I want to get to know her better. I can't remember ever feeling this curious about a woman.

Chapter Eight

Sumiko

"I googled them. Look."

Sarah hands me her phone as she runs on the treadmill next to mine. There are only a couple hits for the Kutsenko name, but they're all for high-end commercial real estate deals or pharmaceutical company buy outs. I scroll until I find a listing for Bear Imports. I see Pasha's name in the description, so I click on it. I hit the About page, but there's nothing mentioning him. I click a few other pages until I find the senior executives. It lists Misha as COO, and Pasha is the CFO. They must run it together because I don't see anyone above them as CEO.

I go back to the About page and read more carefully. It says they're in agricultural imports and exports. What the hell does that mean? They don't strike me as farmers or ever having seen a farm. Does this mean pot? Do they import and export cannabis? Or is it something boring like avocados? And why Bear Imports?

Because they're Russian. It takes me a moment, but then I get it. I can't help but smile. Not entirely original, but definitely not obvious. I hand the phone back as I concentrate on not tripping over my own feet. I told Sarah about the disaster with Steven. She's not easily shocked into silence, but she was. Then she swore up a storm that would make a sailor blush. After that, she apologized profusely. Obviously, she wouldn't have set us up if she'd known he would be a DB. I don't blame her. I changed the subject and told her that Pasha asked me out, and I said yes.

That's when she started searching. I thought she was pulling up a new playlist. I should have known better. She'll have his entire social media life compiled before we're done running.

"Look."

I was right. I take the phone back and stand on the sides of the treadmill, the belt running between my legs. I scroll Pasha's Instagram account, and it's filled with photos of him working out. I can see Anton, Sergei, and Misha in several of them. Aleks in some too. The other guys all look just like Aleks. I swear, a geneticist would have a field day with them as research subjects. It's uncanny.

But there's nothing more than gym photos and a few from other diving trips. It's boring and completely uninformative. I try a couple other social media platforms, but I can't find any accounts. I suppose it would feel odd for a woman not to have them, but I can sorta get why guys don't. He doesn't seem like the type to waste time scrolling or posting.

"It's weird that he doesn't have anything personal or professional about him."

Sarah's more skeptical than I am. But she also lives her life through Instagram. She's a self-proclaimed foodie and influencer. I can barely remember to take photos of anything. I have way more on my social media than Pasha, but nowhere near Sarah. Tiffany's somewhere between us.

"No LinkedIn profile came up, either. Maybe he doesn't want his personal life splashed all over, but why doesn't he have anything professional coming up?"

That observation makes me stop and wonder, but then I shake my head.

"I never use my LinkedIn."

I don't. I made the profile ages ago and never look at it.

"At least you have one. Weird."

"I checked Steven's profiles, and nothing made me think he was a creep. Look at how that turned out."

"I suppose."

Sarah shrugs as I give her back her phone and jump back onto the belt. We run for another thirty minutes before we head into the locker room. I say nothing, but Sarah's got me wondering. She has a point about not having anything professional online. You can usually find something about people. I search the name Kutsenko some more while I'm on the subway to work. A lot more comes up when I put in Maksim Kutsenko. There are photos of him and a gorgeous brunette at their wedding reception and at a gala at the mayor's home. I zoom in and spot Anton in both, but I don't see Pasha. It takes me a moment to remember his other cousins' names, then I search them individually. Nothing interesting comes up. I don't know Sergei's and Misha's last name.

I drop my phone in my bag as I get off the train and head up to the street. I have a full day ahead of me because it's almost the end of the quarter. Some days I love my job, and then there are days like today when I wonder why I chose something so boring. I remind myself of my job security. People will always need accountants. I'm a Certified Forensic Examiner, so I specialize in digging through companies' records to find irregularities or discrepancies. Most often, I'm looking at records before potential buy outs or bankruptcy. I have uncovered more than one juicy scandal, so it's not all bad all the time. But the hours are going to drag today. I just want to get to seven o'clock, and my date with Pasha.

"You look beautiful, *malyshka*."

Pasha's waiting for me at the restaurant door with a bouquet. They're peonies. Beautiful pink ones, and I like them way better than if he'd gotten roses. I mean, I would have appreciated roses, but it seems less trite or cliché. I sniff before stepping closer. I'm not sure what I planned to do, but he wraps his arm around me, and we brush our lips together.

"Thank you."

I whisper my gratitude before he kisses me properly. It's as though we're a couple that's already been dating for a while. Not two people going on a first date. I suppose when you've spent hours naked with someone in bed, a first date isn't going to be too traditional.

He confirms that when he slides his hand into mine as we follow the host to our table. Pasha pulls out my chair for me and waits until I'm ready to scoot it in.

"What do you recommend? I thought about it, and I definitely don't think I've ever had Brazilian barbeque before."

"You're in for an experience. We call it *churrascaria*. It's not like American or Korean barbeque that's smoked. It's slow-cooked and more grilled than anything else. There isn't any sauce on it. They just use *sal grosso*. It's like a coarse rock salt, so it brings out the natural flavors in the meat. Just know that it can be a little crunchy, which is usually weird to Americans who expect meat slathered in dry rub or sauce. But what makes this fun is that they bring the meat by on these swords, and it's carved tableside."

"Do you have a favorite?"

"All of them."

I can't help but laugh. I enjoy food. A lot. It's likely why I look nothing like Sarah or Tiffany, never mind that I'm Asian. Sarah modeled in high school, and Tiffany was a beauty pageant queen since she was seven. I hardly consider myself ugly, and it's clear Pasha likes what he sees. I've never had trouble getting dates. But when I go out with Sarah and Tiffany, I become invisible to most men. It's why I assumed Pasha bought Sarah's drink, not mine. When the three of us are at bars or clubs, I'm usually the last one picked like we're playing dodgeball, and I'm the least desirable team member. Pasha makes me feel like I'm the star player.

"Is it mostly beef?"

"Yeah. There are three cuts here. Filet mignon, babe beef—we say bebe beefey, and *picanha*. That's leanest to fattiest." I point to a passing waiter with a long skewer. "There's also pork loin, and there's usually lamb. But some nights they run out."

This isn't quite a hole in the wall place, but it's well known in the neighborhood. I think it's the best Brazilian restaurant in New York, but that's also because it's three blocks from my place. It reminds me of visiting my grandparents. It's comfort food.

"I'm glad you picked this place. It's nice to learn more about you."

"That I like a marathon of meat."

Pasha nearly chokes on his water, unprepared for my quip.

"And there's the sense of humor that made me look up to see who made the raunchy comments. I know you like a marathon of meat. I meant, it's nice to learn more about what you must have grown up with if your family is Brazilian."

"I didn't think anyone heard me."

I blush. I remember saying something about being wet, taking a pounding like a drunk college girl, and taking it up the ass. Not my finest moment for someone to overhear.

"It made me curious. Then I saw you. I think you know how I reacted to that."

"Not at first."

I think I'm blushing even harder. Why have I suddenly gotten nervous? He slides his hand across the table to me and rests it palm up. I place mine in his.

"I wish your friend hadn't assumed the drink was for her."

I shrug.

"It usually is."

"If I say good, that will not come off right. I'm just glad that I got your attention."

"You definitely got my attention. I almost fell off my stool."

He flashes a smile at me, and it's like the heavens part. It's the broadest one I've seen from him, and he looks completely relaxed. He's smiled plenty of times, but he's never appeared this at ease.

"And I was happy to catch you."

We pause as the waiter comes to take our drink order. We both get a glass of wine. I wonder if he'd rather have vodka. Is that too much of a stereotype? He and his friends did have back-to-back shots at the club.

"What type of accounting do you do? I'm assuming that's what you do if that's what you majored in."

"I'm a forensic accountant now, but I started out as a regular CPA."

"Are you a fraud investigator?"

"No. I've done a little of that, but mostly I investigate companies before potential mergers and acquisitions, or if a company intends to file bankruptcy. Exciting stuff. Let me tell you."

I raise my wine glass as it arrives.

"What made you decide to get into that?"

"Certainly not the sex appeal. I like numbers and puzzles. I like job security. People will always need someone to handle their money, whether it's an accountant, a banker, or a financial advisor."

"Practical. But I get the sense that's your nature. Let me guess. You had one small suitcase, and your friends had like four each."

"Not that bad." I laugh. "I had a small roll aboard, and they each had a checked suitcase. I'm frugal and impatient. I don't enjoy waiting at baggage claim."

"I guessed that.

"I saw you getting off the jet."

I'm not sure if I should have mentioned that. I hope it sounded like an observation and not that I was looking for him.

"You did?"

"Yeah. A car service got you, and off you went without needing to go in the terminal. You had a town car waiting last night, and you offered to send one for me tonight. Do you always have a driver?"

"Often. But I like to drive my car if I don't have to do it in Manhattan."

That's rather vague. I don't want to ask what kind of car he drives after mentioning the jet. I don't want to sound like a gold digger.

"Are you the type who works in the car, so the driver is more convenient?"

"It allows for that. I don't enjoy maneuvering traffic."

Just how rich is he? He could take the subway if he doesn't like traffic. I remain quiet, waiting for him to continue the conversation. He doesn't seem to want to talk about himself. How am I supposed to get to know him?

"Do you have siblings? You've met Anton."

"Yeah. I have an older and younger brother. They live near LA."

"Did you go to school out there? Or did you come east for college?"

"I came east. I went to Dartmouth. You?"

"Columbia."

He's certainly not dumb.

"You're pretty much a local. But you still have an accent."

"Yeah. We came here when I was twelve."

"How old are you?"

I'm back to asking the questions. Damn.

"Twenty-eight."

I thought he was older. I thought at least thirty. He seems too serious to still be in his twenties.

"Me too."

"When's your birthday?"

"It was Saturday. That's why we went on a girls' trip. To celebrate the auspicious occasion of turning a very bland twenty-eight."

"So was mine. That's why we went away, too."

"We have the same birthday. That's random."

Okay. We might get somewhere now.

"It is. Have you been in New York since you graduated college?"

"No. I lived in New Jersey for a couple years and commuted to Columbia for grad school. Much, much cheaper."

"Were you born in Brazil?"

I don't have time to answer since a waiter brings over the first selection of meat. I know the guy, and we greet each other in Portuguese. I explain the options to Pasha, and he agrees to try the *picahna*.

"*Como novo namorado?*" Hot new boyfriend?

I shake my head as I look at my friend.

"*Você quer que ele seja?*" Do you want him to be?

"*É o nosso primeiro encontro.*" It's our first date.

"*Pena que ele não é gay.*" Pity he isn't gay.

I'm certain I'm blushing to my roots. There is no way Pasha didn't understand that last word. He's watching us, but his expression is inscrutable. It's usually like that. I can't tell what he's thinking unless he wants me to. His unguarded moments are really just times when he lets me in. I realized that when we met, and I saw it last night when he found out what Steven said. But I get a sense of how he feels. Right now, he's just curious, which is a relief.

"A friend?"

"Yeah. He's the owner's son. I've been coming here for years, so we've gotten to know each other."

I wonder if he's going to ask what we talked about, but he doesn't. Not nosey. Hmm.

"You were on the surf team in high school, but Dartmouth isn't near the water. Do you play any other sports?"

"I run, but only because it's good for me. I used to play soft-ball, but only until high school. You?"

"Diving, American football, and soccer in high school, and diving in college."

"I'm the only Brazilian I know who doesn't play soccer. My parents say it's sacrilege."

"Do you speak Japanese as well as you do Portuguese?"

"Yes. I grew up with both at home and English at school. My parents wanted to be sure I could speak to all of my family wherever we visited."

"Did you speak one language with one parent and a different one with the other?"

"Yeah. I spoke Japanese with my mom and Portuguese with my dad. But it overlapped as I got older. We also spoke a lot more English at home once they knew my brothers and I were fully trilingual. Do you speak any languages other than English and Russian?"

"French and German fluently. I'm pretty proficient in Polish. I can understand some of the other Slavic languages, but only enough to get the gist of conversations."

"Do you do a lot of business in France and Germany?"

"Sometimes. I like languages, so I studied them through college."

Vague again. I don't even know what he does, but he knows I'm an accountant.

"It's embarrassing to ask this, but I don't even know your last name, Sumiko. You heard me introduce myself to Steven."

"I did. My last name is Kimura."

I hadn't wanted to give my last name to a stranger, but now it feels a bit slutty to have hooked up with a guy who barely knew my name. Oh, well. I don't regret it. His next observation reminds me of my conversation with Sarah this morning.

"We both have unique last names in America. Even so, I know there's not much to find about my family."

He assumes I checked his social media and Googled him.

"*Malyshka*, you're a young woman in a big city. I expected you to look me up."

"I did. Sarah started and got me curious. You're right that there isn't much to find."

I wait for him to offer more, but he doesn't. I know he has a brother and moved here when he was twelve. I know he went to an excellent university; the same one where I went to grad school. He speaks four—nearly five—languages fluently. He

71

played sports. Those are all benign things about his past. I know nothing about his present.

"What do you do?"

"I work in the family business."

Do I give away that I know about Bear Imports? I feel like I'll sound pushy if I ask what kind. Too bad if he does. I want to see what he says.

"What type of business?"

"Imports and exports. Misha and I own a company we started, but our fathers were in the same field."

Why doesn't he sound like he wants to talk about that? It's not like me, who thinks my work would probably put him to sleep. His tone says he won't tell me more. We're interrupted again as another meat options come by. Then we're quiet as we eat.

"This was a delicious choice. Thank you for suggesting it. Do you cook?"

"Yes. But mostly American food now that I'm on my own."

"No slow-cooked meat marathons at your place?"

"No."

I shake my head. He smiles again. The one where he looks completely at ease.

"What types of things do you import and export?"

The smiles still there, but it's faded.

"A variety. Too many to list."

He shut me out.

"Are your parents in New York?"

He asked about mine. I want to know about his.

"Yes."

He takes another bite, and I think it's an excuse. This is getting frustrating. One moment he's forthcoming, and the next, he shuts down.

"What do you do for fun?"

I have to think about that. I can't tell him my favorite pastime is sleeping. I'm up before five to meet Sarah at the gym, and I rarely get home from work until close to seven. The days are long, and I catch up on my sleep on the weekends.

"I read, go for runs, travel when I can, go out with Sarah and Tiffany or other friends. You?"

"Work out."

He grins, as though the answer is obvious. It is. I've seen what's under the snug charcoal shirt and trousers. The suit coat he wears accentuates his broad shoulders.

"Maybe we could go for a run together sometime."

I wasn't expecting that offer, but I nod. I bet I'm like a slug compared to him, but I can run for a long time. Maybe a run would get him to be chattier than a crowded restaurant.

"I can tell you're close to Anton, and I guess Misha's your best friend if you run a business together. Are you close with your cousins? That was Aleks last night, right?"

"Yes."

He takes another bite. I wait for him to elaborate, but he doesn't. Instead, he turns the question around on me.

"Are you close to your family?"

"Very, even though we live across the country from each other. We try to alternate years between trips to Brazil and Japan. All my great-grandparents immigrated to Brazil at the end of World War Two. Some of my family remained there, but others have returned to Japan. Did your family come here because of the fall of the Soviet Union?"

"No. That happened three years before I was born. My family stayed for more than a decade, but life is better here. What brought your family to America?"

He definitely doesn't sound like he wants to talk about that.

"A biopharmaceutical company offered my dad a job."

"Which one?"

"Davidson Global Bio." His expression is even blanker than usual. "Have you heard of it?"

"In passing. I think I heard about some R and D they were doing a while ago."

There's that purposely vague tone. It's almost dismissive. Why won't he tell me anything about his work? If he's heard about their research, does it have something to do with what he does?

"You mentioned you studied languages in college. Was that your major?"

"No. My minor was Modern Languages, though neither French nor German are particularly modern. Not when they've been around for centuries."

This is like pulling teeth.

"What was your major?"

"Accounting."

What the fuck? We studied the same thing, and he knows I'm an accountant. He didn't think to say, 'hey, me too.' Maybe he wasn't meant to be more than a hook up.

Chapter Nine

Pasha

This is why I don't date. She wants to know things anyone would want to know when going out with someone. But it's a constant juggle of what to admit and what to hide. I don't want to hide a damn thing from her, but she's intelligent. It wouldn't take her long to piece it all together. I'm not ready for that yet.

I haven't brought a single woman into my real life. I've never admitted to anyone that I'm bratva, and I'm scared shitless to ever do it. That admission could ruin everyone I love and everyone I'm responsible for. I'm an *avotoritet,* a brigadier. When we run large-scale operations, especially ones where there's plenty of danger that bullets will fly, I'm a leader. Men depend on me to stay alive. If she told the police—told anyone —I would end up on death row. The best all the men in my family could hope for is life in prison. Though, that's probably a far worse fate.

"I'm a CPA too. I became one to help with the family business. You know what that's like. It's not exactly exciting stuff handling taxes. Do you think you'll stay in New York, or do you want to move back to the West Coast?"

She's annoyed. Super annoyed. I can see it. She's got a good poker face, but I can read it. I'm asking these questions because I genuinely want to know, not just to deflect. But I don't think she believes that.

"I'd planned to stay out here."

She shrugs one shoulder. A shoulder that I've kissed and stroked. Now it's dismissive. She's withdrawing. Isn't that for the best? Why am I on a date if I know I can't get closer to her? Because that's all I want. I've gone long enough without sex that it's not just wanting to get laid. Her face can be so expressive. I like her sense of humor. I'm intrigued by her obvious intelligence. I want to know her hopes and goals. I want to know what she wants in life. But I can't tell her any of that about myself. But I can offer something.

"I travel when I can, but I'm definitely a New Yorker."

There. Is that a little better?

"For work or just for pleasure?"

And now that's not better.

"Both. Sometimes it's checking out merchandise to import. If it's something very high end, then I might travel with it for its export."

"High-end agriculture?"

Shit. She must have found Bear Imports' About page.

"Since we work mostly on referrals, we haven't updated the website in a while. We started out with things like pineapples, jalapenos, coconuts, and other tropical fruits and vegetables."

Because we could hide drugs in them easily. Bear Imports brought them in legally. Then we created bills of sale that made it look like we legally sold them. Our bratva business used them for smuggling.

"Oh. I thought—"

"Pot?"

"Yes. Or cannabis."

"Hemp plants and seeds. They're legal in the U.S. We import places other than the U.S., so different laws apply, and we can import cannabis. We can't in the U.S."

Marijuana is the least of the DEA's worries with what we handle. But that's bratva business, not Bear Imports. Nowadays, we stick with what's purely legal as far as anyone knows. We branched out a few years ago to legitimize ourselves and distract attention.

"We also handle textiles, ceramics, and other home goods."

She nods. I think she believes me. My cousins' wives have a pretty good idea of what we do, but Maks, Niko, and Bogdan have never told their wives explicitly what our illegal operations handle. Laura has the best idea since she's our corporate lawyer. She only conducts our legit business, but she must have put the pieces together.

"And that's what your dad and uncle did before you?"

No. They ran guns and drugs. They never had a legal front for their smuggling. Vladislav Lushak didn't care about that when he ran our bratva before Maks took over. The sociopath believed the law would never catch us, and he was willing to sacrifice anyone if it did. He's the one who trained all of us. He forced us into the bratva despite how our families fled Russia to avoid it. He still sucked us in. Maks, Niko, Bogdan, and Aleks bore the brunt of his training because their father was already dead when they arrived. My father and Sergei and Misha's protected us longer. We didn't have to join until we were teens. Bogdan was in by the time he was twelve.

"They mostly focused on domestic shipping. Misha and I expanded it internationally."

They were in charge of getting drugs to New York from Miami and Dallas. That's not something I can share.

Dinner's over, and it's both a blessing and a curse. I don't want to end the evening, but I also don't want to talk about my family or me anymore. I settle the bill and take Sumiko's hand again. She's not holding as tightly as she was before. She seems stiff and unwelcoming compared to when she arrived. She's carrying her flowers, hanging from her hand by her thighs. When I gave them to her, she held them close to her chest. She considers this a disaster.

"Will you let me walk you home?"

She hesitates. Fuck.

"Sure. Thank you."

"How long have you lived in the neighborhood?"

"About three years. Do you live in Manhattan?"

"Yeah. I have a loft there."

She points out a few stores and restaurants before we get to her building. I know she won't invite me up, so I stop at the bottom of the steps leading to the front door. I slide one arm around her waist and tunnel my other hand into her hair. I refuse to give up completely.

"I had a nice time, *malyshka*."

"Me too."

No, she didn't. But I lean forward to kiss her, and she lifts her chin. This isn't the casual kiss from when we greeted each other at the beginning of our date. This is the kind we shared in Anguilla. This is the kind we couldn't stop giving while we rolled around in bed all night.

"Goodnight, Pasha."

"Sweet dreams, *malyshka*."

She nods and offers a tight smile. Neither of us says anything about a next date. I want one desperately. But it's foolish. That doesn't stop me craving more of her time, more of her attention. I watch her walk up the steps. She looks back and waves before she goes inside. With a sigh, I turn back toward the road. Ilya is waiting with the car. I ride home with my eyes closed. How do I get a woman to be as into me as I am with her if I can't tell her anything real about me?

"Chill out."

"Don't tell me to chill out, Anton."

I've been snapping at everyone for days. I'm throwing real punches in the ring today, and it's pissing Anton off. Fine. I'm a rubber band ready to pop. I haven't felt this on edge since I was a teenager, terrified of what Vlad was going to make me do next. I resented that bastard with every breath. Anger and frustration used to come out in the boxing ring until I learned to control it. He beat any reaction out of me, but boxing was the one place I could let it all out. But I was never as controlled and methodical as Maks. That's why he was a prizefighter, and I used to bust people's lips.

"What is your deal? You've been a little shit for days. Ever since you went out with Sumiko."

I step back and lower my fists as I look at my brother. He hasn't had this type of romance issue. Oh, there's been a shit ton for him and Sergei, but never did they doubt their feelings for each other.

"She ghosted me."

"Won't answer your texts?"

"Yeah, and the three times I've tried calling over the past week, it's gone to voicemail after two rings."

"I didn't think she was the type to just ignore someone."

"She didn't exactly."

I jump down from the ring and go to my gym bag. I unwrap my left hand and grab my cell phone. Anton's standing over my shoulder when I unlock it and pull up my texts.

Me: Goodnight. Thank you for a wonderful evening.

Sumiko: Thanks for dinner.

Me: I'd like to see you again.

Sumiko: I don't think that's a good idea. I don't think we have much to talk about. Goodnight.

Me: There's plenty I'd like to talk about and get to know you.

Then there's nothing.

"This is why no one dated before Maks met Laura. I mean, Bogdan used to have girlfriends, but he hadn't had one in three years before Christina. Niko had a few here and there, but nothing serious. Maybe she isn't the right woman."

"Or maybe I was an idiot to think she could be."

I've been miserable for the past week. I tried sending Sumiko a couple more texts, but she never responded. I remember when Maks first started dating Laura. They got into some argument and didn't talk to each other for nearly a week. I thought Maks was going to kill someone. No one wanted to be around him because his fuse was nearly nonexistent. I feel the same way. I'm one wrong word away from losing my shit completely.

"You'll know if and when you meet the right one."

"The problem is, I thought she was the right one. I wasn't going to divulge everything to her during our first date, but I could see letting her into my life more. It sounds lame to keep saying there's just something about her, but there is. We all have strong intuition. We've lived to our ripe old twenties, you've even made it to thirty-one, because we listen to our guts. Mine's telling me she's special."

"Then find her. Don't be a stalker about it. But try for a second chance. If that doesn't work, then respect her wishes.

She didn't strike me as the type to spend the night with a guy she wasn't really into. I think she senses something about you. She's probably disappointed because you weren't forthcoming. She was probably hoping for more."

"Maybe I should send her flowers. She was happy to get them when our date started."

"Find something less cliché."

"She knows I've imported fruit. Maybe I send her one of those arrangements. Maybe she'll think it's sweet or funny or at least make the connection. Fuck if I know."

I run my hand through my hair. I'm driving myself crazy. It's probably infatuation, even if I tell myself it's not, or that it's something more than it is. I just can't get her out of my mind.

"We need to get ready if we're going to pick Christina up on time. She and Bogdan spent the night at the penthouse to make it easier for us. We still have two more accounting firms to interview. She arranged to go to them today."

"I'll be ready in five."

Anton and I hit the showers before saying goodbye to the rest of our family, who're working out too. Maks and Bogdan were in the ring when we left. Maks doesn't compete anymore, and Bogdan's the only one who really enjoys the sport. They spar together pretty often. The other guys were lifting weights.

Half the time, Anton and I are security for our cousins and their wives, so we sit up front with the driver. But today, we're in the back when we pick up Christina. She hands me a couple of files, and I review them again. I feel prepared by the time we exit the elevator and walk to the reception desk.

A shiver goes down my spine as I see a woman with black hair in my peripheral vision. I spin in her direction, and even though I can only see her back, I know her. What's she doing here? I'm staring when she turns around and walks toward me.

She blinks several times before her gaze darts to Anton and Christina.

"I'll be back in a minute."

I mutter, and don't care if Anton or Christina hear me. I approach Sumiko with purpose, but I don't want to be entirely obvious.

"Do you have an office?"

I keep my voice low, and she nods. She leads me past all the center cubicles until we get to the last office. It has a solid door, and no one can see inside. Good. She lets me in, and now I prowl toward her as she retreats.

"What're you doing here, Pasha?"

"We're interviewing your firm."

"I didn't know."

"Neither did I."

I wrap my arm around her waist and pull her back against my chest before she can hide behind her desk.

"You've been ignoring me, *malyshka*. That hurts."

I speak against her neck, punctuating each sentence with a kiss. My free hand draws the hair out of my way as I kiss the crook of her shoulder and make my way up to the spot behind her ear that I know makes her shiver. The arm around her middle holds her in place, but she's not trying to escape.

"I—You were too evasive, Pasha. I don't want to play guessing games about who you are. I don't want to date a guy who only wants to fuck me."

I spin her around, but I pin her against me again. My hand in her hair keeps her head in place.

"That's fair, but you could have told me that. You could have texted me that if you didn't want to say it over the phone. Instead, you left me in knots for a week. You would have let me fear the worst if I hadn't shown up today."

"I doubt you're still thinking about me."

"Bullshit. You know I am."

I kiss her. Her arms come around my neck as she opens for me. I squeeze her ass again until I'm certain it hurts. It only makes her rub her pussy against my hard on. Her practical skirt is far longer than the one she wore in the club, but I gather it in my hand.

"When I finger you, I know you'll already be wet. But I want a shit ton more than to just fuck you, Sumiko. If all I wanted was to fuck, I wouldn't bother texting you when you ignored me. I wouldn't want to apologize and try to make it right. I wouldn't be ready to snap everyone's head off because I can't get you off my mind."

I give her a moment to refuse me, to pull away, to push me away. She hikes up her skirt instead.

"Fuck. You're so hot and smooth, *malyshka*. I'm going to make you come, then I'm going to spank you."

"I'm sorry, sir."

She's speaking barely above a whisper. I growl as I squeeze her ass again. I work her pussy as she clings to me. I kiss her to swallow each moan. She's so tight, and all I can think about is getting my dick in her and feeling her come on me.

"May I come, sir?"

"Yes, baby girl."

She buries her face against my chest as she trembles. Her pussy grips my fingers as my thumb rubs her clit. When she looks up at me, her cheeks are flushed, and her eyes are glazed.

"Pasha, I want more. I need you. I've been miserable for a week."

"Then why didn't you respond to me, *malyshka*?"

"Because I thought you'd break my heart. That I'm way more into you than you are with me."

"I promise you that is not the case. I haven't dated anyone in a long time, Sumiko. I'm rusty at letting people into my life. My family is everything to me, and I'm protective of them. It's not that I don't want to, but I have to think about them too. You need to know that you don't just get me, you get all of them. I work with them. I spend all my time with them. My brother and cousins are my closest friends. Our parents still see each other every weekend and half the days of the week."

"And you're all very rich. I get it now. I think you trust me and know I'm not interested in your money. But I can see how bringing someone new in can be hard when I'm going to be judged by so many."

"No, *malyshka*. They will not judge you. That's one thing I can guarantee. I'm just cautious, and I'm not used to talking about myself. The last few women I dated were happy to just talk about themselves. I don't really know what to say that's interesting."

That isn't a lie. And it's a vulnerability that I wouldn't share with just anyone. People outside my family have always seen me as good looking and not much more. Even Anton and Misha assumed I was too shallow to notice Sumiko. I know what I offer my family and our bratva, but I'm not so convinced I know what I can offer anyone else.

She cups my cheek and presses the softest kiss to my lips. She rests her forehead against mine before she speaks.

"I'm more than just my weight. And you're more than just your pretty face. I get it."

"I know you do. I think that's part of why I'm drawn to you. I felt like you understood."

"You don't feel that way anymore?"

"I wasn't so sure after you ghosted me for a week. You wouldn't have stopped if I hadn't shown up here."

She shakes her head and looks down.

"I went to Ivy Friday night and Envy Saturday night. I

know your cousins own those clubs. I hoped you might have been there."

"I was working other clubs they own. I wish I'd known."

"I wanted to see you, but I was embarrassed. I thought maybe you weren't that into me beyond sex, so I wanted it to look like a coincidence."

"I have never wanted to have sex with a woman more than I do you, *malyshka*. But if you wanted to date for a year before we ever had it, I might die, but I would certainly agree."

"I don't want to even wait five more minutes."

I grin and tease her.

"Do you only want me for my body?"

"No. But I enjoy it."

"Will you go out with me again?"

"Yes. And I'll be more patient with you."

"Thank you."

Our kiss explodes once more. I let her lead this time, her hands sliding beneath my suit coat until she becomes frustrated. She pulls my shirt free from my pants, and her fingers sweep along my chest.

"I'm serious, sir. I don't want to wait another five minutes."

"I'm clean, Sumiko. It's been months since I've been with anyone, and I tested after that."

"I am too. I've never had sex without a condom, and I have an IUD."

"I don't have one with me. Do you?"

She shakes her head.

"What do you want, baby girl?"

She looks me in the eye before she answers.

"You."

I push her skirt up to her waist and yank down her thong. She reaches behind her and pushes papers out of the way before unfastening my belt. I unbutton and unzip my pants, before lifting her onto the desk and leaning her back. My hands find hers, and I lift them over her head. Our fingers entwine as I thrust into her.

"Holy fuck."

We whisper it at the same time. I hold both of her wrists with one hand as the other grips her hip. I pound into her over and over as she rolls her hips to meet me. I bury my face against her shoulder and inhale her jasmine scent. My fingers dig into her flesh as I fight not to come yet.

"More.. Please.. Harder."

"Anything for my baby girl."

I thrust and circle my hips until she's struggling to get her hands free, but I won't release them.

"I control this, *malyshka*. Do you understand?"

I'm growling as I keep working her pussy. It's effort and concentration mixed with a need to dominate and pleasure her.

"Do you understand?"

She moans instead of answering. I grow more demanding.

"Do not make me ask a third time, *malyshka*. You're already due a spanking. Now answer me."

"Yes, Daddy."

We both freeze. She's lying on her desk, looking up at me, and blinking like an owl. Neither of us knows what to say for a moment, then I can't stop.

"That's right, *malyshka*. Daddy's in control, and after I make you come, I'm spanking you. You were a naughty baby girl, and I expect you to understand you don't run from me. We talk if there's a problem. If you want to end this, you tell me."

"I don't want anything to end, Daddy."

She's barely louder than a whisper, still unsure about calling me that. I release her hip and rest my hand on her throat. There's no pressure, just a reminder that I dominate, and she submits.

"I have never called another woman baby girl in any language. No woman has called me Daddy. I'm not a dom, Sumiko, but you know what I like. And hearing you call me Daddy is about the hottest fucking thing ever. I'm trying not to come, but you make it fucking hard."

"I know I make it hard, Daddy. I can feel you."

"Cheeky, *malyshka*."

"Just for you, Daddy." She grows serious as we move together. "I've never called a man that before. Only you."

And that's all it takes. I feel her coming, and I struggle to hold on until she's done. The moment her body relaxes, I snag some tissues from the box on her desk and pull out. I want to come on her again, but I remember—barely—that she is at work. Fucking in her office is bad enough. I don't need to leave her sticky with my cum.

"I know why you did that and thank you. But next time, mark me again. If we're dating, then there's no one else for me. I'm yours."

"There isn't anyone else for me either, Sumiko. I'm all in."

"Already?"

"That's where I stand. If you need more time and aren't ready to commit to more, I understand."

She considers me for a long moment as she pushes her skirt back down after she stands. Then she nods.

"I'm all in, too."

Now I have to figure out exactly what that means. I know what I want, but I have to figure out how. I don't want to hide from her, but I don't want to terrify her, either. I want her to have a more gradual introduction to my world than Laura, Christina, or Anastasia received. Emergencies and danger forced their welcome. Not surprising, but it's also not how I want things for Sumiko.

"I have to go back out there. Christina and Anton have probably started the interview already."

A knock interrupts us. I hurry to get my shirt tucked and my pants fastened as Sumiko darts to her chair. I drop into the one closest to me.

"Come in."

"Sumiko, we need you in this meeting, please."

"Sure, Greg. Which one?"

"With the Kutsenkos. Mr. Kutsenko, your brother and Mrs. Kutsenko are in the conference room."

I look back at the man in the doorway. From the look on his face, I think he believes Christina is my wife, and he wants to know why the fuck I'm in a closed office with another woman.

"Sumiko, I think you're going to like Christina. I'd trade my cousin for her, but she insists she loves her husband." I shrug and grin. "She knows way more about construction."

I step aside as Sumiko follows Greg, and I follow her as I make sure my clothes are back in place. Anton looks at me as we enter. His expression looks blank to everyone else, but it's reproving to me. Christina is struggling not to laugh. She definitely doesn't hide her thoughts as well as Bogdan or the rest of us. She sticks out her hand to Sumiko as I walk around the table to the open chair between Christina and Anton.

"Ms. Kimura, I see you're a CFE with a master's in accounting. How long have you been in forensic examinations?"

Christina launches straight into her questions as she looks down at Sumiko's company profile. She's all business now, and Sumiko focuses on her.

"I've been a licensed accountant since I graduated undergrad, so six years. I've been a certified forensic examiner for four."

"What's your experience with value assessments?"

"I work mostly with potential mergers and acquisitions, so I'm very familiar with finding hidden assets and potential causes for insolvency. I handle mostly bank account assessments, but I have done inventory evaluations."

"Fraud investigations?"

"I haven't done any in a couple years, but I'm qualified and experienced."

Christina looks at me. This is where I usually come in and ask questions specific to accounting.

"Ms. Kimura, please describe your process for locating the financial information you need during a valuation."

"I can examine the readily available banking and investment information, but I usually discover what I can about the businesses' customers or partners and what I can about the stakeholders. Then I consider where they might hide information. It might be offshore accounts or through relatives. Children's education funds tend to be popular for those who don't understand how they work. They usually trap their money in them, which makes it easy to find."

"What types of reports are you most comfortable with?"

"Most. Whether it's a simple profit and loss statement and regular quarterly reports or quantifying losses to establish valuation, I can do those and most things in between. When I'm considering a potential buy out, I run reports on the already established losses as well as projected ones between present day and the expected date of merger or acquisition."

"How would you conduct investigations for us?"

This one I really need to know. How hard will she push for us, but also how nosey might she become?

"If you're talking about an investigation rather than an assessment or valuation, I would start with the physical evidence available. Usually if there's enough suspicion to warrant a forensic examination, then there's usually a crime.

Discovery of one crime often leads to others. People leave footprints, even when they think they've hidden things well. If there's no obvious physical evidence, then I ask questions. Who's gone without a raise the longest? Who's taken the most days off? Who has family outside the state or the country? Who has the cleanest record, or most recent promotion, or most recent bonus? Where did the executives last work, and were there any noted issues companywide there? Those sorts of things."

She'll be thorough with our legal operations, but if I bring her into this world for good, then I'll have to explain enough for her not to follow too many scents. She'll end up discovering things I want her kept away from. I don't want to endanger her with knowledge that could get her killed.

"Do you prefer to work alone or in a team?"

"I can work in either situation."

"What do you do to decrease the likelihood of error from conflicting information?"

"I assess the sources of information and their inherent validity. Then I rule out obvious reasons for contradiction. Finally, I investigate what's least explicable. I don't file reports until I can reconcile the information."

"How long does the average valuation or investigation take?"

Sumiko turns toward Christina as I sit back. I've finished my questions, and Christina knows it, so she takes over.

"That depends, Mrs. Kutsenko. It could be as quick as a week. Or it could take me several months. It depends on the scope of the audit and the evidence available. I can't give you an exact number of days or hours."

The conference door opens, and a gentleman steps inside. I recognize Sumiko's confusion, but it's Greg's surprise that makes me dart a glance at Anton. Why is he surprised that the firm's owner just arrived?

"*Kak prodvigayutsya dela?*" How are things progressing?

I answer since Christina doesn't speak Russian, and I led the interview, not Anton.

"*Chto zh. My dovol'ny tem, chto uslyshali.*" Well. We are happy with what we've heard.

"*Grigoriy, a ty?*" Grigori, and you?

"*Ya dumayu, partnery Kutsenko budut khoroshimi kliyentami, papa.*" I think Kutsenko Partners will be good clients, Dad.

Ah. Grigori Balandin, not just Greg. The owner's son. He might have introduced himself as that. Christina's expression tells me that isn't a surprise to her. I wish I'd known. Sumiko is looking at Arseniy Balandin, Greg, and now me. Did she not know her company was owned by Russians?

"Ms. Kimura, we haven't met, even though I know you've been with firm for several years. I haven't been part of day-to-day operations in decade. But I thought I would say hello to Kutsenkos."

Arseniy walks toward Sumiko, who rises. She accepts the older man's hand and shakes. His English is excellent, but not like a native. He misses some small words in English that we don't use in Russian like the, an, and a.

"Thank you, Mr. Balandin."

"Ms. Kimura, I'm certain Greg will let you know if Kutsenkos hire us. Thank you for your time."

Sumiko glances at me before she smiles and nods to Arseniy.

"I look forward to working with you. Mrs. Kutsenko, Mr. Kutsenko."

She nods to us before she walks out of the conference room.

But she glances at me again through the glass before turning the corner to go back to her office.

"Mrs. Kutsenko, I believe you don't speak Russian, so I will speak English."

"Thank you, Mr. Balandin."

"I know who you are." Arseniy looks at me, then Anton. "I know your father. It's no coincidence that my son shares same name."

This is news to me. I can tell it is to Anton as well. Christina is wisely remaining quiet, like a fly on the wall. Arseniy slips off his suit coat and rolls up his sleeve. Fuck.

"You know what this means. I left your world when I moved here before end of Soviet era. Grigori was baby when we immigrated, but I was your father's best friend growing up. Kirill was like little brother to me. I think of him often."

My uncle Kirill died in the Second Chechen War, only feet away from my father. My father has never mentioned this man.

"Does our father know you live here?"

"Yes. I assumed he recommended us." Arseniy's brow furrows. "That's why I took interest. We will take you on as clients, but strictly your legitimate business. If you bring bratva to us, we end our ties. I will not have it."

The steel in his voice tells me he might have left the bratva behind in Russia, but he is still every bit the *boyevik* he must have been as a young man. He still has the lethal edge of any foot soldier. I turn my attention to Greg, and he looks completely lost.

"My son doesn't know your world, and I expect it to stay that way."

"Dad?"

"My past is meeting my present. As long as they uphold their end of this agreement, you need know nothing more. It's better for you and family if you don't."

Arseniy looks out the conference room window and down the hall Sumiko walked a moment ago. He meets my gaze.

"You are involved with Ms. Kimura. Does she know yet?"

"No, she doesn't."

"I don't want to be nosey, Pavel. It's not my business, but she is my employee. She handles nothing you do. I already know you're *derzhatel obshchaka*."

The bookkeeper. He knows I'm our accountant. How does he know that?

"I don't see your father often, but we are still friends. He is extremely proud of you two, just as he is your cousins. Our lives went in different directions because of that war. I fled when I could and brought my family with me. I know that wasn't option for your family, even though I tried to help. I wish I'd done more, and I'm sorry that I couldn't. Like I said, Kirill was like my little brother. I don't doubt Galina raised your cousins to be honorable, just like their father. It's why I'm agreeing to this arrangement. Keep Ms. Kimura far from your dealings. I don't want her in danger, and I don't want my company destroyed. Consider that my only warning, Anton, Pavel. Good day, Mrs. Kutsenko."

Arseniy doesn't wait for a response, and I know I have none to give. What can I say? I certainly won't argue and say I'm eager to risk everything he has and put Sumiko in danger. He knows our agreement goes without saying.

But the path to hell is paved with good intentions. What if I can't keep them?

Chapter Ten

Sumiko

I head back to my office and leave the door open. That's not entirely unusual, but I hope Pasha sees it. It's an invitation to him more than it is anyone else. When I get to my desk, I pull my phone out and pull up my web browser. I don't know who that man was, but I'm guessing Greg's father. I thought Greg owned the company. He's the CEO.

Balandin: Russian surname
Meaning: A small crater on the moon.

That's not what I expected when I search their name. Not that it's Russian or its meaning. Greg has no accent, so I never guessed he spoke another language. Is it a coincidence that Pasha and his family interviewed this firm? Do they like to keep their business within the Russian community? I don't know that we have any other Russian clients. This isn't a large company, and there are only ten accountants on staff. Even if I'm not working with a client, I know about most of them. Did I miss something? Why does it matter?

A knock makes me look up. I smile at Pasha, and he comes in. He shuts the door behind him, and I'm out of my seat. I'm back in his arms, and it feels like I arrived home after a long day. It's comfortable and familiar already. It's where I want to be.

"*Malyshka*, I didn't know your firm—the owner of your firm —was Russian. Turns out he's my dad's childhood friend. Only Christina knew the owner was Russian."

"You like to keep your business within the Russian community. I thought you might."

"We do. It's not that we think your company needs our support, but we like to support other Russians."

"I can understand. My parents feel the same way about shopping at Japanese owned stores. There aren't too many Brazilian owned businesses near us, but they look for them. Maybe it's an immigrant thing."

"I suppose so."

"I have to work, Pasha. But you still—"

I glance toward the door before meeting Pasha's gaze once more.

"I still owe you your spanking."

"You know I'm not a little, right? I don't even know where that came from."

"I know, and I'm not a Dom. I may like to be in control, but that's not the type of relationship I want with you, *malyshka*."

"I think between that and you calling me baby girl, it just seemed to fit."

"Seemed?"

"Seems, Daddy."

I try it out when we're not in the middle of having sex, and it still feels foreign, but not wrong. Heat flares in his eyes before he devours me. His tongue thrusts into my mouth, and I don't stifle my moan. We're fumbling with each other's clothes, the air of secrecy and discovery heightening our excitement.

"I'm going to fuck you, *malyshka*. And this time I will mark you. You are mine."

"And you're mine."

"I am."

We abandon each other's clothes and tug at our own. I look back at my desk and notice my thong on the floor beside it. Holy fuck. Did Greg see that? I don't think so. I didn't notice Pasha dropped it there. I didn't even notice I sat through the entire meeting with no panties.

Pasha lifts me off my feet and carries me to one of the chairs in front of my desk. It's a tight fit, but we manage as I straddle him. I might be on top, but he guides me as I rise and fall on his cock. More like a fucking Coke bottle. I've seen enough dicks in real life and in movies to know he's more than average.

The chair creaks as we move together, and I have a moment of doubt that we're too heavy. That I'm too heavy. But Pasha's let go of my hips and is moving his hands over my thighs, pressing his fingers into me before gliding them over my hips to my ass to squeeze it, then to my waist. His fingers trail over my belly.

"Fuck, *malyshka*. Every inch of you is temptation. I want to strip you and kiss all of you. I want to mark all of you as mine."

"Tonight?"

"Every fucking night."

He must be exaggerating. I look into his eyes, and he's revealing his feelings to me. There's earnestness there, and now I think he might mean that.

"I told you I'm all in, Sumiko."

He presses my head down so he can kiss me. I expect it to be ravenous again, but this one is tender. It's as though he needs me to know that even though we're fucking, this is about more than just that.

"I am too, Daddy. If you're willing to let me in more, then I want to see you whenever we can."

"Baby girl, are you close? I can't last much longer. You're too tight and so fucking smooth and hot."

He's pressing me onto his cock, rubbing my clit against him. It's all I need to detonate. I throw my head back as I come. It's a struggle not to make a sound. He pulls my blouse from my skirt and pushes it until he can kiss my ribs. He yanks the waistband down as he kisses my belly. I feel him pulse inside me. He's coming too. I don't get up, and he doesn't lift me off. Half an hour ago, I had sex without a condom for the first time, and now he came in me. Thank God for my IUD. I believe what he said about being clean. I get the feeling he might not always be forthcoming, but he won't lie to me. Not about something like that.

He draws me into his embrace as we try to catch our breath. He kisses my cheek and temple as I kiss his neck. It's that affection he showed in my hotel room. It's unexpected, but so welcome.

"I wish I could stay, Sumiko. I don't want to have sex with you then leave straight afterward, but I have another interview. I'd like to come back and take you out to lunch, though. Are you available?"

"I am. Today's actually my half day. I work long hours, so I have every other Friday off, and only half days when I'm in on a Friday."

"Really?"

"Yeah. I started doing it when I trained for a triathlon a few years ago, and it's just stuck. Greg doesn't mind because I get more than enough done while I'm here. Sometimes I take work home with my on my half days, but usually I'm just off. I'm done at one."

"Can I come back and pick you up then?"

"I'd like that."

He kisses my forehead before I stand. He steps past me as I turn to retrieve my thong. He snatches it from the floor, sniffs it, waggling his eyebrows, and sticks it in his pocket.

"Mine now. And I don't think you'll need to bother with any in the future. They won't stay on."

Between his cum that I can feel on my thighs and my own reaction to that comment, I'm soaking again. I might need them after all.

"I'll walk you out. I need to freshen up."

"Sumiko, I have to talk to Christina and the others about whether they're comfortable still considering your firm since we're together now. I don't know what they'll say. If we hire your company, I don't know whether they'll assign you to us after all."

"It would be a conflict of interest, but I think it can still work legally."

"I'll see how the next interview goes, but I don't know that I'll have a decision by lunch."

"It's all right, Pasha. I don't expect anything either way."

We exchange a quick kiss before I walk him to the elevator. I duck into the restroom to tidy myself before returning to my desk. I dive into the work I need to complete, and it's one o'clock before I realize it. I look up for the first time in hours to find Pasha at my door a third time. I'm quick to gather my things. We don't talk until we're outside.

"What are you in the mood for?"

"I picked last time, though, I've never had borsht."

"You're not missing anything. I hate it."

"And I thought you were a true Russian."

"That is hardly our best dish. Do you eat sushi?"

I watch him, and he looks like he wants to swallow his tongue. I laugh. I can't help it.

"Yes, I do. If that's what you want, I'm sure I'll find something I like."

"That was so stupid."

"No, it wasn't." I kiss his cheek as I take his hand. "I'm glad to know you like raw fish. Not everyone does. I eat more Japanese food than I do Brazilian, so it works."

"But it was so stereotypical."

"And my comment about borsht wasn't?"

"You were joking. We can get something else."

"I'd like to have sushi. If you aren't too starving, there's a great place in Jackson Heights."

"Queens?"

He seems to hesitate a moment, but then he nods.

"Yeah."

He guides me to the car and waits for me to climb into the back of the town car before he follows. Once he's settled on the seat, he lifts me onto his lap.

"I don't think I'm going to get used to you picking me up whenever you want."

"You should. It will happen often. I don't enjoy having you out of reach. You belong right here."

"You're not worried that I'm going to ignore you again, are you?"

"No. You hide the hard on I get every time I see you, and I don't mind you knowing now that it happens."

"Every time?" I scoff.

He maneuvers me to straddle him again.

"Yes, every time. You're so damn hot, and now I know what it feels like to be inside you. You've ruined me."

I run the back of my fingers against his temple before

tunneling them into his dark hair. Our kiss is slow, but it's still hot. Can we have sex a third time today? He's unfastening his pants again. Thank God. I reach between us and stroke him, making him groan as he keeps his eyes closed. What felt like iron a moment ago turns into what must be titanium or something. How did he get even harder?

"You do this to me, *malyshka*."

He speaks as though he reads my mind. He pulls my hand away from his cock, and I rise onto my knees before sinking onto him.

"Baby girl, that's almost better than coming. It's like I've found where I've always been meant to be. Inside you, with you in my arms."

Neither of us moves. We just sit there, joined, looking at one another.

"I feel the same way, Daddy."

He twitches inside me, then stills. I lean forward, unsure suddenly. But he wraps his arms around me and strokes my back. It's so soothing that I soon find myself so relaxed I could almost fall asleep. But he's still buried in me, and we're not moving. It just feels so incredibly right.

"What's happening between us, Pasha? I don't understand."

I whisper, afraid that I'll shatter the mood.

"I don't know, but I've never felt this way before. I want to make you come, but I don't want to come. I don't want this to end, even though I want to pleasure you more than I want anything else."

"I feel the same. A week ago, I felt like you wouldn't let me get to know you. Now I feel like I've always known you. How did sex change that? I mean, I get sex changes things in general. But why do I feel so—"

"Connected to you?"

"Yeah."

"It's like something unlocked in me. I want to bring you into my life when I have never let a woman get this close to me before."

"Why not?"

"It's complicated."

My last boyfriend said something just like that. But not in the middle of sex—or whatever this is. I never felt this close to him. He was distant and evasive, like Pasha was during our date. It's why I broke up with him. I don't want a repeat with Pasha, but he says he wants more.

"Why is it complicated?"

He chooses his words carefully as he answers.

"With a lot of wealth comes a lot of competition and envy. Not everyone is civil in business. Sometimes there are threats. I can work long hours, and sometimes I'm called away for a few days at a time unexpectedly. I have responsibilities to my family and my work that I can never ignore. Sometimes they have to come first, even if that's not what I want. We employ many people who depend on us for their livelihoods and their families'."

His expression and tone are neutral, but I sense regret.

"Can you tell me when something comes up, and you have to put that first?"

"I will always try to. If I have to leave, and I can't let you know myself, someone in my family will tell you. I promise."

That seems really important to him. There's emphasis on those last two words that wasn't there a moment ago. It's like he's trying to convince me of something I still don't know about. Why does he sound so serious if he handles importing textiles and household goods?

"*Malyshka*, Bear Imports is the company I own with Misha. But I have other business ventures besides that. I have stakes in many of the developments my cousins own. They're even wealthier than I am, so I often accompany them when they have to be away. I am an accountant, but I'm also a bodyguard when needed."

"You looked like that when you walked us back to the hotel. All four of you did."

"Because we are. Don't laugh."

I cock an eyebrow, and he smiles. It lightens the mood.

"Maks has twin babies. A boy and a girl. He and Laura have faced some of those threats, so we're all very protective. I'm a bodyguard to a four-month-old. Misha is too."

Now I really try not to laugh. I picture this tall, muscular man guarding a baby. I can picture him in aviator sunglasses with an earpiece while pushing a stroller, better yet strapped into a baby carrier. It's actually kinda hot.

"That's sweet."

"They are, but it's also serious. There are some risks to being involved with me, Sumiko."

I nod before I cup his jaw with both hands. I drop a kiss to his lips. I'm ready to pull back, but his fists my hair and holds my head in place. Our talk is over, and so is the motionless joining. Neither of us can strop. I'm unbuttoning his shirt as he's pushing mine up. We pull apart long enough to shed them, and he unclasps my bra. He dives in as though he's starving. He sucks each. Hard. He's once more setting the pace, and it's exactly what I need. He knows. It's not what he wants. It's always about him giving me what I need. He unfastens my skirt and pulls it up over my head. He draws me up onto my knees before his hand lands across my ass.

"This isn't your real spanking, *malyshka*. I haven't forgotten about that. I will give you that when we're done. This is purely for pleasure."

"Yes, Daddy. I want all of it hard."

"So you know how much I want you? That I can't get enough of you?"

"Yes."

His hand rains down a stinging blow. One after another until he's done it five times.

"Do not doubt me, Sumiko. I've told you from the start that I know what I want. If you want me to tell you or show you because you enjoy it, I will. But don't ever let it be because you need me to prove it. You'll wind up with my hand on your ass, not an orgasm."

"Daddy, that's hot."

"Do you understand me? I am not some teen boy who doesn't know what he wants. I'm fucking balls deep in you because I was ready to tear everything down while we were apart."

"I understand, Daddy."

He continues to spank me, pushing me onto his cock with every slap.

"May I come? I really need to. Please."

"Yes, *malyshka*."

I moan, uncaring that the privacy glass probably isn't thick enough to block it out. I'm loud, and he loves it. He flips me onto my back on the seat. He's rougher now. His hand is on my throat. It's tight but not breath play. I'm not ready for that.

"I want you tied to my bed, so I can worship you and torment you in equal parts. I want to make you come, and I want to hear you beg. I want to claim every part of you."

"I want to give you every part. You've had most of me, but I'll give you all."

Does he get what I mean?"

"I'm fucking buying a rainbow selection of butt plugs, then I'm fucking you there too. Is that what you want?"

"Yes. Fuck, how soon can they be delivered?"

"Tonight. I'm serious. I want you in my bed. I'm sick of looking at the empty spot. I had one night with you, and I haven't been able to sleep properly since."

"Me neither, Daddy. I'm sorry."

He pauses and shakes his head. He doesn't move for a moment.

"I didn't like you ghosting me. You could have told me, and I would have listened. I would have respected your wishes. But I can't fault you for feeling like we weren't compatible. I didn't make it seem like we are. I'm sorry too."

"Kiss me, please."

I pour everything into it. Everything I feel and don't understand. His words were heartfelt. He wants me to know that. He let me in. I hope neither of us regrets it.

Chapter Eleven

Pasha

After I left the conference room, I texted Ilya to pick me up as I walked to Sumiko's office. I didn't think anyone would know from the beginning that we're bratva, but neither did I expect a man to tell me he grew up with my dad. I knew Anton was probably already calling our dad from the car. I told him and Christina to leave without me before I went to see Sumiko. I joined them for the second interview, but that company was owned by an American.

We prefer to keep our money in our community. We can also trust the business owners more easily, and we have leverage if we need it. But that wasn't the reason we're awarding the job to Sumiko's firm. She provided the best answers, and they are the most qualified.

But that's not what I'm thinking about as we kiss. She wants to be with me, but I'm still scared. I've hinted as much as I can, but the day will inevitably come when she discovers it all. She'll either walk away, or she'll accept the danger this life brings. Neither is ideal, and both make me feel guilty. But I'm selfish enough to want her, anyway.

"We're here, *malyshka*."

The car pulls to a stop, and she scrambles for her bra and blouse. I pull my shirt back on. She looks around, anxious that my driver will open the door before we're ready. He knows better than that. When we're dressed, I knock on the window.

"This is the place."

She points to the restaurant, but I'm looking around. Jackson Heights is the heart of the Colombian community in New York. It's not somewhere I go often. It's not wise, and I'm tempting fate. I'm already putting my *malyshka* in danger, but she wanted to come here. I didn't want to tell her no. I never want to tell her no. But I know I will have to and often. Just not yet. I entwine my fingers with hers as we walk to the door, but I have to let go as we enter. It's too narrow for us to stand side by side. It's seat yourself, so she heads toward an open table. She reaches back and takes my hand as I follow her.

"Sumiko."

Fuck. I know that voice.

"Kutsenko?"

"Hi, Pablo."

How the hell does she know Pablo? She's not from this neighborhood. She doesn't even live in the same borough.

"Diaz."

Sumiko is looking between us, but Pablo is looking at our hands. His eyes slowly rise until our gazes meet. She shifts to step between us, but I tug her back gently. I don't take my eyes off Pablo as I guide her to stand behind me.

"What are you doing with my ex-girlfriend, Kutsenko? I'm not the one she needs protecting from."

"Pablo—"

"Outside, Diaz. Sumiko stays in here. Your man and my man both guard her."

"Pasha? What's going on?"

"I'll explain in a moment, *malyshka*. Please wait for me in here."

"Your man and his man? What men?"

She's trying to peer over my shoulder, but I'm too tall. I twist so I can see her, but still keep Pablo in the corner of my eye.

"Ilya, my driver, is going to step outside with me. But Misha is in the far-right corner, near the hallway to the restrooms."

"How—Have you been here before?"

"No, *malyshka*. But I am quick to be observant wherever I go. Pablo's man is near the kitchen."

She looks around and spots Misha, the surprise clear on her face. Then she looks at the kitchen, her brow furrowing until I think she knows which man I mentioned. There are plenty of other Latinos inside, but Pablo's man is obvious once you think about it. Misha blends in much better.

"Pasha, what's happening? I—"

I pull her against my side and whisper in her ear.

"I promise everything will be all right, baby girl. Pablo and I have a long history together. Our families have known each other since mine moved to America. Please let me talk to him, then I'll explain what I can. I need you to trust me."

"Sumiko?"

We both look at Pablo.

"How do you know Pasha? What's going on? Why are you here with him? I used to bring you here. This was our place."

Sumiko blushes to her roots as she looks between us.

"I—"

"Pablo, outside. This is between us."

I try to intervene, but he shakes his head.

107

"I want to know why you'd break up with me just to go out with a man just like me. Why?"

"He's not like you at all, Pablo. And why I want to date anyone is none of your business. Let's go, Pasha. I'm sorry I picked this place."

"No, *malyshka*. I have to speak to Pablo. Please trust me."

Our gazes meet and hold before she nods. I wave Misha over.

"Keep her company while I talk to Pablo."

I kiss her temple, but I don't give anyone a chance to argue. I turn to the door, trusting Pablo won't shoot or knife me in the back. We step outside, each with a man standing close enough to fight alongside us but far enough away to be discreet.

"What the fuck, Kutsenko?"

"I didn't know."

"Now you do."

"And she says it's over. I didn't take her from you, and you know it."

"But now you know she was my woman."

"Was. This isn't the same as with Sean."

Pablo looks like he's ready to murder me. Even more than usual. But I know that's what he's thinking about. He already lost one woman to a syndicate rival.

"I fucking know you're not Sean O'Rourke. I know this is different. But Sumiko doesn't know about this life. It's better that she broke it off with me when she did. She deserves better than me or you, *cabrón*."

"I'm not an asshole, so I'd watch who you're calling names. I'm not your *manito*."

"You're as much of an asshole as I was if you bring her into this life. Does she know?"

"No."

"For fuck's sake, Pasha. Look at what happened to your

108

cousins' wives. It has forced them into the middle of everything. Sumiko is a nice girl. Walk away."

He's right about it all. I should. But fuck me, I won't. I could, but I can't all at the same time. Pablo takes a step back, nodding his head. I see the resignation that I won't listen, but I see the determination to make my life hell if I don't.

"This is only our second date, Pablo. She may not be that interested in me. This might be nothing."

"Bullshit. You haven't been on a date since we were in college. Maybe even high school for all I know. You don't date."

"And you do? You said she was your ex-girlfriend. That's more than just one or two dates. You're a fucking hypocrite."

"Or she might be the only person who makes me have a conscience. Stay away, *cabrón*."

"Or what? You'll send Juan my way? You'll cry to your *tío* that I have something you want? But she doesn't want you. You said she broke up with you. You're jealous."

I know he is. I would be. He hides his emotions nearly as well as a bratva man. But I see the anger in his eyes he's trying to hide. It's anger from worry and jealousy. The worry I can appreciate. The jealousy I couldn't give a fuck about.

"I'm warning you, *malparido*. Stay away."

Badly born. I know enough Spanish to translate that literally, but I also know when someone's slinging one of the strongest slurs in Colombian Spanish at me.

"Do you kiss your *mamasita* with that mouth? I may not speak Spanish, but I learned your curses as a kid. You sound like a criminal, even if you're wearing a custom suit. Maybe that's why she didn't want you. She deserves better than some *hijueputa* off the streets."

Son of a bitch. I can dish it out too.

"Back off, Pasha. I won't warn you again."

"Or what? Come after me and put her in the middle? That

didn't work out so well the last time that happened. Let's see that scar Sean gave you. You didn't get your woman back, but you did spend a week in bed."

"*Coma mierda, huevón.*" Eat shit, asshole.

"Speaking of eating, my date is waiting to have lunch with me."

Pablo takes a step forward, and so does Ilya. I wave my man back.

"You come into my neighborhood. You've always had a big pair of *huevos*, I'll give you that. But you're fucking stupid to do it once. It's suicide to do it again. Leave and don't come back."

"After my rainbow roll with extra crunch. Have a good day, Pablo. I'd spend my time looking for my *manito* if I were you. Maks is getting closer."

I don't wait for him to say anything else. I go back into the restaurant and spot Sumiko and Misha at a table along the far wall. I see Misha scanning the customers as I make my way to them. He nods and stands up, making Sumiko look in my direction.

"Is everything all right? I shouldn't have suggested this place."

"The one you used to come to with your ex-boyfriend in his neighborhood? Perhaps not. But the sushi looks good."

"Pasha—"

"Shh, *malyshka*. I'll explain in a moment. The waitress is coming."

We place our order, and I can tell Sumiko is nervous. She stared at the menu, blinking for several moments before she just pointed to something. I don't know if she's even aware of what she chose. When the waitress takes our menus and moves to another table, I slide into the chair beside her, trusting Misha will guard my back.

"How did you meet Pablo?"

"I met him in college through a friend. We didn't know each other well, but we hung out with some of the same people. A year ago, we ran into each other here. I was with Tiffany and Sarah, and he was with his brother. After dinner, my friends left, and we started talking at the bar."

She shrugs. And the rest is history. But it's not. It's here and now, and it could get really messy.

"How long did you date?"

"Three months or so. I broke it off with him, Pasha."

"I know that, but why?"

She sits back in her seat and looks at the table. I move my chair closer and take her hand.

"Because he wouldn't tell me much about himself or his family. He was attentive, but I soon realized it was so I wouldn't ask questions. When I did, he was evasive."

"Like I was at dinner."

"Yes."

I sigh. This isn't the right place for this conversation.

"I think we better get our order to go. What I need to tell you can't be done in public."

"What's going on? Tell me now."

"Sumiko, in this neighborhood, the walls have ears. I will tell you what I can, but not here. Please trust me."

"You keep saying that."

"Because I need you to. If you want out after I explain, I get it. But it's not safe for any of us right now."

Her eyes widen, and I finally get through to her. She looks around before she nods. I signal the waitress and tell her to make it to go. I gesture to Misha to wait for our food before I lead her outside.

"When did Misha get here? Why is he here?"

I sigh.

"He was in the front passenger seat the whole time. He got

out and went inside while we were getting dressed. I wanted someone else with us, regardless of where we went. It wasn't an option not to have him once you told me you wanted to come here."

"I don't understand."

"I know, *malyshka*. Get in."

I wait until we're both in the car before I say anything else. A knock on the window distracts me. I lower it and accept the bag from Misha. I raise the window and wait for the car door to close. I put the bag on the seat between us but change my mind. I lift Sumiko onto my lap and put the bag where she sat.

"What do you know about Jackson Heights?"

"There's a big Colombian community here. Pablo always knew a lot of people here. He said he spent a lot of time in the neighborhood as a kid."

"Do you know more than that? Like what this neighborhood is really like. What happens here?"

"I don't understand."

"Jackson Heights is like Brighton Beach to Colombians. Brighton Beach has a lot of Eastern European immigrants. One part is even known as Little Odessa. What do you know about the Colombians and Russians? The stereotypes about our communities."

She stares at me before she turns her head and looks at me sideways. Then she shakes her head.

"Are you saying he's a drug dealer?"

I don't answer.

"No. He's no more a drug dealer than you are a sex trafficker. Those are just nasty stereotypes."

"You're only right about part of that. My family will never traffic anyone. My father and uncles did things I will never share with anyone outside my family to protect my mom and aunts from being trafficked in Moscow. My mom—" I have to look away. "They took her when she was fifteen. My dad and Uncle Kirill nearly didn't get to her in time."

It's something we never talk about. But it's why Aunt Galina and Uncle Kirill had my cousins so close together. They were childhood sweethearts. My mother and my aunt Galina were best friends growing up. She and Kirill introduced my parents just like they did Svetlana and Radomir, Sergei and Misha's parents.

"I'm so sorry, Pasha."

I cover her hands with mine and pull her close to my chest, so she leans against me.

"Thank you, *malyshka*. Living in similar neighborhoods, Pablo and I grew up similarly. I've known him since we were kids."

I need to consider what else I can say. We're treading dangerous ground. If I say the wrong thing, not only could I scare her away, I could have her running to the cops.

"Pasha, you said only the sex trafficking part wasn't true. Then you said you and Pablo grew up similarly. Were you both drug dealers?"

I hold my breath for a moment before I exhale slowly.

"It's not that simple."

"Either you were, or you weren't."

"It truly isn't that simple, *malyshka*. The people who controlled our neighborhoods back then made us into the men we are now. But it was through coercion and fear."

I don't want to tell her a thing about Vlad, and I don't want to tell her it was Pablo's father and uncle who trained him.

"I can't tell you more because I don't think it's safe for you, Sumiko. But he was evasive for the same reason I was. There are things about our past and our present that we can't talk about. It would endanger you and everyone else we care about."

"Then why are you telling me this? Why didn't he?"

"That's not an easy question to answer. He didn't tell you any of this because it was safer not to draw you in. But he didn't draw you in because he didn't—"

"He didn't what, Pasha? You're scaring me."

"He didn't feel like he could barely breathe without you. He didn't feel like his world was off balance without you. He didn't feel like he needed you to give him the only reprieve he gets from all this shit."

She sits silently for a minute, but her body is relaxed against mine. Then she sits up, and I'm scared she's withdrawing from me.

"Is that how you feel about me? Do you believe you're being selfish bringing me into your life?"

"Yes, to both."

I look out the tinted window. She tries to turn my head, but I won't budge. I'm a coward. I don't want to look at her when she says she wants out before it's even started.

"Daddy, look at me, please."

I'm slow to turn my head, but I do.

"Am I in danger with you?"

"Yes. I will do everything I can to keep you safe. But being with me brings risks."

"And not just because you're rich."

"No."

She swallows, and I watch as her throat constricts.

"It's more than just a little street hustle, isn't it?"

"Yes."

"Is Christina involved in this? Am I because you're hiring my firm?"

"She isn't directly involved. We all have legal businesses, and she heads the construction division of my cousins' legal corporation. You and your company would only handle our legal assets and evaluate only legal acquisitions. Greg and Arseniy know that."

"Because they're Russian?"

"Yes."

I can't tell her more than that. Not yet, at least.

"If Pablo was—is—a drug dealer, is he part of the Cartel?"

I don't answer. I just look at her.

"If he is Cartel, and you're like him, does that mean you're in the Cartel, too?"

"I am not part of the Cartel. The Colombians and Russians tolerate one another. But his family and my family have a history together. Right now, we're on good terms. We aren't always."

"Are you—like—rivals?"

Again, I don't answer. If I don't give her explicit answers, then no one can force them out of her.

"Why are you telling me all of this? Pablo definitely didn't even come close to this. Do you really feel the way you described?"

"Yes. Sumiko, I'm being selfish, and I know it. I want you to be mine. I want you at my side. But I can't ask that of you and keep you completely in the dark. This is unfair enough without hiding everything from you. But I know I'm asking a lot."

"I want to be yours."

"*Malyshka*, it goes both ways. I am yours. I will do whatever I have to keep you safe and to make your happy."

"And if I want out?"

"I will never force you. If you're my girlfriend, then I need you to accept a security detail. If we break up, then I want you to still accept it, at least for a little while. Or you let me help you set up one of your own."

"This is some scary shit, Pasha."

"I know."

"This is a lot."

"I know."

"Can I think about it?"

"Of course. I know you're going to have questions, and there will be a lot of them that I can't answer. But what I can, I will."

She nods again and leans back against me. She wraps her arm around my waist and nestles closer. I glance down, and she has her eyes closed.

"Daddy?"

"Yes, *malyshka.*"

"Will you take me home? Yours or mine and stay with me?"

"Yes, baby girl."

"Will you tie me to a bed and spank me like you said earlier?"

"If that's what you want."

"Will you order those rainbow butt plugs?"

I feel her cheek move against my chest, and I know she's smiling.

"Maybe we could do a little shopping together."

I hold my breath.

"Breathe, Daddy. Yes, I'd like that. I think you might be as kinky as I am."

I ease her away from me.

"Sumiko, this isn't just about sex for me."

"It's not just about that for me, either. But that's a whole lot easier to talk about right now than the heavy shit you just shared."

I nod and lower the privacy glass a couple inches.

"*Moye mesto.*" My place.

Chapter Twelve

Sumiko

What the fuck have I gotten myself into? Out of the frying pan and into the fire. Pablo was evasive, and I think he lied often now that Pasha's explained what he can. I'm not angry that he lied. I get it. He protected me and everyone else around him. But it also tells me he was never as serious about me as I hoped he would be. I really liked him. But as I lean against Pasha and rest throughout the car ride, I realize it wasn't a fraction of how I feel about Pasha.

And that freaks the fuck out of me. This has to be infatuation. There's no other explanation for such strong feelings in such a short amount of time. It's ridiculous otherwise. Then again, the cliché love at first sight exists for a reason. Same for soulmates.

"*Malyshka*, we're here."

I reach across the seat and grab our food. Ilya opens the door, and I scramble off Pasha's lap. I didn't think about anyone seeing us like that. I'm closer to the curb, so he reaches out his hand. I take it and get out, but I glance back at Pasha just before I release Ilya's hand. He nods to me, but I can tell he doesn't love seeing my hand in another man's. But he says nothing. Perhaps he's possessive, but not unreasonable. I wrap my arm around his, but he pulls loose and drapes his arm around my shoulders. I glance back as we enter the building, but neither Ilya nor Misha followed us.

"Misha lives a couple blocks from here. Ilya lives in Queens. I have security here, *malyshka*."

I look around and see someone in the lobby's corner. A man materializes from I don't know where, as we get on the elevator. He walks behind us until we get to Pasha's door, where there's a third man. I can only look up at him, utterly unsure what to say.

"I know it's a lot. Come inside, and let's eat. I'm sure you have more questions. I'll do what I can to answer them."

"Could I use your bathroom? I'd like to wash my hands."

He points to a door, and I head to it. I hear him getting plates in the kitchen. I turn on the water and unlock my phone.

What is Russian cartel called

Maybe I shouldn't have looked this up. Link after link comes up with things about Russian prisons and tattoos and guns and drugs, and lion, tigers, and bears. Oh, my. I click a link and put my phone on the counter. I lean forward to read while I wash my hands. By the time they're dry, I'm freaked all the fuck out.

Russian organized crime is known as the bratva, which translates to brotherhood. The bratva is involved in narcotics smuggling, international arms dealing, bioterrorism, money laundering, and sex trafficking. Some bratva organizations run as paramilitary operations and are often supported by local governments in Russia. Extortion and blackmail are common. Force is used when other forms of coercion do not work. The bratva is most active in New York City, especially the Brighton Beach area of Queens; Chicago; and Los Angeles. Many branches formed after the fall of the Soviet Union. Members were often former KGB or Russian army.

I don't bother to read any more. I dry my hands and walk back out to the living room. The loft is enormous and open concept. Pasha is waiting by a small table in the breakfast nook. It's more intimate than the larger rectangular dining room table I can see on the other side of the kitchen.

"Are you bratva?"

I blurt out my question. Pasha stares at me for a moment before he sets down the water glass. I thrust out my phone. He approaches me slowly, like I'm a wounded wild animal he doesn't trust. He takes it and skims what I read. When he looks up at me, his face is entirely blank. I have no clue—not even a hint from which to guess—what he's thinking. I'm certain there's plenty going through his mind. There's a fucking whirlwind in mine. But it's as though I'm looking at a mannequin for all the emotion that's on his face.

"Yes."

I asked, and he answered. Now what do I do with that? I should bolt. He'd chase me. He'd try to reassure me and ask me not to tell anyone. But I know he would never hurt me. That is the only thing I can feel all the way to my bones. He will never intentionally hurt me. But what happens when he breaks my heart?

"Sumiko, will you sit with me?"

I nod. I expect him to turn back to the table. Instead, he walks to the living room. He sits in an armchair and points to the sofa. I don't think I like the distance he's put between us. He told me earlier that he doesn't enjoy having me out of reach. He's put me on his lap more than once.

"*Malyshka.*"

That one word is such a relief.

"I have never admitted that before. I've lied any time I've ever been asked. I'm surprised that I answered you at all. I don't want to lie, but that confession could be my death sentence."

"You think I'd turn you over to the cops?"

I'm appalled and insulted, even if I understand why that's a reasonable fear for him.

"Not necessarily. But if you ever let that slip..."

I rest my elbows on my thighs as I bury my face in my hands. I need a moment. He doesn't rush me.

"My ex-boyfriend is in the Colombian mafia, and you're in the Russian mafia. Does that mean you've done all those things in the article? I mean, except the sex crimes?"

"I will not answer that, Sumiko. That is a question I understand, but it is one that will only endanger you if I answer."

"That is an answer. Are you a murderer, Pasha?"

His expression is blank again.

"You won't admit that out loud, but your silence does it. You won't lie to me, so you just won't answer."

"It's never that simple. None of this life is simple. It's why Pablo didn't let you in. It's why I'm fucking selfish to let you come anywhere near it. Good and bad, right and wrong—they're subjective in this life. Our morals and ethics are situational, not absolute. At least, that's how outsiders would see it. For us, it's very clear. I'm twenty-eight and still alive. There are plenty of men I knew who didn't live to be my age. There are reasons I have. That's all I can say."

I swallow. I don't know where to look or what to say. There's a tug of war in my mind, and what I feel should be the clear victor is barely holding on by its fingernails. I should run. I should swear never to say anything and then never see him again. But that's not what I want. I don't notice my tears until Pasha leans forward and wipes them away.

"Sumiko, I wish I were a better man for you."

"Don't say that."

I'm more adamant than I expected. Hearing him—the words and the regret in his tone—they feel so wrong. I shake my head, but I can't look at him yet.

"I knew I would have to explain more over time. But everything has happened so fast today. I can take you home."

"Do you want me to leave, Pasha? Do you wish you hadn't said anything?"

"No, I don't want you to leave. Not at all. I should have known you'd Google this, but—" It's his turn to shake his head. When I look into his eyes, I see it. I see a lifetime of pain.

"You didn't choose this, did you?"

"No, I didn't."

"Were you born into it? Is that how it works?"

"Often, but no, I wasn't born into it. It's the very thing my parents wanted to avoid and why we immigrated. But we knew nearly no one in America. We came to New York because Misha's family was already here, and we followed my father's brother's family. My uncle was already dead, so it was only Aunt Galina to raise and protect my cousins. My parents and Misha's did what they could, but when the bratva came for Maks, Aleks, Niko, and Bogdan, there was nothing anyone could do and still stay alive. My parents did everything possible, but when the bratva decided it was time for Anton and me to join, there was no choice."

"How old?"

I can barely get the words out around the gorge in my throat.

"Fourteen."

"Two years after you moved here."

"Yes. Sumiko, for us, there is no walking away. We're safer here than on our own. But you can—you should—walk away."

"You said you don't want me to leave."

"What I want and what should happen are vastly different."

"And if I want to stay?"

"Then you're free to go when you want."

I sit back and try to absorb everything I've just learned. Pasha watches me, but he says nothing. He's giving me the time I need. I suddenly feel exhausted. I close my eyes. The longer I sit there, the more powerful my reaction becomes. I reach out my hand to him. He takes it without hesitation.

"Daddy, will you sit with me, please?"

His hand trembles for a moment before he moves next to me. I wrap my arms around him and burrow against his chest. I'm testing myself. Being this close to him doesn't make me want to flee. It makes me want to crawl onto his lap and feel safe again.

"What do you need, *malyshka?*"

"For you to hold me while I sort through all of this. Just stay with me."

"I thought I would be asking you that."

He kisses my forehead, and I tighten my hold. He pulls me onto his lap, and I release a shuddering sigh. More tears fall.

"Will I be able to introduce you to my other friends? Can we spend time with Sarah and Tiffany? Do I have to keep you from my family?"

"Yes, you can introduce me to your friends, and we can spend time with Sarah and Tiffany. I don't want you to keep me a secret from your family, but I understand if you do. Most of the time, I live a normal life. I go grocery shopping and work out. I like to go hiking, and I've started biking since Christina enjoys it. I don't mind going with her on her insanely long weekend rides. The woman does thirty miles with a smile. I go to the movies and out to eat. Just normal stuff."

"But your day job isn't normal. And you said sometimes you leave unexpectedly. Will I be waiting for someone to tell me you're dead?"

He sighs, and it's as though the weight of the world rests on him. It makes me shift, but he holds me close.

"Please don't leave."

His request startles both of us. He eases his embrace, but I don't move again.

"I'm not leaving, Pasha. I'm trying to work through all this. But I'm not leaving."

I say it twice because I sense he needs the reassurance. He's vulnerable, and I think it's a position wholly foreign to him. I twist to straddle him, so I can see him properly.

"Pasha." I collect my thoughts as I go. "If this doesn't work out, and I can freely leave, then I will stay. If this is a lifetime commitment because I'll know at least some of your secrets, then I need to think about it. But nothing is making me run. I'm still here, and you're not having to force me. I'm learning, and I'm trying to digest everything."

"Do you want to talk more? Or have lunch? Or—"

"Let's eat. I'm starving. Then we'll see from there."

I stand up, and he follows me as we walk to the table. He has us seated across from each other, but I don't think that's what we need right now. I move my plate and glass to the spot next to his. Just like at the restaurant during our first date, he pulls out and pushes in my chair. He waits for me to take the first bite before he eats. I don't think he's doing it to impress me. I think someone ingrained those manners into him. It's old-fashioned, but I admit it makes me feel special.

We eat in silence for a few minutes, and I can tell it's bothering Pasha. I think he fears I'm withdrawing from him. And I'm worried that he's going to doubt us and do that too. I slide my fingers into his curled hand. He brings them to his lips and kisses the back of mine.

If I'd heard everything from Pablo that Pasha just admitted, I think my reaction would have been extremely different. I'm confident I wouldn't be sitting, eating sushi with Pablo. I think he would have protected me out of duty if I'd stayed with him. With Pasha, I feel safe because it's him. I can see the similarities between them, and it all makes more sense now, but I don't feel the same way. It's visceral with Pasha.

The longer we sit together, the more reconciled I become to this information. But Pasha's vibe is the opposite. He's growing tenser, even if his expression is back to being shuttered. His unease is pouring off him like a flood over a cliff.

"Daddy, I believe you owe me a spanking."

I waggle my eyebrows, hoping to make him smile. It jars him out of his thoughts.

"Is that right, *malyshka*?"

"Yes, Daddy. Then I think there was some online shopping we were going to do."

"You still want that, Sumiko?"

"Pasha, I don't know what the future holds for either of us separately or us as a couple. But I didn't go running out of here screaming bloody murder. I'm going to have more questions, and you're going to have to be patient with me as I learn. But if I'm honest, there's an air of danger about you I've felt from the start. It's hot as hell, but it likely warns most people away. I ignored it—accepted it—whatever, but I've known it's been there since we met. Now it just makes sense."

He nods a few times. He's accepting my explanation. He pushes back from the table, and I stand too.

"Come with me, baby girl. Your ass and my hand have a reckoning coming."

Chapter Thirteen

Pasha

I keep thinking, *what have I done?* We don't admit who we are. We don't bring in outsiders. We don't form attachments. We don't do a lot of things that normal people do.

Laura figured out who Maks was without him having to say anything. She knew before their meeting began. But she was already familiar with the Russian underworld from spending a year there in college, and her career as a corporate lawyer put her on the underworld's periphery. Christina figured some things out, but threats forced her to learn about others. Anastasia's half Russian, but she didn't know about the bratva until she guessed, and Niko didn't lie. I guess I'm in the same boat as Niko.

But no one else has brought women into their lives who weren't already from bratva families. What's Maks going to say when I tell him yet another outsider knows about us? He'll understand, but that doesn't mean he'll be happy about it.

I'm questioning all of this. But the one thing I'm not questioning is how I feel about Sumiko. I never imagined she would handle this so well. When she showed me the website, I panicked. She might not have known because I didn't want her to, but I was scared as hell. Vlad's training came in handy. I never thought I would say that without being in some type of dangerous situation. Then again, Sumiko learning the truth was a dangerous situation. My heart was racing even if my expression didn't show it.

But she asked me to explain. She gave me the opportunity. She didn't lock herself in the bathroom or a bedroom or run to the elevator and call the police or the Feds. She listened to me. And she stayed.

"Take your clothes off, *malyshka*."

I sit in a chair beside my dresser and watch as she looks around.

"Do not make me tell you twice, or your ass will burn for days."

"Yes, Daddy."

She strips, but her eyes are darting everywhere. I get the sense she's just curious. When she looks at the bed, she glances at my side with the alarm clock, but her gaze rests on the pillow I want to become hers. When she looks back at me, I'm certain she's thinking the same thing.

Once her clothes are laying on the end of the bed, I tap my lap. She comes to stand in front of me, and I guide her to lie across my legs.

"Keep your hands out of the way, *malyshka*. Hold my leg or the chair leg if you think you're going to reach back. Have you ever been spanked like this?"

"Not since I was like five, and I broke a family heirloom."

"You said you like it kinky. Do you have a safe word?"

"No. I—"

She looks back at me. I help her up, and she perches on my knee.

"Do you have experience with kinky sex?"

"Not really. I want it, but the other guys I've dated have been pretty vanilla. A few spankings during sex and dirty talk, but none were as adventurous as I wanted to be."

"You set the limits, Sumiko. If there are things you're certain you don't want, then tell me when you think of them or when they come up. If there are things you wish to try, but you're nervous, then we go slowly and learn together. If there's something you like, tell me, and I will try my best to give you what you want. If you need to stop, and you say your safe word, it ends immediately. I will never force you to keep going or try to convince you to do more than what you're comfortable with. I want to be in control, but not at the expense of hurting you. That's not the kind of control I crave."

"I want to submit to you because that power dynamic intrigues me. I trust you, Pasha, and I don't think you'll abuse that. But I don't want to be a slave or even a sub where you make all the decisions."

"We are equals in this. What you do or don't want is as important as anything I might want or don't want. What's your safe word, *malyshka*?"

"Kale. I hate it."

I can't help but laugh.

"Anton makes me eat it. He's a way healthier eater than I am. I think it tastes like dirt. He likes to sneak it into my smoothies and not tell me until after I drink most of it. I love my brother, but he can be an ass because he's older."

"I picture him pinning you down and making you eat it like he might have made you eat dirt as a kid."

"Yeah, well, he's shit out of luck if he wants to pin me

down. We're evenly matched in strength. It took twenty-three years, but I finally caught up."

"You sound like my younger brother."

I shrug. The bane of being the younger child, I suppose.

"Over my lap, *malyshka*."

"Yes, Daddy."

I rub my hand over her ass, appreciating the view. The flesh is soft and supple. There's nothing bony about it, and I'm glad. I love the feel, and I'm struggling not to abandon this and fuck her instead.

"You're already wet, baby girl. Does being over my lap excite you?"

I dip my fingers between her legs, her dew coating them.

"Yes, Daddy."

"Do you think baby girls who earn spankings deserve orgasms, too?"

"Definitely."

I laugh. I'm going to make her come all afternoon and throughout the night. She sounds so certain, but I'm going to edge her for a while before I let her have her first one. I squeeze her ass hard enough to leave temporary imprints.

"You had every right to not want to see me. But ignoring me rather than talking to me wasn't cool. Don't hide from me, *malyshka*. I told you, we're equal partners in this. If something's bothering you, we talk about it. I'm not your Dom. I will not automatically have the final say in everything. The only time I won't relent is if it concerns your safety. That will not be negotiable."

"Yes, Daddy. I'm sorry. I could have told you to stop texting me, but I took the easy way out. It's not like you were harassing me or anything. I just didn't want to make the effort."

"Five spanks on each side, then it's done. But if you put

your hands in the way, or you use your safe word just to get out of this, I will triple it."

"I understand, Daddy. I'm ready for my spanking."

I lean over and kiss her ass. A peck for each cheek before I sit all the way up to land the first slap. The sound rings in the bedroom, and I watch her ass tense. She relaxes quickly. I land the next spanking, and she tenses again. She remains that way for the next two, so I make the ones after that harder. When I finish, her ass is bright pink and so delectable.

"Open your legs, baby girl. Let me see how wet you are. You're dripping, aren't you?"

"Yes, Daddy. Am I forgiven? I need you."

"You want me to forgive you, so I'll make you come? That's not how it works."

"No. I mean, I know. I want to be forgiven because I want you to trust that I'll talk to you if there's a problem. But I need you because you're the hottest fucking man I've ever met, and your dick is making me ache. I can feel you, and I want you inside me."

"I decide when you get to come."

I press my fingers into her as I work her pussy. I start agonizingly slow, only building the force, not the speed. She's gripping my ankle like it's her lifeline in a typhoon. When she tries to look back at me over her shoulder, I press down between her shoulder blades. She tries to rock her hips to press her clit against my thigh. My elbow goes between her shoulder blades, and my hand spanks her. I pull on one globe, and I look at her tight rose bud.

"Have you worn a plug before?"

She shakes her head.

"Have you had anal before?"

"Yeah."

She pants her answer. For a flash, I wonder if it was with Pablo. I wonder if she's comparing me to him.

"Daddy, don't think about him. I'm not."

"What?"

I meet her gaze, and I realize she was watching me while I thought about fucking her in the ass.

"I can tell what you're thinking, Pasha. The answer is no. But I don't want to think about anyone but you. Are you comparing me to someone else?"

"There is no one to compare you to. You exist in an entirely different, better universe than anyone else."

I give her a quick, hard kiss. I can feel her core quiver, so I pull out. She wails and kicks her feet.

"I was so close."

"I know."

I spank her once again, my hand covering both cheeks. I fist her hair and pull back enough to make her back arch without hurting her.

"And you weren't going to ask. Who decides, *malyshka*?"

"You, Daddy."

I rub her clit.

"That's right."

I feel, as much as hear, her breathing change. I pull my hand away. She cries out again.

"Pasha, please. I need to come."

"Are you going to die?"

"I might."

I laugh.

"I doubt it, baby girl."

I thrust my fingers into her, working her faster and rubbing her clit again. Just as she starts to come, I pull away yet again.

"Pasha. Daddy. Please."

"Go lie on the bed, face up."

I help her up. As she hurries to follow my directions, I go to my closet and pull out four ties and four belts. Her eyes are as wide as saucers as she watches me.

"No more spankings, baby girl. Not unless you ask."

I work quickly. I have way too much experience restraining people, but only a small portion comes from sex play. I bind the ties around her wrists and ankles, then I use the belts to give me enough length to attach them to the bedframe. An under the mattress restraint system will be one of our first purchases. I come to stand at the foot of the bed and examine her as I yank my clothes off. I thought about a tie for a blindfold, but I want her to watch every moment.

I climb onto the bed and settle my shoulders between her thighs. I peel back her pussy lips and lick. My touch is gentle, so she's unprepared for when I latch onto her clit and suck hard. She bucks on the bed and cries out.

"Please."

It's a begging wail.

"Not yet."

"Daddy!"

I graze my teeth over her sensitive skin, the nerves already ablaze with sensation. I nip at the insides of her thighs when she tries to squeeze them around my ears. She's trembling as I thrust my tongue into her, my fingers following. When she's on the cusp of pain and frustration rather than aching anticipation, I shift upward, my forearms beside her head.

"Do you want me to wear a condom?"

"Don't care."

She's writhing with unspent lust.

"Sumiko, look at me. Do you want me to wear one?"

She stills and looks up at me. She takes a moment before she shakes her head. She waited long enough that I believe she thought about it, even if only briefly. I surge forward and pound

131

into her. I'm unrelenting as she strains against her restraints, trying to wrap herself around me but at my mercy.

"Daddy, I can't stop. Please may I come? Please don't punish me."

"Shh, *malyshka*. You can come. It's all right, baby girl."

I pull her wrist cuffs loose, and she clings to me.

"Kiss."

It's a hoarse request that I'm happy to indulge. The moment my tongue enters her mouth, its rhythm matching my cock's, I feel her clamp around me.

"Fuck, Daddy... Fuck... Arrgggh."

"I'm going to come inside you, *malyshka*. You're mine. You're going to take all my cum, and you're going to take me."

I fist her hair and move faster, harder, until I fear hurting her. But my need for her consumes me. I want to possess her as much as be possessed by her. I want the euphoria of coming, but I want to watch her pleasure continue. I want to be inside her and never leave.

"*Malyshka!*"

It's more a roar than anything else. I hold myself deep within her as I come. My cock pulses over and over. Every time I think there's nothing left to spend, another wave of pleasure rolls over me, and another jet of cum shoots from me. I feel completely depleted by the time the bliss wears down.

"Daddy, don't pull out yet."

I don't like how timid she sounds asking for what she wants.

"Baby girl, you're not being clingy, if that's what you want. I want to hold you, but I don't want to crush you."

"I'm a big girl. You aren't going to crush me."

I narrow my eyes at her. It wasn't said in jest or with confidence. It was like she was admitting a fault. I don't like it at all.

"I am heavier than you, taller than you, and broader than you.

Your size has nothing to do with that. I could crush Anton, and he weighs fifteen pounds more than me. I know because I've done it. You didn't say that as though you mean you're all grown up."

"Pasha, I am no waif."

"Good. I wouldn't have looked twice if you were. This is the fourth time today I've been buried balls deep in you. I plan to spend most of the night inside you if you're not too sore. I know exactly what your body is like, and I know just how much I desire it. I do not want you any other way than you are now. You're perfect."

"You are a sweet man."

She cups my face and kisses me. I pour all the affection into it I can. I brush the hair back from her sweaty temples. She strokes my back, and I feel my cock coming back to life. I wasn't this horny or ready to go this often when I was seventeen. I'm nearly thirty. Holy fuck. Who the fuck needs a little blue pill when they have a woman like Sumiko?"

"*Fofinho*, are you getting hard again?"

There's a playfulness to her voice that makes me grin.

"What does that mean?"

She swallows her laughter before she can answer.

"Cuddly."

"Cuddly? I'm going to do a shit ton more than just cuddle with you."

I circle my hips, and I'm about to nibble her lip, but my phone rings. Fuck my life.

"*Malyshka*, that's Maksim's ring tone. I can't ignore it."

I drag myself away from the bed.

"*Privet*."

Maksim responds in Russian when I answer in it.

"I need you now."

"I'm in the middle of something."

"Bring Sumiko here. Laura saw Juan at the park. He was watching her with the twins."

"Fuck. All right. We're on our way."

"What are you going to tell her?"

"She knows, Maks. She figured it out."

"I guessed as much. Misha told me you ran into Pablo and that he said she was his ex-girlfriend."

"She didn't know about him. But she knows about us. I need to get dressed. Are you in Queens?"

"Yes. Hurry."

"We will."

I toss the phone on the end of the bed. I was already unfastening Sumiko's ankles as I talked to Maks.

"We need to go to Maks's in Queens. Something's come up."

"We? I can go home, Pasha. You don't need me in the way."

"You are not in the way. This fucking sucks for timing, but this may be one of those times where I'm unexpectedly away for a few days. I want you with Laura and my family. Maks knows you know. That means everyone else will soon, too. He guessed after Misha said we ran into Pablo."

"Is this about Pablo? Did something happen because of me?"

She rolls off the bed and hurries to grab her clothes.

"No, *malyshka*. I swear this has nothing to do with you at all. This is about Maks and Laura. But I want you with Laura, Christina, and Anastasia. They know what to do when we're away. I think it'll be easier for you to be around the other women. I don't know if this will be a few hours or a few days."

"Where are you going?"

I pause as I get ready to pull my sock on.

"I can't tell you."

Chapter Fourteen

Sumiko

I hurry to keep Pasha from waiting. There's an urgency in the way he moves. He tells me to wait in the living room, and he'll be out in a moment. I hear a drawer open and close, then the closet doors. He'd taken off his suit coat while I was in the bathroom washing my hands. He's wearing a different one when he comes out. I notice he's not wearing his watch anymore, and he pulled his belt from his trousers. I glance at his shoes, and they're not the ones he wore earlier. They're still dress shoes, but they appear to have rubber soles.

Why did he change? And why can't he tell me where he's going?

He's on the phone speaking Russian when he leaves his bedroom. He reaches out his hand, and I take it without hesitation. The man guarding his door moves aside when Pasha opens it. There's the same guy at the elevator who rode up with us. Misha's waiting for us in the lobby, but there's another man there who looks like Aleks. I recognize Christina. I glance at

Pasha, but he hurries me out of the building. There's a limo idling at the curb instead of a town car. Misha, Christina, and this mystery man climb into it before us.

"Sumiko, this is my cousin Bogdan, Christina's husband."

He reaches across Misha to shake my hand.

"It's nice to meet you, Sumiko."

"You too."

"Hi."

Christina offers me a warm smile with her greeting, and Misha nods with a smile. Bogdan wraps his arm around Christina, and she sags against him before she catches herself. She darts a glance at me, and I'm watching them. I look up at Pasha, much more nervous than a moment ago. He's holding my hand with them resting on his thigh. He wraps his arm around me just as Bogdan has his arm around Christina. Pasha kisses my temple as we ride in silence. It becomes deafening, but Bogdan, Misha, and Pasha probably can't discuss anything in front of Christina and me. Christina clearly knows what's happened and has guessed what will happen. I have no clue.

"I spoke to Maks after the second round of interviews. Bogdan, Niko, and Aleks were on the call, too. We're going to hire your firm."

Christina breaks the tension. I nod, but I look up at Pasha again before looking back at Christina.

"Arseniy and Greg know we'd like you to handle our account, but now—if you'd prefer not to, we understand."

"Um."

Pasha gives my shoulder a squeeze. I lean against him as I shrink into the seat.

"I'd like to. Isn't it a conflict of interest, though? Won't people question my valuations and investigations if I find in your favor?"

"They can try."

Christina says it with the same warm smile as she had when she said hi. But it feels like a veiled threat now that I know about them. Christina must sense it too because her smile drops.

"Sumiko, your experience, and record vouch for you. It has nothing to do with us. If anyone questions your assessments, it's because of us, not you."

Christina slides closer to us and jerks her head toward Bogdan and Misha. Pasha trades places with her. I can barely hear what she says when Bogdan speaks Russian because she's keeping her voice so low. I can tell Pasha isn't paying attention to Bogdan, and Bogdan knows it. He talks to Misha instead.

"I know how crazy this is. It's terrifying and confusing. But Laura, Ana, and I will keep you company. You can ask us anything, and we'll do our best to help."

"Thank you. I'm not sure what to make of all of this. We had one date and a lunch that was interrupted. Now..."

I shrug. Christina meets Pasha's gaze before she turns back to me. I think Pasha has to really strain to hear her because she's practically whispering. I can tell he's nervous about what Christina will tell me. I feel bad for him, but I'm curious and scared, all wrapped up in one.

"The men in this family will do anything to protect their women and to make them happy. You're here because Pasha wants you in his life, and not just for a little while. You need to think about whether you can commit and make that choice. If you have any doubts, then he'll understand. But if you stay, know that he's completely committed to you. There won't be anyone else for him. Ever."

"He said he was all in, and so did I. I'm just not sure what that means."

"It means accepting there are things you will never know about him or this family. You might guess, but no one will ever confirm or deny. You have to live with that. But the parts of him he can share, he will do without reservation and with his whole heart. He's a good man, Sumiko. I don't know what your future holds any better than I knew what mine held when I met Bogdan. But these men, when they find the right women, they're completely devoted. He risks everything bringing you into this world. It's obvious he trusts you more than any other woman he's known."

"I trust him. You must know how insane that is. But I just know it."

"I do. I felt the same way when I met Bogdan. I freaked out at first, but it didn't take long for me to realize there was no point in denying how I feel. I'm happier with him than without."

"We barely know each other, though. Maybe we're rushing things. How do I know he's not just infatuated?"

"Because they don't do infatuation. At least, they don't bring women into our family if it's only that. It may have seemed hurried, but I promise you, he's thought long and hard about this. None of them are impulsive. They don't have that luxury."

I sense Pasha knows he shouldn't be listening so intently. But he's scared. When our gazes meet, he lets me see it. I don't think Christina is trying to warn me off. But he's worrying she'll say something that makes me want to end this.

"I don't think I'm infatuated either. This—I don't know what this is. But I've liked guys before. I was even in love with a guy in college and thought we would get married."

I'm sure Pasha doesn't enjoy hearing that. I wouldn't, but I still have to talk loud enough for Christina to hear over Bogdan and Misha.

"But something always held me back. There was always a niggling doubt. With Pasha, even learning what he's a part of, there isn't the doubt about him as a person. I'm not sure about everything I'm getting into because I don't understand it all. But I don't doubt Pasha."

"Good. This isn't an easy life to live. But they are easy men to love. You will discover that all the men are devoted to our family. Loyalty and honor are everything to them. He will never intentionally hurt you. It isn't in his nature, and he has seven very large men he's accountable to, plus his father and Misha's. If you didn't know their kinder side, you'd never guess that they're really just teddy bears."

Bogdan snorts. I don't think it has anything to do with what Misha just said, because Misha isn't smiling. Bogdan's listening to his wife. But I saw the way he was holding her a few minutes ago. He is a teddy bear to her. I wonder if Maks is with Laura and Niko is with Ana. Now that Christina has said that, I realize Pasha is with me, too. He's affectionate and lets me nestle close to him when I need it. It's what we both need. I hope I can give him the comfort he provides me.

"Think about what I've said. I hope you don't think I overstepped, but I'm protective of my new family. But I also know what it's like to be in your shoes. There was a lot going on for Laura and Maks when Bogdan and I got together. She wishes she could have offered me this support, but it just wasn't possible all the time. But she and I have tried to help Ana now that she's Niko's wife. She's like a sister to us, just like the men are brothers to us. Pasha is as much my cousin as anyone on my parents' sides of the family. We'll treat you like family, too. Just prepare yourself. It can get really noisy. There's a lot of us."

"How many of you are there?"

I'm trying to do the math.

"Eight cousins between both sides of Bogdan's family. His mom, Galina, Pasha's parents, and Misha's parents. Plus three wives. That's sixteen, and you make seventeen. Actually, it's nineteen if you count the twins."

"Wow. That is a big family. How do you all fit in one place?"

"Maks and Laura bought an enormous house. Bogdan and I bought one just as big. Niko and Ana just closed a few months ago on theirs. We all want to have room for both sides of our family to gather, and people can stay over any time they want. And chances are there will be more cousins in the future besides just the twins."

That makes me pause. Children. Could I bring children into this world with Pasha? What does that mean? Do they become bratva too? Will my sons or daughters be mafiosos? Is it mafiosas for girls? My heart is racing, and I feel genuinely scared for the first time.

"Christina, switch with me, please."

I look at Pasha, and I realize my hands are trembling. He saw them. He moves aside and lets Christina have his seat before he comes back to sit with me.

"What just happened? You were fine talking to her, and now you're trembling."

"She mentioned children. If we—will our sons and daughters have to do what you do? I don't even know what that is."

"I honestly don't know how to answer that. I don't know what's in store for the next generation. None of us wants this life for our children. I don't know how we're going to change things, of if they will change. It would be sons, not daughters. Russians are—old fashioned. But so are the Italians and Colombians. The Irish can be—unpredictable right now. But I don't think they'll welcome women into our roles. I'm all for equal opportunity, but this is one area where I'm glad it doesn't exist."

We're entering Queens, so I look out the window.

"There's even more for me to think about than I realized. I haven't changed my mind, Pasha. But I have more to work out."

"I know, *malyshka*."

He drops a light kiss on my lips, and I twist to nestle closer to him. I close my eyes because I need the moment of rest. But I also need the affection, and I'm embarrassed for the others to see me. I don't want to be weak, but I feel so adrift. We hit a bump, and I open my eyes. I see Christina sitting the same way as I am. Her eyes are closed, and Bogdan is rubbing her back. I settle back against Pasha and wait for the car ride to end.

When we pass through gates and pull into a circular drive, I look at the mansion in front of me. This is more than enormous, like Christina said. It's practically a palace. And the guards patrolling the grounds remind me of the paramilitary description in the article. The men have semi-automatic rifles, earpieces, sunglasses, and are all decked in black.

"Is this really necessary?"

I think about the three armed guards I saw at Pasha's place. I thought that was excessive. This. This is like pulling into a diplomatic compound or something. Does the White House even have this many guards?

"Yes."

Pasha doesn't say more, and I don't press him. This isn't the time. We stop in front of the door, and Pasha climbs out before the driver comes around to open the door. He helps me out, and the others follow. He doesn't bother knocking and walks into the house. I look around at the foyer and the cathedral ceilings. I hear a baby cry, then another.

A striking brunette hurries down the stairs, one arm around a baby, and the other hand holding the banister. A man follows her, and he's a mirror of Bogdan and Aleks. He has the same dark hair as Pasha, but the Kutsenko brothers have the same icy-blue eyes as Misha and Sergei. I look around, and there's a willowy blonde standing with the man who must be the fourth Kutsenko brother.

"Sumiko, this is Maksim and Laura."

I shake hands with each of them when they join us.

"That's Ana and Niko."

They smile as they come to join the rest of us.

"Where's Aleks?"

Pasha looks toward a closed door as he asks.

"He's in there with Sergei and Anton."

Maksim kisses Laura and hands the baby he's holding to Ana. The men head toward the closed door, and I'm left standing there with Laura, Christina, and Ana. The babies are still fussing, and Laura looks exhausted. My guess is they're about four months old.

"Will you come sit with us? These two are in a growth spurt. They won't stop eating. Mila's worse than Konstantin. She's two inches longer than him and three pounds heavier."

Laura leads the way into a family room with sofas that look like you should take a nap on them. There's a rocker-recliner near the fireplace. She soon situates herself with a nursing cover over her shoulders. It isn't long before the fussing ends, and happy gurgles escape from beneath the light blanket.

"Anton said your met Pasha on vacation."

Laura rocks gently as she looks at me. She appears completely at peace now that she settled her babies. She makes juggling two look easy, but I doubt it is.

"I was with a couple friends and had just finished surfing. Pasha and the guys just finished scuba diving."

"It's such a small world that you're both from New York and both accountants. What's the likelihood of that?"

I look at Ana as she speaks. We couldn't be more opposite. She's fair haired and fair skinned with the beauty Eastern European women are known for, but she's supermodel thin.

Like Kate Moss in the early 90s without the cocaine thin. It makes me feel like a whale. Laura doesn't look like she had two babies a few months ago. Christina is athletic. I can tell from her build without knowing about the long bike rides she enjoys. I'm certain they must wonder what a man as handsome as Pasha is doing with someone like me.

I don't have the chance to answer Ana because the men come out of whatever room they were in. Sergei and Anton are now with them, and they're already in clothes like the men outside. My eyes widen and dart to Pasha. He's moving around Maks and Aleks to reach me. He steers me toward a window and pulls me into his arms. He doesn't care who's there. He kisses me, and my toes curl in my shoes. I don't pull away. I give myself over to the kiss. Whoever's watching be damned.

"*Malyshka*, I know how Anton and Sergei look. I'm going upstairs to change. When I come down, I'm going to be dressed like them. We all will be. Something's happened that's more serious than I realized. Bogdan and Niko are going to stay here with you and the other ladies. I don't know when we're going to be back, *krasivaya*. It might be tonight, or it might be tomorrow. But I need to warn you it could be a few days. If you want to go to your place, then Bogdan or Niko will take you. But I want two men outside your building around the clock if you're home. If you leave, then at least one guy is with you."

"Am I in danger? What's going on?"

"I can't tell you yet. Not until we sort things out. But a safety detail comes with dating me. It's not negotiable, and it's not up for discussion if I'm not around."

I remember him saying that before. I nod. What else can I do?

"I'll be back as soon as I can, baby girl. Then I'm tying you to my bed again, so I can finish having my way with you. I'm going to text you a username and password. It's my Amazon account. Pick out whatever you want. You can order it, or we can look at the cart together. But when I get home, we're disappearing for a few days. I had way too much time to imagine everything I want to do to your body. Fuck. I'm getting hard just thinking about it."

He kisses me once more, and I press my body against his. When we break apart, I rest my head against his chest. I can see his family trying not to notice us. Husbands and wives are in similar positions, but they're still glancing at us. My emotions are about to get the better of me. I'm embarrassed and insecure, and I'm scared.

"*Rad videt', chto ty vyros, kuzen.*" Glad to see you've finally grown up, little cousin.

"*Kakogo khrena eto znachit, Maksim?*" What the fuck does that mean, Maksim?

"*Vy mozhete videt', chto krasota glubzhe kozhi..*" You can see beauty is more than skin deep.

I don't know what Maksim and Pasha are saying, but Pasha is angry. Like really angry. He's glaring at Maksim, and his hold on me has tightened to where I can barely breathe. I tap his chest to get him to ease his grip.

"*Yesli by eto kasalos' tol'ko tebya, a ne Lory i bliznetsov, ya by posovetoval tebe poyti na khuy. Vse vsegda predpolagali, chto znayut moi predpochteniya. Nikto nikogda ne sprashival. Ya vsegda predpochital takikh zhenshchin, kak ona. Ya ne khochu lomat' tonkuyu devushku popolam.*" If this were just about you and not Laura and the twins, I'd tell you to go fuck yourself. Everyone's always assumed they know my preferences. No one's ever asked. I've always preferred women like her. I don't want to snap a thin one in half.

"*Chto, chert voz'mi, ne tak s khudymi zhenshchinami?*" What the fuck's wrong with thin women?

Niko tucks Ana behind him and crosses his arms. What's happening?

"*U tebya svoi predpochteniya, u menya svoi. Nikto ne dumal, chto s toboy chto-to ne tak, poka ty ne dokazal, chto vneshnost' — eto yeshche ne vse.*" You have your preferences, and I have mine. No one thought something was wrong with you before you proved looks aren't everything.

Niko lunges forward, and it takes Maks and Aleks to hold him back. Anton and Sergei rush forward and stand between us and Niko and Ana. She looks hurt, and Niko looks ready to murder Pasha. What just happened?

"*Prosti, Ana. Ya ne dolzhen byl tak govorit'. Ne stoilo mne tak. Ya prosto syt po gorlo tem, chto vse dumayut, chto ya poverkhnostnyy. Ya ni s kem ne vstrechalsya s tekh por, kak mne ispolnilos' dvadtsat'. Kak, chert voz'mi, kto-nibud' iz vas znayet, chto mne nravitsya?*" I'm sorry Ana. I shouldn't have said that. It was unnecessary. I'm just fed up with everyone thinking I'm superficial. I haven't dated anyone since I was twenty. How the hell do any of you know what I like?

Pasha looks down at me before sweeping his gaze over his family, who are stunned by whatever he's saying during this outburst.

"*Ya vstrechayus' s devushkoy, kotoraya ne khudaya, i vdrug ty dumayesh', chto ya povzroslel. Ty polagayesh', chto vneshnost' dlya menya bol'she ne imeyet znacheniya. Ya dumayu, chto ona velikolepna. Niko, ty dumayesh', Ana velikolepna. No ran'she nikto ne dumal, chto ty pustoy. No ya, dolzhno byt', byl. Davayte razberemsya s etim, togda vy mozhete ostavit' nas v pokoye.*" I date a girl who isn't thin, and suddenly you think I've matured. You assume somehow looks don't matter to me anymore. I think she's gorgeous. Niko, you think Ana is gorgeous. But no one thought you were shallow before. But I must have been. Let's deal with this, then you can all leave us the fuck alone.

He kisses me again, but it's quick.

"I'll be back as soon as I can. I won't be able to call or text. If anything happens, Bogdan and Niko will know what to do."

"Pasha—"

"I have to go, *malyshka*."

He kisses me a last time before he steps away. He doesn't look at anyone as he walks up the stairs. Everyone stares at him before the men follow him. I don't hear any voices, and it's only a few minutes later that they all rush back downstairs. He looks at me and offers me a smile before he opens the front door. The husbands say goodbye to their wives, and then they're gone.

I don't know what to say or where to look. I imagine whatever just happened was because of me. I look at the other ladies. Christina looks confused, but Laura and Ana appear stunned.

"You both speak Russian, don't you? You understood, didn't you?"

"Yes."

Laura looks at the door that's now closed. We can hear cars pulling away. She moves back to the rocking chair. Christina and Ana go back to where they were sitting, but I stay by the window.

"Maksim's comment hurt Pasha. I would have stuffed a rag in Maks's mouth if I'd known what he was going to say. But Maks said what the others were thinking, and that only made it worse."

"Do they not approve of me? Am I not—"

I'm trying not to cry. Ana and Christina rush over to me. I think Laura would too if she didn't have the twins. Ana hugs me, and Christina rests her hand on my arm.

"No. Just the opposite." Ana leans back. "Maks said Pasha had finally matured. I don't know anything about Pasha's private life. But basically, Pasha thinks everyone's always seen him as shallow. It's not that you're not good enough. It's more that Pasha feels like no one thinks he was good enough."

"Because he's dating a fat girl."

"He called you beautiful. That's what *krasivaya* means. He said he thinks you're gorgeous, just like Niko thinks I am. But no one gave Niko a hard time for falling in love with someone so thin she looks like a twelve-year-old boy. No one thought Niko was shallow before me and matured when he fell for me."

"Sumiko, all the men are handsome. I think Maksim is the hottest in the family. But I've heard them tease Pasha. He's known as the pretty one in the group. He said he hasn't dated since he was twenty. As far as I know, that's true. But I've seen women fawn all over him. My guess is, when he did date, he went out with women who approached him or who he thought people expected him to be with. Now he's almost thirty, and he wants to be with who he wants."

"And a fat girl isn't what people expected. Dating me proves he's not shallow. So if he was with one of you, or one of my friends he met, then everyone would still think less of him. Dating someone beneath him proves he's better than everyone thought. I get it."

I want out. I look around and I try to figure out how I'm going to get home. Niko and Bogdan come back inside as the women watch me.

"I'm going home. I'll get an Uber."

"Pasha said—"

"Thank you, Niko. But I can get myself home. If someone has to come with me, fine. But I'd like to go back to my place."

"Sumiko, I'm sorry. This isn't a reflection on you. It's the shitty way his cousins have treated him."

"Stasia, what happened?"

Niko demands rather than asks. It confuses me for a

moment, but I realize he doesn't call his wife Ana like everyone else.

"We tried to explain what happened. We hurt Sumiko's feelings."

Niko and Bogdan come to stand in front of me. Christina and Ana step back.

"Did Ana or Laura tell you he called you beautiful earlier? That he said he thinks you're gorgeous?"

Niko softens his tone as he asks.

"Yes."

"We hurt Pasha, and we've insulted you in the process. That wasn't anyone's intention. He and I are the closest of the cousins. We're the same age, and we've always done things together. It's not the same as with our own brothers, but we've always been best friends. He's even closer to Misha these days because they were both single until he met you. Of all of us, he's the one who's always been most adamant about not getting involved. He said he has dated no one since he was twenty, and it's true. He's gone a date here or there, but he hasn't had a relationship since college. It's when we all realized that having serious relationships wasn't possible with our lives. But before that, he went out with girls everyone expected him to be into. It didn't surprise me at all to meet you. I'm probably the only one who's known his preferences. We played American football in high school, and he asked a girl out freshman year of high school. The other players were merciless. He stopped seeing her because the guys were hurting her feelings as much as his. He tried again senior year, and it was the same thing. Bogdan and I went to college together, so we saw each other all the time. We lived together. But I hung out with Pasha on the weekends. I knew what types of girls he preferred, but it didn't matter when we both realized that dating was pointless. I had a few girlfriends in college, and Bogdan had a couple after

148

college. But until we met our wives, neither Bogdan nor I ever imagined marrying."

"So you're saying he's a chubby chaser, and he caved to other people's opinions."

I have my arms crossed as I put up a physical barrier to the rest of them.

"No. He didn't cave to anything. He was aware of how people's comments were hurting the girls he liked. He didn't want to stop seeing either of them, but he knew going out with them would only mean people were cruel to them. Our paths were decided when we were still boys. Once we were in college, he saw no point in getting attached to someone he didn't think he could be with. I feel like shit for not speaking up sooner. If I'd known Maks was going to say anything, I would have set him straight. I guess I figured everyone else knew his preference."

Niko looks miserable. I get the feeling he hides his emotions as well as Pasha, so he's choosing to let me see them. It almost feels welcoming, like he's allowing me into the inner sanctum of their family by putting down his guard.

Laura's expression is kind, and it puts me a little more at ease when she speaks.

"I'm so sorry for what Maks said. He's the least communicative of all the men, which makes him the worst at it. According to the others, he's practically a chatterbox now that I'm with him. He was incredibly thoughtless, but it wasn't intentional. I guarantee you Sergei and Anton are ripping him a new one. Anton in particular. He's pissed."

"Please don't go home."

Christina finally speaks up.

"I—"

"No. I really hope you'll stay, Sumiko. If this draws out and you're alone, it's going to get scary for you. We'd much rather you stay with us. You're going to have questions, and your mind is going to run wild if you have no one to ask. Please stay."

I look at everyone and finally nod.

"Would you come outside with me for a moment?"

Ana's smile is shy, and I think she believes I'll refuse. I nod. She and I head to the backyard, which is far bigger than anyone would guess in New York. There's a swimming pool and a long stretch of grass. I can picture a swing set and toys strewn across it.

"Why did Niko look like he wanted to kill Pasha if they're so close?"

"Because Pasha said no one thought Niko was shallow before he dated me."

"Oh. Okay. No wonder Niko was pissed. Did Pasha really mean it to sound that bad?"

"No. It stung, and Niko knows I get a little intimidated around Laura and Christina. I'm an avid runner, but even when I don't run for a few months, I can't gain weight. Usually, I feel fine about my looks. But Laura and Christina are both so beautiful. I know I'm not most people's idea of pretty, but Niko doesn't care. He can barely keep his hands off me. He usually doesn't. That was the point Pasha was trying to make. No one thought Niko was suddenly a better man because he chose a thin woman who's practically flat chested and has nearly no ass. If Pasha was dating me, not you, he would have reacted the same way to what they said because everyone would have thought the same thing. It really hurt Pasha."

"Do looks really matter that much to everyone?"

"No, not really. I know it doesn't seem like it. It's just a super fucked up way of saying they respect Pasha even more than they realized. I swear, sometimes men shouldn't be allowed to talk. They fuck things up more than they fix them. We all have something that makes us insecure. Christina hates her freckles. She embarrassed by how many she has, but she says Bogdan likes to pick out patterns and says they're like constellations. Laura was really self-conscious about her ass and thighs. Apparently, Maks bought some bathing suits when they went on a trip together, and she hid in the pool for over an hour rather than have Aleks, Niko, or Anton see her in one of them. Now that she's had the twins, I know she feels even more self-conscious. Now that I think about it, Christina said Bogdan bought her a super skimpy bikini for a trip and she burst into tears. These men—they love with their whole hearts, and they will defend us to their last breath. They see us in ways we don't see ourselves. They don't mean to be insensitive, and it's not that they can't see our faults and flaws. But to them, we're each perfect. They don't get how we don't see ourselves the same way. It's sweet."

I listen to everything Ana says, and I feel better for it.

"Today's been super overwhelming."

"I bet. I found out about Niko and our family a month after I met him, but it was the day after we slept together for the first time. It freaked me out so much that I quit—I'm Laura's paralegal—and drove home to Baltimore. A shit ton more came out when I saw my parents, and I still have a hard time talking about it. But I get it. It's too much to take in all at once. That's why we really want you to stay with us."

"Thank you. Thanks for talking to me, and thanks for the offer."

I look down at my clothes before I look at the house.

"Do you think they'll be home tonight?"

"I honestly don't know."

"I have nothing else to wear. I can't borrow anything from the rest of you."

Ana laughs.

"One benefit of an obscenely wealthy family is how fast

things can be delivered. If you want to send someone to your place to get clothes, we can do that. I'm certain Niko or Bogdan would take you to pick up stuff. Or we can order it for you, and it'll be here within an hour. Whatever you want."

"I can't—"

"I was a broke recent college grad when I met Niko. I couldn't have just ordered a bunch of stuff either. They don't flaunt their money or throw it around, but the men are generous. It's share and share alike in this family. If you want to order something because you don't want to leave or don't feel comfortable with someone in your place, we'll take care of it."

"Thank you. I—"

My phone pings at the same time Ana's does. I pull mine out of my pocket and look down. It's an unavailable number that sent a text. We both unlock our phones and open our text messages.

"Come inside! Stasia, Sumiko! Now!"

Niko is running toward us. We strolled past the pool while we were talking, and Niko is sprinting across the grass.

"Niko, I just got a text."

"I know. I think Laura got the same one."

"I got a text too, but I don't understand."

The text I got makes little sense to me. I show it to Niko and Ana.

You made a big mistake.

"That's the same one I got."

"So did Laura and Christina. Come inside."

Niko's behind us as we rush to the back door. I glance back and see his hand at his lower back. I notice there are more men patrolling the backyard than when we came out. Their guns are raised and ready to fire.

"Who is this? How'd they get my number and know to send me a text, too?"

"We don't know." Christina moves closer to Bogdan on the sofa to make room for me. "We probably won't until Sergei gets back."

"Sergei?"

"Our cousin has a background in information technology."

Bogdan's explanation is vague. As I look at everyone, I get the feeling it's more than IT.

"Is he a hacker or something?"

No one answers. My eyebrows shoot up for a moment.

"He's responsible for collecting information."

Bogdan's response doesn't help. Information about what? Enemies? I keep those questions to myself.

"Sumiko, I know you said you want to go home, but I don't feel comfortable with that. Please stay."

Laura struggles to stand with both babies. Bogdan and Niko are at her side in an instant, taking a baby each. The uncles sway and make faces at the infants, and it might be the sweetest thing I've ever seen. They look like pro bodybuilders, but they're doting on the babies.

"I'll stay. I don't feel so comfortable leaving now."

"Aunt Alina is coming with Mama and Aunt Svetlana. She said she'll bring some things with her for you."

Bogdan explains as he looks at his phone, juggling it with a baby. No one seems to know what else to say. Ana and Niko offer to make dinner, so they disappear into the kitchen. Laura takes the twins upstairs to the nursery. Bogdan whispers something in Christina's ear before he disappears. She suggests a movie, so I stay in the living room with her. How the hell am I supposed to watch a romcom right now?

Chapter Fifteen

Pasha

I need to get over how pissed I am. I can't blame Niko for defending his wife, but we've never come close to fighting outside a boxing ring. I said what I did to prove a point, but I also lashed out. I feel like a complete jackass toward Ana, but I don't feel guilty about standing up to the others. I've volunteered as often as I've been volunteered to chat up women to get information or distract them. I don't think I'm any better looking than the rest of the men in my family, but apparently I am. I couldn't give a shit. Except that I do, at least when it comes to how my family sees me.

I could have knocked Maks's teeth in and made him swallow them. I'm just glad he spoke in Russian. But I'm sure Ana and Laura have already told Sumiko what happened. Niko and Bogdan better not have apologized on my behalf. I don't regret defending her.

"He was an ass, but you know what he meant."

Aleks is sitting next to me as I drive. I look straight ahead and don't respond. Maks is in the third row, as far away from me as he can get. Misha is next to him. Anton and Sergei are in the second row.

"I'm sorry."

"Not now, Maks. Let's deal with Juan. Where am I going?"

"Mott Haven."

It's Sergei who gives me the information I need.

"What's he doing in the Bronx?"

I head toward Whitestone Bridge that'll take us from Queens into the Bronx. Mott Haven is hardly where most people want to visit, but it is where most people want to leave.

"Hiding from us and his family."

I can hear Sergei typing as he talks. I have no idea how he's tracking Juan, but I don't doubt he knows where we need to look. No one would guess he and Anton are practically computer geniuses. Sergei can hack anything without a trace. He took what he learned in college and ran with it.

"Why's he back in town? If we don't kill him, Enrique or Pablo will."

"I don't know. But Laura is certain she saw him. He was gone by the time she could point him out to Anton and Sergei. Anton went after him, but he disappeared."

I hear the frustration in Maks's voice, and I realize I should cut him some slack. His wife and children were likely followed by a guy who nearly got Laura killed. I can only imagine how I would feel if someone threatened Sumiko, and we're not married. I can't fathom Maks's fear and anger about his children being in danger. I can understand why he spoke without thinking. Maybe he thought a joke would lighten his mood. I glance back at him in the rearview mirror. He's looking out the window, and he looks a wreck.

Misha and I will lead whatever's going to go down. But Maks would never send anyone into something where he wasn't willing to go first. As *avotoritets,* we're the brigadiers who'll carry out Anton's strategy. The others will follow our orders. We each have our roles, and mine weighs heavily on me. We aren't defending millions of dollars of contraband. We're defending our family.

"Any idea where he's hiding?"

I'm going to need more specific directions soon.

"In that part of the Bronx, probably in plain sight."

"He'd stick out. He won't look like most people there."

There's no diplomatic way to say a Colombian's coloring won't match most people who live in Mott Haven. There are plenty of Latinos, but he won't blend in.

"Laura said he looked rough. Homeless. He probably won't stand out as much as we think."

Sergei glances up as I look back at him in the mirror. He runs his hand through his hair, one of the few signs that's he's not having much luck and is frustrated. He's hacked into the city cameras and is searching for this big bag of ass.

"Informants told us Juan was back in town, and it was a former bouncer at one of our strip clubs who called Maks and said he saw Juan getting on the subway near Maks and Laura's. We put out feelers, and a guy matching his description popped up near the subway in Mott Haven."

Aleks explains because Maks is lost in thought. Every time I look back at him, my anger cools. I'm still hurt, but I'm not livid. I'm hurt by what Maks said, but I'm even more hurt that no one stood up for me. Not my brother, not any of my cousins, not Sergei or Misha. Anton hurts the most, and Niko knows what women I'm attracted to. He knows my type. He could have spoken up, and he might have if I hadn't launched into insulting his wife. I feel like an asshole all over again about that.

Anton turns in his seat to talk to Maks.

"We'll find him. He's going to stay in the Bronx. He won't

come back to our part of Queens if he thinks Laura spotted him. And he sure as shit isn't going to Jackson Heights. He's way too noticeable as the *jefe's* nephew. He won't want any of his cop buddies to see him in Manhattan. And why the fuck would he go to Brooklyn or Staten Island?"

He's right about which borough Juan's most likely in, but he will have gone underground. I don't know how easy this is going to be.

"Why's he back? Or did he never leave?"

I've been wondering that since Maks called, but no one's offered that information, so I ask. All I know is it's bigger than him spying on Laura at a park.

"He left. I believe Enrique and Pablo sent him away rather than go to war with us." Maks finally looks forward. "But he came back. Our first informant said he's running with the Etas."

"Puerto Ricans? Is he really doing everything he can to piss Enrique off?"

Fuck. He has a death wish. He'll blend in with Puerto Ricans, and the Etas run southeast Bronx. But Enrique will never forgive him for any connections with a gang. I can guarantee he's using his insider knowledge to help increase their drug trafficking through Puerto Rico. The Etas will never let a Colombian former cop into their gang for real. He'll serve them, but he won't benefit from their protection or loyalty.

"I think he couldn't survive wherever they dumped him. I think he's back because he knows New York and thinks he can blend in. But he couldn't help but look for Laura. He believes he's in love with her. I don't trust him not to punish her again for choosing me over him."

He already proved he's vindictive. Maks is probably right.

"Are we taking him straight to the warehouse?"

I assume so, but as the driver, I need to know our final destination. The warehouse is where we go to take care of our less than savory business. We control the situation there. No one comes or goes without our knowing. Unless they're bratva, no one comes and leaves alive. They wind up as ooze in a vat of acid or ash disintegrating in the Flushing River. It's where we put Vlad's real training to use.

"Yes. I haven't decided whether I'll tell Enrique after the fact."

"Do you think that's wise, Maks?"

As Maks's second-in-command and as a member of the Elite Group, Aleks has the right and responsibility to question Maks.

"I'm not turning him over to them again. Clearly, they didn't do what needed to be done. For Laura's sake, I didn't push them to end him. But I warned them I wouldn't be merciful again. Laura wants him gone now that we have the twins."

"But as a courtesy so we don't start a war."

"No." Maks is emphatic. "I'm not giving them the chance to attempt bargaining or to threaten me if I won't turn him over. Better to ask forgiveness than to ask permission."

Forgiveness. Hardly. Maks doesn't give a shit whether the Colombians forgive him for anything and neither do the rest of us.

"Where are we parking?"

A tinted black SUV is a target in this part of the Bronx. No one's breaking any windows since they're shatterproof, and no one's gunning us down because it's bulletproof. But it draws way more attention than we need, especially when we get out and stick out in this neighborhood. Never mind our race, our accents will give us away. None of us have lost it.

"Nowhere yet. I want to scout."

Anton is sitting on the right side, so he has a clear view of the sidewalks as I drive. I'm scanning for anyone paying too much attention. We have our rifles in the back, but I hope it doesn't come to that. Our handguns should be enough.

I drive us around for ten minutes before Anton points.

"There. That's him."

I squint, trying to see who Anton's pointing to among a group of homeless people. Then I spot him. He looks like complete shit. He was suave and always well-groomed when he was a detective. His clothes were a little too expensive for his position, and he radiated arrogance whenever he dealt with us. Now his hair is long and shaggy. He has an old military surplus jacket on, and his jeans are filthy. He looks thin since his clothes hang on him. That or these were the best he could find.

I slow down as I come to a light. He's looking around, jittery. He looks strung out now that I can see his face clearly. He hands something to a woman who looks like a hooker. She reaches out and cups his cock. I guess she is. He follows her toward the back of the building.

"Go now."

Misha gives the order, and Aleks and Anton jump out of the car with their balaclavas in place. The woman screams, but Anton already has a sack over Juan's head, and Aleks has his wrists bound with zip ties. Juan tries to fight, but Anton knees him in the groin. He doubles over, and Anton's upper cut snaps his head back. Aleks's blow to his temple makes him crumple.

He's seated between Sergei and Anton before anyone on the sidewalk knows what to do. I pull away and flip a U-turn. I don't wait for instructions. We need out of the Bronx now. I don't expect any police sirens to follow us, but we don't need anyone catching our license plates. They're stolen, but we still don't need anyone looking for us.

"What the fuck, Kutsenko?"

Juan comes around and grumbles. He should have kept his

mouth shut. Maks has his belt wrapped around Juan's throat and cinches it tight as he pulls backwards. He practically yanks Juan over the seat back.

"What the fuck is I'm going to kill you slowly. You came near Laura and my children. Now you die."

"I didn't."

"Bull-fucking-shit."

Anton puts his hands over Juan's mouth and nose as he snarls his curse. The cloth hood still covers his head. He thrashes, so Maks tightens the belt. He goes still, so Maks eases his hold.

"How about you try not lying, and Anton might let you breathe?"

Sergei has his knife pressed to Juan's ribs. I only know because we're stopped at another fucking light, and I can watch in the mirror. Juan nods as best he can, and Anton releases his face.

"Stay the fuck quiet."

Maks sits back and pulls the belt free. He knows he needs time to calm down, or he'll kill Juan in the car, and we won't get any info from him. It takes us nearly any hour to get to the warehouse in Queens when it only took half that time to get from Maks's place to where we picked up our prisoner. He's no hostage because there's no chance he's going free.

I pull into an open bay, and Anton yanks Juan out of the SUV. Misha and Aleks strip him while I pull a meat hook down. The zip tie isn't strong enough to bear his weight, even if it would cut into his wrists nicely. Once Misha has a rope around his wrists, he cuts the plastic band. I hook him, and Maks cranks the lever that drags him onto his toes. He comes over and swings a lead pipe against Juan's right ribs. A crack echoes in the expansive warehouse. Juan bellows in pain, then whimpers.

"You reek, *el caño*." Pussy. "Been bathing in your own piss? Not so brave now that you don't have your gun and badge."

Maks lands the pipe in the same spot a second time.

"You thought you could come back to *my* neighborhood, watch *my* wife and *my* children, and get away with it. You're a dumb motherfucker to think I wouldn't find out. I own that neighborhood, and now I own your ass."

Maks isn't speaking figuratively. I can guess what he's going to do to torture Juan. Castrating him won't be all that happens.

"What I want to know is why. It has to be more than just jealousy or morbid curiosity."

"Fuck you, *puta*." Bitch.

"I'm not the one strung up. I'm not the little bitch ready to piss himself. You're going to have a hard time doing that after I cut off your dick."

"You're just pissed because I was fucking her long before she met you."

"But who's she fucking now? Who'd she marry? Whose children did she have? She didn't want you, and you're too pathetic to get over it. Were you watching her, wishing those were your kids, and whacking off?" Maks pulls his knife from his pocked and slashes Juan's dick. "You don't need that anymore. You won't be fucking your hand, thinking about my wife ever again."

Maks slashes again and again until Juan's dick is practically shredded. Aleks hands him a knife that's more like a small machete. He ends that torment by leaving none of his junk. But he spins him around.

"Unless you want it up the ass, you'll start talking. Why are you back?"

"Fuck you."

"No thanks. But this pipe will. Without lube."

Maks pokes him, and Juan tries to pull away. Except the

hook just swings him back toward Maks and the pipe. He howls.

"Wanna try again?"

"Fuck you."

"If you're offering."

Maks pokes him again. Misha and I step forward to hold Juan in place. Maks kicks his feet apart.

"Bend over and say ah."

I laugh as I taunt him. But I'm asking the questions now.

"You know you can't go back to Enrique, so you went to the Bronx. Where did Pablo take you?"

Juan says nothing. Maks nods to me. I wrap my hand around his throat. We don't have too long to torture him before he bleeds so much he passes out.

"Minnesota."

Juan croaks his answer. I look at my cousins. None of us expected that, but Maks said he had to be out of our time zone.

"How'd you get back?"

"Pablo gave me some money to get by until I could get a job. I took the bus back."

"That didn't take a year. Have you been back for months?"

Juan laughs. So he has.

"You've been hiding. Why not stay out of sight?"

"Because I didn't come back here to hide for the rest of my life."

"What did you think you were going to do? Kill Maks and get Laura?"

Aleks swipes his blade across Juan's broken ribs as he takes over the interrogation. It's not a deep cut, but it hurts.

"Just the first part. I don't want her saggy *el caño*."

"Liar." Misha flicks him in the eye as Maks calls Juan out. "What were you going to do after you killed me? And just how did you think that would happen?"

"There are plenty of people willing to kill you."

"And you can't afford any of them."

I know how much it costs to take out a hit, and we all know he couldn't arrange one, even without me pointing that out.

"You want more than just to kill me and screw Laura. You want revenge on Pablo and Enrique. That's why you're sucking Etas' cock."

I drag the flat side of my knife along his collarbones as Maks surmises the situation. Aleks and Anton mangled his face from the punches he took on the street. But he's more alert than I thought he would be. I have more questions.

"I think you want to fuck your uncle and brother over by expanding the Etas' drug ring. But what the fuck does your family care about some small time Puerto Rican gang? If you wanted to fuck them over, you should have gone to the Mexicans. But they wouldn't take you, would they? They'd be cop killers before letting a Colombian pig into their ranks. A little pot won't make Enrique blink, and you sure as shit aren't running coke. He'd let you rot in the Bronx."

"You can rot here for a while."

Maks signals all of us to fall back. He and Aleks clean their blades while the rest of us go into the office. They soon join us, and we look out the two-way mirrored window as Juan dangles. His toes barely touch the floor, so his arms and shoulders must be in agony. He can hang and stew for a while.

"He's been gone for a year. Why's he come out of hiding now?"

Maks talks so quietly that I'm not sure if he's talking to us or himself.

"If Laura hadn't known him all her life, I doubt she would have recognized him. Anton only knew what to look for because she described him out at the park. I'm not sure I would have recognized him."

Misha's standing next to Maks as he talks. He turns to look at Maks rather than through the window as he continues.

"He was banking on her not noticing. This might not be the first time he's watched her. Easy."

Maks's entire body goes stiff, and he looks like he's ready to kill Juan now. But it's not time yet.

"Misha's right. He didn't say it to piss you off, Maks. But he's been on the streets for a while."

Sergei rests his hand on Maks's shoulder as he speaks. It's not a reassurance; it's keeping him in place.

"Let Sergei keep digging with our informants. If I need to bring anyone else in here to talk, then I will."

Anton's offer makes Maks relax. But we all turn as the door to the warehouse opens. Bogdan rushes in, and we're back on edge. He glances at Juan, who passed out. He runs to the office, and Misha has the door open for him by the time he gets to here.

"Maks, Pasha, you need to come home."

"What happened?"

Maks and I demand at the same time.

"The women received a text. All four of them. It was from an unavailable number. Sergei, we need you too."

"What'd it say?"

Maks, Sergei, and I are stripping as Maks asks what we all want to know.

"You made a big mistake."

"What the fuck does that mean?"

I ask, but I'm barely thinking straight as I step into one of the four showers. Aleks, Anton, or Misha will take care of our clothes. We never leave here without showering and changing. We leave with nothing. I noticed Maks took his wedding ring off at the house. I'd taken off my belt, watch, and put on other shoes before Sumiko and I left my place. But it didn't matter since I changed into my tactical gear. We have clothes we keep at the warehouse. It's a never-ending rotation, but we're all close enough in size that they're interchangeable. It's a good thing we're rich because our wardrobe alone costs us the equivalent of a small nation's GDP.

We scrub ourselves clean while Bogdan waits. He's pacing, and it's not putting me at ease. I don't know that I've ever showered so thoroughly, so fast. Maks, Sergei, and I are still buttoning our shirts as we follow Bogdan out to the car. We button our pants once we're inside. We wear loafers most of the time since they're easy to get on and off in a hurry.

"What were they doing when the text came in?"

Maks is in the backseat with Sergei and me when he asks. It's a tight fit in a town car. Bogdan is up front with our driver, Ilya, and the privacy glass is down.

"Ana and Sumiko were in the garden talking."

"Why?"

"Easy, Pasha. They were straightening things out. She asked Ana and Laura what was said. Niko and I apologized for putting her in the middle of the fight. Whatever Ana said helped."

"Is she still at the house?"

"Yes. She wanted to leave before she talked to Ana, then she agreed to stay."

"Because of the text?"

"No, Pasha. I think she'd already decided she would. The text confirmed it."

"She must be freaking out."

My knee is bouncing as I look out the window. I need to get to my *malyshka*. She barely finds out who I am, then she's forced into this shit, and I'm not around to help her deal with it.

"She's scared, but she's handling it well. I was on the phone with Christina the entire way here. Mama and your parents are on the way with Uncle Radomir and Aunt Svetlana. She knows she's safe at Maks and Laura's."

"Yeah, because she entered Fort Knox without knowing it."

Now my other foot is tapping along with my knee bouncing.

"I'll look at their phones as soon as we get to the house. I'll figure this out, Pasha."

I look at Sergei, and I try to believe him. He doesn't lie, but I don't know how he'll figure out something like this. The drive wasn't as excruciatingly long as I feared it would feel. Maks and I are scrambling out of the car before Ilya has it in park. Bogdan and Sergei are on our heels.

"Laura!"

Maks bellows as he bursts through the door.

"I'm here, Maks. Shh. The babies just went down for a nap."

Maks pulls Laura into his arms and lifts her off her feet as they kiss. I'm looking for Sumiko. I'm getting frantic when I realize she isn't with the others.

"Where is my girlfriend?"

"Pasha? I'm right here."

I spin around and see Sumiko walking out of the half bathroom. I don't hesitate to scoop her into my arms and carry her to the sunroom. I kick the door shut before putting her back on her feet. I devour her. My hand is in her hair as I ravish her mouth. My other hand is unzipping her skirt. She steps out of it as my fingers thrust into her. She's wet, thank God. She's pulling my pants open, then her legs are around my waist. I thrust into her as her back bumps against the wall. Anyone nearby must know what we're doing. I don't give a shit.

"*Malyshka,* I'm so sorry I wasn't here for you. I'm so, so sorry."

"It's all right, *fofinho.* I'm safe. You're here now, and I feel better."

"Because my cock is in you, and I'm going to let you come whenever you want?"

"That too. And thank you. But I feel better because I'm in your arms. I was so scared something was happening to you. I—"

Tears well in her eyes, and I hate that I'm making her cry. Our kiss is desperate as I continue to surge into her. I feel her cunt tightening around me as she comes. I'm fighting the urge to spend. I'm not done pleasuring her. There's a loveseat near the window, which has its sunshade pulled down. I carry her to it and sit. She rides me as I pull her blouse off and practically tear her bra.

"Daddy, this is hot."

"What is, baby girl?"

"I'm naked, and you're not. It's hot."

"Yeah, it is."

I land my hand across her ass, and her pussy nearly squeezes the cum out of me.

"Are you safe for real, Pasha?"

"Yes. Nothing happened to me. Just let me taste you and hold you. I'll explain later. I need you, Sumiko."

I roll us, so she's lying down, and I'm on top. I'm sucking her tits like a starved man. I want all of her, every inch, like she's my next meal.

"I'm coming again, *fofinho*."

She's breathless as she pants her admission. I can feel her. Not yet. I'm not ready to be done yet. I keep working her until I feel her come a third time. Then I can't hold back. I groan as I finally let myself go.

"Fuck. You feel so good. I want to stay buried inside for forever. You make me feel—"

"What, Pasha? Tell me. I want to know."

I look into her nearly black eyes, and I see worry as she brushes back hair from my forehead.

"You make me feel safe."

We stare at each other. I've never said that to anyone other than my parents, and it's been at least twenty years since I have. It's been longer than that since I was truly safe. I wasn't in Moscow. I was for only a heartbeat here in New York, but it wasn't long before I realized each of my actions could endanger or protect my parents. I have spent my entire life in danger. I'm too old to sit on either of my parents' laps. With Sumiko, I feel like the world can't touch me, even if for only a few minutes.

"Good. You make me feel the same way."

"How can you when I'll always be the reason you might be in danger?"

"Because I trust you to protect me."

"Always, *krasivaya*."

"How do you say sexy as fuck in Russian?"

She makes me laugh as I kiss her cheek.

"*Chertovski seksual'nyy*."

"Yeah, I'm not going to be able to say that without serious practice. How about handsome?"

"It's close to beautiful. *Krasivyy*."

"That I can manage."

My heart melts as I listen to her practice the word four times in a whisper. My two girlfriends in high school learned a few Russian phrases, but I never tried to teach any of the women in college or after that I hooked up with.

"We need to go back to the others, *krasivyy*."

"I know. But I don't want to."

"You sound like you're five."

"What five-year-old can do this?"

I flex my hips and circle them. She clenches her cunt around my dick, and I'm growing hard again.

"Oh, all right, *fofinho*. One more time."

She giggles, and it lightens my mood further to hear her call me cuddly. Never would I have imagined such a pet name and liking it to boot. But I was so scared of what I would find when I got here. When she wasn't with the others, I thought she'd left already. This round isn't as frantic as the last one, but we know it has to be a quickie. We come together, and I feel like I could keep going for a third time. But we sit up, and she puts her bra and shirt back on. I fasten my pants while she grabs her skirt and finishes redressing.

My arm is around her shoulders as we go back to the others. Except it's only Sergei who's in the living room. He glances toward the stairs and rolls his eyes. I guess the other three couples are doing what we were. Sergei's on his laptop with four cell phones on the coffee table in front of him. Sumiko sits on my lap as we get comfortable on one of the other sofas. Sergei says nothing until the others come downstairs.

"It was from a sat phone. I traced its GPS to here in Queens, but I can't get an exact location. It definitely wasn't the Bronx."

"He wouldn't have a satellite phone, anyway."

Maks speaks as he strokes Laura's hair, trying to reassure her it wasn't Juan. She's curled against him in a tight ball, and he's holding her as though she might fly away if he doesn't. I know they're the most freaked out because we don't know if this is related to Juan or something entirely separate. He won't have told her the gory details, but she'll know that we got him.

I glance at Niko and Ana. She's sitting on his lap, but she isn't as anxious as Laura. Christina is sitting the same way with Bogdan. I look down at Sumiko, and she has her eyes closed. I think she's embarrassed again.

"*Malyshka,* open your eyes. We're not doing anything different from the others."

I whisper to her, and her eyes flutter open. She looks around at the other couples, then at Sergei as he works. He's doing something to Laura's phone as he scrolls and taps the screen. He puts it back on the table. He does the same to Christina's and Ana's. He looks at Sumiko once he picks her phone up. She nods her permission, and he unlocks it with some code he punches in. Sumiko sits forward, shocked at how easy it was for him to access her phone.

"Sumiko, whoever this was, cloned your phone. Basically, they made their phone act like it was yours. The message didn't come through as a regular text. You all have the same messaging app. Whoever this was didn't need your phone numbers, just your social media profile name. They blocked your number from being the one that showed up. It took hacking towers to figure out that it came from a satellite and to track its GPS. But it was easy to find the cloning on your phone."

"Me?"

Sumiko looks around, horrified.

"You wouldn't have known what to look for, so you couldn't have known. It's probably been on there for a while."

"Why send the message to all four of us?"

Christina sits up as she asks. She offers Sumiko a sympathetic smile, which Sumiko returns. The women clearly feel better for having us all home, but they're still rattled.

"My guess is to confuse us, so we don't know who the real target is."

"But why me? And if it's been there for a while, then how could anyone other than me be the target?"

"I don't know. That's not something I can tell just from tracing. If you don't mind letting me have your phone for a while longer, I might figure out when the cloning happened."

"Whatever you need. I just want to know how I got involved in this if I only met Pasha a week ago."

Chapter Sixteen

Sumiko

How did someone get a hold of my phone and clone it? How does that even work? Why me? To what end?

One question after another swirls through my head, and I'm dizzy. It's been one of the longest days of my life. It's hard to believe that this morning began with Christina, Anton, and Pasha interviewing me to be their accountant. Since then, I've had sex with Pasha like seven times today. Not that I'm complaining about that. I don't think I've ever had this much sex in one day, and each time gets better.

But I've also learned that my boyfriend—I guess that's what he is since he called me his girlfriend earlier—is part of the Russian mafia. He went on some kind of—mission. I've received an ominous threat that somehow went through my phone and was sent to my boyfriend's cousins' wives.

A knock sounds at the door before it opens. The most beautiful woman I have ever seen walks in, followed by two couples. She looks remarkably like Maks and his brothers, but she also looks enough like Sergei and Misha that she could pass for their mom. The woman behind her must be her sister. They look very similar, but the second woman has red hair. Sergei and Misha are undoubtedly her sons. A third woman, with dark hair and green eyes, follows them. She must be Pasha's mother. I scramble to get off his lap, but he won't let go. None of the other couples are separating, but they're married.

"Pasha."

I practically hiss his name as I push his hand away from my thigh. Thank God I'm wearing my work skirt, so it completely covers my legs to my knees. Pasha sighs and lets me stand. He follows me and slips his hand into mine. He heads to the couple who must be his parents.

"Mama, Papa, this is my girlfriend, Sumiko. These are my parents, Alina and Grigori."

Like my boss. Small world.

"It's a pleasure to meet you, Mr. and Mrs. Kutsenko."

"It's Alina and Grig. Please."

Alina's accent is thicker than her sons' or nephews'. But she has the kindest eyes, and her smile is so maternal that I nearly burst into tears.

"Thank you."

My voice trembles, and Pasha pulls me against his side. I can see his worry, and I try to nod that everything is all right, but it's not. I'm suddenly way too overwhelmed with so many new names and faces, too many emotions, too many shocks and surprises. It's just too many of everything. Alina takes pity on me.

"I imagine you've had a long day, Sumiko. Galina, Svetlana, and I are going to go make dinner. Galina called and caught Niko before he and Ana started cooking. Would you like a cup of tea while I'm in there?"

I nod.

"Why don't you and Pasha come, and you can pick out what type you want?"

I feel like an idiot, but all I can do is nod again. The other men came back not long after Pasha got here. Now I watch as the beautiful blonde, who must be Galina, greets her sons. The massive men embrace her while Sergei and Misha hug their mom. Anton hugs Alina and Grig before father and son disappear into the room Anton was in when I arrived earlier. Radomir is talking to Sergei and Maks once Alina, Svetlana, and Galina head toward the kitchen. Pasha's arm is around my waist as we follow the women. He pulls a bar stool out for me at the breakfast bar.

"Pasha, why don't you get us some fresh mint?"

"Ma—Yes, Mama."

I can tell he doesn't want to leave my side, but his mother's expression tells him, even at twenty-eight, he'd be wise to do as he's told the first time. I find it endearing. The moment he leaves the kitchen, Alina engulfs me in a hug. I'm taken aback for a moment, then I'm sinking against her. She smells like fresh flowers, and she's soft in all the ways a mom is supposed to be. I burst into tears.

"*Rybochka*, cry if it'll make you feel better."

"Pasha will get upset if he comes back and sees me crying. I don't want to worry him even more."

"Pasha understands. It's why he didn't argue with me."

"I thought that was because he's still scared of you."

"I'm a Russian mother. He should still be scared."

Alina's soft laughter eases some of my tension, but the tears are still streaming down my face. Galina and Svetlana come to stand behind me. They join our hug, and I finally feel safe for the first time in hours without Pasha with me. I wipe my tears as the women ease their hold on me. Galina and Svetlana start cooking, and Alina makes me a mug of tea.

"I don't know what it's like to be in your position and learn about the bratva as an adult. I've known about it my entire life, but that doesn't make it any easier. I know you and Pasha just started dating."

"He's told you about me?"

"Yes, *rybochka*. He told me about you before he got back to New York. Then he told me about the mess he made of your date and how he hadn't talked to you in days. If you're here, then you must be dating. Besides, he introduced you as his girlfriend."

"He's called me that twice this evening. I suppose I am."

"You're here, so you're far more than just a friend."

Alina's voice is lilting as she teases me with a wink. My cheeks must be on fire.

"We—we decided this afternoon that we want to be together."

"I'm glad. He spoke highly of you. I told him to give you space, but I don't think he listened at first."

"He sent me a few texts I didn't answer. I feel badly about those."

"Don't. He had his own lessons to learn from that. It made him consider what he truly wants, and he realized it's you as his girlfriend. That means a lot to men like ours."

"That's what Christina said earlier."

I glance toward the living room. I can hear Pasha's voice, and he sounds irritated, but I don't understand what he's saying. I think that's his father who's speaking to him.

"Grig is mostly retired now, but I've been a bratva wife for thirty-two years. If you have questions, I will do my best to have answers."

"Will I ever know where he goes when he disappears?"

Alina's smile fades. She looks past me to the living room before her gaze meets mine. She shakes her head.

"There is somewhere they go where they can do what they must without interruption. He will never tell you where it is, and he will never take you there. But he and the others are safe when they work there."

"Work?"

Alina's gaze doesn't waver from mine. My mind whizzes back to the article from earlier this afternoon, then seeing how Pasha and the others dressed before they left. I look over my shoulder and realize that he's back to wearing a suit, but it wasn't what he wore when we left his apartment. He's changed clothes more times than a beauty queen.

"When they go there, they don't have their cell phones on. If you call or text, and he doesn't answer, it doesn't mean anything bad happened."

"His GPS is off when his phone is off. Is it so no one can track him?"

Once more, Alina doesn't answer me with words. Her expression tells me everything. I don't want to ask any more questions. I'm teetering on the edge again. I nearly jump out of my skin when Pasha kisses my cheek and places the mint in front of me on the counter.

"*Rybochka*, wash those, please. Sumiko can't put them in her tea while they're dirty."

"What does that mean? *Rybochka*. You called me that too."

"It means little fish. Mama has called Anton and me that since we were babies. It doesn't sound right in English, but it's a term of endearment many parents use. Galina calls her boys and now her daughters-in-law *pchelka*. It means little bee."

"Svetlana calls her boys *lisichka*. Little fox. Sergei and Misha were always the least likely to get caught doing whatever they shouldn't have been."

"That's because Sergei used to make Maks and Anton go

first. And Misha claims to be the baby of the family, so who would blame him?"

Pasha rolls his eyes.

"Don't be jealous because my brother and I are smarter than you and your brother."

Misha calls from the living room. The man must have ears like a dog. Pasha grumbles something under his breath that makes Alina tsk.

"I heard that!"

"Shut up, Misha. You did not. You saw my mouth move."

"Whatever. I'm still smarter."

"We just let you think that, so you won't cry to your mama."

Bogdan elbows Misha as he walks by. Misha grabs his ribs and doubles over.

"Mama!"

I listen to the cousins tease one another as the three mothers ignore their sons and nephews. It eases much of the tension that's gathered between my shoulders and in my neck. The headache I've had off and on for hours dulls. Pasha drops a couple of mint leaves in the teacup Alina placed before me. He pulls a barstool next to mine, and I sag against him.

"Are you hungry, *malyshka*?"

"Yes. But I'm just tired more than anything else."

"Do you mind spending the night here? Or we can go back to my place."

"We need the security?"

"I'd prefer it. But your place is farther than mine. You look exhausted. I thought you might like a bath and to go to bed early."

I tilt my head back to whisper in his ear.

"Will you tuck me in, Daddy?"

"After I give my baby girl a bath. If you're really good, I'll tell you the story about the Big Bad Wolf who eats out the *malyshka* he finds in his bed."

"I don't think I know that story."

"It's best acted out."

"If you say so, Daddy."

Pasha kisses my forehead and shifts on his stool. I glance down and see he's hard. I rest my hand high on his thigh, letting my fingers run along the inside seam of his pants. He catches my fingers and gives them a squeeze.

"Do you need a spanking?"

His question makes me stop and think. The idea of relinquishing control right now and putting my trust in him to protect me and pleasure me sounds divine. I don't want to make any decisions tonight because I don't feel like I can. I want Pasha to take the lead, and I'll gladly submit.

"I do."

His surprise is clear. When our eyes lock, I know he understands. His hold on my hand loosens before he lets go. He tucks hair behind my ear, then trails his fingertip along the bridge of my nose. He tips my head back with his forefinger beneath my chin. His kiss is little more than a peck, but it's incredibly tender. We continue to whisper to each other

"I think everyone will go to bed early tonight. Every bedroom has an ensuite. You can have that bath, then I'll do whatever you need, Sumiko. I'll take care of you if you'll let me."

"I need that."

"I know, baby girl. I'll always take care of you."

Something shifts in me. It's been building all day, but now I can feel the clarity that I hadn't earlier today. He didn't say that in passing or flippantly. He truly means it. Christina said the men aren't impulsive and Pasha likely thought hard before deciding to bring me into this life. He's said he's all in. Neither he nor Christina was exaggerating. Pasha means always. And I know now that I want the same thing.

"Will you help us carry these out?"

Galina's request intrudes on my introspection. We help carry dishes to the dining room table. It's enormous. It's like something you'd see in a medieval castle. Then again, I thought this place was more like a palace than a house. The table seats twenty, so there are only a few open seats. I notice there's one next to Galina. As I watch the other couples, I wonder what happened to her husband. I know he died, but I don't know how. Aleks sits on her other side and dotes on his mother. He fills her wine glass and serves her far more food than she could eat. It's more like a serving for him than for her. She taps his arm and swaps plates, taking his empty one. She serves herself this time. He tries to pass her another dish, but she puts three large spoonfuls of some type of vegetable on his plate. His nose curls, and I can almost hear her admonishing him to eat his vegetables.

I look around at everyone else, and it's like something out of a Christmas movie. People are laughing, and couples are sneaking kisses. Husbands have their arms around their wives as the women lean against them. It's the picture of domestic tranquility. No one could guess that the men left looking ready to go into battle a few hours ago or that there were two threats to the family today. They've put that aside for this family meal, and it's a welcome reprieve.

"We can get a little noisy. I know your family is much smaller, so I'm sorry if it's a bit much."

"Don't be. Brazilians aren't exactly known for being quiet, and neither are the Japanese. Not really. This reminds me of visiting family, but I've always had to travel to do that. I feel like this is a pretty normal evening for you guys."

"It is. I mean, we don't get together every week. But some

weeks, we do it a few times. It just depends on what everyone's up to and whether we all wind up in the same place."

"This is really nice, Pasha. Thank you for including me."

"Of course."

"You could have taken me home or even sent me home."

"No, I couldn't have. That would mean saying goodnight and going to bed without you. I refuse to do that."

"You know what I mean."

Pasha looks like he wants to say something more, but he asks if I want any wine. The meal continues with plenty of laughter. Maks goes upstairs to fetch the twins when we hear them through the monitor. I don't think a man could look happier holding his children than Maks does. He's been fierce since the moment I met him, even when he was kissing Laura and his children goodbye. Now he's laughing and making faces at his son and daughter. His son latches onto his nose, and he pretends to snap at the tiny fingers. Konstantin kicks his legs, hitting his sister, who swats both arms hoping to make contact with something.

I glance up at Pasha and find him watching me. It makes me wonder about having children with him. I feel better about the idea than I did the first time.

"One day, *malyshka*."

I swallow and nod. He's right. One day, he is going to be the father of our children.

Chapter Seventeen

Pasha

It's been two weeks since Sumiko and I had sex in her office, then had an interrupted lunch, followed by incredible sex at my place. It's been that long since we picked up Juan and the women received the threat. We spent that night at Maks and Laura's. My mom and Sumiko have a similar build, so my mom brought over a pair of pajamas for Sumiko. She didn't wear them that night, but she was glad for them in the morning when everyone came downstairs for breakfast.

She's spent every night since then at my place. It's been blissful. The first five nights, we were inseparable. We couldn't be out of each other's reach, and it was a sex marathon each night. By the sixth night, we still wanted to be close to each other, but she watched TV while I did some work in my office. We cooked and cleaned up together like a couple that's been together far longer.

Since the day after everything happened was a Saturday, we

went to her place. She picked up clothes and toiletries. I also met her chinchilla, Pandora. I have never been fond of rodents, but that little cutie is enough to make me rethink my opinion. I didn't know rodents of any species could be playful or affectionate, but Pandora is. We brought her back to my place, and she now squeaks when she sees me, just like she does when she sees Sumiko. I've discovered that Pandora likes to sit on my shoulder while I work. The first time she ran up my arm, I nearly squealed like a little kid. It creeped me out. I was certain she was going to chew on my hair, shit down my back, and eat my face. Sumiko saw my terror and laughed. Pandora fell asleep. Now I don't mind.

"Would you feed Pandora, please? Her water bottle needs refilling."

Sumiko just went into what I consider our bedroom to change out of her work clothes. I'm already in sweats since I worked from home today. I was a normal accountant, looking at invoices and account statements. They weren't for any of our legal businesses, but it was as typical a workday as I get.

"Sure. What do you want for dinner? I can grill some salmon, or I can do baked chicken breasts."

"You pick."

"Salmon, since it'll be faster. I'm starving."

I put my hand over my stomach as it growls.

"You're always starving."

"For my dessert. I can't have it until I've eaten my vegetables."

"And I suppose I'm that dessert."

She steps out of the bedroom with a grin. Her yoga pants and tank top make me want to skip dinner. I finish feeding Pandora and join her in the kitchen. Her phone pings, but she ignores it. We try not to look at our phones during dinner, but I've had to take a call or two.

"Do you want a salad? Or do you want me to steam something while you grill?"

Sumiko heads to the fridge as she asks. These normal conversations are something I never imagined having. Sitting down to dinner with the same person, who isn't part of my family, is unexpected. But I love each evening. Perhaps the novelty will wear off in a few decades, but for now, I cherish it.

"Both?"

"All right. I should have known. It's a good thing you're a healthy eater. I don't know how you pack so much away."

"Mama says I still have hollow legs. Aleks is the one who can really eat. I've never seen someone put away as much in one sitting as him. It's unreal."

"I saw him serving Galina at dinner at Laura's. She swapped plates with him because he served four times as much as she ended up taking. He also didn't look happy about those beets that I liked."

"When we left Moscow, he thought he would never have to eat beets again. He thought they only grew in Russia. Aunt Galina set him straight the first time she made dinner in their apartment. He's hated them for as long as I can remember."

"Did you move here together?"

I haven't told her that much about my family's past, but I know she's curious. This is the first time she's asked.

"A few months later. Radomir and Svetlana came here first, with Misha and Sergei. We came after Aunt Galina and my cousins."

Sumiko looks at me, waiting for me to fill in more details. When I don't, she grabs what she needs from the fridge and moves to the sink to wash the vegetables. If she's going to be with me, then she deserves to know more. She's told me plenty about her family. There's so much I can never share that I feel guilty keeping anything reasonable from her.

"Uncle Kirill, Radomir, and my dad were all KGB before the Soviet Union fell. They were still young men when that happened. They'd been recruited—conscripted, really—so they served the government for years. When communism ended, they wanted to find regular jobs. But a bratva that relished having three former KGB members who were young and strong ruled our neighborhood. There are a few men there who escaped being sucked into the bratva, but my dad and uncles were ideal conscripts. It wasn't long before they sent the three of them to fight in the Second Chechen War. They weren't Russian army, but they were paramilitary."

I watch Sumiko as she washes the vegetables. She's listening and keeps glancing at me. I don't know if she's even heard of the Chechen wars, and I don't know if she knows the crimes against humanity and atrocities committed during those years. When she nods, encouraging me to continue, I don't think she does. But I'm certain she'll search the internet when she can.

"Uncle Kirill died when he stepped on a landmine. Radomir had just been sent home with an injury. My dad watched his brother die. He had to tell Aunt Galina and my cousins what happened. Radomir and Svetlana fled with Misha and Sergei as soon as he was well enough to travel. Radomir, Uncle Kirill, and my dad were already trying to get us to America before the bratva sent them to war. After Uncle Kirill died, my dad helped Aunt Galina and my cousins flee to St. Petersburg, where they hid until they could get a flight here. The bratva discovered what my dad did within a couple days. We had to go into hiding until we could leave, too."

"So your family escaped war and the bratva only for you to wind up in it here."

"Yes. The Podolskaya bratva was one of the most well organized and well-trained organizations in Moscow. They were paramilitary like that article described. That's why they wanted former KGB operatives. When word reached the former leader of the Ivankov bratva, our branch here in New York, inevitably, they came knocking. My cousins had no father to protect them. The man who ran the bratva before Maks—"

"Wait. Maks runs your branch or whatever."

Fuck.

"Yes. He's known as *pakhan*, or boss. He oversees everything."

"Are Niko and the others pretty high up there?"

I need to consider how to answer these questions. How much is safe for her to know? How do I phrase all of this?

"Pasha, I shouldn't have asked. Never mind."

"No." I turn off the faucet and take her hands as she turns to me. "I want you to know, but I'm deciding as we go what's safe to tell you."

"Do you think I'll tell other people?"

"No. I don't think that at all. But what you know—how much you know—could endanger you far more than just being associated with me."

"If I know nothing, there's nothing for people to get out of me. But I've always thought that reasoning was pointless when I hear it in movies. If people assume I know stuff, won't they just torture me endlessly, believing I'm hiding stuff?"

Fuck my life. Hard. I tilt my head back. I can't look at her as I answer that.

"At a certain point, it becomes obvious when someone truly doesn't know."

"How—"

"You don't want to know how I know that."

"That means you've tortured people." Her eyes widen. "Or does that mean you've been tortured? Your scars! Are they from—"

184

"Sumiko, I think you already know the answers to all of that. I really don't want to say it."

"Your mom said there is somewhere you go to work. Did she mean that's where you go to torture people?"

The wall goes up. My expression is blank. I'm back to hiding all my thoughts and emotions from anyone and everyone who isn't my family or family friends. My dad can do the same thing. My mom and aunts can read all of us because they learned to understand their husbands. I'm not sure I want Sumiko to have that skill.

"Answer me, Pasha. I need to know."

"I am a monster, Sumiko. I am the things you assume a mafioso is. I can't change that. I can't change the past, and I can't change my future. I won't."

Her phone picks that moment to ping again. Except it isn't once. It's three messages that come in. She looks at me before drying her hands and going to her phone. She glances at it once the screen lights up. It was face up, but she puts it down with the screen on the counter. Why didn't she unlock it and read the texts? Why is it now screen down?

"You say you're a monster. Do you enjoy it?"

"No."

"Then why?"

"Because what choice do I have?"

"There's always a choice."

"Spoken like someone who's never had that privilege taken from them."

"There's still a choice."

"All right. Here's the choice I've been given: do these things or be the reason my family's murdered. There. That's been my choice. Tell me. What would you do?"

I'm too harsh. Sumiko retreats from me. She doesn't know. She doesn't understand. She can't, especially if I don't explain.

"Sumiko, the man who came before Maks was a sociopath. He was the stereotype of a Russian killer. He did it without remorse and for pleasure. I was fourteen when he dragged me into this life. He did things to coerce us all. He hurt my brother and cousins, and our friends, to force us to comply. We were all so young that we believed he would make us kill our parents if we disobeyed. We believed he would kill each of us. We didn't understand that eight athletic boys were a dream come true for him. We were the *boyeviks,* or foot soldiers, he needed. By the time we realized our value, he'd already made us do—things. He'd already trained us. The robbing convenience stores, stealing cars, running illegal gambling rings were nothing compared to the skills he forced upon us."

"And now? You could walk away."

"To what? A world that exists and knows who I am, knows who my family is. I'm safer with them than without. I'm a target without them. And my family wouldn't let anyone hurt me without retaliating. That makes them all targets too. I won't desert them, Sumiko. I will do whatever I have to, to protect my family and the people I'm responsible for."

"Responsible for?"

"Sumiko, the bratva is an enormous organization that legally and illegally employs thousands of people. People who rely on us for their livelihoods and providing for their families. People who depend on us to protect them from the other syndicates."

"Your illegal businesses. That's gun running and dealing drugs."

"I will never answer that, Sumiko. Do not ask me. I wish you wouldn't assume because I will neither confirm nor deny if you tell me your thoughts. I can't. It's not just you who that endangers. It's everyone."

I run my hand through my hair. I knew this conversation

was inevitable. I know Maks had it with Laura, Bogdan had it with Christina, and Niko had it with Ana. But that doesn't make it any easier. And I don't know what they said during any of them. My cousins didn't exactly give me any pointers.

"What happens if you get arrested?"

"One of two things. I'm home and not even booked. Or I wind up on death row."

"You say that as though you know from experience."

"I have a rap sheet, Sumiko. We all do. But it's been at least eight or nine years since my last arrest. We were poor when we moved here. We came basically with the clothes on our backs. Aunt Galina was a widow with four sons. We all did things to help our families get by. I did things thinking I was helping my cousins. We were all forced to commit crimes for Vlad. Sometimes we got caught. Most of the time we didn't."

"Vlad?"

I inhale deeply before I sigh.

"Vladislav Lushak. He was the old *pakhan*."

The name means nothing to Sumiko. I can tell.

"What happens if I'm with you when you get arrested? Will I be too?"

"The police usually leave us alone. They know better than to get involved between syndicates, and it pays better to let us conduct our businesses. I will always do whatever I can to make sure that never happens to you. If something happens, and I get arrested, you go to my family immediately. If you're not with me, someone will come to you."

"I suppose you don't go to hospitals either."

"Not if we can help it. Anton and Sergei are both trained paramedics who keep their certifications up to date. They can handle most things, but we have a doctor on staff in case it's more serious. The same thing applies. Get to my family, or they will come to get you."

Her phone goes off again, but she ignores it.

"Do you need to get that?"

"No. It's just Tiffany and Sarah."

Something about her tone makes me think that's not who's texting her.

"If Maks is in charge, and his brothers are pretty high up there, are you the same?"

"No. Maks is the boss. His brothers are part of the Elite Group. They help run things with him, and they're his advisors. Anton and Sergei are just beneath them and head up security and intelligence."

"Anton's the chief enforcer?"

I don't answer.

"That's why Sergei knows how to track our phones and texts."

"They both have degrees in Computer Science from UPenn."

"What are you?"

"I'm the *derzhatel obshchaka*, or bookkeeper."

"Did you become that before or after you became an accountant?"

"I became an accountant because that's where Maks wanted me. He was already being trained to take over."

"You didn't study it because that's what you wanted."

"No."

"That must have been hard to accept at eighteen."

I shake my head.

"Not really. I have a head for numbers. And I was doing my part. Misha studied entrepreneurship, and Niko and Bogdan studied finance. We did that because we knew we needed those skills to run things better. Vlad was too old-world. He made poor choices about everything, using violence to maintain his control. We have far more stability now that our business affairs are in better order. That's what people want."

"What did Maks and Aleks study?"

"They didn't have the luxury of going to college."

I think that surprises her. From how Maks and Aleks present themselves, I guess she assumed they had. Our athleticism and build usually makes people think we're some type of pro athlete. Our wealth often makes people think we're trust fund babies. Rarely do people believe us when we say which universities we attended. Anton and Serge: went on athletic scholarships. Bogdan and Niko went on academic scholarships. Misha and I got some scholarships, but mostly we worked to pay our way through.

"You haven't had to suddenly take off in the past two weeks. Does that usually happen more often?"

I haven't told her anything about Juan, so I haven't told her I've been to the warehouse three times to visit him. He's still alive, but barely. We've learned a little more, but mostly Maks is punishing him.

"It's unpredictable, but not that often. I'll be home with you most nights."

I say that to test the water. Is she ready to break up with me?

"Do you still promise to tell me if you're going to be away for more than a day?"

"I promise to try. It might not be me who tells you."

I lick my lips as I prepare for my next—warning.

"There might be a time when something goes wrong. Where things aren't under our control. If I tell you to stay away from the condo, or I ask you to stay in a bedroom, I need you to do that. It means I don't want you to see me. It isn't the other way around. It's not that I don't want to see you."

"What does that mean?"

"It means I need to get cleaned up. It means I need to calm down. It means I'm the man I never want you to know."

"Cleaned up. That Friday, you wore three outfits. Why?"

"Sumiko, you know the answer to that."

"No, I don't. You left your suit coat out here. Why did you put on a different one? You took off your watch and belt. You wore different shoes. Why?"

I scratch my eyebrow before I reach behind me. I'm slow as I withdraw my gun. She gasps.

"That's why you always have me put my arms around your neck."

"Yes. That afternoon, I couldn't leave the bedroom without a suit coat on. You would have seen the one at my back and the two in my shoulder holster."

"You had three guns?"

"Yes."

"You didn't have one when we arrived."

"Yes, I did. You didn't notice me slide it out of my waist holster while we were having sex or put it back afterwards. I put that one away while you were in the bathroom."

"But you were in the kitchen. You said you couldn't come out of the bedroom with three of them."

"There are a lot of weapons in this apartment, Sumiko. They're hidden, but in easy reach."

She shakes her head. She grabs her phone and looks for her purse.

"No. This is where I draw the line. There is no point in getting serious. I am not raising a family in a home with an arsenal. No."

"Plenty of Americans have guns in the home."

"Not in my home. You've made it clear that you see us having a future. You see us together for good. That won't happen if it means my children could stumble upon guns hidden all over my home."

"Our children, and our home, Sumiko. I have been a bachelor the entire time I've lived here. I haven't had to consider children finding my weapons. I didn't know my dad owned a single gun until the night we ran away from our apartment in Moscow. I never once saw a gun or a knife. He had plenty. I'm not careless. I know full well the power they have. I've understood since I was fourteen and—Sumiko, when we have children—everything will change. That includes baby proofing electrical outlets, the chemicals under sinks, and this. I'm not reckless. But I can't protect you or our children without them. No one has ever broken in, but it's always a possibility. There was an incident right after Laura and Maks started dating. There were men on Maks's rooftop. I can't afford not to be prepared."

"You—you speak as though—it's a foregone conclusion. That us having kids—that's going to happen no matter what."

"Unless nature keeps us from it."

"You see us together, married?"

"Sumiko, not only have I let you know that I'm bratva. I've told you plenty of my darkest secrets in the last half hour. Things that could absolutely destroy me and devastate my family. It could endanger every person I know. Do you really think after all these years of pushing women away, keeping friends at arm's length, that I just spilled all of this for no reason? I want and need you to understand, so it's your choice whether you stay. But I told you because I want you to stay."

"I need to think about all this. Can I go for a walk?"

"Stefan and Timofey will go with you if you don't want me to."

"I need space."

I nod. It's not what I want to hear. But it's not like I thought she was going to jump into my arms and demand I fuck her. I speak to the guard at the door, Timofey, and give him instructions. She kisses me, and the same passion is there as before this conversation. But she still walks out the door. It feels like she's walking out of my life.

Chapter Eighteen

Sumiko

Everything is always so heavy with Pasha. When we talk about anything to do with his life, it's like this oppressive weight bears down on me. He must carry that with him all the time. He shocked me with how much he revealed. I didn't think he would. Part of me is glad that he told me as much as he did. I'm glad he trusts me and opened up to me. But part of me wishes I was as ignorant as I had been an hour ago. I can't unhear any of it.

There's a park two blocks from Pasha's place, so I head there with my two shadows. They're discreet, but I know they're there. They're as unobtrusive as they can be as they watch everyone and everything in the park. I find a bench and pull my phone out.

Pablo: Sorry I had to hang up so abruptly earlier. When can we finish our conversation?

That was the first text that came in while I was talking to Pasha.

Pablo: We really need to talk.

Pablo: This is important. You need to know who he really is.

Pablo: Don't be stubborn. You can't ignore this.

I was still talking to Pasha when Pablo sent these. I hate that I lied to Pasha. I couldn't tell him Pablo's called and texted me several times this week.

Pablo: I told him to stay away from you.

Part of why I wanted to go for the walk was so that I could escape before Pablo sent any more texts. I know Pasha didn't believe me when I said it was Tiffany and Sarah. He hasn't lied to me. He's been honest when he can't tell me things. No lies by omission. But I lied to him. I've been lying by not telling him Pablo's contacted me.

"Hi."

"I didn't think you were going to call, since you didn't answer my texts."

"I couldn't, Pablo. I was in the middle of something."

"Fucking him?"

"I'm going to hang up."

"No. I'm sorry. Sumiko, you don't understand how dangerous he is."

I've been evasive the few times I've responded to Pablo's texts. I answered two of his calls just to say that I was too busy at work to talk. The one call when I could talk, he had to go. I sent his calls to voicemail when I was with Pasha.

"Yes, I do. You and he are a lot of alike. At least your occupations are. But only he told me the truth, Pablo."

"What does that mean?"

"It means I know. I know about him and his family. I know about you and yours."

"What did that fucker say about my family and me?"

"Calm the fuck down. Nothing beyond saying it's a similar situation to his. Believe it or not, but my ex-boyfriends don't come up in conversation."

"It is not the same."

"You mean you aren't Cartel?"

"*Hijueputa.*" Son of a bitch.

"I heard that. I guessed that, Pablo. He only confirmed it. You let me go out with you for three months and didn't think I needed to know the danger I was in, the risk of being arrested. He hasn't lied to me, Pablo. He's given me the choice to stay or go. You didn't. It was your evasiveness that broke us up."

"So you'd still be with me if I'd told you things that could get you killed."

"No."

"But you said—"

"I still would have gone on that vacation. I still would have met Pasha. I would have—I would have broken up with you for him."

"Bullshit. You wouldn't have let him chat you up if you had a boyfriend. You aren't that kind of girl."

"Pablo, you and I both know we weren't destined to be together long term. If we were, you would have been more forthcoming. You would have trusted me and wanted to let me in."

"And you're so sure about your future with him."

"I am."

"You're making a mistake."

"The same one you would have let me keep making until you dumped me?"

"I—"

"No. I think you're acting like a spoiled child who's pissed that a kid you don't like is playing with your toy."

"I kept you out of all of this to keep you safe. How can you respect him if he's brought you into danger?"

"Because he hasn't left me ignorant, and he's given me choices."

"You think he's going to just let you walk away if you change your mind? You're stuck now. He will never let you walk away. Never."

"You make it sound like he'd kill me if I broke up with him."

Pablo's silence is deafening. It's also infuriating.

"Don't call or text me."

I hang up. I put the phone on the bench next to me and tilt my head back. This is all too much again. Today's been a lot to take. It's all or nothing right now. It's all wonderful or pretty fucking horrible. It's all really heavy or practically perfect. There's nothing in between, and it's emotionally and physically exhausting.

What Pablo said pisses me off. Especially implying Pasha would hurt me if I tried to leave him. I think they know each other pretty well. I know Pablo knows Pasha is not that sort of man. He's possessive and protective, but that also means he would never hurt me. Not intentionally. And the men in his family would never condone it. Nothing about Maks makes me think he would order me dead if Pasha and I broke up.

But as angry as Pablo's made me, I can still see the soundness in what he said. I get why he didn't let me get closer to him. Part of me thinks maybe he cared about me more than Pasha does since he tried to protect me. Then I remind myself that we dated for three months, and he never once ensured I had a safety detail. He never once thought to warn me that people might take notice when we were together. I feel vulnerable when I think back on that time. And that makes me angrier.

Pablo: I'm sorry I pissed you off, querida.

Darling. He used to call me that.

Pablo: I'm worried about you. I didn't want us to break up. You decided that. I thought we were good together.

Me: We were in the beginning. But you were never going to let me get closer to you. That's why we broke up. I'm not rehashing this.

Pablo: I was protecting you because I care about you. I'm still protecting you.

Me: Except I don't want your protection. Stop texting me. I won't keep answering.

Pablo: You don't want to hear what I have to say because you know I'm right.

I don't respond. We keep going around in circles. I'm over it. I tuck my phone into my yoga pants' pocket against my thigh. I look around before I stand up. I can't go back to my place without my purse, which I left at Pasha's. And I don't want to. I don't want to run away and pretend like nothing is wrong. And I don't want to ignore Pasha. But I'm not exactly excited to continue discussing things with him.

Timofey or Stefan must have texted him because he's waiting at the door when I return. We thank Timofey, who goes back to guarding the door. I can smell the salmon cooking, and the salad is already in a bowl. The microwave dings, and I know the vegetables are done. Pasha steps onto the balcony to get the fish while I wash my hands.

Neither of us brings up our earlier conversation. We chat about our day and what we want to do this weekend. He has to work Friday and Saturday nights at his cousins' nightclubs. He said Christina and Ana are taking Laura out for the first time since she had the twins. Maks is staying home with them. He suspects Galina will go over once Laura leaves. He asks if I want to join them. I let him know they already invited me, and I accepted.

"*Malyshka*, you look exhausted. Do you want to go to bed early?"

"Yes. But not alone, *fofinho*."

I watch him relax. I didn't realize how tense he'd been throughout the entire meal until just now. He hid his emotions like he often does. But he suddenly looks younger and more at ease. We've had a lot of sex, but it hasn't been that kinky since the first time we did it here. But a box of goodies arrived today.

"Are you too tired to play for a while before bed?"

"I think I can stay awake for that."

It was mortifying to pick up the package from security in the lobby. It was already open, so I knew they'd searched it. Pasha had warned me that all packages are, but that still didn't prepare me for how badly I wanted to be invisible when I realized someone saw the ten pounds of sex toys we bought.

"Strip, *malyshka*. Slowly."

Pasha sits in the armchair where I got my first spanking. I ease my tank top up, inch by inch, until my tits are bare. I lean forward as I lift the shirt over my head. I toss it aside before cupping my tits and squeezing them together. I lick each nipple, and I watch him shift in the chair as he adjusts himself. I slide my hands down my ribs until I hook my thumbs into my waistband. I turn away from him before I pretend to pull down my pants, but I stop after an inch of my lower back is revealed. I look over my shoulder and wiggle my hips. He's rubbing his cock through his pants.

"I said slowly, *malyshka*. I didn't tell you to stop. Naked. Now."

I don't hurry, but I push my pants down over my hips, letting my hands trail over my ass. I bend in half as though I need to when they get to my ankles. I'm wearing a thong, which

I know he both loves and hates. I remain leaning forward as I reach back and move the material aside before I run my finger along my pussy.

"*Malyshka.*"

I love the warning in his voice. He likes my teasing, even when he doesn't. I know he enjoys watching me. I also know he's impatient. I slide the thong down my legs, spreading my ass cheeks as I step out of it. I snag it from the floor, twirl it on my finger, then launch it toward him. He's out of his seat the moment it hits his chest. He slings me over his shoulder and starts spanking me.

"You, baby girl, should know by now not to bait your Russian bear."

"My Russian teddy bear?"

"Maybe after I've fucked you for a few hours. You offered me your ass, and I'm taking it tonight."

A shiver runs through me at the idea. He twists the plug I put in before dinner.

"You didn't mention this little jewel, *malyshka*. When did you put this in?"

"When I got changed earlier."

"You were already planning for me to fuck your ass."

"I was hoping."

"I'm going to fuck your mouth, your cunt, and your ass tonight."

"Yes, please, Daddy."

He twists the plug then lands another spank. He does this three more times before he puts me on my feet. He spins me to face the bed.

"Lean forward."

He goes to the open box on his dresser and pulls out a blindfold. He comes back to the bed long enough to slip it over my eyes. I'm unprepared when he comes back a second time and eases earbuds into my ears. There're soft ocean waves playing, but the volume is high enough that I can no longer hear him moving around.

I scream when the riding crop lands across my ass. I wasn't prepared for that. I didn't know he was standing next to me or that he would use something to spank me. He pulls one earbud out.

"What's your safe word, *malyshka?*"

"Kale, Daddy."

"You do not take more than you can handle. Do you understand me?"

"Yes, Daddy. I want this."

"I know you do, baby girl. I will give you everything you want. Tell me what you need, and I will give you that too."

"Pasha?"

He slides the blindfold from my eyes. His concern is obvious. I never call him by his name when we're like this. I rest my hands on his chest.

"I'm not going anywhere without you."

He wraps his arms around me and pulls me close. His kiss is so gentle it almost makes me cry. It's enough to make us both consider abandoning the kinky, but we both want it. I slide the blindfold down and my body against the mattress. He puts the earbud back as I cross my wrists and keep them against my lower back. I feel cuffs snap around them, and I never even noticed he had them. Then the crop lands across my ass, and I go onto my toes.

Fuck. That smarts.

He lands ten more, some on the meatiest part of my ass, and some on my horizontal crack. He uses one hand to rub my ass, taking some of the burn out of my skin. But then he squeezes. Hard. Like really hard. Enough for me to catch my breath and whimper. Then I feel a vibrator against my clit. It's there for only a second before I feel him pressing it into me. I'm a fucking slip and slide already. I'm surprised it doesn't fall right back out.

He moves the vibrator and butt plug at the same time. My fingers are opening and closing while my toes curl and uncurl. When he alternates the rhythm, I'm panting.

"Please, Daddy. I need to come."

The ocean sounds keep me from hearing him if he answers. But I don't think he does. He knows I wouldn't be able to hear.

"Daddy, please."

I'm begging. I'm too close. I try to wriggle away, and that earns me a slap across my already tender ass. He turns up the vibrator, and I'm stomping my feet, trying to distract myself.

"Daddy, I can't stop. I'm going to come. Please. I'm trying. I can't st—"

I'm mid-sentence when I feel his tongue on my clit. The moment he sucks it while still working the plug and vibrator, I'm done for. I can't stop. I'm practically convulsing as I come. He doesn't relent until I'm spent. I come twice, and I'm winded. The moment he pulls the vibrator from me, I twist toward him and lower myself to my knees. I open my mouth.

He pulls the earbuds out.

"As gorgeous a sight as you are, and as much as my cock wants to feel the back of your throat, I didn't tell you to kneel. Who decides, *malyshka?*"

"You do, Daddy. I just really want to get you off."

"I'm not ready to get off."

"You made me feel so good. I need to—Daddy, I just want you to feel that good too."

He slides the blindfold off and stares at me. My brow furrows, and I suddenly feel really unsettled. He smooths the hair back from my face, and I turn my cheek into his hand. I close my eyes, savoring his tenderness.

My voice is a hoarse whisper.

"Please."

He unfastens his pants, then sits on the bed and opens his legs. I shuffle forward and open my mouth again. He guides his cock to my lips and runs the head over them. I lick him over and over until he presses forward. Then I barely stop short of inhaling him. I suck him, my eyes closed even without the blindfold.

"You don't know how fucking hot you look with your lips around my dick, *malyshka*. Fuck. Your mouth feels so good."

He fists my hair and presses me forward. I relax my throat and take him as he thrusts. He's not applying much pressure. He's not trying to gag me. His hand in my hair is more a reminder than actual control.

"Let go."

It's a command I know I don't dare ignore. His tone tells me. He's quick to unfasten the handcuffs, and they fall to the floor.

"Jerk me off."

I stroke him until his cum splatters across my tits, neck, and lips. It's like a fucking porn. I always thought the women looked so ridiculously happy lapping up the guy's jizz. Now I'm happy doing it.

"You're fucking mine, *malyshka*. My cum is on you, and soon it'll be in you. Your mouth, your pussy, your ass. They're all mine to pleasure and to punish."

"Your punishments are pleasure."

He laughs, but it's not humorous.

"Then I haven't punished you enough. They are two very different things, baby girl."

"Does punishing me give you pleasure?"

I look up at him, and I'm surprised to see sadness. He's

letting me see it. He's being open with me. I stand up and take his hands.

"Pasha?"

"The answer to that question isn't simple. So far I have meant the punishments to give you pleasure eventually, and in turn, that gives me pleasure. I'm not looking for true domestic discipline, Sumiko. I'm not that controlling. But if I ever give you a punishment because you've done something that's endangered you or you've hurt yourself, then there won't be pleasure for either of us. I will never strike you out of anger, and I will never hit you. But I will punish you if you put yourself or anyone else at risk."

"I understand, Pasha."

He looks as though there's more he wants to say, but then he thinks better of it. But I don't want him to keep things from me.

"What's wrong? You want to say something, but you aren't."

"It's nothing."

"That's not true."

"Let it go for right now."

"Now I really want to know. Is this something that I really can't know, or are you holding out on me?"

"It's something we can talk about later."

"I want—"

"No. It will ruin our evening, and I refuse to let that happen."

"But—"

"Who decides, *malyshka*? I haven't said I won't tell you. I've said this isn't the right time."

That's fair. I nod before I stand on my toes and peck his lips. He lifts me off my feet, and I wrap my legs around his waist. He tosses me onto the bed before he grabs my wrist. He reaches down and pulls up a restraint.

"That wasn't the only package that arrived today."

He's referring to the one on the dresser.

"Oh?"

He moves to my ankle and uses a cuff he pulls from the bed frame. He straightens and has a bar in his hands. It's a spreader that he extends all the way. He attaches it to my right ankle, then my left, before he cuffs my left ankle and wrist to the bed. I'm spread eagle for him. I'm vulnerable, and I'm excited. I trust him, which I already knew. But I keep discovering my trust runs deeper than I expected. When I'm tied to the bed, he slips the mask back over my eyes and puts the earbuds back. This time, there's classical music playing. I assume he's using his phone, but I don't know since I haven't seen him with it. Nothing happens for what feels like forever. It's building the anticipation, and I also hope it means he's getting naked.

The first drip of hot wax on my belly makes my abs contract. The temperature isn't enough to burn, but it hurts for a moment. Then it's nothing short of erotic heaven. He trails it over my tits, covering my nipples before he pours it over my bare pussy. I got a fresh Brazilian on Monday, and I'm glad I did. I writhe as the hot, sticky liquid hits my pussy. The air shifts, and I know he walked away from the bed. My senses are all heightened and grow more attuned as I get used to the loss of my sight and not being able to hear anything but the music.

I tremble and tense when the ice cube slides up from the arch of my left foot, along my calf and over my thigh. He trails it across my pussy lips. Another glides over my tits, swirling around the nipples. He's pressing the first one inside my pussy. I can feel it melting. Where the hell did he get ice cubes from? He doesn't have a bar or a fridge in here. He planned this before I arrived or while I was at the park.

I moan when his warm mouth latches onto my nipple. He flicks it several times before pulling back and peeling the wax off my belly and mons. Then he sucks on the other nipple as he climbs onto the bed. He runs another ice cube over my pussy before pushing it into me. The cool is refreshing as I overheat with unspent lust. He kisses my tits, my shoulders, my neck. He does it over and over before he thrusts into me. I wasn't expecting it at that moment. I scream and try to wrap myself around him to hold him against me, but I can't do more than jerk my arms and legs.

He pounds into me, unrelenting as he drives me wild with the need for more. He pushes the blindfold from my head and pulls out the earbuds again.

"I want to see all of your face when you come. I want to see the look in your eyes."

"May I come, Daddy?"

"Yes, *malyshka*. As many times as you want."

I strain against the cuffs, and my legs fight unsuccessfully against the spreader. I want to hold on to him, but soon my back arches off the bed.

"Daddy!"

He grunts as he keeps fucking me. I'm expecting to feel him pulse inside me, but he just thrusts. I draw in a ragged breath and close my eyes until I hear a bottle snap open. He pulls out, and my eyes pop open. He's rubbing lube on his cock as he twists to unfasten my ankles. He draws my legs over his shoulders, positioning me so he can remove the plug. He sets it aside, then lifts my hips higher off the bed. He pours the lube over my asshole, spreading my cheeks so it drips inside, the plug having gotten me ready. He snaps the bottle closed before easing into me. He's incredibly gentle and careful.

"Tell me if it's too much, Sumiko. Say no or use your safe word. Do not do this if I'm hurting you."

"Daddy, I'm all right."

"That doesn't mean you agree with my instructions."

"I understand, Daddy. I'll tell you if it hurts. It's never been—"

I could bite my tongue. We never talk about our past sex experiences. He asked me if I'd ever had anal the first time I was here. Beyond that, we have kept our past to ourselves.

"You can tell me, baby girl. You don't have to hide anything from me."

I feel like that's loaded with a whole lot more than just what's happening right now.

"It's never been this painless. You're being so careful, and I'm ready for it."

"You know I don't want to bring you every kind of pain. There are some types that I will do everything in the world to avoid."

"I know. Will you please unfasten my wrists? I really want to hold you."

He slides all the way into me, rocking forward, so he can reach to unfasten me. His hips circle, and his thrusts are shallow. He's letting me get used to him, and I appreciate his consideration so much that I'm choked up. But I force myself to swallow my gorge, lest he think he's hurting me instead of making me fall in love with him.

That's what he's doing. He's making me fall in love with him. Not just tonight as he fucks me in the ass. It's every day that we're together. It's everything about him. I hate what I'm discovering he does. But I admire and respect his loyalty to his family. He's thinking of me ahead of himself as he decides what to share with me. He's scared, even if he won't let me see that. But he has been vulnerable, and I think that's a state he's wholly unused to being in. He trusts me, and in return, I respect him.

"May I kiss you, Daddy?"

"Yes, *malyshka*. We're done with our roleplaying for tonight. You don't have to ask for anything you want or need. Take it. I'll give you anything, Sumiko."

I raise my head until our lips meet. This isn't the way I thought we'd have anal, but it's incredibly intimate, even if I am contorted. As our kiss lingers, I hear a buzz. He reaches between us and rubs a pocket vibrator that's shaped like a bowtie over my clit. Everything tightens from my belly button to my knees.

"I'm coming."

My head tilts back, and my back arches.

"I am too, *malyshka*."

He spills inside me as my pussy spasms. But I'm left achy, not enjoying coming without him in my cunt. It's not that I didn't enjoy what we just did, and I'm happy that he enjoyed it. But I'm left emotionally unsatisfied.

"You didn't enjoy finishing with me there."

"But you liked it."

"That's not what I'm talking about. You wanted me in your cunt."

"I prefer it."

"I do too. Your ass makes me so fucking hard, and you're so damn tight. But I missed the connection we have when I'm in your pussy."

"Me too."

"Next time, I'll be back where I belong. Come, *malyshka*. Let me give you that bath."

He pulls back and looks at me for a moment. My brow furrows as I watch him try to decide something.

"I'll give you that bath, and you can tell me what Pablo had to say."

Chapter Nineteen

Pasha

I'd already guessed it was Pablo who texted her. When she turned her phone screen down, I knew she didn't want to risk me seeing his name flash. Timofey confirmed it when he radioed me from the park. I didn't tell him to report what she did while on the walk. He thought I should know that she was talking to a rival. I let sleeping dogs lie when she returned. I wanted us to have a normal dinner like we've been having, and I wanted—needed—the intimacy that kinky sex would bring us. We've had sex a lot of different ways in two weeks. I know it hasn't all been fucking. The rawness of my emotions tells me we've made love several times. I'm falling in love with her.

She shows the trust she places in me throughout this when she lets me restrain her and spank her. She submits to me, and it allows me to feel like I have control over the situation again. Every time I divulge something to her, the world feels like it's spinning out of control. For a man who has survived by dominating every situation, it's terrifying to relinquish it. Her

208

submission resets the balance and restores my equilibrium. I don't know if she understands that's what she does for me, but I need it.

I think she gives me control because being with me is one overwhelming experience after another. I hate that. But when we're having kinky sex, she doesn't have to think about the outside world. She doesn't have to be scared. She doesn't have to choose anything. She doesn't have to decide anything but whether to safe word. It frees her.

But I can't ignore the nagging need to learn what she and Pablo talked about. I gave her a moment of privacy before I ran us a bath. Now we're soaking together. She's facing me as she leans back against one end of the tub, and I lean against the other. I'm turning into a stage five clinger. I don't like her being that far away, only our legs touching.

"He's been texting and calling me."

She sounds scared, and I hate that even more. That's not what I want.

"He's your ex-boyfriend, and you seem on friendly terms with him. I won't control who you can and can't talk to, who you can or can't be friends with."

She nods, but she looks no more reassured than a moment ago.

"Has he been warning you away from me?"

"Yes."

Fucking asshole. I mean, he's right. But he's still a fucking asshole for interfering.

"Do you agree with what he says?"

"I'm still here, aren't I?"

"That doesn't mean you don't disagree. Are you afraid I'm going to hurt you, that someone will hurt you, if you break up with me?"

"There are a lot of things I fear that I knew nothing about

two weeks ago. But the one thing I have never, and will never fear, is you hurting me. You would never allow anyone to hurt me, either. You lost your shit when you thought Maks insulted me. We'd been together less than a day."

"Do you agree with him that I'm selfish for being with you?"

Her face screams distrust now. Her brow lowers, and she cants her head.

"Sumiko, I'm not tapping your calls or reading your texts. It doesn't take much guessing to know what he's saying to you. He's trying to break us up."

"He's concerned."

"He's trying to break us up with that concern."

"How would you feel if you were in his position? He didn't tell me about his life to protect me. I dumped him, not the other way around. We're friends."

"It sounds like he still wants you. He breaks us up, then he swoops in. He tells you he can protect you better than I can. He swears he's not being selfish like I was, and now you need real protecting."

Something flashes in her eyes, and I know I'm right. Even if he hasn't said it in so many words, she knows that's what he means. Motherfucker.

"He hasn't said a thing about getting back together, Pasha. But nothing he's said has been untrue. I am in danger knowing what I do about you and him. He's pissed that I know. He doesn't agree with your decisions. He doesn't agree with my choices. But that's the thing. They're my choices, not his. I don't really give a shit that he disagrees."

"But you do. Because you're still talking to him about this. Five texts came in while we were talking. You were on the phone with him for a while. You said he's been texting and calling. Tonight wasn't the first time. You've encouraged him by engaging."

"No, I haven't. I've sent him to voicemail."

"I bet that's only when you're with me. Maybe when you're at work, too. Otherwise—"

"Otherwise nothing, Pasha. When am I not at work or with you?"

"I don't believe today is the first time you've talked to him about this."

"Fine. I returned a call a few days ago, but he suddenly had to go, so we didn't get very far. I was going to tell him to quit trying. I don't want to hear what he had to say."

"Suddenly had to go." I snort. "He's telling you to dump your bratva boyfriend and gets interrupted by Cartel business."

"You don't know that."

"Did he say why he had to go? Did he say more than just 'I gotta go,' then hang up?"

"No."

She looks at the bubbles floating between us.

"Then that's exactly what happened. Was someone speaking Spanish in the background?"

"Yes."

I know I look smug. Good.

"You're pissed that he's called and texted, and you're pissed because I've talked to him. But never have I said I agree with him or that I'm going to take his advice. I'm here, naked, in a tub with you after letting you fuck me in the ass. I think that says a lot, Pasha."

"That we have great sex."

She stares at me, and I've gone way too far. She stands and reaches for a towel.

"Don't talk to me like that. Don't dismiss me."

I grab her hand before she can snag the towel. I step toward her, then pull her into my arms.

"I'm not used to feeling jealous, Sumiko. I've never been territorial about anything. I've shared almost everything I've ever had with seven other guys since I was a baby. This is very new to me. You've had boyfriends before. I haven't really had a girlfriend since I was seventeen. You know I wasn't a monk. There were women I saw from time to time, but neither of us wanted anything serious out of it. I don't know how to do this. I don't know how to be a boyfriend with some other guy trying to steal my girlfriend."

"Pasha, I don't want to keep doing this. I—"

My ears are ringing. No, no. no. No! She's leaving me. I went too far.

"Pasha, fuck."

She wraps her arms around me and nestles close to me.

"I'm not breaking up with you. That wasn't what I meant, *fofinho.*"

She places her hand over my heart. I'm certain she can feel it racing. She kisses my chest.

"I meant, I don't want to keep having these conversations about if I'm staying. You just hurt my feelings, but it didn't mean I was going to dump you. I haven't run away, despite everything you keep revealing. I'm certain there's more that will come out. And it might be worse than what you've already told me. I'm still all in, Pasha. My heart won't let me walk away. And even though part of my mind is still wrestling with this and coming to terms with everything, I decided two weeks ago that I'm staying with you. The gun thing freaked me out today. I got scared. But I came back. This is where I want to be. I don't want to live without you."

I cup her face and kiss her as tenderly as I can. I'm not falling in love. I'm already in love. It's been fast, but that seems to be the way things happen in this family. Uncle Kirill and Aunt Galina introduced my parents, and they were engaged a week later. There is no doubting they are soulmates. Radomir and Svetlana were almost the same. Aunt Galina and Uncle Kirill fell in love as children. They got married as soon as they were old enough.

"It's us against the world, Pasha. No more you versus me. We'll probably argue, and I probably will hate some things I learn. I'm probably not done freaking out about shit. But I am not walking away."

"Neither am I."

Her smile makes me melt. She's radiating happiness, and it warms what's left of my frozen heart.

"Let me finish taking care of you tonight, *malyshka*."

She nods. I release the plug and lead us to the stand-up shower. I wash her hair and run the poof over her entire body. I kneel before her like a supplicant then guide one leg over my shoulder. I worship her pussy, reverent in every stroke of my tongue and every thrust of my fingers.

"Daddy, may I come?"

"Yes, *malyshka*. I told you, our roleplaying is done for tonight. Take whatever you need from me. I give it all to you."

She shudders and grips my hair as she presses me to her pussy. She grabs my upper arm and tugs until I stand up. I lift her, and she wraps herself around me. We love bath and shower sex. We're slow this time, our lips trailing over any part we can reach when our mouths aren't fused together. We last much longer than I expected. But when we come together, it's such euphoria that I'm lightheaded.

"*Malyshka*, I want to take you away. I want us to go on a trip where the rest of the world doesn't exist for a few days. I want to spoil you and make love to you."

Neither of us has used that phrase before. She tightens

around me, squeezing her arms, legs, and pussy as we cling to each other.

"I want that."

"Where do you want to go?"

"I've always heard Croatia is beautiful."

She flinches as soon as she suggests it. She looks like she wishes she could suck her words back into her mouth. I smile and kiss her temple.

"*Malyshka*, plenty of Russians vacation on the Adriatic. They don't loathe us or anything. Our history with all the Slavic countries is complicated, and I can't hide my accents completely. I can't change my place of birth on my passport. But I'm wealthy enough that most places are very welcoming. If that's where you want to go, we'll go."

I gear myself up for the one part she's going to hate.

"But no matter where you choose, we have to take security with us. This is non-negotiable. Even with Anton, Sergei, Misha, and me, there was an incident when Ana and Niko went to Greece. I won't risk a repeat. There aren't any direct threats against us, but I won't risk your safety."

She looks at me for a long time before she nods. She's coming to terms with this too. A romantic getaway with body-guards doesn't sound romantic at all. But I will make it wonderful. We dry off and climb into bed.

"You're going out with the girls on Friday. Do you want to leave Saturday?"

"That's in three days. We have to book tickets and find a hotel."

"*Malyshka*, Kutsenko Partners owns a jet. It's my cousins', but the rest of us can use it at our leisure. Aleks owns a house just outside Dubrovnik on the Dalmatian Coast. He hasn't been in ages. I'm certain we can stay there."

"Really?"

"Yes. If that's where you want to go. Do you think you can get the time off work?"

"Pasha, you're our biggest client. I'm dating that *pakhan's* cousin. I don't think Greg would dare say no."

"Maybe we wait a week or two then. I don't want him to feel threatened into giving you the time off. I'm not looking to intimidate him."

"I can ask."

"All right."

She snuggles closer, and we're soon asleep. I'm dreaming of the private beach with my *malyshka*. She might not surf, but we can go diving if she wants. Or we can just have sex on the beach. The drink too.

"They know Juan came back."

Maks is sitting behind his desk in his office in downtown Manhattan. We rarely come here. It's a front for the Kutsenko Partners' many shell corporations. It's a mailing address and a place to hold meetings if my cousins are forced to host them. But we're here today because it's not something we want to discuss at Maks's house around Laura and Ana. I don't know if Laura already knows, but I still don't think she wants to talk about it or hear about it.

"How'd they find out?"

Niko asks before anyone else can.

"The Etas. Someone tipped them off. They're pissed because they think they got played. They think he's taking what he learned back to his family. When Enrique argued Juan was long gone, they told him about how some white guys grabbed him. It didn't take long for Enrique to deduce it was us. He called this morning. He wants Juan back."

"Fat fucking chance."

Bogdan was the last one to see Juan before today. I haven't been to the warehouse this week. But I can bet what kind of shape the fucker is in. I'm certain he's wondering why his body has betrayed him and kept him alive so long. I'm certain he's praying for death. Anton got stuck sewing up the damage Maks did with the knife. But he didn't bleed to death, which was the point. His ribs are still broken. He's missing fingers and toes, which were cauterized with a branding rod. He'll never hear out of his right ear again, but that hardly matters.

"That's what I told him. He didn't push too hard. It was more out of duty than any real wish to get his nephew back. If anything, I think he feels badly that Pablo won't get a turn with him."

"Yeah. That's the only fucked up part of it. Pablo would kill his own brother. None of us would."

I speak the truth. Vlad learned early on not to pit us against each other physically. He would hurt one of us—or several of us—to coerce us into doing things. But he tried to get Anton and Maks to fight, and it was the first time they ever refused Vlad anything. Four of his men tried to force them. Those men didn't survive. He tried again with Sergei and Misha, and the same thing happened. After that, he gave up pitting us against each other. We wouldn't do it. We didn't hurt women or children—at least, not children who weren't bratva and in the same position as us—and we didn't touch our family. The same rules still apply.

"In this case, blood isn't thicker than water. Pablo would do it for Laura's and the twins' sake. She might refuse to have anything to do with that family, but Pablo regrets losing their friendship. He'd pick her over Juan in a heartbeat."

Maks talking about Pablo brings back all my anger from last night. I have told no one about Pablo's interference. Mixing business with pleasure is inevitable when your business permeates every ounce of your life. I won't keep this from the others, but now doesn't seem the time to bring it up.

"We've learned nothing new from him in days. He doesn't know more about the Etas to be useful. It's clear he knows nothing current about the Cartel. Is there any point to keeping him?"

Anton's question is on my mind too. Maks shakes his head.

"I'll take care of him. I want that smug bastard to see me when I do it."

No one is going to contest Maks's right to end the threat to his wife and children. I don't mind because I don't feel like going to the warehouse today. We discuss a few more business-related things before we all get up to leave.

"Hey, Papa said he tried calling you this morning, but it went to voicemail."

"Yeah. My phone died last night. I was playing music, and it drained it. I didn't realize until this morning."

"Arseniy called him after Greg called Arseniy. They want to know if Sumiko's time off is a request or an order."

"It's definitely a request. I want to take her to Dubrovnik, but we're both happy to wait a few weeks if we need to."

"I told Papa it was probably a request."

"Thanks."

"Going on a getaway?"

Aleks comes to stand with us.

"Yeah. I was actually hoping we could use your house."

"Of course. I'll need to get a staff in there a couple days early to open it up and dust everything off."

"I'm hoping to take her on Saturday if Greg gives her the time off."

"You know he will, even if you say it's a request."

"I don't want him thinking I'm strong-arming him, Anton."

"How long do you want to be away?"

Aleks already has his phone out, and I know he's ready to help me plan.

"Ten days. Maks?"

"Yes."

"Can I use the jet? I want to take Sumiko to Croatia for a few days."

"Of course. None of us have trips coming up. I can do a videoconference with the people in Montreal. I don't need to go up there if you need the plane."

"Thanks. Aleks, Anton, I was hoping you and Sergei and Misha would come, too. I'm thinking about Ilya, Stefan, and Timofey as well."

"I can come."

Aleks nods and steps away to make a call.

"We can come."

Anton answers for him and Sergei, who is on a call in Maks's office.

"Misha? You up for a trip to the Dalmatian Coast?"

"Yeah. It's beautiful, and the weather is always perfect."

"Great. Anton, do you think I should talk to Arseniy or Greg?"

"It probably wouldn't hurt. Papa's probably already talked to Arseniy but hearing it from you would be better."

"All right."

I need to head to Bear Imports' warehouse, so I call Arseniy from the car while Ilya drives. He's our most reliable driver, and we take turns with him. He's usually assigned to the wives before anyone else.

"Arseniy, it's Pasha Kutsenko." I speak to him in Russian. "Sumiko and I were worried that you might feel obligated to give her the time off. I know it's very short notice. If it isn't convenient, we can wait and travel in a few weeks."

"Thank you for calling. I spoke to your Papa, and he said same thing. He said you and Sumiko are very serious."

Alarm bells are going off like a five-alarm fire. He sounds fatherly, so I can guess where this is going.

"Greg says she's very nice young woman. Hard worker and extremely intelligent."

He's right, but what can I tell him without giving away everything? The last time we talked, I told him Sumiko knew nothing, which was true back then.

"She's both, and far more. We are very serious. She understands she will always have a choice about this life."

"Good."

He says nothing else, but I'm waiting to know if she can take the time off.

"Would you prefer we wait a couple weeks, so she can arrange her calendar?"

"No. Greg has already given her time off. We just wanted to be sure we also understood our choices."

"Thank you. I'm sorry if this put Greg in an awkward position this morning."

"Not to worry. We would have done it as favor for your father. Enjoy your trip."

We hang up, and I sit back as I plan. Bikinis and a toothbrush are all she needs. I might pack a few other things we didn't get to last night. My mind is working overtime.

We're at Ivy tonight, and the place is packed. I'm glad Sumiko accepted Christina's invitation to join her, Laura, and Ana. I get why they're close, not only because they genuinely like each other, but because they aren't as close to their old friends as they once were. It must be hard for them to juggle. Tiffany left last week to move back to her parents' place. Sumiko told me her mom is only getting worse. They went out with Sarah and had a last hoorah, but it was a pretty somber night. She came back to my place and felt better snuggling with me. She had lunch with Sarah a couple times since they work near each other. They aren't meeting at the gym that often because it isn't convenient. But she explained how she found herself being evasive with Sarah, and it makes her feel horrible. Sumiko suspects she's starting to notice. With these ladies, she doesn't have to watch everything she says.

Laura's the natural ringleader just like Maks.

"Let's get a drink! I pumped before I left. I'll pump and dump when I get home. Whisky sour, please."

I can see the ladies from where I stand across from the bar. Laura looks back at the rest of them, making sure the bartender hears their orders. They move away from the bar once they have their drinks, since Laura practically had to elbow her way between three guys.

"Are you having fun, *malyshka?*"

She knows it's me before I say anything. She knows the feel of my hands on her waist. She knows the goosebumps she gets whenever I'm near her. I wrap my arm around her waist and pull her back against me. We sway to the music as Christina kisses Bogdan. Maks and Laura are whispering to each other, and his hand is practically on her ass. Niko and Ana disappeared. My guess is to Bogdan's office. Lucky fucker. I was hoping to disappear there for an hour or four. But I'm working. Even as I stand with Sumiko, my gaze is roving the crowd. Bogdan manages the nightclubs and strip clubs that he and his brothers own. Misha and I are head of security for all of them. I spot Misha near the door, working with two of the bouncers to check IDs and to make sure no one skips the cover.

"I have to go back to work, but I'll check on you in a while."

"All right, Daddy."

She whispers it in my ear, and we both grin at our little secret. I suspect my cousins have similar arrangements with their wives since I've heard all three call their wives *malyshka*. We may share most things in our lives, but the intimate parts of our relationships remain private.

Maks and Bogdan move off to the side, and I make my rounds. I see the ladies on the dance floor, and they look like they're having a great time. Laura is living it up, enjoying her parole from motherhood. Galina and my mom ended up going over to babysit. They wanted Laura and Maks to have a night out. I think Maks enjoys watching his wife dance, and I also think he doesn't like knowing men are ogling her. I've seen some wandering eyes landing on Sumiko, and I'm fighting the urge to gouge them out.

She's in a halter dress that shows off her tits enough that I bit my tongue to keep from demanding she change. I can tell she's nervous around the others. She looks amazing, and the dress flatters every part of her. But after my argument with Maks, I think I made things way worse. She waves to me whenever our eyes meet.

I try to keep her in my sights and know where she is, but it's extra crowded tonight with three bachelorette parties. Each of them has a group of like fifteen women. Then there are the regulars who are here every weekend. They're enough to fill the place. The drinks are flowing, and it's the point in the night where people are going from buzzed to hammered fast.

I spot the ladies back by the bar. I notice Bogdan, Maks, and Niko staring at the women. Ana joined them not long after they went on the dance floor. Her face was already flushed. I could only shake my head. Niko was a lucky bastard. I follow my cousins' gaze and see a group of guys checking out the women. My cousins are inching forward, but I'm the closest.

"*Pochemu tol'ko tri iz nikh dolzhny byt' goryachimi? Blondinka khuden'kaya, no seksual'naya.*" Why'd only three of them have to be hot? The blonde's skinny but bangable.

A blond guy elbows one of his friends as he jerks his chin toward the women. I recognize him. Mikhail.

"*Ya zametil ikh. Ya ne zastrevayu s tolstukhoy.*" I spotted them. I'm not getting stuck with the fat one.

His friend pushes the blond guy's elbow away and points to Sumiko. I went to school with this guy too. Dominic.

"*Zatknis'. Ty znayesh', o ch'ikh zhenshchinakh ty govorish'? Nas iz-za teba ubyut.*" Shut the fuck up. Do you know whose women you're talking about? We'll get killed because of you.

It's the third friend, Boris, who is the voice of reason. It doesn't matter. I'll kill all fucking three of them. I'm pushing through the crowd as I watch Laura and Ana step forward. The fourth guy with them sees me approaching and disappears into the crowd.

"*Krutee peedalee paka nye dale.*"

Laura's using her "fuck with me and find out" voice that she usually reserves for business negotiations. What she says translates to pedal away while still not beaten up. It means fuck off. Ana points to the door before pointing over her shoulder toward Niko and the others.

"*Nikto iz nas ne stal by trakhat' tebya, dazhe yesli by my byli ne zamuzhem. Ukhodi, poka nashi muzh'ya ne uslyshali tebya.*" None of us would fuck you even if we were single. Leave before our husbands hear you.

"*Davay, malyshka. Tvoy tolstyy podruga mozhet posmotret'.*" Come on, baby girl. Your fat friend can watch.

Mikhail reaches for Laura before any of us can get there. Her fist lands against his left eye. I pull her back and push between her and Ana. I wrap my hand around his throat and lift him onto his toes. My fist drives into his gut. Dominic swings at me. I pivot, and his friend takes the punch. I squeeze Mikhail's throat tighter as I knock out Dominic's two front teeth out. Boris backs away. Little bitch is going to abandon his older brother and friend. He's going to run like their other friend did.

"*Govorite o moyey devushkemne v litso. Yeshche raz nazovi yeye tolstoy, ublyudok. Ty znayesh', kto ya, chert voz'mi.*" Talk about my girlfriend to my face. Call her fat again, mother-fucker. You know who the fuck I am.

By now, my cousins are standing between the women and me. Niko's got Dominic, the guy whose teeth are now missing, by the hair and shoulder. I drag Mikhail by the arm. We're going out to the alley behind the club. This isn't over. Niko's right behind me. Maks is talking to Ana and Laura in Russian, and Bogdan is with Christina and Sumiko.

"*Misha, prinesi.*" Misha, bring that one.

Misha came to see what was happening since we don't allow fights at all. I doubt he knew I was involved at first. But he grabs Boris and follows Niko and me. I practically throw Mikhail through the back door.

I continue speaking in Russian since it's easier when I'm this pissed.

"You're a stupid fucker, aren't you? You must not give a shit about your family. Your dad's working on a mini mall project right now. Your mom's a maid at a hotel here in Manhattan. That sweet little sister of yours still needs braces."

"Stay the fuck away from my family."

"You should have stayed the fuck away from our women."

"I never guessed you liked fucking cows."

He's egging me on. I accept the bait willingly. My fist breaks his nose. The eye Laura punched is already swelling. My fingerprints are all over his neck. He's not going to the cops. He won't tell a fucking soul he got in a fight with a Kutsenko.

No one would ever talk to him again. They won't want to be guilty by association.

"Did you say goodbye to your mama? You're not going home again."

"My brother's drunk. He's going to regret this in the morning. How can we make it up to you, Pasha? He'll apologize to your girlfriend. I swear."

The quiet one, Boris, is suddenly chatty when he realizes he's about to watch his brother die.

"Regret is useless."

I punch loudmouth Mikhail in the ribs.

"Since your parents didn't do a good job teaching you manners, maybe we'll have a talk with them about that. How about that, Dominic?"

Niko shakes the guy he's holding up. He's worked Dominic's face over. He recognizes these guys, too.

"Please, let them go. I'll take Mikhail and Dominic home. We will never come back to a Kutsenko club again. I swear."

"Boris, shut up."

I glance back over my shoulder as I snap at Boris, who Misha is standing next to. He doesn't have to restrain this one. Boris looks like he's about to piss himself.

"I thought you could do better. How do you even find her pussy with all those rolls?"

"Now you're fucking dead, Mikhail."

I pull my knife from my pocket and press it against his throat. I watch him get sober real fast now. Too late. I press and break the skin. He pisses himself. Just what I wanted.

"Cat suddenly got your tongue, Dominic?"

Niko's holding his knife toward Dominic, the tip level with his eyes.

"I'm sorry. We didn't know—"

"Shut the fuck up, you motherfucking liar."

Niko slams Dominic's head against the wall and puts the knife tip just beneath his left eye.

"The fuck you didn't know who those women are. You're fucking Russian. Your father's bratva, and you've been our little errand bitches since we were in school together. You fucking piece of shit. Pasha's going to kill Mikhail, and then he's going to kill you. Boris, you get to watch and tell your friends who the fuck to stay away from."

Niko presses the knife to Dominic's face, and he pisses himself too. The moment he does, Niko and I back off. We let go of them and put our knives away.

"We're going to visit your families in the morning. They're going to make this right. If they can't afford it, then we're coming for you."

I shove Mikhail toward the door.

"Walk."

The six of us go back into the club. People stare at the wet stains on the front of Mikhail's and Dominic's. Their noses are bloody, and Mikhail's eye is turning black. They'll look a shit ton worse in the morning. Boris darts around us and is hailing a cab by the time I throw Mikhail out, and Niko does the same with Dominic. Our bouncers will be sure they leave.

I heard voices in the office as we walked by, so I know Bogdan and Maks took the ladies in there. Niko punches in the code, and Misha and I follow him inside. Ana rushes forward, but Sumiko hangs back. Laura and Christina have their arms around her, and it's clear she's been crying. Someone translated. That or she guessed just what I was doing outside and thinks I'm a monster.

I ease my way toward her. Her tear-filled eyes meet mine, and she launches herself at me. I pull her close as she cries against my chest. The others leave us alone in the office, and I walk her to the soft sofa. There's one that's more like a bench. That's for employees and others who wind up facing Bogdan.

"I'm so sorry, *malyshka*. Are you upset because of what I did?"

She shakes her head.

"Are you upset because someone told you what they said?"

She nods. I rub her back. I feel her pain as it radiates from her. People have preferences. Some women like chest hair. Other women don't like guys with too many muscles. I'm attracted to women with meat on their bones. Yeah, Sumiko caught my eye because I think she's fucking hot as hell. But I care about her for so much more than just looks. Half the world looks at me and thinks I'm the male version of a bimbo. She could have assumed I was shallow, like my family clearly thought I was. But she sees more in me than my looks. This just fucking sucks.

"Do you want to go home, *malyshka*?"

Chapter Twenty

Sumiko

I lean away from Pasha, ready for a new set of tears to fall. I don't want him to send me away. I need him.

"No. I want to go to your place. I don't want to be by myself."

"Baby girl, I didn't mean your apartment. I haven't thought about that place since I went with you to pick up some clothes and Pandora. Home is my place with you in it. I want you to move in with me, Sumiko. Or we can move into your place. But home is where we're together."

"It's been three weeks."

"And it feels like three years. A lot's happened in those three weeks. But we've already said we're committed to each other. You've been back a couple times during the day to get more stuff. But you haven't slept at your place once since we got together. Do you want to sleep alone there?"

"No."

"Do you want us to live at your place?"

"My place is a shoebox compared to yours."

"So? Do you like your place better? Or do you want a place we get together?"

"This is impulsive, don't you think? A couple guys insult me, and now you want to move in together."

"You know those douches had nothing to do with this. I've given you half the closet and half my dresser, even though your clothes haven't filled them yet."

"I know. I've been so happy living with you for the past two weeks. It feels so natural, and it doesn't feel like it's just a visit with an end date. I've liked how indefinite it is."

"Does that mean you don't want it to be permanent?"

"No. Just the opposite. It's felt like it could be permanent. I want it to be permanent."

"Will you move in with me when we get back?"

I nod and wipe my tears as I look up at him. This feels like the soundest, rightest decision I've ever made. I can't even decide what to have for dinner this fast. There's only one thing that makes me hesitate for a moment.

"Pasha, I've met all of your family. You have met none of mine. This is a huge step, and they barely know anything about you. They know we're dating, and it's getting serious fast. But that's it. I haven't even shown them a photo of you."

"When's the last time they visited you or you went home?"

"Christmas. I went back to California."

"Would your parents and brothers be comfortable if we flew them out here and put them up in a hotel?"

"Uh—"

I'm not sure what to say about that. That's an expensive offer when they know we've only been dating a few weeks. I don't know how to tell them I want to move in with him after dating for less than a month.

"There's no rush, *malyshka*. If you're not ready to live together or to have me meet your family, that's all right."

"No. I am to both. I don't want you to feel like I'm backing out or don't want them to meet you. It's just it costs a lot to do all of that."

"Sumiko, I'm not as rich as my cousins. But I don't think you realize how rich I am. The bulk of my wealth is from legitimate ventures. I admit I paid my way through college with money I earned from the bratva. But now, most of that money goes back into our community or it's my cousins'."

"Just because you can spend it doesn't mean you have to on my family."

He weighs his words, and it makes me wonder what he's thinking. His expression isn't blank. It's thoughtful, but I still can't read it easily.

"My family already considers you a part of it. I hope one day your family will think the same way about me. I'd like to think that any offer I make to your family is the same as making one to my own. If they'd like to fly in the private jet, then I'll send it for them. If they'd prefer commercial first class, then I'll arrange that. If they want a hotel, then I'll reserve rooms. If they want to stay with us—see what we're like together—you know I have the space. But I won't be able to fuck you in the kitchen or on the dining room table again until after they leave."

"I'm not super eager for them to stay with us, but I think it would help if they saw how normal we are."

"Think about it while we're in Croatia. If you want them to come, we can invite them and let them pick the dates that work best. We can hold off on making our living arrangement official."

"Thank you, Pasha."

"Anything for you, *krasivaya*. Are you ready to go home?"

"Yes. I still need to pack."

"No, you don't. I already put your bathing suits in a bag. You can put your toothbrush in it in the morning."

"I need more than just swimsuits."

"Fine. A cover up. I don't want you to burn."

"That's what sunblock is for. But I need real clothes. I can't be in front of your family in just a bikini all week."

"They'll stay out of sight."

"Don't be obtuse. You know what I mean."

"If we aren't on the beach, in the pool, or in the hot tub, you're going to be naked in our room. No need for clothes."

"Are you taking anything but board shorts?"

"No. I might just be a nudist."

I run my eyes over him. If anyone could be, it's him. His body is perfection. Not just by my standards, but every person with eyes.

"I might only pack your bikini bottoms. Plenty of beaches are topless."

"No. You know I won't go for that. Are you trying to keep me in the bedroom? We don't need to go to Croatia for that."

"Hmm. On second thought, I'm too possessive for you to go topless."

"Pasha, about tonight. You didn't have to defend me like that. You could have just had the bouncers throw them out."

He sighs and shakes his head.

"If they hadn't been Russian, then that's what would have happened. I know them. Their dads are bratva and work construction for our companies. They've worked for us. They knew who Laura, Christina, and Ana are. They knew who you are. To allow the slight is to appear weak. If I can't protect what's mine, people will think everything of mine is for the taking. If they think I'm weak, then they'll think my cousins are susceptible. And I will let no one think I'm not the proudest man alive to have you on my arm."

"It was about reputation."

"And pride. I want people to know that I will do anything to defend you. You are the most important person in my life, Sumiko."

That steals my breath. I feel that way about him, but he has so many people that he's close to. I lean forward and kiss him. It's another tender moment, and I wish it could last forever.

"You're the most important person to me, Pasha. I'm just—I know most people couldn't understand, but your family could. It was humiliating, and I'm embarrassed that people look down on you for being with me."

"I know it was. And I hate people see us and react that way. I'm scared you're going to get tired of that and tired of people hurting your feelings. I'm scared you're going to break up with me over it."

"Of all the reasons I might leave you, that's what you're scared about?"

"I'm scared of a lot of things that might drive you away. I know we said we won't keep going back and forth about this, but who knows if you'll get to where you've had enough?"

"What about when you get fed up with people looking down at you for being with me?"

"Fuck them. They don't know shit. I'm never going to stop desiring you, Sumiko. I want to be inside you around the fucking clock. There's a fucked-up part of me that thinks this means I can keep you to myself, that I'll never have to worry about you leaving me."

"That is fucked up. No one else would want me, so you get to keep me. But I get it. It's endearing in its own twisted kind of way."

"I told you, I'm not used to being territorial or possessive. I've had to share everything with at least Anton, if not all the other guys. You're all mine. I'm selfish enough and childish enough to love that."

"As the only sister, there were a lot of things I didn't have to share. I have little practice, and I don't like to do it."

"You will never share me with another woman, Sumiko. It's bad enough how much time this life will steal from us. I'm not letting anything else get between us."

"*Fofinho*, can I be all yours in the backseat on the way home, then in our bed?"

"Yes, *krasivaya*."

We stand, and he takes my hand. I sort of guessed something linked those guys to the bratva. It's not that I now assume every Russian in New York is, but I got that sense from how Pasha reacted. The same with Niko. I understand what he means about reputation and not appearing weak. Not that anyone looking at him would ever think that, but I get the machismo of it all.

We join the others back in the main area of the club.

"I'm taking Sumiko home, Bogdan."

"Okay. I'm sorry about everything tonight."

Bogdan gives me a quick hug and winks at me. I know he's doing it to annoy Pasha. I don't think Pasha's snarl is a joke. Never mind that Bogdan is blissfully married and Christina is standing beside him. He makes good on my request as we ride home. We climb into bed, and he shows me how much he appreciates every inch of me until we can barely keep our eyes open. It doesn't take away the humiliation from earlier, but it sure as hell boosts my confidence.

Calling Aleks's place in Dubrovnik a house is an understatement. It's not as big as Maks and Laura's house, but it's insanely large. The entire wall facing the Adriatic is windows that slide open. I was unprepared for Pasha to reassure me they're bulletproof. I tried not to think about all the weapons that were likely stored in the plane's hold once I saw the seven men come aboard with us. The master suite is bigger than my entire apartment without counting the bathroom. The sheets must be a gazillion count. I've never felt anything so soft. Everything is exquisite.

We've been here six days, and it's a fairytale. We've gone kayaking and snorkeling. We've swum in the Blue Cave, which is incredible. It's a mixture of light and darkness with crystal clear water. We picnicked on a nearly empty beach on a nearby island. We toured the old town and went souvenir shopping. We ended up with a mountain of gifts for our families. His amounted to Everest, and mine was a close Kilimanjaro. We saw the filming location for *Game of Thrones*. We've had Michelin star quality meals served on demand at the house. We've eaten on the private beach, on the patio, and in our bedroom. I'm beyond spoiled.

Pasha packed more than just my bathing suits, but barely. From what the ladies warned me, the men have a habit of buying skimpy bikinis. Since none of them have any experience doing it, they don't have the forethought to understand why we might be uncomfortable prancing around in front of anyone nearly naked. Pasha told me as I opened the box that it was something for his eyes only, so at least his possessiveness kept me from arguing with him. I've only worn it in the pool and hot tub. I haven't even worn it to our private beach since the men come with us.

They're ghosts at the house. I never see them. But they're

with us the moment we step out of the front door. I think we draw far too much attention with that many bodyguards. People want to know which famous person is there, and it's just us. But I feel safer.

"Let me see your phone, please, Ms. Kimura."

Sergei's formality seems pointless, but I appreciate the respect. I know the men in Pasha's family refer to me by my first name when they're not talking to me. Only Aleks and Anton use my first name with me here. The men who work for the Kutsenkos definitely don't address me by it.

"Is it that sat phone again? Is it coming from the U.S.?"

I received three texts this morning from an unavailable phone.

You made an even bigger mistake.
You're in danger.
This won't end well.

The messages came in while we were on a scuba diving excursion. I spotted them when we came back onto the boat. I showed them to Pasha and Sergei immediately, but there was nothing anyone could do on the chartered boat. We came back early. Sergei, Pasha, and I are sitting at the dining room table while the others patrol the neighborhood or are stationed at the doors and on the beach.

"It's definitely a satellite phone. They're not bothering to spoof your phone. The other ladies haven't received any messages."

Pasha's holding my hand as it trembles. Pasha and the others assumed that since the first message coincided with that guy Juan coming back to town that it must have been directed at Laura. But I've had a phone call each day since we've been here. The person doesn't speak. They're just there, but not long enough for Sergei to track it. After the third time, I sent the unavailable number to voicemail. The caller lets it ring until the voicemail picks up. They're silent on the recording, but once again, they aren't on the phone long enough to trace it. Pasha and Sergei are handling this, so I refuse to let it put a dent in my fairytale. At least, not until now.

"This is about me. Sending the first one to all of us was a distraction. They cloned and spoofed my phone for a reason."

"We don't know that for sure."

Pasha's not reassuring me at all. Okay. Maybe we don't know for sure. But come on. Who else is it about? No one else has received more texts or any calls.

"It's going to take me a while to get an exact GPS on these. They don't want to be tracked. It looks like they sent them from three separate locations, but that isn't possible given how close together they arrived."

I watch Sergei as he works on his laptop. I trust he'll find the location, but will it do any good? He traced the one before our trip to an abandoned house in Queens. He and Anton went to check it out. There wasn't a single clue to who was there or why. It was part of Queens that Pasha said is like no-man's-land. None of the syndicates claim it.

"I'm going to take a shower."

Pasha looks at me. I shake my head. I want to be alone for a while. I need to sort through all of this, but I don't want to think right now. I know he would gladly distract me. But I just want to stand under the showerhead and zone out. I rarely take long ones, but I'm in there for twenty minutes. I feel better now. I wrap a towel around my hair and put a robe on. I pad back out to the dining room. The mood is entirely different.

"Pasha?"

"Go into Anton and Sergei's room. Lock the door. Ilya and Stefan are outside the windows. Stay away from them."

"Pasha?"

"Go, Sumiko. I'll be there in a moment. If you hear anything, you do not leave that room. You do not open the door unless it's me, my brother, Aleks, Sergei, or Misha. Not to any of the other men. Do you understand?"

I stand and blink.

"Sumiko, do you understand?"

I nod.

"Go. I'll be there in a minute."

I rush into the bedroom and lock the door. I look around. Do I hide under the bed? Do I hide in the bathtub with the bathroom door locked? Do I hide in the closet? What the fuck is going on?

It truly is only a minute before Pasha knocks on the door. I let him in, and he huddles me into the bathroom and shuts the door. He holds me against him as I try not to lose my shit.

"*Malyshka*, another text came in while you were in the shower. Whoever this is knew you were taking one. No one can see into the bathroom unless you had the door open. But they must have seen you come in and out naked and guessed."

"I went in naked, but I had the robe and towel on when I came out."

"Either way, they guessed. It means they're way too close."

"Is the house bugged or something?"

"No. No one comes and goes from the house without Aleks knowing. He has around the clock security. The men swept the house and all the grounds when we arrived. They looked for cameras and audio recorders. One of them always stays behind when we go out."

What he says reassures me.

"No one came onto the property. They'd be dead or running for their life."

"*Malyshka*, it would only take high-powered binoculars or a telephoto lens to see into here. There are curtains on the windows, not blinds. Anything heat-seeking would make it easy to watch you."

"I hope it's just that and not binoculars or some camera. I can live with being a red blob. I don't want to think about anyone actually seeing me."

"I know, baby girl. I don't like any of it, but I feel the same way."

"What do we do?"

"That's up to you. Do you want to go home or stay?"

"Stay."

I blurt that out without thinking. I take a moment, but my mind doesn't change.

"I want to stay, Pasha. If you feel like the guards are enough, then I don't want anyone ruining our vacation. If they're watching me here, then they'll watch me at home. I'd rather keep my fairytale."

"Fairytale?"

"Yes. You're my Prince Charming. The one from Cinderella, not Shrek."

"I'm closer to Shrek's size."

"But you have the perfectly chiseled looks from Cinderella."

"Didn't he have blond hair?"

"You're also not green."

The banter eases some of my tension. I can almost forget that we're hiding in the bathroom to talk.

"Are you comfortable going back to that room, or do you want to move to another one?"

"I am not giving up that bed. That is the comfiest bed I've ever touched."

"I thought I was the comfiest thing you'd ever slept on.

That's what you told me yesterday when you woke from your nap on the beach and on me."

"I said it's the comfiest bed. You are still the best thing to sleep on or with."

He strokes my temple and looks like he's about to say something, but he thinks better of it.

"Do you want to eat inside?"

"No. Unless you think it's dangerous to eat outside, I don't want to change anything we don't have to."

"You're stubborn. Recklessly stubborn."

"Do you think it's too dangerous? Or do you think I'm not taking this seriously enough?"

"Neither. But you're determined, even in the face of a threat that's entirely new to you."

"Pasha, I'm with you."

I speak as though my response is obvious, but he looks confused.

"You're here with me. I know that doesn't guarantee our safety one hundred percent. But I feel completely protected with you. If you weren't here, I would be packing. I trust you to know what to do. If you think it's okay to eat outside, to stay here, then I won't ask for something else."

"Get dressed, *malyshka*. I have a surprise for you."

Pasha takes me back to our room. I take my clothes into the bathroom, but neither of us says anything about it. When I come out. Pasha's wearing light tan pants and a white Cuban shirt. He's gotten even darker while we've been here. He's stupid gorgeous. Like I can't believe he's real kind of gorgeous. But it's his smile. The way he lights up when he sees me. I feel like the most precious thing in the entire world, like I'm the only thing that exists for him.

He confessed he asked Sarah to go to my place before we left. She has a key, and he hoped she would pick up my best dress. It's a cocktail one that I haven't worn in years. I'm lucky it still fits. It's an empire waist halter dress that comes to just above my knees. It's a deep ruby, and I feel like a million bucks in it.

"Come, baby girl. It's time."

Chapter Twenty-One

Pasha

My mind feels scattered. It's racing as I evaluate the danger we're in, whether I should honor Sumiko's request to stay. I'm trying to plan contingencies in case there's another threat, or God forbid an attack. But I also can't stop thinking about how amazing she looks. Sumiko has an aura about her that glows. It radiates from her whether she's in a cocktail dress or yoga pants. It doesn't matter whether or not she's wearing makeup, whether her hair is done or in a messy bun. Every time I see her, she takes my breath away because of how happy she makes me. No one, not even members of my family, makes me this happy.

"It's a bit of a distance, but it won't take long."

"Where are we going?"

"You'll see."

We get in the car, and it's a rarity, but we both look out the windows rather than paw at each other. It's been years since I've been to Croatia, so it's like seeing it for the first time all over again. We point things out and add to our list of things to do before we leave. It's a brief tender ride to Lokrum, but it's worth it.

We're at one of the highest points on the island. We came here the day we arrived, and Sumiko fell in love with it. We're beyond the city limits with a view over the lights and the sea. The stars are coming out, and it's a brilliant full moon. We've come up to an old fort that's closed to tourists for the night. But wealth has its privileges. The chef I hired is an experienced caterer and has everything under control for our dinner outside.

"How did you arrange this?"

"Magic, *malyshka*."

I waggle my eyebrows at her. She just shakes her head and smiles. We make our way to the table that's set with candles. There are peonies on it, just like the ones I brought her for our first date. She leans forward to sniff. She looks back at me while still bending over, and I can see how pleased she is. She steps in front of me and presses a soft kiss on my cheek.

"Roses are beautiful, but I'm so happy you picked something more unique. Thank you."

"I'm glad you like them."

"I like all of it, Pasha. You've planned the most amazing adventures. You asked my friend to help you, so I had a dress I like for such a special night. You arranged this incredible evening. It's only just begun, and it's the best one I've ever had. Thank you, *meu carinho*."

She's spoken no Portuguese around me except for at the Brazilian BBQ restaurant. I wait for her to tell me what it means, but she doesn't offer a translation. I'll look it up later.

We sit down for dinner, and it's one course after another. The wine flows as we look out over the water and the city on the mainland. By dessert, we're holding hands, and our chairs are closer. A breeze stirs her hair, so I slip my suit coat off and wrap it around her shoulders. I don't fear her seeing my guns holstered beneath my arms. She's gotten used to them. We walk to the retaining wall, where she stands in front of me. I wrap my arms around her, and she rests her head back against my chest.

"This is bliss, Pasha. I wish every day could be as easy as these have been so far. We've had a dose of reality every day, but it's still been perfect. Even with the texts today. I wish we never had to leave. This time with just you—you make me so happy."

"I feel the same way, *moya lyubov'*."

She turns to face me.

"What does that mean?"

"It means my love. Sumiko, I love you. You're brave and resilient. You adapt to whatever is happening. You're intelligent and witty. You're determined and understanding. You're forgiving. You show me your vulnerability, and you trust me. You put so much faith in me, and it makes me want to be the man you want and need. You know I'm attracted to you. Sex is an important part of our relationship. But it's these qualities that make you so beautiful, so desirable that I can't get enough of you."

"*Meu carinho* means my love. I wasn't sure you'd want to know that, but it's how I feel. I love you, too. You've trusted me in a way no one else ever has. The stakes have been so much higher for you. You've seen these qualities in me, and I know how precious your trust is. I know you don't allow others to see your vulnerability. You allow me in, and I know what that costs you. I want to be the person you can lean on. I want it to be more than just you trusting I won't tell anyone or that I won't leave. I want to support you the way you have for me as I learn about this new world."

"I've never been in love before. I won't get this right half the time, but please know I will always try."

"I know, *meu carinho.* I thought I'd been in love before. Maybe it was, but it wasn't like this. I've seen your faults since the beginning, and I've seen the challenges. This vacation has been perfect, but our regular life hasn't been. We aren't going into this with blinders on or rose-colored glasses. My feelings are so much more mature than they were when I was in college."

"I'm excited that your parents will arrive just after we get home. I want to know your family because I think you know I want more than just living together. I want cur future together to be permanent."

"Do you mean marriage? Or do you mean just a committed couple?"

"Marriage."

I wonder if I've jumped the gun on this. It's probably way too much too soon. But I've known what I wanted since the beginning. This was the end goal all along. I wouldn't have let her into my world if I didn't want to marry her. Just living together isn't enough commitment for me. It's too easy for one of us to walk away. I want her to know that I'm not leaving. That I'm always hers.

"There's an ancient Japanese legend that everyone has a red string attached to their pinky. This string will one day lead you to the person you're destined to be with. Part of the legend is that there was a man who lived in the moon. He would return to Earth every night to connect kindred spirits with this unbreakable red string. Each person follows their string until they meet the person on the other end. The person they're meant to create a history with, a memorable story that prevails over time and adversity. The pinky has an artery, the ulnar, that runs to the heart, so the string binds the hearts as much as it does the fingers."

"Do you believe the man in the moon has tied our pinkies together?"

"Yes. The string might bend and twist. It might get stretched, but it never snaps or frays."

"You're my soulmate, Sumiko. I don't doubt that at all."

"Neither do I. And it's not too soon to talk about marriage. I've pictured it since we met."

"I have too. My family will understand, but would yours? If we talked about it this soon, would it upset them?"

She shakes her head.

"It's my parents who told me the legend. My older brother is married, but I don't know that he believes in soulmates. I hope his wife is his, but I don't know. My younger brother hasn't met a woman he can date for more than six months, so he definitely hasn't. They might not understand, but my parents will."

I lift her off her feet as we kiss. She wraps her arms around my neck, and I don't have to lean forward. I marvel at the various kisses we share. There are fun, lighthearted pecks, deep sensual ones, frantic and needy ones, and those that tease. This one is my favorite kind. It's tender, languid, and I can feel her emotions as though they're my own. They are my own. Our hearts are beating in tandem.

"Come, baby girl. I have something for you."

"Really?"

"Mhmm."

I lead her to the table and gesture to Sergei. He picks up a box that he placed on a low wall. He hands it to me, and I feel like I did when I was five and wanted to see what Anton got for Christmas. I hand it to her, watching as she unwraps the silver paper. She lifts off the lid of the gift box and moves aside the tissue paper before she lifts out the gift. I see her curiosity and pray she likes it. I watch her eyes widen as her fingers trace the engraving on the lid. She opens the antique box and covers her mouth with her fingertips.

"Pasha, where did you find this? It's exquisite."

"I have connections, *malyshka*. Do you like it?"

I believe she does, but I have a moment of self-doubt.

"This abacus must be from the nineteenth century."

"Eighteen eighty."

"It's—I—thank you for my *soroban, fofinho*."

She gently places it on the table before she launches herself at me. She smatters my face with kisses. When our lips meet, it's the type of kiss that makes me want to order the men to leave, so I can strip her bare and sink into her under the stars. I scoot back my chair and pull her onto my lap. She shifts to straddle me. I know where my men are, but she looks around.

"Do you want me, *malyshka*?"

"You know I do, Daddy. But your men will see us."

"They know better than to watch. If you want me, baby girl, I'm yours."

She glances around as she unfastens my pants. I push my boxer briefs down over my cock, and she pulls her skirt out of the way. She knows better than to have bothered with panties. I banned them for the trip. She sinks onto me and stills. I hold her against me, kissing her cheek and hair.

"*Malyshka*, this is where I belong. I just want to be inside you, so there's no you and no me. There's just us."

"I know, Daddy. Can we sit here like this for a little while?"

"Yes, baby girl. For as long as you want. Tell me when you want to come, and I'll pleasure you anyway you want."

"What about when you want to come?"

"Honestly, I'm content the way we are."

I am. I never thought that I would want to bury myself in a woman and not try to get off. I'll make her come because I enjoy giving her that pleasure, sharing that with her, knowing

I'm the only man with that privilege. But I don't have to come right now to be satisfied. Holding her is what I want.

"Pasha, there's a depth to your tender side that I know you don't let anyone know exists. Thank you for letting me see it."

"I love you."

She cups my jaw and kisses me again.

"I love you, too."

We sit together until I lose track of time. I can't believe I stay hard as long as I do. But when we both feel needy for more, I carry her to the shadows. I perch her on the edge of a flowerbed wall. Our movements are slow as she braces one hand on the ledge and the other on my shoulder. We watch together as I slide in and out of her until she grabs my ass and pulls me forward. Then I pound into her until she throws her head back, her hair cascading down her back. She grips my shoulder and the wall again as I feel her cunt spasm around me. I come, panting and euphoric.

Whatever happens next, whatever happens in the future, we're tethered to each other, red string or not.

"An abacus? That's what you gave your girlfriend on a romantic getaway. What're you going to do? Give her a graphing calculator on your honeymoon? You're a boring accountant. Is she going to give you pocket protectors in return?"

"Hey. I like my abacus, Anton."

I turn to find Sumiko in the doorway to our bedroom. We didn't return to the villa until after three. She fell asleep in the car, so I waited with her while the guys did a thorough sweep, and Timofey gave Anton a full report. Then I carried her inside. She's been sleeping late since we arrived, and I'm glad she's able to be lazy. She's usually up at five and at the gym with me within the hour.

"But you're not a boring accountant."

"Maybe not. But it reminds me of the one I saw in a museum with my Japanese grandparents as a kid. I mentioned it once, and Pasha remembered. I think it's sweet. And he's hardly boring."

She waggles her eyebrows at me as she comes to stand beside me. She snags a piece of bacon from the chafing dish. She eats three-quarters of it, then offers the last bite to me. When I open my mouth, she drops it into hers instead.

"I have something better to eat, anyway."

I whisper in her ear, certain no one else heard me. But she flushes, and Anton rolls his eyes.

"Whatever you said was gross, little brother."

"If anyone is boring, it's you, old man."

Sergei snorts but says nothing. It's my turn to be disgusted.

"Gross."

It's not. They're good together, and I'm happy when we can travel, getting away from our complicated and restricted lives. I was nervous since I hadn't discussed my brother and Sergei before we left. I tried to broach the subject delicately, but she shrugged and said they're cute together.

Timofey, Stefan, and Ilya have rooms in a different wing. As far as they know, Anton, Sergei, Aleks, and Misha each have their own room. I was angry at the world for a long time, wanting to rail against the injustice of our community's rigid and antiquated beliefs. But it was Anton and Sergei who helped me accept that none of us were going to change the people around us. It still hurts my heart, though.

"What're we doing today?"

Sumiko reaches into her robe pocket as she asks about our plans. Her brow furrows as she looks at her phone screen.

"Sarah?...Sarah? I can't hear you if you're talking. Can you hear me?...Sarah?"

She glances to make sure the call is still live. The volume is loud enough that I can hear the voice come through the speaker. Sergei holds up his phone to show he's recording it. Something isn't right.

"You should have listened when I told you this was a mistake. You were safer when you didn't know about your boyfriend."

I grab the phone from her.

"Pablo?"

I want to keep him talking.

"I wasn't talking to you, Pasha."

"But I'm talking to you. Why do you have Sarah's phone?"

"She should have believed me. She was and never will be yours."

There's a click. The call ends. Sumiko snatches the phone from me and taps the screen twice.

"Sumiko? Are you back already?"

"Sarah, where are you? Are you with Pablo?"

"What? No. I haven't seen him since you broke up. What's wrong?"

"Nothing. I just got a weird call, and I thought you were with him."

"No. I'm at my place. Are you home?"

"Not yet. We're still in Croatia for a few more days. Thanks for picking up my dress."

She watches me as she scrambles to distract Sarah, so she doesn't have to explain her panicked call.

"I expect to see tons of photos."

"You know I'm useless at that. I have a few."

Mostly ones I took of her. They aren't nudes or topless, but they aren't meant to be shared either.

"All right. Let me know when you get back."

"I will."

"Love you."

"Love you, too."

She hangs up and looks at Sergei. She gives him her phone without him asking.

"What the fuck? Is he trying to start shit like Sean did?"

I'm gripping the back of a dining room chair, and my knuckles are white. I'm ready to lose my shit. Other than my knuckles, no one who isn't family could tell the rage I'm in. Sumiko wraps her arms around mine and squeezes. She's fearful of my suppressed reaction. She's probably wondering when I'm going to explode.

"Who's Sean?"

"Sean O'Rourke. He's part of the Irish."

"The Irish? Like the mob?"

"Yeah. He's sort of equivalent to my cousins. He's up there."

I don't want to say too much. I shouldn't have said anything at all. That goes to show how pissed I am.

"What happened with him and Pablo?"

"It was several years ago. They had a thing with a couple girls. The one Pablo was dating left him for Sean after cheating on him with Sean, so Pablo dated Sean's ex-girlfriend. The girls were cousins."

"Ew."

"Yeah, well, it took a long time for the dust to settle on that."

"They were just pissed at each other?"

I look at Anton, whose expression is muted to Sumiko, but it's screaming at me.

"They got some other people involved. It was ugly, but it's over now."

I reach for a plate and scoop eggs onto it for Sumiko. But she twists to meet my gaze.

"Are you saying things are going to get ugly between you and Pablo? I don't want that."

I open my mouth, then snap it shut.

"Don't do that."

Sumiko's voice is barely a whisper, and she looks like she's about to cry. She lets go of my arm and hurries into our bedroom. I follow her, getting to the door as it shuts in my face. I ease it open.

"*Malyshka?*"

"Don't shut me out like that. I might have to wait for you to let me see how you're feeling, but don't put up that wall where I can't even remotely guess. It makes me scared about what's going to happen. I know whatever it is, you won't tell me. It makes me feel alone and vulnerable. I don't like that you can tell everything about me, and I can't tell a damn thing about you unless you deign to let me."

"You want to know what I'm thinking? Why the fuck would you protect him? Why the fuck do you still care about him? He keeps getting in touch with you because he knows you'll keep going back to him. This isn't about me not wanting you to be friends with some guy you've known longer than me. This is about you letting your ex-boyfriend into our life. This is about you choosing him."

Her head jerks back as I unleash.

"If you think I'm protecting him, it's because I'm scared you're going to kill him and get killed for doing it. If I'm trying to protect anyone, it's you. I care about him only so far as he's a danger to you. He can go fuck himself. He has no right to interfere. As for going back to him, the fuck I am. Pasha, I don't know how the fuck any of this works. If I piss him off, and he's already territorial, is he going to put a hit on you? Are you going to die because of me?"

Fuck my life.

I open my arms to her, and she falls against me. She doesn't know how the fuck this works. She's seen movies and probably looked up a ton of shit she hasn't told me.

"I saw what you did to those guys who insulted me. They work for you. I can only imagine what you'd do to rival or enemy. Is that what Pablo is? An enemy?"

"No. He's a royal pain in my fucking ass. He's a rival. I don't consider him an enemy. But he's pushing to become one. I already told him this isn't like what happened with Sean. Yet he keeps pushing. He wants it to turn into an open conflict. He knows that's where things are headed from what happened with the Irish. If anything, the Colombians are pissed about something else. This is just an excuse."

"What something else?"

"I don't know if I can tell you that. I need to think for a moment."

She remains quiet as I consider what's safe to tell her. If I stick to the basics...

"This is all I can tell you: Pablo and his uncle know we found Juan. They didn't want us involved. They wanted him to come home. We disagreed, and Juan didn't see his family."

"Didn't see them? Before what? He left?"

I don't answer.

"Oh. Did you..."

I don't answer that either.

"I know how scared Laura was. She told me what happened. As far as Juan is concerned, good. But I don't want to push Pablo to where he does to you whatever you or your family did to Juan."

"Sumiko, this isn't your cross to bear. If he's pissed about

Juan, and this is how he's getting back at us, then he's really fucked up. Women and children are off limits. Juan said fuck it to that rule, and that is why he landed himself in the situation he did. If Pablo's using you, then he's violating the agreement that the Kutsenko women are untouchable."

"I'm not a Kutsenko woman."

"You might not have my last name yet, but you are definitely my woman."

Heat flares in her gaze, and I fear it's anger. But the way she presses herself against me tells me otherwise.

"I am yours, Daddy. Always."

She knows that helps calm me. It gives me that moment of feeling like I have control again in what's turning out to be an uncontrolled situation.

"Thank you, *malyshka*."

"So what happens now?"

"You have breakfast, then we go to the beach. Anton and Sergei will stay back and talk to Maks and our cousins. They'll fill Maks and the others in. Maks will probably talk to Enrique, and hopefully, the *pakhan* and the *jefe* will sort things out, so it doesn't go any further."

She nods, but I know she's not confident with my response. Not surprising since I'm not either.

Chapter Twenty-Two

Sumiko

Being back to work after a ten-day getaway with Pasha is the most anticlimactic thing that's ever happened to me. Our last few days were just as wonderful as the first week. But I got more texts. The calls with no one there continued. Sergei pinpointed the GPS location before we left, and Bogdan and Niko went to check it out. But it was just like the first time. An abandoned building in Queens. It made no sense.

I know things are bad because Pasha doesn't want to discuss what's going on. He's been evasive for the past two days, and it's pissing the hell out of me. But I know he's trying to figure out what's safe for me to know. As best I can tell, Maks and Enrique spoke on the phone. It erupted into a massive argument, and Enrique denied the entire thing. I suggested I talk to Enrique, but Maks and Pasha shut that shit down right snappy. Pasha warned me not to take matters into my own hands and try to contact Enrique or Pablo. He said I wouldn't be able to sit for a month, and I believe him. This is now bratva business. I don't want or need to be drawn in any further.

"Hi, *mamãe*." I hug my mom. "Hi, *papai*."

My family just got off the private jet, and we're still on the tarmac. This wealth and luxury are going to take some getting used to. Pasha and I came in one of the Kutsenkos' limos, so there is plenty of room for my parents, my two brothers, and my older brother's wife, along with Pasha and me. I can tell my dad is sizing him up, and I can tell Pasha is doing the same. I happened to glance at Pasha as my dad took the last step. Something like surprise and recognition flashed in his eyes, but I don't know why. Then again, the Kutsenkos own pharmaceutical companies, and that's my dad's field. Perhaps their paths have crossed.

"Sumiko."

My mom hugs me again after my dad lets go. It's not as comforting as it used to be. I think it's because I know there are things I'm going to have to hold back from my family. There are things they can never know. Whereas Alina already knows everything. I saw her before we left for Croatia. Pasha must have told her what happened at Ivy because she gave me a hug that made me want to never leave her arms. Guilt gnaws at me that I find it easier to be with someone else's mom than my own.

"*Mamãe, papai,* I'd like you to meet my boyfriend. Pasha, these are my parents, Afonso and Akiko."

"It's nice to meet you, Mr. and Mrs. Kimura."

Pasha shakes my parents' hands, and I can tell they appreciate his more formal greeting. They may have grown up in Brazil, but both of them are Japanese. I know Pasha addresses them that way because that's how his parents raised him. It's not for show, which I believe my parents can tell.

"These are my brothers, Cristiano and Davi. This is Cristiano's wife, Helena."

"It's Cris. Nice to meet you."

I watch Helena size up Pasha, and I'm annoyed. She loves my brother, and I don't doubt her faithfulness, but the way she looks at Pasha makes me uncomfortable. If she were a firefighter, she'd slide down his pole. But he looks at her only long enough to shake hands. His other hand is holding mine, and he gives it a squeeze. He can tell, even if everyone else is oblivious.

Davi is the last one to shake Pasha's hand.

"Thanks for sending the jet. Never in a million years did I think I'd ever fly in one. It was amazing."

"You're welcome. We're glad you could visit. We can head to our place, and you can rest or get freshened up. We can eat in or go out for dinner. Whatever you feel up to."

I internally cringe when he says, "our place." My parents don't know yet, but from the way my dad's jaw clenches, he caught it. Pasha and my dad are staring at one another, and I don't understand what's happening between them. It's not exactly a staring contest, but there's a vibe that's—I don't know—charged. I don't think it has anything to do with my living arrangement. It started when Pasha saw him.

I climb into the car first because I'm closest to the door. But Pasha waits until everyone else is inside. I'm seated next to my mom, and Pasha is at the other end of the car. We've never sat apart in a vehicle. I can tell he's not thrilled, and frankly, neither am I, since something is going on. I'm uneasy as my mom chatters about what's been happening at home. I answer when I'm supposed to, but I'm watching Pasha with the men in my family. My brothers have picked up on the tension, but they don't appear to know what's happening. Helena is watching the New York skyline.

"This is the building."

I point out the window as we stop in front of Pasha's condo. We talked for hours about our future living situation as we flew home. We agreed to let my lease end, and I would move into Pasha's loft. But that would only be temporary. It seems like everyone is drifting back to Queens as more couples marry. Sergei and Anton will stay in Manhattan, but Pasha says whenever Misha and Aleks find women to marry, they'll probably want houses in Queens too. We plan to look at homes in the same neighborhood as the others. Some people might think it's odd that the three already married couples are practically neighbors, but I love the idea that they're all close together. The few times the family has gathered with me, things have been a bit rocky, but I love that they're so close.

"Wow. It's beautiful."

My mom and I have to wait for everyone else to get out before we can. Pasha offers my mom a hand because he's waiting by the door for me. As soon as I step out, his arm goes around my waist, and I lean against him. We do it without thought, but my family notices. No one says anything, but I feel scrutinized.

"Don't worry about your luggage. It'll be brought up."

I glance up at Pasha, and I wonder if the bags are going to be run through the x-ray machine I know is in the security room. It's for Pasha's private use. He has his own security detail that has nothing to do with the building's concierge. Nothing comes up to his loft without being examined first. That's why the sex toy package mortified me. I still get flustered when I think about it.

Pasha meets my gaze and shakes his head. His smile is understanding, and I feel better knowing he isn't suspicious of my family. The tension has eased slightly between him and my dad. Perhaps it's a truce. The bodyguards are more discreet than usual, so there isn't one posted outside Pasha's door when we arrive. There's a guy near the elevator, and if I didn't know, I would think he was a resident waiting to go downstairs. It's not Timofey, but someone I don't know.

Ana brought Pandora back the night we returned. Apparently, my chinchilla and Niko's African gray parrot became the best of friends. She said I should be glad that chinchillas can't talk, or Pandora would have a salty vocabulary. When we come inside, she stands on her hind legs and chatters. I think she believed I was never coming back. It's Pasha who takes her out of her cage and pets her. Seeing my hulking boyfriend with my tiny pet melts my heart every time. She's clearly content.

"Pandora's here?"

My mom looks at Pasha, then me.

"Yes. Pasha and I decided while we were on our trip that we want to live together. I haven't ended my lease yet, but for all intents and purposes, this is my home, too."

My parents say nothing, and my brothers and Helena look out the window. I thought we might have a little more time before I made that announcement. But it just sorta flew out of my mouth.

"You haven't known each other very long, and you already want to live together. Wasn't it enough to go away to another continent for nearly two weeks only a few days after meeting?"

My dad's arms are crossed, and his dislike it clear. My mom is a little more circumspect, but I can tell she's not happy either. Pasha puts Pandora back in her cage and comes to stand behind me. He rests his hands on the outsides of my shoulders, and their weight is reassuring.

"Mr. Kimura, I think you and I should talk in my office."

"No. Pasha, why can't we clear the air here?"

"*Malyshka,* we probably will, but it would be better if I have this conversation alone with your dad."

"No."

I shake my head. It's not like I think they're about to have a father-son chat that leads to Pasha asking my dad for my hand. There's something really off, and I'm worried it's only going to devolve.

Someone knocks, and Pasha tells them to enter in Russian. I recognize the word. Two men from the concierge arrive with the luggage. I stand and watch as Pasha shows Cris and Helena their room, then he points out Davi's.

"I think we'll unpack."

Helena suggests it, but my brothers are just as eager to escape.

My mom and I sit on a sofa while we wait. My dad is like a statue. When Pasha returns, he sits beside me.

"Does Mrs. Kimura know?"

"Know what?"

My mom and I respond to Pasha's question at the same time.

"Yes."

My mom's eyes widen for a fraction of a second. Mine narrow.

"Will you tell Sumiko, or do you want me to?"

"This doesn't concern my daughter."

"I think it must. *Papai*, what's going on? How do you and Pasha know each other?"

"We don't."

I look at Pasha, completely confused by his answer. What is going on? His gaze has hardened as he stares at my dad. My dad is unwilling to back down, either.

"Mr. Kimura, Sumiko knows who I am."

"Pasha."

I look back and forth. How the fuck does my dad know what that means? Why did he phrase it that way? My father sat in an armchair when Pasha came to sit next to me, but he jumps out of it like a scalded cat.

"I said nothing when she dated Pablo, and I said nothing when she told us about you. But he didn't put a target on her. My daughter is not living with you because the two of you are done."

"*Papai*, what are you talking about? And you don't get to decide. I'm twenty-eight."

"Sumiko, your dad recognized my last name."

"So? I figured you knew of each other, but I assumed it was because of the pharmaceutical industry. I know Kutsenko Partners owns several companies."

"They do. But that's not how he knows me. He knows I'm bratva. He knew Pablo was Cartel."

"*Papai?*"

"Yes. Pablo didn't bring you into his world. He cared enough about you to keep you safe."

"No, he didn't. He let me go around telling people he was my boyfriend, and he left me unprotected once people started seeing us together. He never warned me about the danger being associated with him put me in. He didn't bother to give me any choices. Pasha has been honest since the beginning."

"Your drug-dealing mafia boyfriend has been honest?"

My dad's laugh is mocking, and it grates on my nerves.

"Those who live in glass houses, Mr. Kimura."

"I'm so lost. *Mamãe*, what's going on?"

She looks at me, and her face is completely white. I turn to Pasha. He takes my hands.

"*Malyshka*, your dad and his brother look enough alike that I recognized your dad."

"*Tio* Ignácio? How do you know him? He lives in São Paulo."

"We do business, Sumiko."

I turn my head away from Pasha, but I'm still looking at him. I get the definite sense that it's not legal business. I shift my gaze to my dad, and he looks ready to murder Pasha.

"*Papai*, why did you call Pasha a drug dealer? And why did Pasha say those who live in glass houses?"

My dad's eyes turn to slits as he glowers at Pasha.

"If you don't explain, I will."

Pasha draws my hands to his lap and covers them with his. I don't notice they're trembling until he stills them. Neither of my parents speak.

"Sumiko, you told me your father works for a global bio-pharma company in sales. But that's not where he started. When he still lived in Brazil, he was a chemist. He worked with his brother."

"I know that. But that was more than thirty years ago."

"Do you know what he worked on?"

"No. Medicines, I suppose."

"Officially for his day job. Sumiko, your uncle is one of our main South American suppliers of cocaine."

Pasha's looking me in the eye as he speaks. I'm starting to understand his expressions more. I can see his anxiousness in his gaze, even though he appears steady. He's just confessed something that could destroy his entire family. It takes a moment to dawn on me that what he said could destroy mine, too.

"What? No. My uncle is in real estate."

"He is. That's so he can have plenty of locations for his labs."

"Labs?"

"Yes. Cocaine's made through a process that has several steps and involves a lot of chemicals. It's not like pot that gets picked and dried and then is practically ready to use. Brazil is one of the largest drug trafficking countries in South America.

The raw materials come from Paraguay and Bolivia, then they're made into cocaine in the Amazon. The forest is so vast that there are plenty of safe places for the labs to go undetected. Much of the cocaine in Brazil goes directly to Europe, but not all of it."

"Some of it comes to you."

"Yes."

"And my uncle is—what—a drug lord?"

No one answers. I look at my dad.

"And you used to make cocaine?"

My dad takes a long time to nod. I look at my mom, and she's still pale. But nothing seems to surprise her. She's known all along. I can tell.

"Are you Brazilian mafia?"

"Cartel, and no. I met the wrong people in college and had a foolish sense of immortality that comes with youth. I didn't think it was a big deal. Ignácio saw the potential with the formula I developed for a cartel. I never got sucked in, but he got more involved. That's when your mom and I moved to California."

"But I know *tio* Ignácio. We've stayed with him when we've visited. I never would have guessed. Do Avó and Vovô know?" My grandma and grandpa. Holy hell.

"Yes. It was a family secret until today. One best not talked about."

"You used to make coke. My uncle sells it to Pasha and his family when he doesn't sell it to people in Europe. You knew Pablo is Colombian Cartel, and you knew Pasha is Russian bratva. You didn't think either time that maybe you should warn me away from either guy? Dad, you don't get to be upset about Pasha bringing me into this world since you knew and did nothing. Mom, did you know who Pasha or Pablo are?"

"No. I know about the family secret, and I know about your

dad's past. But I don't know any details. It's too dangerous to know these things."

"I—"

My phone rings in my pocket. I pull it out to silence it, but I look down and see it's Pablo. I show it to Pasha, who takes my phone and marches to his office.

"We'll be right back."

I run to catch Pasha, and I close the office door behind us. He hands me back my phone, and I put it on speaker when I answer.

"I told you to stop calling and texting me, Pablo."

"Hello to you too. And I did stop. Your boyfriend is making up bullshit lies about me."

"What lies, Pablo?"

"He's telling Maks I've been threatening you. He's trying to start a war with my uncle. He's probably hoping to shoot me."

"I wasn't until you gave me the idea, *puta*."

"Pasha?"

"I don't lie. Stay the fuck away from my girlfriend, or what happened with the Irish will look like a fucking Sunday picnic. Threaten her again, and I will fucking eviscerate you."

"Threaten her? Sumiko, what the hell has he been telling you?"

"He hasn't told me anything. You know he isn't lying. You talked to him the other day. Stop calling and texting."

"I haven't. What are you talking about the other day?"

"When you called me while I was in Croatia."

"You were in Croatia? I haven't talked to you in over two weeks."

"Stop lying, Pablo. And stop calling and just sitting there, silent. You know I can't block your number since you make it unavailable. But I'm going to keep sending you to voicemail."

"Slow down, Sumiko. Pasha, whatever is going on, is not me. Is Juan still alive?"

"What do you think?"

"He's the only person who would dare call someone and pretend to be me."

"It couldn't have been him on that phone call."

I look at Pasha and know that means, without a doubt, Juan is dead. It only confirms what I already knew, but it still makes me feel ill. Pablo doesn't sound fazed when he continues.

"What did this person say?"

"You know—"

"Sumiko, wait." Pasha's staring at the phone in my hand.

"Pasha, what did this person say?"

Pasha pulls out his phone and unlocks it. He opens his texts and taps one. Pasha's voice plays, followed by Pablo's."

"Pablo?"

"I wasn't talking to you, Pasha."

"But I'm talking to you. Why do you have Sarah's phone?"

"She should have believed me. She was and never will be yours."

There's a moment of silence after the recording ends. It's Pablo who breaks it.

"Pasha, we have a big problem. That wasn't me. Can you play it back to me again?"

"Pablo—"

"Sumiko, let him hear it again. There's something to the recording that sounds off. I didn't notice it when the call was live."

Pasha turns the volume all the way up and he puts his phone's speaker to my phone's mic.

"Play it again."

Pasha follows Pablo's instruction. Then we hear something garbled from Pablo's end. After that, it sounds like two voices speaking at the same time. One sounds just like Pablo, but the other is muffled and hard to distinguish.

"I'm calling Maks. You need to call Enrique. We need to meet."

"I know. I'll have my uncle call Maks. I can meet as soon as they pick a place."

"Same."

"What about Sumiko?"

"That's a shitstorm too. Did you know Sumiko's uncle is Ignácio Kimura?"

"What the fuck? No."

"Yeah, I didn't make the connection either. Sumiko's family is here. Her dad knows about both of us. I'm taking them to Maks's."

"Good."

"I'm still standing here. Why are we going to Maks's? Why do you two have to meet? You sound like allies when a moment ago you were enemies."

"The enemy of my enemy is my friend. Right now, someone is fucking over the Cartel and the bratva by pitting us against each other. Pablo, Sumiko's dad needs to be at that meeting. Someone knows who her family is. I guarantee her uncle has something to do with this."

"You think my uncle is doing this?"

"No, *malyshka*. I think someone is using you to bait us, so they can get your uncle's business."

"Who?"

"The Italians or the Irish come to mind."

It's Pablo who answers, but Pasha wants to know more.

"I thought you were on good terms with both of them. Something go wrong?"

"Nothing that I know of, Pasha. But it seems like there's a

fuck ton I don't know. Go to Maks's. I'm calling my uncle. Bye."

Pablo hangs up before Pasha or I can say anything. My head is spinning, and I'm so lost.

"Baby girl, your family needs to come with me to Maks's. It's safest there. The calls and texts obviously weren't from Pablo, after all. But I couldn't recognize the voice. I need Pablo to get that audio to Sergei, and I need to get you protected. Someone is trying to start a war between the Russians and Colombians to keep us distracted. I'm worried whoever this is plans to strike soon to take your uncle's business from us. Your dad needs to talk to his brother."

"What about my brothers? They don't know any of this. Neither does Helena."

"And hopefully, it can stay that way. We're going to tell your brothers and Helena that my family invited us over for dinner. Then something is going to come up. My cousins can keep your brothers occupied while their wives entertain you and Helena and your mom. Your dad can make the call in Maks's office. But we need to go now."

Chapter Twenty-Three

Pasha

The entire ride to Maks's, Sumiko, her parents, and I try to keep up the façade that everything is fine. Her brothers and sister-in-law are excited to meet my family. Despite our conversation being heated and my rapid explanation about our call with Pablo, we'd kept our voices down enough that I'm sure Cris, Helena, and Davi didn't hear us. They seem none the wiser. The enemy of my enemy is my friend holds true. Afonso no longer seems so hostile toward me. He sees the way Sumiko turns to me, and how I do what I can to support her.

She and I are sitting next to each other, and she's telling her family about our vacation and the abacus. She's valiant in her effort to sound normal, and she does. But the nervousness pulsates from her. When her family talks amongst themselves, I draw her against my side and whisper in her ear.

"I don't know what's going to happen tonight, but I will do everything I can to be with you before you go to bed. Do you need Daddy?"

She nods.

"Do you want to submit and not think about all of this?"

She nods again.

"When we get there, you and I are going to slip away for a few minutes."

She sags and rests her head on my shoulder. When we get to my cousin's, Anton and Sergei are already there. Aleks arrives with Misha as we're walking through the door. Niko and Ana arrive in a limo with Bogdan and Christina. They could have walked, but I know neither Niko nor Bogdan would permit that until we know what's happening. I stand next to Anton and keep my voice low.

"Sumiko and I need a couple minutes. Keep people from noticing we're not here."

"Is she all right?"

"She will be."

Anton doesn't ask anything else. I lead Sumiko up the stairs to one of the guest bedrooms. I lock the door. She's looking around and squeaks when I grab her arm, spin her toward the door, and press her against it. She's wearing pants, which I hate. I push them down and slide my fingers between her thighs. She looks back over her shoulder at me.

"Do you need Daddy, *malyshka*?"

"Yes."

"Why?"

"Because everything is a mess. I don't know what to do, and I don't want to have to figure it out. I'm scared. I don't want to think about this for a few minutes. I don't want to have to make any choices right now. I just want to focus on doing what you tell me to do."

"What's your safe word?"

"Kale."

I press my cock against her ass, pinning her between me

and the door. I squeeze her ass as hard as I can. I know I'm going to leave marks.

"Does my baby girl want her daddy's cock?"

"Yes, Daddy."

"Do you want it hard and fast? Or does my *malyshka* need it slow?"

"Slow. But we don't have time."

"You told me what you need. Now who decides?"

"You, Daddy."

"I'm going to spank you, *malyshka*. It is not a punishment. It's a distraction. Come, lay across my lap."

I back away and walk to the bed. She kicks off her shoes and leaves her pants as the door. Her top only comes to her waist, so I have a glorious view of her legs and pussy. My fucking balls ache. She drapes herself over my lap, and I rain down ten rapid slaps on each side. The speed makes it sting and burn, not the strength of each blow. Her ass is glowing red by the time I'm done. She kicked her feet a few times, but her body is completely lax over my legs by the time I'm done. She didn't cry, but she sighed several times. Fuck me. I need to come.

"Stand up, then bend over the bed. I'm going to give you that fuck you need. I'm going to come in you, and you're going to keep all of it inside you until I let you move. You're mine, and my cum says so."

"Yes, Daddy. I want you to finish in me."

Once she's bent over the bed, I unfasten my pants and thrust into her.

"Whose cunt is this?"

"Yours, Daddy."

"And what do I get to do with it?"

"Whatever you want, Daddy."

"And if I want to fuck it one moment, then make love to it the next, what will you do?"

"Enjoy every minute. Daddy, I really want to make you come."

"Why, baby girl? I thought Daddy was taking care of you, not the other way around."

"Because I love you."

Those words will never lose their potency over me. I lean over her, and our fingers lace together near her head.

"I love you, Sumiko. You're going to make me come. You're so fucking tight when you do those Kegels. Come when you want to, baby girl. I want you to spend tonight thinking about how I feel inside you. Concentrate on that if I'm gone."

"I will. I'm so close. I can feel it."

I keep working her pussy until her fingers tighten around mine. I shoot my load inside her as she shakes beneath me. I help her stand while I'm still inside her. I turn us, so I can sit, and she's on my lap.

"We're going to get cleaned up. Then I have something for you that we haven't used yet."

"What is it?"

"I said we're going to get cleaned up first."

"You didn't say you couldn't tell me."

"*Malyshka.*"

I infuse warning into my tone. She stands up and turns doe eyed as she looks at me. We both know she's pretending. I scoop her into my arms and carry her into the bathroom. We're quick to tidy up. Then I lift her onto the counter and pull her hips toward me, tilting them up. I pull a small velvet sack from my pocket.

"Open it, *krasivaya.*"

She pulls the top loose and drops two shiny Ben Wa balls into her hand. Her eyes light up.

"These will give you something to focus on tonight. You can't let them fall, and you can't make yourself come."

"Thank you, Daddy. If I can't have your cock in me all night as a distraction, then maybe this will help."

I press them into her cunt and draw my tongue along her plump pussy lips. I kiss her clit. I carry her back into the bedroom and to the door. I help her put her pants back on before I open it. We make our way downstairs, and only a couple people look our way. Laura had just finished a tour of the house. I see Helena's speculative gaze, and it irritates me. She doesn't want to actually fuck me, but that's all she thinks I'm good for. I know that look. I've received it too many times. Sumiko sees it too because she seems to shrink as we walk with our arms around each other's waists.

"*Malyshka*, don't. I just had my cock up to your belly button as I came. If our families weren't here, I'd still be inside you."

"She's really pre—"

"Do you need a spanking that's a real punishment?"

"But she's—"

"*Malyshka*." I turn her toward me. "Do you need more time?"

Her eyes fill with tears as she nods. I don't give a shit about keeping anyone from noticing we're gone. I steer her back up the stairs and into the same bedroom. I lift her onto the bed after she kicks off her shoes. I do the same and follow her. Once I'm settled against the headboard, I position her on my lap, and she curls into a ball.

"Do you need a good cry?"

She nods.

"Then cry, Sumiko. You've held it together admirably. You're not weak because you're struggling right now. You know

I may not show my emotions, but you also know I still feel them. I'm upset too."

"Do you need a good cry too, *fofinho*?"

"I probably do. I'm scared for you, *krasivaya*. You might not want to make decisions and be in control right now, but I crave it. I hate feeling like I'm not. You helped me as much as I helped you. You let me feel like things were normal for a few minutes. Let me take care of you still. Let me feel like I can do something for you and not feel useless and helpless."

"That's how you feel, Pasha?"

She leans back to look at me. I let her in. I let her see my fear as I nod and swallow. She shifts to straddle me and cups my jaw.

"You are not useless. Not ever. And there is nothing about you that will ever make me think you're helpless. Frustrated, sure. Stuck between a rock and a hard place, practically every minute. But not helpless."

"I couldn't get whoever this is to leave you alone. I didn't figure out that it wasn't really Pablo. I—"

"And neither did Sergei. He's a hacking genius, and he didn't figure it out. You're an accountant. He's the one with the skills and knowledge, and even he didn't put it all together. You are not useless, Pasha. I only feel safe when I'm with you. You are so attentive and loving. You are doing everything you can to give me what I need, to make me feel better. And it's working. I'm sorry that I got insecure."

"Never apologize for that, Sumiko. You are entitled to your feelings, and if you don't feel good about something or about yourself, don't dismiss it. Let's fix it together. I don't know what Helena's deal is, but she sure as hell doesn't respect me. There's nothing attractive about her to me. I don't think she's that pretty, and her attitude is ugly. To look at me like I'm some man whore while she's standing next to her husband and in front of my girlfriend is pathetic."

"You know she's pretty. She's beautiful."

"She's thin, with no ass and flat lips. The lines around her mouth turn down. She frowns more than she smiles. She doesn't have your glow."

"My glow?"

"Yes. You radiate your beauty. It's your appearance, but it's also your personality. It comes out, and together, it makes you so fucking hot. Damn it, I'm getting fucking hard again."

"You're always hard."

"That's entirely your fault. I would really have to think to remember the last erection I had before I met you that wasn't one I gave myself from jacking off."

"Really?"

"Yes. I'm like a fourteen-year-old boy, whose dick wakes up when the wind blows. I think about you, and I'm hard. I see you, I'm hard. I hear you, I'm hard. I touch you, I'm hard. I smell you, I'm hard. I taste you, and I'm ready to fucking blow."

"Maybe I should blow you more often."

She waggles her eyebrows before leaning forward. She rests her head on my chest as I wrap my arms around her.

"Do you need that cry?"

"Not anymore. Can you just hold me for a bit?"

"Forever."

She nods and sighs. But she soon shifts restlessly.

"Daddy, I can't keep those balls in sitting like this. My pussy isn't strong enough to keep this Kegel going."

I wondered how she was doing it. I move her, so she has both of her legs to my left. We sit in silence for a few minutes before she pulls away. She wipes under her eyes and pulls her hair to one side. She gives me a tender kiss before getting off my lap.

"I know we have to go back down. I don't want to worry my parents."

"I know. If you need another break, just let me know. I don't care what anyone thinks. If you need it, we take it."

"I love you, Pasha."

"I love you. I will always take care of you, just like you always take care of me."

We rejoin the others for a second time. Afonso and Akiko watch us. They're worried until they observe us for a while. My gaze meets Afonso's, then Akiko's. They both smile, and it's genuine. I have their blessing. Good. Because I'm marrying their daughter within the week, regardless.

Enrique wasn't available until nearly midnight. My family tried to come up with reasons for Sumiko's to spend the night at Maks and Laura's, but her brothers and sister-in-law were getting suspicious. We ended up coming back to the loft, but Aleks, Sergei, Anton, and Misha followed us. I already have my regular safety detail there. Afonso and I are on our way back to Maks's. My brother and the others are staying at my place but not in my loft, since I loathe leaving Sumiko somewhere that isn't as secure as any of my cousins' Queens homes. I'm in the middle of fucking Manhattan with strangers in my building.

"Have you ever met Enrique or Pablo?"

"No. But I know Pablo's father, Luis. We met while I was in college. It was back when Colombia was the main South American trafficker. I learned how to make coke from a chemist at one of his family's labs."

"That's why you didn't object to Sumiko dating Pablo. You know the family."

"Yes. Maks and my brother have done business, so I know

your family's reputation. That's why I didn't object about you either. But I never imagined you'd bring her into your world. I thought you would keep her at a distance like Pablo did until she tired of it and broke up with you."

"Sumiko is my soulmate, Afonso. She told me the legend of the red string. She's on the other end of mine. I do not doubt that for a second. I would never bring her into this if I wasn't committed to be by her side until my last breath."

"And the danger you bring with you?"

I shake my head.

"I can't change that. But someone knows who you are. They knew using Sumiko to get between the bratva and Cartel would distract us from our ties to your brother."

"You don't know that it's to get to Ignácio. Maybe it's one of your local rivals just wanting a bigger share of New York."

"That's not high enough stakes for someone to start a war. Not unless they have something personal against Sumiko to put her in the middle. Whoever th—"

Gunshot riddles the car, and I look out of the town car window as I push Afonso to the floor. Headlights are blinding me. I shield him as I get down. I look around, and headlights are flooding us from three sides. I push the button to lower the privacy glass. I see headlights in front of us too.

"I'm going, boss."

Ilya slams on the gas, and the car charges forward. My shoulder rams into the divider as the town car rams into something. The sound of grating metal is ear piercing. More bullets hit the side of the car. Fortunately, all of our vehicles have shatterproof windows. The doors are reinforced, but they aren't entirely bulletproof. These aren't our SUVs. Those are veritable tanks. Ilya's still gunning it as a tire pops. We skid, but he doesn't slow down. When another tire blows, Ilya swerves, trying to regain control. The car screeches to a stop just as one vehicle nails the hood and another hits the trunk. The car crunches, then more gunshots. Crowbars pry open the rear doors. Just before a sack goes over my head, I look up to see who's on Afonso's side. Motherfucking son of a cock sucking cunt bitch.

Chapter Twenty-Four

Sumiko

I can't sleep. I think about getting out of bed to pace, but what's the point? It won't ease my nervous energy. I can't stop picturing Pasha in a shootout, then his body riddled with bullets, left for dead on some street corner. The image is so vivid I keep thinking I'll vomit. I'm driving myself crazy. I've been doing this for an hour and a half. I can't torture myself anymore.

I throw back the covers and pull on pajama pants and a t-shirt. I wonder if my mom's sleeping. Cris, Davi, and Helena don't know my dad and Pasha left. They sneaked out like phantoms, but I saw Aleks and Anton outside the door. Pasha told me they would stay there all night, even if he and my dad return. Misha and Sergei are in the security room. Sergei was going to keep working on the audio. He looked excited when Pablo sent the file to him. It's clear he was eager for the challenge, but I know it's no game to him. He wants to protect his family and me. If Pablo hadn't heard the recorded conversation, we would have been none the wiser that it was someone else. Fortunately, Pablo had the tech to separate the two voices. I don't ask why he did.

I slip out of the bedroom and creep to the door. I open it a crack and find Aleks's back to the door, but Anton's looking at me. Both men face me in an instant, guns raised. I put my hands up, even though they can't see them. I take a steadying breath, then ease the door open before I step into the hallway.

"Nothing's wrong. I can't sleep."

Both men offer me sympathetic nods. They lower their guns. Aleks moves, so I have a wall to my back, and he can see the hallway to the elevator. Anton is still looking at the door. I realize he's positioned to rush in if someone enters the loft from the outside. We're ten stories up at the equivalent of the penthouse. I don't want to know how someone could get in through a window. But he's prepared, nonetheless.

"I can't stop imagining Pasha's been shot and left somewhere." Tears well in my eyes as a tsunami of guilt crashes over me. I swipe at them as they fall. "Fuck. I wasn't even thinking about my dad being with him."

Anton draws me into his embrace.

"I'm worried about my little brother, too."

It sounds so weird to hear Anton call him that since they're nearly the same size. They're the same height and build, but Anton's got a few extra pounds of muscle. I can only tell because Pasha told me. I never feel this protected when Cris and Davi hug me, but then again, when have they needed to?

Pasha and I talked for a few minutes before he left. We agreed Davi is too young and immature to be trusted not to let Pasha's ties slip, and we don't trust Helena not to brag about Pasha's mafia life. We don't expect Cris to keep secrets from his wife.

I pull back from Anton and offer him a weak smile.

"Do you know if they're at Maks's yet?"

"They should be, but we haven't heard anything."

Aleks keeps his voice low, and it makes me wonder if I should have whispered. But I've already learned he's the most stoic of the group. It's not that he can't be easygoing and funny, but he's the most reserved. I suspect the weight of being Maks's second-in-command weighs heavily on him. If anything happened to Maks, he would step into being *pakhan*. He's also supposed to be the loudest voice of dissent if the Elite Group disagrees with Maks's decisions.

"Would one of you text me when you hear? Or is this one of those times where they won't have their phones on?"

"We'll know, then we'll let you know."

"Thanks."

I don't know that I can sleep now, but that's more reassurance than I had a few minutes ago. I head back to bed and climb in. I don't realize I've fallen asleep until my phone wakes me. I glance at the clock. It's been three hours since I stepped into the hallway.

"Hello?"

"We need to speak to you. Come outside."

"Anton? What's wrong?"

"Come out in the hallway."

There's urgency to his voice, so I scramble out of bed.

"Where's Pasha? What happened, Anton?"

I'm running to the door, which is already open. I step into the hallway, and Aleks closes it behind me. There are at least ten men in the hallway, all in dark fatigues. They have rifles and earpieces. I shift my gaze to Anton when he speaks.

"Your dad and Pasha were in a car accident."

"What? Are they alive? What hospital are they at?"

I'm ready to run inside and get my purse before we go.

"They're not at a hospital. It was an attack, Sumiko. They were taken."

The world stops. I stare at Anton, but it's like he's a statue, not a person. It's like everything else is frozen, and all I can sense is myself. Pain radiates from my chest as though a massive vise clamps my heart. Fear makes me break into a cold sweat.

"Who?"

My voice is hoarse as I look back at the men swarming the hallway.

"We don't know. Ilya didn't see who it was. They shot him and left him, assuming he was dead. By the time he came round, it was two hours later. He called Maks, then me. I called you. I don't know any more than that."

"What happens now?"

I'm asking questions, but it's as though I'm hearing someone else's voice. I don't feel like it's my body producing the sound.

"Stay here with your family. No one leaves."

I keep watching the men as I try to formulate my thoughts. Pasha was taken. He's gone. He could be dead. I might never see him again. I'm alone. What am I going to do without him?

"Sumiko, we know nothing yet. Don't go down that road."

I turn to look at Aleks. Tears slide down my cheeks.

"Are you saying they might ransom him or something? Is that how it works? Or will we know he's dead because he never comes back, or they dump his body somewhere?" I think of something else as I look at Aleks. "Is he important enough for them to ransom? Or did they do this because they think he's disposable? He's not as high up as either of you."

"Sumiko, everyone in our world knows Pasha is my cousin and Anton's brother. There is no doubt they know just what they're unleashing. Taking him has started a war. Hurting him or killing him will cause more bloodshed than anyone will risk.

Everyone—I mean, *everyone*—knows how close our family is. They also know how my brothers, cousins, and I were trained. They know what we're capable of."

"Because of that Vlad guy?"

Aleks's expression turns grim. I glance at Anton, and I feel like he could turn me to ash.

"Am I not supposed to know about him? Please don't be mad at Pasha."

"We're not mad at my brother, and the other wives know about him. We're not surprised you do. But he was our judge, jailor, and executioner. He killed our childhood and made us what we are. When it comes to our family, I truly can't believe anyone thinks they'll come out of this the winner."

"Is this like a blood feud now?"

"Yes."

Both men answer, and it sends a shiver down my back. Anton continues to explain.

"Sumiko, the other syndicates are violent. There's no sugar coating that. But they aren't Russian. Former Soviets trained none of them. They don't have our skills or organization. We are paramilitary. Pasha told me about the website and how you found out. We have conducted other recovery operations."

"Laura and Ana."

"Yes. And they are our family, and we love them like they're our sisters or cousins. But Pasha is blood. I can't explain how that makes it different. It makes it sound like we don't love the wives as much as I say we do. It's the things we've been through together. It's what we survived. It's the communal rage. They have my brother. He is coming home, Sumiko."

Anton's conviction offers a measure of relief. And it scares the shit out of me for whoever did this. I force my mind not to conjure images of torture. I know I can't even scrape the surface of what they will do.

"What do I tell my family? I just thought about saying he had something come up with a shipment for Bear Imports. But that doesn't explain why my dad is gone. Do I say they left much later than they did and say they wanted a father-groom chat? What happens when they aren't home soon?"

"Tell them that. Pasha got called into work early this morning. Your dad was getting a glass of water, and Pasha offered to take him so they could get to know each other better."

"Okay, Anton. How are you not losing your shit?"

"I am, Sumiko. But you know how we are. This was part of our training. Showing any emotion caused others to get hurt. Vlad made sure we could see the worst and not blink. Just because we don't show our emotions doesn't mean we don't feel them. They have my baby brother. My shit is already lost."

"He told me the same thing. The part about still having feelings. I wish I knew how to make this easier for you. I'm sorry that I don't."

Aleks gestures between Anton and him as he talks. I gave up trying to dry my tears, so they continue to trickle down my cheeks.

"Sumiko, you didn't do any of this. We appreciate your compassion, but you're only entering this world. No one expects you to fix anything. We're sorry we haven't fixed this."

"Do you or your men need anything? Drinks? Food? What if someone needs to use the bathroom?"

Anton shakes his head.

"We have what we need in the security room, including a bathroom. Thank you. My brother is a lucky man to have you as his soulmate."

"How do you say that in Russian?"

"*Rodstvennaya dusha.*"

"That's going to take me a while to practice. Hopefully, I can say it right by the time Pasha gets home."

I offer a watery smile.

"Pasha will love it. Like I said, my brother is lucky to have found you."

I look at the men before I go on my tiptoes and whisper in Anton's ear.

"I truly hope we have what you and Sergei have. I want that kind of partnership with Pasha. You give me something to aspire to."

Anton's smile breaks through the ice forming inside me. There is so much sincerity and warmth in it. I wonder if he doubted my acceptance.

"I finally have the sister I wanted. It makes up for having a little toad for a brother."

Aleks looks at us.

"I want what Anton has."

Aleks nods. No one will ever say it out loud, which breaks my heart. But I'm glad Anton and Aleks know how I feel. I hope they tell the others.

"You do. Pasha is devoted to you. He will not give up trying to get home to you. I know my cousin because he's like all the men in this family who have fallen in love. He will not stop until he knows you're safe, which means he'll fight for forever if he has to."

"Thank you."

I inhale deeply. It's a fortifying breath that I release slowly. I turn toward the door, but I stop.

"Tell me everything. Don't wait to find a good way. Just tell me."

"We will."

It's noon, and we still haven't heard from Pasha. I went into my parents' room and woke my mom. I had to tell her the truth. If I kept it from her that someone took my dad, it would be a wound too deep. But I was terrified. It shocked me at how calm she was. She said my uncle's old rival took my dad once before. That was the real reason they moved to the U.S. The fucking secrets coming out are mind-boggling. She's more of a support to me than I am to her. She goes along with my story when I tell everyone else. Blessedly, it's pouring. It gives my mom and me an easy excuse for keeping everyone at the loft.

I made a big breakfast to keep myself occupied. Except everyone ate so much, they're not that interested in lunch. I have nothing to occupy me right now. We're watching a movie, and I'm trying not to fidget too much. I have Pandora in my lap and petting her gives me something to do. She might not be much to look at, but she's been the perfect pet since I moved to New York. I don't have to worry about getting home to walk her. She doesn't shed all over the place. She doesn't destroy any of my stuff. She just likes to cuddle.

"Pasha doesn't mind rodents?"

Davi has always given me a hard time about my pets. Before I left for college, I had a mini lop rabbit named Bunny. I had hamsters before that. I like low maintenance pets. I get the comfort and fun of having an animal without too much fuss.

"Pandora may love him more than she does me. She likes to sit on his shoulder while he works."

"Is he a workaholic? He and Dad have been gone a long time."

Cris is a complete workaholic. He's in high end real estate in one of the wealthiest counties in the country. He's not Kutsenko kind of rich, but he and Helena have everything they want and then some. She's his interior designer, so she works just as much. But since they work together, they say they always have enough time for each other.

"Not really. Something must have really gone wrong with the shipment. He handles a lot of agricultural products, so if stuff is spoiled or something, it's probably a big deal. It's not like they could easily replace it. I don't know."

"He hasn't texted or called you?"

Helena sounds scandalized. Maybe she and Cris spend too much time together if she can't imagine a couple going a few hours without talking to each other.

"We don't talk that much during the workday. We're usually too busy. I know I'm with him every morning and night." I shrug. "It's not like I'm unsure when we'll see each other again."

No one needs to know how desperately I want him to contact me, how much I don't know whether I'll see him tonight. I think about what it must take for Pasha not to react, and I try my damnedest to channel that. My thoughts keep racing, but I must do a decent job hiding them because no one's asked me if something's wrong. My mom looks completely normal, but she covers my hand with hers every so often. Do I want to know why this looks so easy for her?

I just put Pandora back in her cage when my phone pings. I pull it out of my pocket and notice the number is unavailable.

Pandora kale R.S.

"I'll be right back."

I go through the kitchen and slip out of the front door.

"Pasha texted me."

Anton and Aleks swivel toward me as I stick out my phone.

"Pandora? Like your pet?"

Aleks glances at the door as he asks.

"Yeah."

"What's kale? He hates it."

Heat singes my ears at Anton's question.

"So do I. It's just a thing between us."

Both men know what I mean. I can just tell. Fucking mortifying.

"But what's R.S.? I get the first two. He wants to be sure I know it's really him. But I don't know what the initials mean."

Anton pulls out his phone as Aleks answers me with information that doesn't make me feel better.

"We do. You and your family need to go back to Maks's."

Chapter Twenty-Five

Pasha

Robert Simms, mercenary extraordinaire. I catch sight of him just before the sack goes over my head. We thought he was involved in the trouble Maks and Laura had when they got together, but as far as we know, the ghost had nothing to do with it. That's why this is so fucking infuriating. I don't know who hired him or why. Someone outsourced their dirty work. Even the kid who got me doesn't give me a clue.

The man-child has a dragon tat on his arm that I spotted. It links him to the Triad, but I can tell he's not a member. Wishful thinking or a family connection, but this kid is not part of the Chinese mafia. He's all fingers and thumbs from what I can tell. He and Simms traded once they pulled us from the car, and now the man-child's having a hard time getting Afonso to cooperate, and Robert is trying not to blow his stack.

I'm resigned to my situation. Robert won't kill either of us, but Afonso doesn't know that. Robert leaves no trace, and that's how we know when he's been on a job. The man's bank is his mattress. He trusts no cell carrier, so he uses burner flip phones. He has no social media presence and doesn't even use email. His lack of traceable identity makes him obvious. But as good of a mercenary as he is, which means he's accepted death, he doesn't want to die at any Russian's hand. He knows he needs to keep me alive, which means Afonso by extension.

I'm not sure where we are yet, but I nearly took a header coming down some stairs with this fucking bag over my head.

"Who're you turning me over to, Simms?"

"Shut up."

"You won't kill me, Simms. You don't want to die the way my family would end you. So who are you working for, Simms?"

I know he hates me saying his name so many times. He probably hasn't told any of the people working for him his real name. I only know because of how we met. He was—an "associate"—of Vlad's. The closest thing Vlad probably ever had to a friend. I met him as a kid, and some of the techniques I know are what Robert taught me. This means he also knows what my family and I are capable of. He doesn't want that kind of tortuous death. But if tossing his name around means someone hears and remembers, well then, he should have left me alone. If it means he ends up killing the mercenaries he hired to help, that's a few less for me to deal with later.

"You'll know soon enough."

"You might have cleaned up the mess you made, but I haven't heard Ilya. If you left him for dead, you left evidence. Tsk, tsk. That's not like you."

"How do you know I didn't bring his corpse with us?"

"Because I don't smell blood."

I can't smell shit under this sack.

"You can't smell shit under there."

Hmm... So much for that bluff.

287

"Doesn't change the fact that you will have cleaned up any shell casings. You will have swept my car for anything to identify me. The fact that there will be nothing for the police to work with will tell my family that it was you."

"So? They don't know where you are. I have your belt, remember? Your buckle is done."

We all have trackers on our belt buckles. Only someone who knows us well would know that. It also means my family can't find me as easily. But holy fucking shit when they do.

"You must be making more money that God for this job, Simms. But what the fuck are you going to spend this fortune on? You don't see daylight, you fucking vampire. And my family is going to kill you before you can give it away. Or does someone have something of yours? I could see you going after a Mancinelli, a Diaz, or an O'Rourke and believing you'd survive, but us? Robert, what the fuck happened that you're willing to die the way Anton will kill you? And that's if you get lucky. If my dad is the one who gets to you...KGB and bratva. Fuck, I might start praying again because if you have a soul, you're going to need it."

"Your dad is old and soft."

"He's still my dad. If he has to tell my mother I'm dead, he will make you suffer beforehand. Someone must have something of yours or know something you don't want them to tell."

"You talk too much, Kutsenko."

That is not something most people would accuse us of. Most people call us uncommunicative.

"I already know it's you. Taking the fucking bag off my head. It's not like it's a secret that you took us."

Robert rips the sack off my head. I blink in the dim light. I glance around and spot Afonso to my left. He's doing the same thing I am, blinking and looking around. We're in a basement. I see stairs leading up—they're the fuckers I nearly fell down—

and there are bare wood beams holding up the ceiling. Someone moves behind me, but I don't react. I won't let Robert think I'm jumpy. I glance at Afonso again, but he's watching something off to his left. I squint, but I can't see anything. There's no sign of anyone else, but to shoot up the car and pin it from both ends was more than a two-person job.

"I'm surprised to see you. I thought the rumors were true. You're too old to go on missions anymore. Or some injury keeps you out of the field. You look fine to me."

"Who says I haven't been on ops? Maybe I was in plain sight, and people just didn't know who I am."

I catch sight of the guy who's barely twenty. He was behind Afonso, so I didn't see him when I first looked. Now that I can see his face more clearly, he looks familiar.

"Triad, how'd you wind up with Simms?"

The guy startles, and I learn several things. The Chinese haven't trained him. They're almost as precise and controlled as we are. Thank you, communism. He depends on Simms because the kid looks at Robert, not me. He's looking for reassurance. The last thing I learn is that I can break him.

"Cat got your tongue? Or is it a dragon? Robert, you need to teach your son to wear long sleeves if he's going to have such distinguishable tats."

I switch to his first name. I pray the informality will lull him into relaxing, since it only took me a fraction of a second to know why he seems familiar. He looks just enough like Simms to be sure of his paternity, even if most of his features must come from his mom. Oh-ho-ho. I have leverage now.

"I didn't know you had a son, Robert. Clearly, you left some evidence behind somewhere."

"Shut up, Kutsenko."

He wishes to maintain the formality. Doesn't mean I'll give up.

"You're not denying his paternity. You confirmed it. Useful."

"If you don't shut the fuck up, I will knock you the fuck out."

"Seriously, Robert. You shouldn't have involved him. You know what's going to happen. Send him away, and I'll make sure no one touches him. If he's here..."

"I don't need your pity offer that's already useless."

"He's not ready for what's going to happen when my family finds me—finds you. I can see it, and you know it. Send him home before you get him tortured and murdered."

I sense the bravado of youth come into the kid's eyes. Stupid motherfucker. That shit'll guarantee he's dead. At his age, I knew I wasn't immortal. I'd been shot more than once before I was twenty. I'd been stabbed a couple dozen times by then. I had no bravado because I knew I could die. I almost did a few times. I remember the first time I got shot. I was sixteen. My mom spent a small fortune on my funeral suit. It pissed her off when I got shot again at nineteen because I was nearly twice the size. I couldn't fit in the expensive suit. That time, fortunately, she decided not to get a suit until she was sure I would die. I lived, and she saved a few hundred dollars. She loves me unconditionally, but she's also Russian, which makes her inherently practical and thrifty. The stabbings always hurt, but they were never serious enough for her to consider my funeral apparel.

"Are you my executioner or just my chauffeur, Robert?"

"Fuck, you talk a lot."

"Ah, chauffeur."

"How'd—"

It's the kid who talks, but he snaps his mouth shut when Robert pushes him away from Afonso.

"You mean besides you confirming it? Your dad's threatened me, and he's bitched. But I'm still alive. Someone else wants me, so your dad can't do anything."

"I can beat the shit out of you. You won't look so pretty soon."

It's a weak threat from Simms, and it doesn't take my attention away from his son.

"Chicks dig scars. How'd you wind up with your dad? The tats tell me you're connected to the Wo Shing Wo, but there is no way you're an active member. Who's your mom?"

The Wo Shing Wo is one of the oldest crime organizations in Hong Kong, and often the most powerful.

"Don't answer that."

Robert snaps as he glares at his son. I narrow my eyes as I study the kid, trying to think if I know anyone in the Cantonese mafia who could be his mom. They aren't super active in New York these days, and they mainly stay out of the other syndicates' business. They prefer to deal in meth rather than cocaine. But I've known members for years.

"You're Wing-hung's nephew. Your mom must be the dragonhead's sister. Not bad, Robert. She was hot back in the day."

"Don't talk about my mom—"

"Shut up."

"You haven't trained your puppy very well, Robert. Does he still piss on the rug? Maybe you should send him back to Hong Kong and let his uncle housebreak him. That's where Ju was last I heard."

The man-child looks like he wants to say a shit ton more. He wants to know how I know about his family. He wants to know more about his dad, who I get the distinct feeling he doesn't know well. If he did, he would shut up. I decide now's a good time to dial it back for a while. I've learned plenty from my questions. It's time to learn by observing.

Robert gestures to his nameless son, and they head up the

stairs. Afonso watched and listened to most of my exchange, but he kept staring to the left.

"What do you see?"

I keep my voice low. We're each tied to a chair, our arms behind our backs. Robert is getting lazy in his old age. He should have gagged us.

"Nothing. Just thinking. That guy is a mercenary, isn't he?"

"Yeah. The best in the business."

"Then why'd he bring his son into this?"

"I don't know. But you can see the resemblance, can't you?"

"Yeah. Is Simms known for ties to the Hong Kong mafia?"

"No. Just the opposite. Simms has no loyalty to anyone. He's loyal only to himself. The moment the job is done, and he gets his money, he's done. If someone hired him to kill the man who just paid him, he would. In a heartbeat."

I switch back to Robert's last name, following Afonso's lead.

"He doesn't strike me as paternal."

I look toward the stairs and consider the body language I saw. They didn't seem in tune at all. Even if they aren't the affectionate type, it was like they were strangers.

"Me neither. I don't think they know each other well. Maybe the kid showed up as an oopsies. But I don't know how he would have found Robert. Sergei usually has an idea of where Simms is floating, but it's practically impossible to pin him down."

We fall silent for a long time. I don't have a clue how much time goes by. It drags though. By the time Robert returns, I'm starving. It has to be mid-morning, if not later. I'm unprepared for him to unbind my hands from behind my back. He cuts the existing zip ties to do it, but he immediately puts on a new one. At least, now they rest in my lap. I'm extra suspicious, though. He does the same for Afonso. He still has our legs and bodies tied to the chairs, but I can use my hands to an extent.

The man-child has a gun pointed at each of us as Robert repositions us. They disappear, but it isn't long before Robert's son returns with food trays. That's a shock. I'm not eating shit from it, despite how my stomach grumbles. I'm not drinking anything either.

"What's your name?"

"John Doe."

He hands me a tray, then gives the other to Afonso. My future father-in-law and I exchange a glance. He's not touching his tray either.

"Really? Already accepted your death. Good to know. Your dad's going to get you killed. Leave before my family arrives."

"Your family isn't coming here. I know my dad is a ghost. No one is finding you."

"You might know a couple things about your dad, but you don't know him well. Otherwise, you'd know he lied. My family will find me, and the amount of jobs your dad's done for us won't gain him any forgiveness. As his son, and being in this house, you're as good as dead if my dad and brother find you."

"House? How'd you know?"

"I guessed, and you just confirmed it. You don't know what you're doing. You aren't ready for something like this. You are not trained, so you will die. If Simms is willing to have you here, then he's willing to let you die. He knows he could die on any mission."

"If I die, my uncle will avenge me."

"Maybe in Hong Kong, but your uncle isn't coming near the Russian bratva in New York. There's a reason they already keep their distance."

"How do you know they're not the ones who hired my dad?"

"Because they gain nothing and will lose everything. You

should call your uncle. Tell him what's happening. I guarantee he gives you the same advice. Get out while you can."

"I don't believe you."

"Fine. Then prove me wrong. Call him. Put him on speaker, so I can hear him tell you I'm wrong. I might not speak Chinese, but I'll tell from his tone."

The man-child considers what I say. He's slow, but he pulls out his phone. He doesn't put it on speaker, and I don't understand a word he says. But the kid's expression tells me everything I need to know. His uncle is pissed. Man-child darts his eyes to the stairs several times when he isn't looking at the floor in front of him.

"I was right, wasn't I?"

I ask the moment he hangs up.

"It doesn't matter. I can't leave."

"You should find a way."

"No. I'm staying. I'm not ditching my dad."

Stupid kid. Fine. Play macho. I let the things on my tray slide to the ground.

"What the hell?"

When he reaches to pick them up, I swing the tray and hit him in the head. I can't put as much force into it as I want since my upper arms and chest have rope around them. But it's enough to knock him over. I lean as far as I dare and almost topple over, but I snag his phone from his back pocket. I drop it onto my lap and cover it with my hands.

"What? Gonna cry to your daddy that you got too close to the mobster, and he knocked you on your scrawny ass with a tray? Run away, little boy. This Russian bear will eat you for dinner."

"Fuck you."

"I'd prefer your mom."

"Motherfucker."

He draws the knife I saw attached to his belt. He swings at me, but he's incompetent. He isn't holding it right. I get one hand around his wrist as he aims for my heart. I squeeze until the knife falls. He lunges for it, which puts his throat within reach. I wrap both hands around it and choke him. I hold him until he passes out. I'm not looking to kill him. Afonso maneuvers himself and grabs the knife, but he has to rock forward. He lands hard on his hands and knees. He gives it to me, and I'm soon sawing through the zip tie at his wrists. With his hands free, he shreds the zip tie binding my hands together. He works on getting the rope off of him while I pull up the text app. The burner phone is shit. It doesn't have any type of lock. I type Sumiko's number because reassuring her I'm alive is the most urgent thing I can think of.

Pandora kale R.S.

I know she'll show it to someone in my family. I trust she isn't alone. They know I'm missing by now. They will have found Ilya and the car. She'll know it's me from the first two words, and my family will know I mean Robert Simms. Once the text is sent, I delete the record. It takes a few minutes, but the response comes.

Sumiko: Where?

Me: Basement but don't know where we were already in Queens car ride was quick can't be far maybe five minutes his son is here mom is Wing-hung's sister

I know Sumiko is showing this to someone in my family. They'll understand it, even if she doesn't.

Sumiko: Hurt?

Me: No Afonso fine

Sumiko: U alone?

Me: Don't know simms and son here maybe

others but haven't heard them

Sumiko: Call. Sergei will trace.

I dial Sumiko's number. Thank God we're old fashioned and still memorize numbers. It's for situations like this. I can feel my phone isn't in my back pocket, and I'm certain the man-child took Afonso's, too. I say nothing to Sumiko or whoever has her phone. I suspect Robert has the basement bugged. He isn't running video feeds, or he would be down here already.

Sumiko: Got it, little bro. Coming.

Anton. I close my eyes. Never have I been happier to be reminded that I'm the kid brother. I hang up and delete the texts and call entry. I untie myself before slipping the burner into my pocket. Mine now. But in case I can't hold on to it, I don't want Sumiko's number easily traced. Afonso frisked the kid while I was texting. He hands me the kid's wallet.

James Hu Simms

His name is in the Roman alphabet on his Hong Kong driver's license. I can't read anything else except for what I assume is an expiration date. There's no photo and nothing that looks like a date of birth or age.

"Anton responded. I called, and Sergei traced it."

"I heard it ring. Sumiko is with them, then?"

"Yeah. They'll all be at Maks and Laura's. It's like our head-quarters, I suppose. We just all end up there, even though it's not official."

"Will they come for us?"

"They're on their way. I don't know who else is here, but when they arrive, you go to those shadows and stay in them until we get the all-clear."

"What about you?"

"I have a hostage."

Afonso glances at James and nods. Now we wait.

Chapter Twenty-Six

Sumiko

"The issue at Bear Imports' warehouse was a bigger deal than Pasha thought. There was an armed robbery. A guard got hurt, so he would feel much better if we went over to Maks and Laura's again."

That's the best I can think of. And from what Anton and Aleks told me, the attackers injured Pasha's driver. It hadn't been easy explaining away the intense security at my future in-laws' home, but once my family was inside and realized just how rich the Kutsenkos are, it made sense. Especially when they met the twins. They understood why new parents would worry about their infants. I don't know how I'm going to justify the added guards in the hallway.

But by the time we leave, only Aleks and Anton are in the hallway. I know the men must be in the security room or already in cars that will escort us. Sergei and Misha are in the lobby. I glance at Sergei as he looks at Anton. I shift my gaze to my future brother-in-law, who is looking at his partner. Sergei sends him some type of silent message because I can tell Anton relaxes. Or maybe it's just the reassurance of being back in Sergei's company.

Life is cruel, and this family has had too many servings.

"Pasha's building seems pretty secure. Why can't we just stay there?"

Helena is eying Sergei, Misha, and Anton with the same assessing look as she did Pasha when she met my boyfriend. It's laughable. Obviously, Sergei and Anton have no interest. Misha is like the rest of the men in his family. He will never look in a married woman's direction. I look at Cris, who seems oblivious as he holds Helena's hand. She redeems herself when she turns to my brother and pulls his raincoat closed and huddles next to him under the umbrella I gave them. It's a loving gesture, and her smile appears sincere.

I point out more of the sights as we make our way to Queens. I'm on edge as we drive. I don't know if I'm waiting for us to be attacked or what. My soon-to-be in-laws—that's how I think of them, even though Pasha and I aren't engaged. *Yet*— keep up the conversation when I run out of things to mention. I'm sitting next to my mom again.

"Sumiko, when this happened in Brazil, we had none of the resources the Kutsenkos do. It took nearly a month before your dad came home. They will find *papai* and Pasha, and we will put this in the past."

"What if whoever this is still wants to hurt Pasha's family to sabotage their deals with *tio* Ignácio?"

"Then the Kutsenkos will handle it."

When we get to the house, it's crowded. I recognize Anton's parents and Sergei and Misha's, but there are two men I don't know. They're introduced to me as Christina's and Ana's dads. Why the hell are they here? There's an air about them that matches the bratva men. I wonder in particular about Ana's dad, since it's obvious he's Russian.

"Where are you all going?"

Davi sees the men gathered in the foyer, and it's clear they were waiting for us before they left.

"There was a lot of damage done, and we're going to check our other warehouses and businesses."

Maks answers, and his voice downplays this crisis. I wonder if any of them are staying with us, but it looks like they're going as a family. God help these people. There are eleven huge, muscular men who I'm certain are all armed, standing together. There isn't a dad bod among the older men. I watch the husbands and wives say goodbye while I stand with my family. The couples keep it short, but there's no missing the passion between any of them. The men are all in their suits, just like they always are. But I don't doubt they'll be in tactical gear before they reach their destination.

"Have you had lunch yet? Are you hungry?"

Laura comes to stand with us, Konstantin in one arm and Mila in the other. It was particularly poignant watching Maks kiss each of his children's head before he kissed Laura a second time. He's intimidating on sight. They all are. No one would guess how Maks dotes on his children and Laura. I saw Pasha holding Mila the first time I came here. I'm confident he'll be the same with our children. I just need him to get home, so we can get married and work on those babies. We can at least practice for a while.

"We had a big breakfast, so we didn't have lunch before we left. I can help you in the kitchen."

Laura nods as she hands off the babies to Ana and Christina, and Alina joins us. The moment we're in the kitchen, Alina wraps her arms around me. I burst into tears. I'm so fucking terrified. I don't want to admit it to anyone, but I know the wives understand. They must be just as scared for their husbands. But I don't understand this life yet. I don't know how they live with it. I don't know what to expect when the men leave like this.

"Will they go to that place once they get Pasha and my dad?"

"The warehouse?"

Alina whispers as she glances to the doorway.

"Yeah."

"Some will. They'll bring Pasha and your dad here. They know I'd kill them if they didn't."

I try to put myself in Alina's shoes. It's her son who's missing. Now her other son and husband are off to do Lord only knows what. I tighten my arms around her. She strokes my hair down my back and kisses my forehead. She's a pillar of strength, and I feel like a leech. She's struggling too, yet here I am, taking comfort from a woman who might lose her entire family. I try to pull away, but she doesn't let go.

"I know this life, Sumiko. I accepted it thirty years ago. Time doesn't make it any easier, but I know what to expect. It takes time to learn how to do that. It's unfair and terrifying. None of them chose this life, but it's the one we live. Take comfort from those of us who already know."

"Thank you. How do you do it?"

"I love my family more than I fear their death. It's a struggle at times like this. But what choice do I have? I would never walk away. They never can. So I accept it, and I pray. Often."

"I love Pasha. This is a trial beyond anything I ever imagined. But I want him in my life too much to walk away. He makes me too happy to give him up."

"That's how I felt about Grigori as soon as we met. I knew he was my *rodstvennaya dusha*."

"Soulmate." I smile up at her and see her surprise. "Anton taught me."

"Russians have written some of the greatest and some of the most tragic love stories. We believe in a love that overcomes adversity."

That's true. At least Pushkin had some optimistic tales. But regardless of their outcome, they're all passionate and dramatic. That feels familiar.

"Alina is right. It doesn't get easier, per se. But you realize you love the man too much to live without him. The happiness outweighs the fear."

Laura moves around the kitchen with ease now that her sisters-in-law are watching the twins. I'm in awe of the woman. She's a brilliant lawyer, a loving wife, a doting mother, and a compassionate friend. She gives me a quick squeeze before getting out plates. The three of us are quick to make lunch for my family. My brothers and Helena must sense not to ask too many more questions. We watch movies and play cards and board games as the afternoon passes into the night.

I don't understand what's taking so long. If they knew where the attackers held him, and it's in Queens, why aren't they back? I want to demand answers, but from whom? None of the women's phones have made a noise or vibrated. They know nothing either. Galina arrived just before dinner. She'd been at work and unable to leave since she's a pharmacist. She, Alina, and Svetlana are holding it together and making it look so easy. It's giving the rest of us courage. My mom fits in with them like they've been lifelong friends. I can tell my mom is anxious, but she's keeping herself occupied. She keeps looking at the twins, then at me. I had no idea she was so keen on grandchildren.

We finish dinner, and I can tell my brothers and sister-in-law are getting suspicious. How do I explain why no one is back or why we have to spend the night?

When my phone rings, I nearly jump out of my skin. But it's Pablo. He's not who I want to talk to right now, but he might know something. I slip out of the living room and up to the room where Pasha took me the night my family arrived. Holy shit, that was last night. That feels like ages ago.

"Hello?"

"Sumiko, *dios mío*. You're safe. I was scared you were with Pasha. Maks called and said the meeting was off. He thinks we did this. He thinks agreeing to the meeting was a trap, and that we were coming to his house to attack."

"Were you?"

"What the hell? I can't believe you just asked that. Laura was like my sister for nearly thirty years. She has babies now. I would never target her or her family. Half of this fucked up shit started because my brother got dick hurt that she didn't want him. He broke a sacrament. Women and children are untouchable."

"So I've heard. Yet you were scheduled to come here, and now my boyfriend is missing. Did you lie to us about that recording, Pablo? Are you playing me?"

"No. Are you at Laura's? Please tell me you are. You need the extra security. I know what Pasha has at his place, and it's not enough."

"How do you know?"

"For fuck's sake, you really think any of us doesn't know what kind of security our rivals' have. Are you safe?"

"Yes."

"That's all that matters."

"No, it's not even close. Pablo, they have my dad too. Pasha isn't home and with me, so what matters is finding them and bringing them home. If this isn't you, then who did this?"

"I truly don't know. It's most likely the Irish or the Italians, but no one is claiming this. Both sides deny any involvement."

"Some other Eastern European group? Other Russians? People from another city?"

"It could be any of those. This is why I said you needed to stay away from Pasha. They've had trouble with the Irish and Italians within the past year, and the fucking Russians reached across the ocean to get them."

"But you're innocent in all this."

"Personally, yeah. But my family is up to its fucking eyeballs after Juan dragged us in."

I don't want to give away that Pasha's family is on their way to rescue him and my dad. I don't know who to trust, but if they aren't a Kutsenko or related to them, then I won't even consider it.

"I have to go. My family is here, and we're busy."

"Doing what? Do they know?"

"Playing games. And not the type you're playing with me. You don't care. You're fishing for information that I don't have or won't give. If you want me to believe you—to trust you—then find my dad and boyfriend. If you can't do that, then leave me the fuck alone."

I hang up. I know I'm taking a lot of this out on Pablo, but I truly don't know if I can trust him. I know now that the calls and texts weren't him, but someone knows he wanted me back or at least wanted to break Pasha and me up. It doesn't negate the texts before Pasha and I went to Croatia or what I received while we were there. Despite the few distractions, Croatia was perfect. I want to run away with Pasha and go back. Go anywhere that isn't here and in the middle of a shitstorm.

I go back downstairs, and the women except for Helena look at me. I shake my head and mouth, "Pablo." Laura's eyes widen, and she's out of her seat. She practically drags me into the office she shares with Maks.

"What did he say?"

"He wanted to be sure I'm safe. He didn't think Pasha's security was enough."

"What else?"

"I don't remember half of it. I was too annoyed and distracted. He said it wasn't them, but no one else has taken responsibility. He doesn't know who it is. He agreed it could be foreign syndicates or someone from another city."

Laura pulls out her phone and unlocks it. I wait as she listens to it ring.

"Where the fuck is my cousin?"

She puts it on speaker.

"Laura, I don't have him. I swear."

"Why should I believe you?"

"Because I left Juan for dead in Minnesota because of his choices. I nearly killed him, gave him enough money to last him a couple days, and left him there."

"Yeah, and he used that money to come back here and stalk me and my children. He wasn't so dead until Maks took care of what you couldn't. He was your brother. It never should have been yours or Enrique's decision what happened to him. He nearly got me and my babies killed. You did a shit job punishing him."

"You're right; he was my brother. What the hell was I supposed to do? Would Maks kill any of his brothers? He wouldn't even abandon them somewhere."

"He and his brothers would never have done what Juan did."

"I still don't know where Pasha is. You and Maddie were my sisters until a year ago. *Tío* still has yours and your sister's initials on his arm. He—"

"Is that Laurita?"

I recognize Pablo's uncle's voice from calls Pablo took when we were together.

"*Si*, Enrique."

"Are you safe?"

Laura doesn't answer.

"Laurita, answer me. Otherwise, I will think you aren't, and I will come to make sure you are. If you don't want two dozen Colombians on your doorstep, answer me."

"I'm fine. But where is my cousin?"

That's the second time she's called Pasha that. Not cousin-in-law. Not my husband's cousin. Her cousin. I could see Maks and his brothers as my cousins. I've already sort of started thinking of Anton as my brother. It's the one bright spot today.

"We don't know. But whoever this is, is trying to fuck shit up with Ignácio if they took his brother."

"Has anyone talked to my uncle? Does he know what's going on?"

"I spoke to him this afternoon, Sumiko. He's heard nothing from anyone, but he had three hundred kilos of product stolen from a ship on its way to Valencia."

"Spain?"

I think that's where Valencia is.

"Yes. He's been dealing with that. He didn't know about Afonso and Pasha. He's pissed and threatened to come up here."

"That's probably exactly what whoever did this wants."

"Laurita, that's what I told him. I know Pasha is your family. Pablo and I are doing what we can to figure this out."

I tap Laura's arm and shake my head. I mouth, "They don't know."

She nods, understanding that they don't know there's a

rescue team already in action. But why haven't they gotten home yet? I can't let my mind race down that path right now.

"Enrique, call me if you learn anything. If I have to find out from Maks that you knew something or learned something and didn't tell me, you may as well laser Maddie's and my initials off your arm. We will be at war."

Laura hangs up. We stare at each other, neither knowing what to say. My gaze wanders over the bookshelves and the computer on each desk. I think about Pasha's laptop at our place. As scared as I am that he's not coming home, it solidifies one thing for me. He is my future, and we are home wherever we are together. I'm moving into the condo completely. I don't care what happens to my furniture and stuff at my apartment.

As I look around, a thought niggles at the back of my mind. It's like a kernel waiting to pop. It's not quite ready for me to know what it is, but it's trying to take root. We hear nothing by the time we're all tired enough to go to bed. It's my mom who saves me the trouble of trying to figure out a lie. She claimed a headache while Laura and I were in the office. I don't know if she was pretending or really asleep, but she looked passed out when Ana checked on her. No one wanted to disturb her.

I sit cross-legged on the bed as I try to get my thoughts in order. Seeing Laura's laptop made me think of Pasha's. Since he's the bratva's accountant, I wonder if there's anything on there that might help me figure out what's going on. I close my eyes and think about what might be on it that could be of use. He probably has software like what I use on my work computer. He can probably data-mine. If he has the tools I suspect, he can run massive amounts of data through the program, and it'll spot irregularities.

Could I get into his computer and into the program? I don't know what his passwords could be. They're probably twenty characters long. Even if I could figure that out, it's at the loft in

Manhattan, and I'm at his cousin's place in Queens. I know I can't leave. Only a Kutsenko brother or cousin, or Sergei and Misha, could authorize it. I'm not even sure if Grigori and Radomir would have the authority. There's no way off this property without going past guards.

I get dressed, but I have no clue what I'm doing. I slide my shoes on and slip downstairs. I find my raincoat, and I glance up the stairs as I put it on. I never thought to ask if there's an alarm system. There probably is. How am I going to get out of the house?

Laura said some tycoon built this house during Prohibition. He had something to do with the railroads, but she said he used to run gin he distilled in the basement. She joked it was kismet that they lived here, especially since Maks didn't know until Laura stumbled upon a tunnel. I don't know the last time anyone's been through it. I don't know if it's even open. And I don't know where it ends. But I'm about to find out. Please don't let me get trapped or set off the alarm. Pasha's going to kill me as is.

Chapter Twenty-Seven

Pasha

Afonso and I can hear people moving around upstairs, but no one has come down for James. He woke only a couple minutes after I knocked him out. He's now bound and gagged to a chair. It makes me wonder if Robert left, and whoever is upstairs doesn't know about James. He watched the stairs for the first hour, but now he just stares at the floor.

I know it takes time for surveillance and to strategize, but where the fuck is my family? With the burner phone, I can keep track of time. It's been hours since Sumiko texted Sergei had my location. My estimate is that it must be night by now. I want to text someone and ask what the fuck's happening, but I don't trust the unsecure line. It was risky enough doing it once. I don't need anyone else tracking this phone to know who I'm contacting. And I need to keep the line open and not drain the battery. One of the few character traits Vlad drilled into me I don't loathe about myself is my patience. I have an abundance of it. I might let myself lose my patience from time to time, but even that is calculated.

A strategy is always better than an impulse. We had to repeat that mantra for hours. Vlad was a shit businessman, but his years in the KGB taught him to be a strategist. Anton was his best student. I trust my brother to get me out without getting anyone killed. I know they have to wait until the best time, and that might not be right now.

"Who's upstairs?"

I fist James's hair as I ask. When he doesn't make a sound immediately, I yank back, practically snapping his neck. He mumbles something, so I pull the strip of his shirt from his mouth.

"The guys from the op, probably."

"How many?"

"I don't know. I've never met them before. I was in a car with my dad. I don't know who else was there. They were on bikes and in cars."

I recall hearing motorcycles revving over the gunshots. It's how they surrounded us so easily and left so fast.

"Where's your dad?"

"He got a call. He said he would be back in a few hours. I think it was to get the last payment."

"And these people just walk into his house?"

"It's a safe house. He doesn't live here."

"Does anyone know about you?"

James shakes his head and winces since I'm still holding his hair as I grill him.

"I'm still willing to give you the chance to go free. If you're here when my family comes, I won't protect you. You'll face them like the man you're pretending to be. You want to work for a mercenary, then you'll die like one."

James struggles with the decision. It's written across his

face. I know the moment he chooses life over his father.

"Get on a plane and go home. Go back to your uncle or go wherever you want. Either you have money, or someone gives you a generous allowance. Your clothes tell too much, poor little rich boy."

"How do I get past the people upstairs?"

"Carefully. That's your problem."

"How do you know I won't tell?"

"Because you know they'll keep you here too. You want out."

He nods. I'm rolling the dice, and I am not feeling lucky. Like, not even a little. No one ever showed me mercy. No one ever gave me the chance to get out. I spent years praying someone would. It took twice as many years to understand I couldn't beg, barter, or bribe God. We all still believe. We were raised Russian Orthodox and were altar boys. But lapsed seems a rather benign word. I don't think God has forsaken me, but forgiveness from my sins might elude even Him. I've come to terms with never being offered an out.

I untie him, but I keep his phone and his knife. He bolts for the stairs, but he goes up them quietly. He eases open the door and listens. Voices filter down to us. I listen and count. I hear at least three guys and two women. The amount of noise from people moving around makes me think there are more. Shit. I should have asked how many floors the house has. Could there be more on a second story?

He slips through the door, and no alarm goes up. I creep up the stairs and open the door a hair's breadth. I can't see anything but a sliver of lamplight, but I can hear more. Everyone speaks English, and no one has an accent.

"When's he supposed to be back from the drop?"

"He said like midnight. We're supposed to wait here if we want to get paid."

It's a guy and girl talking, and they both sound young. Younger than me, but not as young as James.

"You leave and he gets back, there's no payday for you. More for the rest of us."

A second guy joins the conversation.

"Who hired him?"

The woman asks the sixty-four-thousand-dollar question.

"Don't know, don't care. Money is money as long as it's in my pocket."

"But are we sure Simms will get paid? What if they kill him?"

It's the first guy who sounds antsy.

"Simms has lived this long and hired me for other jobs. I'm still here. He'll get paid, and the man is like immortal or something. He'll live."

Once more the bravado of youth, a trait I lost at fourteen. What they say grates on my nerves because, to my ear, they sound stupid. But I remind myself that normal people, even normal mercenaries, don't have the same history I do.

"Just drink your beer and stop worrying."

The second guy's voice trails off, so he must walk away. Where's he going? Who's he going to talk to next? So many more questions than answers.

I join Afonso, and we move the chairs into the shadows. I give him James's knife. Neither of them checked me. Simms is getting lax these days. I have my blade in my right pocket. I pull it out and flip it open. I rest it on my right thigh. The waiting continues.

A cacophony brings me awake from a doze. Another follows a moment later. They're flash bangs. Stun grenades. It's time.

"Afonso?"

"Yeah."

"Stay behind me until it's all clear. They will shoot first and ask questions later. We wait."

I know better than to charge into the fray with no bullet-proof vest or gun. A knife won't do shit against one of my family's semi-automatic rifles. There's gunfire and screams, but none sound like ones someone in my family would make. How do I know? Because none of them would ever scream. That shit got a brother or cousins beaten within an inch of his life when Vlad was alive. How the fuck Bogdan is even remotely normal is beyond me. He bore the brunt as the youngest Kutsenko brother. Vlad used to fuck with Maks and his brothers by hurting Bogdan first. He has an unnatural pain threshold now. I worry that's what will kill him. He won't admit when he's near death, and we won't know how serious a wound is until he's gone.

My mind fills with thoughts that are useless right now. I chide myself for being distracted. But I know my mind wanders, so I don't count the seconds until someone finds us.

"Pasha!"

The almighty roar can only come from one man.

"Papa! The basement."

Where I'm standing allows me to see the door. It's nearly pulled from the hinges as my dad appears. He takes half the stairs, then leaps down the rest. I may be almost thirty, but my dad's hug is more life sustaining than my next breath. He ruffles my hair, but he doesn't let go.

"Sumiko?"

I need to know before I can do anything else.

"She's fine. She's with her family at Maks's. Afonso, your wife and other children are there. They were going to watch movies when I left."

I hear an accent that makes me lean away from my dad.

"You brought Liam?"

"He's a *vor*, and we didn't know if we would find the Irish here."

Christina's dad became a made man when Christina's life was at risk. He's a former British Royal Marine and a massive Highlander, way burlier than any of my family. His day job puts him in a position to learn about New York's syndicates. He knows some of the Irish mob personally, much to his disgust.

I recognize Yuri's voice, too. Ana's dad is the same age as mine. He didn't escape an upbringing like my dad's. I know he knows what he's doing.

"Let's go. Anton's going to pull this place down around our ears if he doesn't see you soon."

Afonso follows me, and I follow my dad. I see the dead bodies strewn across the floor, but the sight barely registers. But from the way Afonso gags, he's unprepared for the bloodbath. Someone grabs me by the back of the shirt and pulls me backwards.

"About time, old man."

"You were out past your bedtime, little brother. Someone had to bring you home."

One time. Just one time while we still lived in Moscow. Misha, Bogdan, and I stayed out after dark. Our parents flipped. They thought the Podolskaya bratva took us. Anton, Sergei, and Maks had to look for us. They were ready to beat us within an inch of our lives because our moms threatened to take wooden spoons to the soles of their feet and our dads held up their belts to chase them out of the door. We learned later that none of us was ever in danger of corporal punishment, but it convinced all of us to follow the rules.

"Take me to Maks's. I need to see Sumiko."

Maks walks over as I speak.

"We will. We'll get a team in to deal with the bodies. A few are alive and will be our guests. I'll head back to my house with you and Afonso. Laura texted a while ago to say Pablo called Sumiko. They talked to Pablo and Enrique. I don't know the details, but I need them before I deal with *los Diaz*."

Maks looks anything but eager. Anton, Maks, my dad, and I surround Afonso to shield him from the worst of the carnage as we leave the house. We're about to get into one of the SUVs when Maks's phone rings.

"Laura, slow down. I can't understand you. I'm putting you on speaker."

"You need to come home now. I went downstairs for some water after nursing. I felt a draft as I passed the basement. I went down there to check. The tunnel was open. I ran upstairs and checked all the rooms. Sumiko's gone."

"What?"

I'm ready to snatch the keys I see in Misha's hand. He and I usually drive on ops because we're the perfect mixture of reckless and purposeful when maneuvering the veritable tanks we drive.

"I don't think anyone took her, Pasha. I looked around, and her clothes are gone. So are her shoes. She's not wearing the pajamas your mom lent her the last time you stayed over. They were laying out on the bed. Her raincoat and umbrella are gone too. She left, Pasha. No one took her."

Why would she do that? Where did she go? I turn to look at Afonso, but he looks horrified. He doesn't know where she went. Where is my *malyshka*?

"Hey, I found your phone and gun. What's wrong?"

Niko joins us and hands me my phone just as the screen lights up.

"Sumiko, where are you?"

"You need to come home, Pasha."

Chapter Twenty-Eight

Sumiko

I should have known Maks and Laura's basement wouldn't be somewhere dank and filled with cobwebs. It's mostly a gym. There's top of the line equipment and weights that look well used. Pasha told me there's a gym with a boxing ring that one of the brothers owns. They usually work out together, but I suppose one workout a day isn't how they got to be their size. I look around for anything that might be a door. I doubt it's going to be obvious.

It takes me fifteen minutes and moving a stack of boxes before I find it. The door isn't easy to open, but I manage. Barely. It's heavier than I expected. Thank heavens phones have flashlights, or I would enter blind. I pull the door most of the way closed, but use the corner of a box to keep it from sealing me in. I don't know how I'll get back into the house otherwise. It's nearly the middle of the night, so I only have a few hours. I have to be back before anyone wakes. I can't just stroll back in through the front door.

The tunnel is pretty straight, and the ceiling is way higher than I expected. They definitely made it for men. There was probably wood planking at one point because some steps are on something smooth. It would have made moving crates easier. I let my mind wander to the bootleggers to keep my fear at bay. But it feels like it was all for naught when I come to the end of the tunnel. It appears sealed. My hand roams as I try to find a handle or release. There isn't one. I'm defeated and frustrated, but I give the door an old-fashioned shove with my shoulder. I practically fly through it. Either I'm stronger than I thought, heavier than I thought, or the builders wanted a fast way out.

As the door swings open into the dark, I fear I wound up in someone else's house. What if it connected to a safe house back in the day? I take a hesitant step out and breathe fresh air. I'm in the wooded area behind the property. I suspect Maks might own it too to keep anyone from building too close to his house. I look around for any men on patrol. I see nothing, so I strain to hear. It's silent, which is freaky. Aren't there any nocturnal animals around here?

I'm not sure which street I'm going to as I find my way out of the trees. I have to walk a long suburban block before I figure that out. I'm booking an Uber as I walk. The middle of the night in a wealthy suburb of Queens means there's a twenty-minute wait for someone to get me. Then almost half an hour to make it to Pasha's building.

Pasha gave me a key to his place before we left for Croatia. I came and went as I wanted because of work and the gym. I didn't think about security until I get to the building's front door. Now what? They have to know what's going on since they're bratva. I nod to the night concierge and try to look natural. His brow furrows, but he says nothing. I wonder who he's going to call to tell I'm here.

I enter the elevator and use the biometric pad to hit the top floor. Pasha had to add me to that as well. I'd never used anything like it before meeting him. Swanky to say the least. Intimidating more than anything.

I let myself in and check on Pandora. She chatters as I lift her out of the cage. She's calming, so I take her with me to the office. As I flick on the light, I wonder if someone might be watching the loft from outside. Should I use my flashlight again? What if someone sees the light? I might not have a security detail like usual, but there is security here. I turn on Pasha's laptop as I sit at his desk. Now what? I don't know any of his passwords. I don't want to try a bunch of shit and get locked out.

It's some type of numeric pin to get in. It won't be his birthdate, and his brother's or parents' birthdates are too obvious. I try the twins', but that doesn't work. Since he and I share a birthdate, it isn't mine. I sit, thinking for a few minutes. I try the date we met. Huzzah! Success! Such a sweet man I have.

The software he might run doesn't have a desktop icon. I have to search a bit, but I finally find it. This password is going to be way harder. If it's one of those auto-generated and suggested ones, it could be anything. For the sake of argument, I open the program to see if it's saved. It isn't. If Pasha wrote it down somewhere, I have no idea where. I don't think he'd keep a sheet of paper or a little notebook of passwords near his computer, but I check all the desk drawers. I feel horrible snooping, and I force myself not to pay attention to anything that isn't obviously a password.

I practically tear his office apart before I move to our bedroom. He has a fireproof safe with things like his birth certificate and Social Security Card. I know the combo because my stuff is in there, too. I pull everything out and go through it all. There are childhood photos in there, and there's a man who looks exactly like Grigori in most of them. I realize it's Kirill,

Grigori's brother and Pasha's uncle. I can see where the Kutsenko brothers get their dark hair and a strong dose of their looks. But their blue eyes come from Galina, and I see her features in them too.

But what I don't see is anything that could be a password. I look through his half of the dresser and find nothing. Then I move to the closet. It took coercing, but he convinced me to learn the combo for the gun safe. Obviously, I'm not opposed to firearms. I'm dating a man who carries one everywhere. I just didn't want them strewn around once we have kids. I'm just not experienced with them beyond an old boyfriend taking me to a range once.

I keep my fingers away from any triggers as I feel around. It's the last case that hits gold. It's a small notebook that matches the color of the gun case inlay. I pull it out and flip through it to the end. I figure that's where the most recent passwords are. It's in fucking Cyrillic. Of course, it is. I swipe my fingers over my eye and along my temple as I sigh. I slide down to the floor and open my phone. I search the internet for a Cyrillic translation site. I finally find one that I can figure out how to use. I start from the back and work forward as I convert the names of various computer programs into Roman letters. I find the codes to all his family's computers and some stuff that must be on Sergei's. I think I've found what I'm looking for, so I go back to the office. Pandora follows me since I'd set her on the floor when I came into the bedroom. She's better than a puppy. I put her on my shoulder when I sit at the desk.

I get into the program, then I hit the next obstacle. What the fuck am I searching? I know R.S. stood for Robert Simms. He's supposedly untraceable. No one in this day and age is completely untraceable. I click around some more on Pasha's computer until I find something that looks like it'll let me search bank records from various places in New York and all the major metropolitan centers in the world. This isn't even remotely legal to use or to have.

Robert Simms

I doubt that's his real name. He's a mercenary, so he's methodical. If he's older than Pasha, then he's lived a long time. I can't imagine longevity—life or career—is part of the profession. He's probably highly intelligent and a problem solver. I don't feel like he would have chosen a pseudonym at random. Maybe, but maybe not. His name might be an anagram for something else. I write out all the letters on a sheet of printer paper.

Then I start arranging them:

Tim Srobrems

Bremroos

Rossborem

Reis Strommb

Brommst

Brommts

Briems Orms

Bo Strimmers

BMT Morrises

Rom Timbers

Berim Storms

Brtims Rose

None of them seem likely at all. They're ridiculous. This was a waste of time. But...Until I come up with another way to think of finding his real name, I consider my list.

I cross out a few that are too outlandish.

~~BMT Morrises~~

~~Brtims Rose~~

I search the names I'm not sure are real. I'm almost to the end of my list when I find something that might be important.

Berim is a mountain in Kosovo.

Okay then. I don't think Storms is a likely choice, but I could rearrange a couple letters.

Stroms: etymology. Means "what towers above" from Proto-Slavic...

I don't know what Proto means, but I recognize Slavic. A mountain in Kosovo and a Slavic last name. I toggle back to the bank record search program and type in Berim Stroms. I wait as the software chugs along. It feels like it takes forever, but I remind myself it might be searching millions of accounts. When it stops, there is a list of hits. London, Madrid, New York, Milan, Cannes, and Belgrade.

Belgrade? I know there was a war in Kosovo, and it gained its independence from Serbia. Which means Belgrade makes no sense to me. If this guy is Grigori or Radomir's age, then he might have been KGB or something equivalent. I don't know too much about the Soviet era, but I know Serbia used to be part of Yugoslavia, and Belgrade was the capital. Maybe that's why a—what's someone from Kosovo called? A Kosovoan?—has a bank account in Belgrade. A left-over connection.

Cannes is the south of France, so either this guy has really rich clients, or he likes expensive vacations. I start with the New York account and run it through Pasha's accounting software. This account has nothing interesting in it. Just living expenses for an average person in New York. I try Belgrade next. Nothing for twenty-five years. It's open but empty. Milan. Not Dublin but Milan. Nothing in Ireland but something in Italy. I run that next.

Holy shit. Jackpot. This program looks for patterns and irregularities. Within the past month, there have been a series of deposits of varying amounts. But just like Robert Simms is an anagram, the amounts are numeric equivalents. They're different amounts, but all made up of the same numbers. They're coming from different sources, and none are sizable. They're more like paycheck amounts, but it can't be a coincidence. I've been doing foreign valuations and audits long enough to convert Euros to dollars easily.

There are other deposits scattered among the transactions, but having the program search and organize them makes them far more obvious than just scanning an account statement. I page back through older data and find similar patterns. I look at where these deposits are from. I have to search the internet for the names. Restaurants, dry cleaners, bars, hotels, convenience stores. All places that handle large amounts of cash. All places where money is laundered.

I go back to the first software and search the name of the most recent deposit source. It's a restaurant, and it's easy to find their bank records. I toggle back over to the data-miner and enter the new information. Hmm. Someone from Palermo likes to eat out in Milan. Sicily. That sure as fuck isn't a coincidence. I dig deeper, and what do you know? This—Palerman? Palermian? whatever—receives wire transfers from a bank in New York. A bank in Queens.

It's not a national chain, so this takes a little more work to figure out, but I'm still able to get into it. Lots and lots and lots and lots of cash deposits. Like lots. There are just as many cash withdrawals. There're only a few debit card ones. Enough to keep the account from looking entirely suspicious. Except for the wire transfers. Maybe it's a minimum wage immigrant sending money home to Palermo. But not when that money winds up in an upscale bank in Milan.

Now to find out who owns this account.

Gabriele Mancinelli.

I know that last name. Why do I know it? I close my eyes as I try to recollect. It hits me like a freight train. *Cosa Nostra.* Pasha has mentioned the other syndicate family names a few times to make sure I know them. I don't recognize the first name, but I know the last.

I dig around in other accounts under this guy's name. Damn. Someone is paying him a healthy allowance every month. The dumbass is trying to launder his own money. He gets these hefty cash deposits into one account, then immediately, there are all these small deposits into the account that originates the wire transfers to Milan. Fucking moron. Whoever pays him has the sense to do it in cash. I look at transactions from the main account, but it's mostly restaurants, a gym membership, rent, and a slew of strip clubs. Classy.

I try to wrack my brain for any first names Pasha told me, but the only one I remember is Salvatore. He's the don. I search his accounts, but they're all legit. They're what I would expect from a man who owns corporations. I bet the Kutsenko Partners' accounts and Pasha's business accounts look like this. This man is doing his dirty work under the table. But he's certainly wealthy enough to be paying Gabriele's allowance. What else is he paying for?

Carmine.

The name comes to me as I digest everything I'm seeing. Carmine Mancinelli. He's one of Salvatore's nephews. I don't know how Gabriele connects to the don, but I remember Pasha saying Salvatore only has young daughters. Carmine was involved in shit that happened to Ana. I look for him next. As the program runs, I glance at the clock. I'm running out of time. I've been here way longer than I thought. I look at my phone, but there are no new notifications.

A transaction from a few days ago comes up, and I don't recognize the routing number at all. It's international though. I do a quick search, and my mouth drops. São Paulo. *Tio* Ignácio. I see the exact same amount return. The transfer was rejected. My uncle didn't take the money. But Carmine is trying to buy or bribe my uncle. I search the Brazilian bank account, and it comes back as a real estate investment firm. Definitely my uncle.

I don't know where Pasha is or if he has his phone back, but it's time to call him.

Chapter Twenty-Nine

Pasha

"Sumiko, what the hell are you doing at the apartment? Why did you sneak out of Maks's place? How—"

"Pasha, you need to come home. I know who did this."

"Is someone there? Who took you? Mother—"

"Pasha, stop. Am I on speaker?"

"No.

"I left through the tunnel in Maks's basement. I took an Uber to the loft. I did a shit ton more that you're probably going to spank me for a month of Sundays over. You may even leave me over it. But I know who did this. I don't know if it's safe to tell you over the phone."

"It's not. I'm coming."

"You should bring your family. My dad too."

"Why?"

"Just please come home."

"All right. I love you, *malyshka*. I'm not going anywhere."

"I love you too."

I've heard my cousins call their wives *malyshka* enough times not to care who hears me call Sumiko that. My heart was still racing from Laura's call. Sumiko's only amped it up. How the hell does she know what's going on? Then it dawns on me.

"She must have found a money trail. She wants us all to go to our place. She says she knows who did this."

"Do any of us wait for Simms to come back?"

Bogdan looks at Maks, who shakes his head before answering.

"He's bound to have seen us by now. He won't come back."

"He might if he thinks his son is still here."

Eleven startled faces turn to me.

"I don't know even a fraction of the story, but Simms had a baby with Wing-hung's sister. The head of Wo Shing Wo is his uncle. His son was with him for this."

"Did we kill him?"

Bogdan looks back at the house.

"No. He's barely more than a kid wanting to be a man. I let him go. Told him to go home to his uncle or wherever he wants. He has a dragon tattoo, which is what tipped me off. But he's untrained. He's not ready for the shit his dad or his uncle are into."

"You don't think he ran straight to his dad?"

"No. He ran away from him. Let's go. I need to see Sumiko."

"I need to see my daughter, and I need to call my wife."

Afonso speaks up for the first time. I almost forgot he was there, but he's standing next to me. Niko gave him his phone as I got mine back. We pile into the SUVs, and I'm behind the driver's seat. We'll see if even Misha can keep up. The streets are fairly empty given the time, but they get more crowded once we cross in Manhattan. Fortunately, I have an underground parking garage. Even if it is the middle of the night, we don't need people staring at nearly a dozen men in black tactical gear. We gain entrance through the elevator and ride up to my floor. I bolt down the hall and burst into my apartment. Pandora peeps louder than I've ever heard before and jumps down from Sumiko's lap and bolts under the sofa.

I'm across the living room in five strides. Sumiko is in my arms, her feet brushing my shins, and her lips plaster to mine before I know what's happening. Her kiss is everything. I'm safe. She's safe. We're home. My heart finally slows, and I feel like my lungs can fill with air again. Our kiss draws out, and I don't give a shit who we keep waiting. When we tear ourselves apart at last, she rests her head on my shoulder. I still haven't put her down. Her voice is barely audible.

"Daddy."

The moment she says it, she cups my jaw and kisses me again. We rest our foreheads together as we catch our breath. I kiss the tip of her nose.

"I'm here, *malyshka*. Daddy's home."

I whisper in her ear, and all I want is to disappear into our bedroom and fully convince myself she's okay. But despite my raging hard on, we can't. I put her down, but she doesn't let go of me. She twists in my arms and points to a stack of papers on the coffee table. I can see they're bank statements. With a sigh, she releases me. I'm not so quick to do the same. She gives her dad a hug before she kneels beside the table and spreads out the sheets.

"Pasha, I broke into your computer. I searched your office, then the bedroom. I found the notebook. I'm sorry I invaded your privacy, but I'm not that sorry. I figured this out because I snooped."

"I don't give a shit. Everything in this place is yours as much as it is mine. What did you find, *krasivaya?*"

I keep nothing incriminating here. Except for my laptop, and she had to crack the codes.

"I found your bank record locator and your analytical software." She slides a page to me. "I guessed a mercenary is probably methodical and even a little nerdy. His name is an anagram."

I see a list of what I guess are supposed to be names. Some she crossed out, but she circled one.

"Robert Simms is probably from Kosovo.'

My pronouncement shocks the shit out of all of us, except Afonso, who looks lost. Simms has never had even a trace of an accent. He sounds American.

"How'd you figure that out?"

It's Christina's dad, Liam, who asks first. He's in national security. The kind that takes him overseas a lot to places the U.S. government shouldn't be seen. He knows of Simms.

"This name. Berim," I point to the page, "is a mountain in Kosovo. The last name is Slavic too. Stroms. Czech or Slovak, I think. Not Kosovar, but maybe."

"Kosovar? I wondered what people from Kosovo are called. He has a bank account in Belgrade that dates back to the Yugoslav days. Are Kosovars Slovaks?"

"No. Most are of Albanian or Serbian descent. Some are Bosniak, Gorani, Romani, or Turkish."

Yuri's better equipped to answer that than I am. I know about the wars in Kosovo because I had to learn about them in school before we left Moscow, but I know little more than that. Losing my dad in the Second Chechen War turned me off to studying anything about Balkan conflicts. They were too violent, even by my standards.

"My guess is his bank account in Belgrade really is a holdover from the Soviet days then. But I found he has accounts in New York, London, Cannes, Madrid, and Milan."

Sumiko points to each page as she names a city.

"Milan? The Mancinellis?"

I make the leap immediately.

"Yes. Someone named Gabriele."

"Motherfucking son of a bitch. I'll fucking skin him and feed it to him."

Niko looks and sounds calm despite what he says, but there's a cat five hurricane brewing. After what happened to Ana, he has every right to have first crack at him. Yuri right after him.

"I traced the money in Milan to Palermo. From there, it wasn't hard to find it here in New York. Whoever Gabriele is, he thinks he's laundering his own money within the same bank. He's receiving large cash deposits, then withdrawing them, and depositing them into another account in much smaller amounts. He's sending it to Palermo from there. Simms—Stroms—got a series of deposits that weren't the same amount, but each amount had the same numbers in it. The only thing I don't know is what's happening to the money after it reaches Milan. It just appears to be sitting there collecting interest."

"In cash?"

Aleks wonders what I do.

"No. But they're amounts that look like they could be paychecks. Gabriele's the one handling suspicious amounts of cash. He's using what I think must be an allowance from Salvatore. There's nothing shady about the don's account. I remembered the name Carmine, so I searched him. He made a huge wire transfer to a bank in São Paulo, except it got rejected. *Tio* Ignácio sent it back."

Afonso pulls out his phone. It must only ring once because he starts a rapid conversation in Portuguese.

"He's demanding to know why his brother got money from the Italian Mafia...he wants to know when they got in touch...

he wants names...he wants to know whether my uncle and their family are in danger...more than usual."

Sumiko whispers as she interprets the side she can hear. Afonso nods several times, and he sounds more relaxed when he says goodbye.

"My brother doesn't know names since no one uses real ones, but he said a young guy, with an American accent that sounds heavily Italian, contacted him a couple months ago to set up a new deal. Ignácio isn't interested. He has a good trade going on with Spain and Dubai, plus what he sends to you and the Colombians up here. Apparently, the guy got pissed and started getting pushy."

"Did he say what names they go by?"

Maks and the rest of us know Gabriele and his friends think they're the second coming of John Gotti. They like having what they think are gangster or mafioso names. It makes them sound even more childish since no one dubbed them the monikers. They made them up.

"No. He said he got some threats a few weeks ago, but he thought they were from a Bolivian supplier. Then there were some supply issues from Colombia, but neither was a big deal. A few calls sorted things out. Then the wire transfer happened, and the young guy calls him back. He demands they do business. My brother hung up on him and canceled the deposit."

"That must have been around the time of that first text that went to all four women."

Niko's glowering as he speaks. We consider him and Bogdan the most easygoing in their family and even among the cousins. But they aren't with family business. I don't try to stake my claim, even though I'm the one they ordered taken this time.

I help Sumiko back onto the sofa, and I wrap my arms around her. I can't handle not touching her. Her head rests on my shoulder, and she closes her eyes. I'm physically content, even if my mind is jumping from one idea to another.

"I'm so proud and grateful, *malyshka*. You are so intelligent and resourceful. No one thought that Simms's name might be an anagram. We've tried to figure him out for decades. You could work for Sergei."

Sergei nods, but everyone knows she never will. Laura doesn't touch any of our bratva businesses, which means Ana doesn't either. All the construction business Christina handles is on the up-and-up. Sergei's hacking is so far from legal, it's ridiculous to compare him to any regular background check agency. Sumiko will never dirty her hands with our business after today.

"I'd like that."

She sits up, and she's dead serious.

"No."

Maks and I respond at the same time.

"We will talk about this later, *malyshka*. But the answer won't change."

"Yes, it will."

I see the stubbornness that I've caught hints of, and it's about to be unleashed in full force.

"Do you still see our future the way you said?"

"Of course."

I'm indignant that she would ask, but I know she's about to launch her attack.

"Wives can't testify against husbands and vice versa. Anything I do goes through you, not Sergei. I handle only financials. But it's obvious I can do a lot of the same background checking Sergei does, but I follow the money. Once we marry, I'm as good as being bratva when it comes to how the law will look at me. I may as well be useful."

"You are. You handle our legal enterprises. This isn't negotiable, Sumiko."

"We'll see."

We aren't arguing exactly, but it's a damn good thing I'm not old-fashioned about anything but women and children not being involved in bratva business. Arguing with me in front of my family would be a horrible choice in other households. But I'm glad she's comfortable speaking up in front of them. She leans back against me.

"I will never argue with you in front of other bratva members. I swear."

I glance down at her as she whispers. She understands it's a matter of appearances. Other members aren't as progressive as my family.

"What now?"

Aleks, the ever practical one, brings us back on topic. Except no one has an answer yet. It's Maks who will have the final say, so he lets us know what he wants for now.

"We can't strike back yet. We need to watch Carmine and Gabriele closely. I'm not telling Salvatore shit this time. He obviously didn't muzzle his dogs, so I don't trust him to deal with this sufficiently. I don't want a full-fledged war with him. We still have unresolved issues with the Irish. Taking Carmine and Gabriele to the warehouse isn't an option."

Sumiko tenses at its mention, but that's where anyone else would wind up if they did this. But as the don's family, it gets messy. If they were Salvatore's minions, then we wouldn't think twice about ending them.

"Afonso, you can come home with me. I'm sure Akiko wants to see you. The rest of you go to your own places. We meet at my place in the morning."

Maks stands and shakes out his pant legs. Sumiko hugs her dad again, and we walk everyone to the door. I can't shut it fast enough. I pull her into my arms, and we're kissing as I walk her backwards to the bedroom. We leave a trail of clothes, but we only make it to the door before Sumiko remembers Pandora. Cute little thing, but a cock block. She gets the little beast out from under the sofa, puts it back in its cage, and returns to me. She takes my hand and leads me into the bedroom. We're a tangle of arms as we finish undressing.

"I need you, *malyshka*. I need to be inside you, but I won't rush you."

"I'm ready, *fofinho*. I have been since the moment you walked through the door. Fuck, it was so hard with everyone around us."

"It was hard."

I waggle my brows at her, and she giggles. It's so good to hear that after I feared I never would again. I knew my family would come, but I feared it wouldn't be in time.

She presses my fingers between her legs. Her dew coats them, so I lick it off. Her breathing grows shallow as she watches. I sweep her into my arms and lay her on the bed, following her onto the mattress. Our kisses are a race to devour one another as our hands roam. She wraps her legs over mine as I thrust into her.

"Fuck, baby girl."

"I know. Don't ever leave my pussy."

"If I could stay here forever, I would."

"A daily dose of the little blue pill?"

"Hourly, if it wouldn't kill me. An erection lasting more than three hours..."

"I know, but I would make sure we put it to good use."

We're moving together, and other than moans and grunts, we aren't talking. But we are communicating. We know how much we crave hearing how we satisfy each other. Neither of us needs to be this noisy, but we love it.

"Daddy, I'm so close. I can feel it."

"Come, *malyshka*."

It only takes a couple more thrusts before she grabs my ass and holds me in place. My cum pulses from me, and I love knowing I'm filling her with it. She's mine. All mine. And one day, we'll make babies with it. But for now, it brands her.

"You're mine, Pasha. My pussy is the only one getting your cum. I like knowing you're leaving part of you in me. I hope that isn't too gross."

"I get it. I was thinking the same thing."

"Branding me with your cum?"

"That's exactly what I thought."

"Good."

"Sumiko, you know you will always be the only one, right? I love hearing you claim me, but I need to know that you believe what you're saying."

"I do. It's still hard to believe sometimes, but you would never lie about this. There's honor among thieves, I guess. You haven't brought anyone else into your world. You wouldn't do anything to push me out. I know how committed you are because of that."

"But you get that it's because I love you. It's not because this is a life sentence for you. If you want to walk—"

"Finish that thought, and I swear, Pasha, you will not sit for a week."

"You'd spank me?"

"If you suggest I leave you, I will. I'm not going anywhere. Pasha, will you marry me?"

"Yes."

I answer without a thought. Then I look down between us.

"Did you propose?"

"I guess I did, *fofinho*. I know what I want, so I said it. Did I ruin it because you should have asked me?"

"Nothing is ruined, baby girl."

"Do you think it's just post sex hormones? Is it wrong that I asked while you're still in me?"

"I don't think it has anything to do with hormones. And I like that this is how we agreed. We're connected with no end and no beginning when I'm inside you. We've joined our bodies. Now I want to join our souls.

"*Rodstvennyye dushi.*"

I melt as I slide my arms beneath her and roll us. She draws her legs up and nestles against my chest.

"You said that perfectly. How'd you know that?"

"Anton taught me. Your mom said we were. I've been practicing it over and over in my head."

"You're more than the other half of my heart, Sumiko. You're all of it. I'll marry you tomorrow if you want."

She leans back and nods.

"My family is in town. Everyone I want to attend is already here."

"I don't have a ring for you."

"Walmart or Target have ones that'll work for now."

I laugh, and my cock twitches.

"I am not getting you a plastic ring for our wedding. There isn't a jeweler in the tri-state area who wouldn't make a ring for me in under a day. I'm very convincing."

"You're going to go all mobster scary on them?"

"No. I'm going to pull out a hundred grand in cash."

"A hundred—No. Pasha, that's ridiculous."

"It's not. If you pick something you like that is that much or more, then we get it. If what you want is less, fine. It's about getting what you want to wear for the rest of your life."

"Somehow, I don't think you're going to compromise with a jewelry store in a mall."

"Not even remotely a chance."

"All right, *fofinho*, if you insist I must have something ludicrously expensive to make you happy."

She tickles me, and I laugh. I roll us again as my cock springs back to life. What this woman does to me. Fuck needing a little blue pill. I have my *malyshka* to keep me hard. We move much slower this time. I suck her tits as she grips my ass. I support myself on one forearm. My free hand skims over her. I want to touch every inch of her. I start with her hair, smattering kisses on her face as I trace her features with my fingertip. I sweep my hand down her neck, over her collarbone. I cup her tits as I move back and forth, sucking and biting. She arches her back and whimpers as I pull away. My hand glides between them until the back of my fingers caress her belly. I draw them over her ribs before my hand sweeps down her thigh and pulls it over my hip. Then my hand finds her ass. I can no longer hold back as I squeeze her plump flesh. I lose control.

"Harder."

I grunt.

"Daddy, more... I need you...Fuck me."

"Gladly."

I pound into her as her nails claw my back. They'll leave marks, and I can't wait to see.

"Fuck, baby girl. I want to make you come."

"I'm so close."

Her head tilts back, and I attack her neck as she spasms around my cock. I don't relent. I'm holding on by a thread, but I don't want this to be over.

"I'm going to make my fiancée scream."

"Call me that again, Daddy."

"My fiancée. *Moya nevesta.*"

"*Meu noivo. Watashi no fianse.*"

She says it in Portuguese and Japanese. I'll be practicing those. She grips the back of my shoulder with one hand as the other fists the sheets. She arches off the bed before thrusting up her hips. She tightens her cunt around my dick, and I explode. Our kiss is sloppy and still ravenous. But we're replete when we finally relax.

We're tired, but neither of us wants to sleep. We don't let go of each other all night. We talk about wedding plans, and we agree we are doing it. We talk about her apartment and moving the last of her stuff here. We talk about a honeymoon as though I wasn't just held captive. We talk as though we're not in the middle of a shitstorm brewing into an all-out mafia war. The world will intrude tomorrow. For now, my *malyshka* is the only person in the world who matters.

Chapter Thirty

Sumiko

I stretch as I come awake next to Pasha. I roll onto my side and find him watching me. He strokes my cheek and presses a tender kiss to my lips. He pulls me closer and pushes down the sheet. I gladly inch closer when he pulls my leg over his hip.

"Ow!"

I'm not prepared for the first spank or the second and third.

"Ow! Pasha, I thought you wanted something else."

"I do. After. This is just getting your skin warmed up. I'm grateful for you discovering so much last night. But I'm not even remotely pleased that you wandered out of Maks and Laura's place through a tunnel. A fucking tunnel no one has used in like a hundred years. Then you took a fucking Uber. You just sauntered into the building. I checked my voicemail a few minutes ago. There are five messages from the guys downstairs, completely freaked out that you arrived without guards."

"I knew, if you'd been there, you wouldn't have agreed to

me leaving with anyone outside your family. With none of your family there, there was no one to come with me."

"And you couldn't wait until morning. You knew Anton and the others were on the way. You knew they were going to bring me home."

"No, I didn't. That's what they told me. But none of us knew that. They could have been taking you to a funeral home."

"If I'd died because someone took me, don't you think that's all the more reason for you not to gallivant on your own?"

"I didn't gallivant. I left your cousin's house and came straight here. I didn't leave here."

"You left without telling anyone and without a guard. Do you have any idea how panicked Laura was when she called Maks? Her voice was trembling."

That makes me pause. Let's be real. I knew I would freak people out if I wasn't back by morning. But I did it anyway.

"And I feel guilty about that. But I don't feel guilty about following the money."

"Which you could be doing right now after me picking you up from Maks and Laura's."

"I—"

"No, Sumiko. I need to know I can trust you, that you won't be impulsive. I need to know you take your safety as seriously as I do. I need to know for your sake and for any kids we have."

That makes me stop in my tracks. I see the fear in his gaze because he wants me to know how upset he is. It was impulsive. It could have waited. I shouldn't have left, and I was lucky nothing happened.

"I'm sorry, Daddy. I do take it seriously. I did it because waiting for you was excruciating. I did it because I wanted to be useful. I did it because I want you to make these people pay for putting you in danger. But it could have waited."

Pasha sits up, naked, and swings his legs over the side of the bed. He pats his lap, and I crawl to lie across it. He's hard, and I'm wet. This spanking is going to test me. I take a deep breath and wait, but the first slap doesn't come. Instead, Pasha runs his hands over my ass.

"*Malyshka*, my life is dangerous. We both know that. Being with me brings danger to your life. I know how selfish that makes me, and I will always feel guilty about that. But I love you too much to let you go. I want you too badly. I need you. I will always do what I can to keep the danger away from you. Please don't go looking for it. I don't know what I would do without you. I don't think I could—"

Pasha's voice cracks, and I glance up at him. He's staring straight ahead as he continues to stroke my ass. There's agony in his expression, and I realize how badly I've scared him and hurt him.

"I'm so sorry, Pasha. I can't keep using I'm learning as an excuse. I was selfish, too. I didn't do it to hurt you. Just the opposite, and I think you get that. I understand your need to be in control of this. This is one thing I won't defy you about ever again."

"I love you, *malyshka*."

"I love you, Daddy. May I have my spanking now?"

His hand lands across my flesh, and I kick my feet. Fuck. That was hard. Fuck. That one was even harder. He really wants me to learn my lesson. If the pained look on his face didn't do it, this spanking will. He rains down one blow after another. Some are on one cheek at a time. Some are across both. Some push my ass up as he lands them on my horizontal crack. It's one after another until I lose track. I stomp my feet and tense. Each time I do, he fingers me. He lets me get close, then he pulls away. It's relief, then torture. I don't know if it's worth

339

tensing, but I crave both kinds of touches. The intimate and the heavy handed.

"Stand up, *malyshka*. Turn around."

His hands go to my hips before he pulls me back. He kisses each ass cheek.

"Get on the bed. On all fours."

It's not a pose I liked before meeting Pasha. It made me feel vulnerable since I've seen myself in the mirror, and it's not flattering. But he loves it. As much as he enjoys looking at me while we have sex, he loves watching us from behind. He loves how he can touch more of me.

I hear him opening a dresser drawer, so I assume he's going to our stash of toys. I close my eyes, not wanting to ruin my surprise. I hear a bottle cap flip, so I assume it's lube. He presses the largest plug we have into me. I relax as it eases in. Then I feel the Ben Wa balls. They'd driven me crazy the other night. They'd been the perfect distraction, but they were a challenge.

"Come, baby girl. Let's have breakfast."

"What?"

I practically squawk. No. No. No.

"We need our sustenance for our wedding night tonight. We also have some calls to make. We should let our family know. We need a priest or minister or someone who can marry us. We need to pick out your ring, and I assume you want a dress."

"But I can be done in five minutes."

Pasha chuckles.

"I could be too, and it's tempting, since this is punishing me as much as it is you. But you'll have to wait."

"Until when? Good God. Not till tonight. Please don't say until tonight."

"Of course not. I can't last that long, and I have a hot bride to make me come. I'm not using my hand when I have your cunt."

"Romantic."

"I know."

He kisses my neck and behind my ear. He tugs my earlobe with his teeth, and I feel his dick twitch between us. I try to reach between us, but he snags my wrist.

"No. And you are not pleasuring me before I make you come."

"When will that be? This punishment blows."

I pretend to sulk as I slip a robe on. Pasha pulls on a pair of sweatpants. We get to the kitchen, and every step reminds me of the balls and the plug. Fucking-a. This is so hard. I pull out food while Pasha calls Maks. Everyone is still at Maks and Laura's. I let him speak to his family in Russian while I call my parents. Even if Maks and the others could tell them, I don't feel that's right.

"*Mamãe?*"

"Hi, sweetheart. *Papai* said you stayed at your place. Is Pasha all right?"

"Yes. They didn't do anything to him."

"Same for your dad."

"Is *papai* there? What about Cris and Helena and Davi?"

"We're here."

I hear Davi chime in. I must be on speaker.

"Pasha's talking to his family right now."

"Yeah. They went into the kitchen. They left us and are speaking Russian."

Helena sounds annoyed. I suppose it is kind of rude to abandon your guests, but Pasha knew I was calling my parents. I bet he told his family to give mine space for this call. I don't know that they'll be as excited as Pasha's family is. He doesn't have it on speaker, but I can hear voices.

"I proposed to Pasha last night, and he said yes. We're getting married today."

"What?"

It's Cris who speaks first. Then there's a jumble of voices.

"It'll be this evening to give us time to make arrangements. Mom, Helena, would you like to come dress shopping with me?"

"We were going to go sightseeing, but this is much better."

Helena sounds surprisingly supportive. I thought I understood her. Then she confused me with her reaction to Pasha and the other guys. But she sounds like the woman I've known since Cris was in college with her.

"Thanks. *Mamãe?*"

"I'll come. I'm just a little—shocked. Are you sure this isn't just being impetuous after yesterday?"

I realize I don't know what my brothers and Helena know. I'm going to have to tread carefully until someone fills me in.

"We've been talking about it practically since we met."

"But it's been a month. Barely. Not even. Please don't do this, Sumiko. I know you believe you're soulmates. If you are, then you can wait. Neither of you will go anywhere."

I glance over at Pasha, and some of his excitement has worn off. He opens a drawer and pulls out paper and a pen.

They're cool with a wedding. But it can't be today. We have to deal with this.

I nod. I take the pen.

My mom wants us to wait. She thinks it's too soon. I don't.

Someone says something to Pasha, and he has to focus on his call.

"*Mamãe,* you're in luck. Whatever went on yesterday with the shipments and break in isn't resolved. People depend on Pasha for their jobs. He has to deal with this. It was a bigger deal than I imagined."

"Good. I know this isn't what you wanted, sweetheart. But it really is for the best."

"Sure. Thanks, *mamãe*."

"Just more time to pick the perfect dress."

Helena's cheer is infectious. It lightens my mood as I hang up with my family. Pasha puts his phone down at the same time as me. He wraps his arms around me, and I sink against him.

"I'm disappointed too, *malyshka*."

"Can we slip away and do it, anyway? Have a reception or something later?"

"Do you really want to get married without your family?"

"No. And I know you don't either. I shouldn't have asked."

"You can always ask me for what you want and for what you need."

"Thank you, Daddy."

"Come with me, baby girl. Breakfast can wait."

He leads me back into the bedroom and guides me onto the bed after I shed my robe. He soon has me fastened into cuffs at my wrists and ankles. He bought the under-mattress restraints, and I love it. I wish he'd put me in them every night.

"*Fofinho*, if there isn't time to get married today, are you sure there's time for this?"

"I can make time. I always will if it's possible. It'll be often enough when I won't have that choice. While I do, nothing else exists beyond us in this room."

"Pasha, you're a good man. You might have to do bad things, but you are everything I could ever hope for. You treat me like I'm the most precious thing in the world. I love you."

"You are the most precious thing in the world. I love you too. As far as I'm concerned, you're as good as already my wife. We will make it official, though. Let me spoil you for a little while, baby girl."

"Yes, please, Daddy."

I grin as I wait to see what he has planned. He has a Wartenberg pinwheel in his hand. They've intrigued me for years. They're tiny, but they're supposed to be incredibly stimulating. I watch him as he approaches, then he takes a few steps back. He's teasing me. He pulls out an eye mask, and my leg jiggles in excitement.

"You're mine to play with, *malyshka*. Now and forever."

"Yes, Daddy."

He slides the mask into place, and I hold my breath, wondering where the pinwheel will touch me first. I wait for the soles of my feet, or maybe my nipples. Nope. It's the space between my pussy lips and thigh. I shriek. My ass is still sore, and the plug and Ben Wa balls are making me hypersensitive in that area. But, fuck, it's amazing. It's not just my leg moving. Now my whole body is trembling as he moves it up one side, over my clit, down the other, and across my pussy. He torments me over and over before trailing it down my thigh. It tickles, and it makes me try to press my legs together, but I can't because I'm restrained. The tip of his tongue follows the pinwheel, his teeth nipping every so often.

"Do you have any idea how much I wanted to wrap your legs around my waist while we were at that pool bar? How much I wanted to do what I am now. Kiss and lick and nip your thighs. I might be a little obsessed with them. Well, all of you really."

"You really like them that much?"

They're hardly what I consider my best feature. I might be fine with my looks and not interested in changing my weight or my appearance, but I still have parts of me I don't like. I do not like my thighs.

"Yes. I don't like skinny legs." He shrugs. "I like how yours fill my hands. I will never get enough of you. I love how I feel like there's always more of you to touch, to hold. It's like a kid who's in front of a buffet for the first time and can't wait to dump everything onto his ice cream. There's more and more to try. What I have with one serving isn't enough. I want it all."

"I'm not sure that I've ever wanted to be compared to a smorgasbord, but I appreciate the sentiment."

"It sounded way better in my head."

The pinwheel slides down my foot, and it tickles my instep. I tense, and the Ben Wa balls move within me. I can't help my moans as I shift. As the little tool of temptation makes its way up my other leg, the ache in my pussy edges toward painful. I try to breathe through it, but I find myself clutching the sheets.

"Do you need to come, *malyshka?*"

"I need you to make me come. I'm not close, but I want it."

"Good things come to those who wait."

"Fuck that."

"Such a dirty mouth, *malyshka.*"

He leans over and kisses me. His tongue swipes through mine. I try to capture it, suck on it, but he's too quick. He pulls back. I can't see what he's doing, so I don't know what to expect. I scream when his mouth latches onto my clit and sucks hard.

"Daddy!"

He doesn't relent. His tongue presses against it as he sucks. The pressure on the nerves is bringing me to the precipice, and I want to jump so badly. He'll catch me. But he pulls me back. He lets go, and I sense him stepping away. I hear the buzz of the little bowtie shaped toy. He has it on a pulsating setting. My pussy clenches and relaxes to the toy's rhythm. That only moves the balls inside me more. He presses the bowtie to my clit and runs the pinwheel over that sensitive crease between my pussy lips and thigh. I'm grateful for my recent wax. Brazilians know what they're doing when it comes to getting a cunt ready for a good fuck.

"Daddy, I'm getting close. May I come?"

"Yes."

I didn't expect that, but merciful saints. Thank the Sweet Baby J. I ball the sheets in my fists as the euphoria washes over me. He doesn't stop, instead moving the pinwheel over the puffy flesh. It tickles, which makes me clench my core again. That sets off another orgasm.

"Daddy, I want it to be you."

"You want my dick?"

I shake my head. That's actually not what I want. I mean, it is. But it's not just that.

"I want you. I want to feel you against me."

His fingers slide into me, and he works the balls, swirling them before withdrawing them. He climbs between my legs and lifts my hips. As he thrusts into me, he turns the anal plug. I clench my ass, which just pulls his cock deeper into me. The double penetration makes it so tight since there is nothing little about Pasha. His cock could win gold medals. He continues to twist the plug as he eases onto one forearm. It brings his body over mine, and I love the feel of him pressing me into the mattress. I love how large his body is. Not just the muscles, which are hot as fuck to look at and touch. But I love how small I feel because I feel protected. With him above me, the world can't get to me. I'm safe with him. I trust him implicitly in life and during sex. I've never trusted this unconditionally before. Considering his life, I think he could say the same about me.

We move together as much as I can, considering I'm still restrained. I love that he's in control, setting the pace, deciding how hard, leaving me at his mercy. I'm vulnerable in this position, but I know Daddy will take care of me, just like I know Pasha will when the roleplaying is over.

"*Malyshka*, I can't hold out much longer without pulling out. You're so fucking tight with the plug. I tempted myself way too much spanking you then toying with you. I'm too close."

"Keep doing what you're doing. I'm close too. Harder, Daddy."

He slams into me, and the bed knocks against the wall. Good thing he doesn't have neighbors. It hits the wall over and over, the sound seeming to encourage him. I dig my heels into the mattress as I tilt my hips to take him.

"Daddy, yes."

It's more like a croak than anything else as I come. Then I feel him. His body stiffens, and he rocks his hips in small motions. There's sweat across his forehead, and his chest glistens. I can see the muscles in his chest and shoulders flexing, his abs rippling with each breath. I glance at the arm that's supporting him, and the bicep is bulging. Then his other hand is cupping my jaw, and the kiss is languid. How we go from wild fucking to gentle lovemaking is beyond me, but we do. He's still moving, and I know that even though he's spent, he's trying to get me off again.

"Come for me again, *krasivaya*."

It doesn't take much for me to do just as he says. He reaches over me to unfasten my wrists. I wrap my arms around him as we hold each other.

"We should shower, baby girl."

"I know."

But neither of us moves. Soft kisses, nuzzling, rubbing our noses together. It's perfect. Until it isn't. Someone pounds on the door, then Anton is calling out to Pasha.

"Stay in the fucking kitchen. Our door is open."

Pasha scrambles off me, and I pull the sheets over me. He unfastens my ankles and tosses me my robe before he pulls on his pants.

347

"You could have knocked, then waited for me to answer."

Pasha holds my hand as we step out of the bedroom. His hair is a mess. Mine can't be any better. I try to run my fingers through it.

"I did knock. Like twenty times. You haven't answered your phone. Neither of you."

"We were busy."

"Little brother."

"Don't fucking scold me, Anton. I don't go bursting into your place when I know you're not alone."

"But Sergei and I answer our phones. We thought—"

I look between Anton and Pasha, who stare at each other. Pasha nods.

"You're right. I'm sorry, old man."

It's something I've heard Maks's brothers call him. I think I've heard Misha call Sergei that. It's kinda sweet, really. Maks, Sergei, and Anton have carried heavy burdens as the oldest in their family. They've had many people looking up to them for years.

"I came by to see how you're doing. I know you wanted to get married today. I'm sorry that won't work out."

"It's fine."

Anton gives Pasha a look that calls him on his bullshit. It's not fine with either of us, but we want our families to be a part of our special day.

"The morning is nearly gone. We have stuff to do."

It's barely nine-thirty. What stuff? Do I even want to know? Morbidly, yes.

Chapter Thirty-One

Pasha

The morning was hardly almost gone, but it was pointless to argue. Sumiko and I hurried to shower and get ready. Her hair was still so wet it soaked the back of her shirt. We got to Maks's, and the reception differed between families. Sumiko's was warm, mine was not. An outsider couldn't tell, but I can. My parents are the least pleased, and I feel badly when I realized they must have been terrified something happened to me for a second day in a row. Much to my chagrin, I had to explain that we'd left our phones in the kitchen and were too distracted to hear them. I pointed out that I'd just gotten off the phone with Maks and my cousins an hour earlier, but my mom's scowl only grew deeper. I apologized and kissed her cheek. I noticed Ana interpreted everything to Sumiko in a whisper.

My mom clearly wasn't annoyed with Sumiko because she enveloped her in a motherly hug and held on. She kissed her cheek and smiled. I pretended to grumble, but I kissed my mom again. With a nod, all was forgiven. My dad merely rolled his eyes and shook his head as I explained why we were late. But his hand clamped on my shoulder told me not to make that mistake again.

Now my brother, my cousins, and I are closed into Maks's office. My dad and Radomir are pretty much retired. They only go on ops when it's personal and our family is in danger. I have my laptop, and I'm going through the financials Sumiko discovered last night. Maks is on the phone with Salvatore, demanding to know where Carmine and Gabriele are. Sergei's surveillance of their places has turned up nothing. They've been missing in action for a couple months.

"Here. Salvatore just sent this. He says it's time stamped to prove it's recent."

Maks hands his phone to Sergei, but he shakes his head.

"Forward it to me by email. The phone screen is too small to do much besides watch."

Sergei's sitting beside Maks's desk while I'm at Laura's. It's not long before his laptop pings, and Italian voices fill the air. I lean to see, but I have to get up and walk around the desk. All eight of us are leaning over to watch men working in a vineyard. The camera zooms in on three men, and we all recognize them. Luca, Carmine, and Gabriele Mancinelli. They look like shit.

All three are deeply suntanned from hours outside. They're sweating, and their clothes look like rags compared to the designer ones they usually wear. Someone is yelling at them, and a man walks over to Gabriele. He grabs his shirt and pushes him toward a vine.

"*Troppo lento.*"

"Too slow."

Niko translates it on his phone and plays it for us.

Gabriele nods and works faster. The Gabriele I know

would have gotten in the guy's face and probably shot him. He, Carmine, and Luca look awfully humbled.

"Salvatore sent another video. This one is time stamped two and a half months ago. I'll forward it to you, Sergei."

Maks sends it over, and Sergei pulls it up. Fuck. The three *amincis* aren't looking so good in this one. They're looking around as they walk into the vineyard. Luca's arm is in a sling, and Gabriele is limping. Carmine hugs his ribs. It's clear they've taken a recent beating. The man from the first video appears and tosses baskets at them. Gabriele and Carmine catch theirs, but Luca's hits him and lands at his feet. The man kicks it down a row of vines and bellows something unintelligible at him. He pushes Luca several times until Luca picks it up. As he straightens, the man's fist drives into Luca's face. Blood spurts everywhere. The man's bellowing something in Italian. The video ends abruptly.

"Here. Listen."

Sergei captured the audio and ran it through a translation program. The synthesized voice speaks.

"You're little bitches crying for your mamas. You're lucky Salvatore didn't kill you. But I might. Work or no food and water. Work or I beat you again. Work or I will kill you. You sacks of shit are my problem now because I owe the don a favor. This is how he calls it in. You lazy fuckers. He knows I'm more likely to kill you than free you, so you're stuck until he calls you home. Worthless turds."

"An Italian gulag. Hard knock life for those pussies."

I shake my head as I go back to my laptop. A Tuscan labor camp. So rough. They should try a winter or summer in the Siberian steppes. Poor little rich boys.

"Are the time stamps real, Sergei?"

Niko leans over his cousin's shoulder, so close his nose practically touches the screen.

"Back off. Are you so blind you need glasses, old man? Or are you going to sniff out a clue like a fucking bloodhound?"

Sergei playfully pushes Niko back and shakes his shoulders. He doesn't need to crack his knuckles, but he does.

"Drama queen."

It's Anton who mutters, but it's said in jest. I keep sorting through files as Sergei works. He takes about fifteen minutes to authenticate the videos to his satisfaction. They're legit.

"So how the fuck is Carmine or Gabriele sending money to anyone?"

I'm wondering the same thing as Misha.

"Do they have someone doing it for them? Managing their accounts?"

Bogdan leans against Laura's desk as he watches me work and asks.

"No. No one else is authorized on the accounts. Someone could make deposits, but they couldn't make these withdrawals. And nothing is on an automatic payment."

"Maybe they have phones or computers when they're not in the fields."

"I don't think so, Misha. I think that would be a luxury, and that guy doesn't seem interested in giving them any. You saw how they looked."

Sergei shakes his head as he points to his computer screen. I can't see what's on there, but it must be a freeze frame of them. I lean on my right elbow that rests on the desk. I scrape my thumb above my top lip as I think. I'm staring into space, but my mind is mulling over the bank accounts. For the sake of argument, I open up Gabriele's accounts at the New York based bank. The one he's trying to launder money into and uses to send the deposits to Palermo is new. I look at the date on the bank account and check the date on the older video. Someone opened the account ten days after they shot the video.

It's a smaller bank, so less visibility, less scrutiny. Who opened this account in Gabriele's name? Someone had to because it wasn't Gabriele. The first deposits were cash and not at an ATM. Someone went into the bank.

"Sergei, could you get into the security footage from Gabriele's bank? Someone else had to have set up this account the money's filtering through. I'm curious who."

"Let me see."

I show him the information I have for the bank's routing number and address. I don't think that does Sergei any good, but it's what I have. He works as everyone watches him.

"I'm in. Now I just need to scroll back to that date. It's going to take a minute since this is twenty-four-hour footage."

A moment later, Maks and Bogdan are swearing so loud the rest of us look to see if our moms are coming.

"Motherfucking Finn O'Rourke. Because Declan and Donovan didn't cause enough shit. Finn's trying to fill their shoes. Fucking dead man walking."

Maks is livid. He fists his hands as he leans forward on his desk. I'm shocked as shit. This was not the twist I saw coming. I thought it might be one of Salvatore's men or even someone else in his family. The O'Rourkes were never on my radar.

"So what's he doing? How does he get the money from the legit account to the one he created?"

Aleks asks me what I'm sure everyone is wondering. I don't have an answer for certain.

"My guess is he opened this account under Gabriele's name with fake identification. He linked the two accounts, and with Gabriele away and without access, no one knew. He's taking the money Gabriele received from Salvatore and making it look like Gabriele's sloppy and can't wash the money properly. That's certainly believable. Fucking ape. Finn's actually stealing from Salvatore to pay Simms to take a hit on me, so we'll blame Pablo. All the while, he thinks his hands are clean. Crafty bastard, I'll give him that."

Bogdan shakes his head in disbelief before he speaks.

"We knew it couldn't be Gabriele. The man is dumber than a dog licking its dick. I assumed it was Carmine. Finn assumed Salvatore would never tell us what he did with Luca, Carmine, and Gabriele."

"True, Bogdan. But I think he also assumed no one would figure out the money in the first place."

"What now?"

Aleks looks at Maks, who's calmer but definitely not calm.

"Let's wait and see if Finn moves any more money. In the meantime, I think Mr. Stroms—Simms. What-the-fuck-ever— has worn out his welcome in New York. If he doesn't want to go to the mountain he's named for, he can go to the Flushing River. I'll give him that choice for his ashes."

"I'll have him picked up."

Anton pats Sergei's upper arm as he walks past. I wait to hear what else Maks says, but I'm eager to see Sumiko. Part of me wants to tell her what I figured out and see if she has any suggestions, but I don't want her to get any more involved. Despite what she said yesterday, she is not working for Sergei or me. Maks looks at me.

"Pasha, it's your choice. Deal with Simms—Stroms— whoever the fuck he is—however you want. Just kill him so we can deal with the rest of this shit."

"Are you going to tell Salvatore?"

Bogdan crosses his arms and leans back against the wall as he speaks. I can tell he's itching to have a go at the O'Rourkes. Finn wasn't involved in any of the shit that happened with Laura and Christina, but he's guilty by association. The Irish are still shuffling their people, trying to come up with new lead-ership since everyone they've had in the past year is dead. I'm proud to say we did that. No women and children. If they'd just adhered to that, they'd all be alive. Or at least they wouldn't be dead because of us.

"Yeah. Now that we know his nephews and that dipshit Gabriele aren't involved, he can know."

"The Irish and the Italians have run together in the past. Are you sure Salvatore isn't covering for them, letting them launder through him? He might get a kickback we haven't seen."

I don't think that's the case, even as I suggest it, but it's possible.

"They've murdered each other as many times as they've broken bread. To be honest, Salvatore is still terrified of Ana. After talking to her here, he believes her that she'll be the one to kill him if he and his people come near our women again."

Niko's beaming with pride. Ana—fuck. That woman is definitely half Russian. She might be thin and not look too scary, but I was here when she spoke to Salvatore, and I saw what she did in Greece. She has some Cold War grade determination. He believes she'll come for him if the *Cosa Nostra* gets near her or any of the other women and children. I don't think Niko would stop her, either. Watch her back and hand her a knife, but not stop her.

"Pasha, you make the call. You understand the financial stuff the best. Explain what you and Sumiko found. Let's hear what he has to say."

I take Maks's phone and hit Salvatore's name in the contacts. I put it on speaker as it rings.

"Kutsenko, two calls in one day. That's two too many."

"Wrong Kutsenko. This is Pasha. The videos were—entertaining. Life under the Tuscan sun. Haven't they made movies about that? They need to head a little north. Siberia's beautiful this time of year."

"What do you want?"

"To know why Finn O'Rourke is using your accounts to pay for a hit on me."

"Shut the fuck up, Kutsenko. Put a grown up back on the phone. I'm not interested in playing games."

"Who's controlling Gabriele's accounts while he's gone?"

"None of your fucking—"

"Business. Yeah, well actually it is. Money Finn O'Rourke ran through Gabriele's account, made its way to Palermo then Milan. Guess who owns the Italian account. It sure as shit isn't the Pope. It's a mutual acquaintance. One who shot at me and either planned to turn me over to Finn or you."

"My hands are clean. My nephews and that *piccolo cretino* aren't even in the country. I told you I would take care of them. I did." Little cretin.

"Your hands aren't clean because I watched Finn O'Rourke on camera walk into Gabriele's bank the day he opened a new account then linked it to Gabriele's existing account."

"How the fuck do you know it's Gabriele's account?"

"You don't need to ask that. Stop distracting. Either you're in on this with Finn or you really are shit running your family."

"Motherfucker—"

"Enough." Maks glares at me. "Pasha's not wrong. You've had a mutiny brewing for months. Sending those fuckers to Italy for a fall vacation didn't do shit. Shit's happening under your nose, Salvatore. You look weak, and you are weak. They're playing you, and now the Irish are too. Get your fucking house in order, or I will do it for you. I've already cleaned out the Irish."

"And look where it's gotten you."

"I didn't say I was done sweeping. I'll take out Finn and his entire family if I have to. But in the meantime, check Gabriele's accounts. If you don't believe Pasha or me, we'll send you the statements. You keep letting Luca and Carmine fuck things up for you. You're wasting Marco and Lorenzo. Get Marco to look. He can get into everything Pasha did. Use your fucking accountant to account for what the fuck's happening to your money."

"We'll be in touch. Call when you see that I'm right."

I end the call before Salvatore can have the last word. Maks looks at me as though he wants to slap me.

"What? I irritated him enough that there's no way he's going to blow this off. He'll call in thirty minutes. Less probably if Marco's around."

Maks rolls his eyes, but he knows I'm right. We've been locked away in the office long enough. We head back to join Sumiko, her family, and the rest of ours. They're outside, enjoying the fall sunshine. Sumiko turns toward me with Mila in her arms. My heart squeezes at the sight of her holding a dark-haired baby. She could hold our baby one day. I never wanted kids before meeting Sumiko. I like them well enough, but I didn't want to bring any into the world. Now, I want a real family. Despite all the fucked-up shit we've been through, I love being part of a big family, and I love the idea of giving Mila and Konstantin second cousins or whatever kind they'd be.

"You look so natural, *malyshka*."

"Mila's such a sweet baby. She makes it easy."

I wrap my arm around Sumiko's waist, and she leans against me. I pull back the blanket and watch a tiny fist pop out. I offer my finger, and Mila grips it with surprising strength. She bounces and kicks her legs in her blanket. Swaddling Laura called it.

My mom joins us and watches before our gazes meet. I've seen so much sadness in her eyes over the years. When it's not there, it's usually fear that replaces it. But at times like this, when I see her happy, it confirms how much I want to keep our family going. She's been an incredible mom, and she'll be an amazing *babushka*.

"Mama."

"*Da?*"

Her brow furrows at my serious tone. I extract my finger from Mila's hand and wrap my arm around my mom. I lean over and whisper to her in Russian.

"*Kogda pridet vremya, vy s papoy nauchite menya byt' takim zhe khoroshim roditelem, kak i vy?*" When the time comes, will you and Papa teach me how to be as good a parent as you are?

"*Moy rybka, kogda pridet vremya, ty uzhe budesh' znat'. YA tak gorzhus' toboy, Pasha. Ty nashel podkhodyashchuyu zhen-shchinu, chtoby sozdat' svoyu sobstvennuyu sem'yu.*" My little fish, when the time comes, you will already know. I'm so proud of you, Pasha. You've found the right woman to make your own family.

"Pasha, we have to go."

I look at Aleks as Maks gestures for all of us to head to the house. Sumiko looks up at me, then at her family.

"*Malyshka*, I hate I keep abandoning you. I'm making a horrible impression on your family. How your parents haven't dragged you away from me is anyone's guess."

"They know I would come right back. My mom said someone took my dad for a month when they were still in Brazil. A night is nothing."

She offers me a reassuring smile before we share an all too short kiss, but I still feel badly that I'm not here to support her since her family flew across the country to meet me and see us together. I hug my mom and give her a kiss. Radomir and my dad come inside with us. It would be too questionable if the men started hugging the dads and uncles. But when it's possible, we never leave on a mission without saying goodbye properly.

"Hurry and get back. I have nothing in common with Davi, but he talks my damn ear off."

"I will, Papa."

Then we're piling into the SUVs. We haven't changed, so neither Maks nor Anton expects a firefight. Maks is next to me in the lead SUV. Aleks and Bogdan are in the second row. Misha's driving the one behind me with Sergei, Anton, and Niko. It's Niko's number that flashes as the car's Bluetooth rings.

"What's going on, Maks?"

"Salvatore called like Pasha said he would. He wants a sit down with us in Harlem. It's pretty neutral ground because he said he convinced Finn to show up. I want us in that restaurant first, so our backs are to the walls."

I've already punched in the address to the GPS. I weave through traffic and look around as we approach the restaurant. I'm not doing valet. Never. That shit takes too long when you need to leave in a hurry. I find a spot large enough for Misha to pull in behind me. The eight of us get out of the vehicles and make our way to the front door. People stare, but we're used to it. It's rare for eight men in suits to walk into a restaurant. At least not men like us. We all look around, but none of us spot any *Cosa Nostra* or mob. Normally, Misha and I would position ourselves near doors or the kitchen, but Maks wants me there to discuss the money trail.

Niko goes to the hallway leading to the restrooms. Bogdan is near the kitchen. Misha is by the fire exit, and Aleks is perusing a menu by the front door. Anton and Sergei follow Maks and me to a large table with a reserved sign. The head of the table puts Maks's back to a wall, so he doesn't hesitate to take the seat. I sit to his right. Anton stands behind me while Sergei stands behind Maks.

It's not long before Salvatore shows up with his other nephews, Marco and Lorenzo. Their relative, Matteo, is with them as Salvatore's security. I scan the restaurant and recognize some of the other Italians.

"I'm the one who called for this sit-down."

Salvatore's scowling at Maks, who just cocks an eyebrow. The air changes the moment the O'Rourkes enter. Both my family and Salvatore's are on edge. Finn appears calm walking into the lions' den, but he'd be wise to squeeze his ass cheeks to keep from shitting himself. He drops into his chair as though he doesn't have a care in the world. He's with his brothers and cousins, Dillan, Sean, Shane, Cormac, and Seamus. Until this shit, I actually didn't mind these guys that much. Donovan, Colin, and Declan were another story. Those fuck faces were lucky not to get their entire family killed.

"What do you want, Salvatore? And why are they here?"

Salvatore nods to me. I push a sheet of paper toward Finn. It's a snapshot of several bank accounts on one page. Salvatore pushes a photo across the table. It's a picture of Finn at the bank when he created the account. He doesn't react before turning a blank stare at Salvatore, then me.

"Why are you using one of our accounts to pay for Robert Simms to kill Pasha?"

"I don't know what you mean."

"But you do." I speak up. "Not only did we trace money you put into an account you opened under Gabriele's name, we tracked it to Simms. He's not such a ghost when the two of you leave so many breadcrumbs to follow."

"So Hansel, what are those breadcrumbs? If I remember correctly, Hansel and Gretel got themselves eaten because there were no breadcrumbs to lead them home. Your Gretel is so pretty."

He's baiting me. I remind myself of that. Let him call me

names. I don't give a shit. But not letting myself lose my cool and not lashing out over Sumiko is a battle of wills.

"We have the footage of you at the bank. One that you don't have any of your own accounts at." I point to the photo, then the statements. "And those show the money moving through Gabriele's accounts to Palermo, then Milan. Where they end up in Simms's account."

"If you say so. A couple pieces of paper and photo are about as shitty proof as actual breadcrumbs in a forest. Salvatore, you told me you wanted to discuss how to strike back at Maks. Now you're sucking his dick. We're done."

"Don't lie, Finn. I recorded our conversation because I don't trust you. I'll play it for Maks."

Finn sighs and rolls his eyes.

"You went to a lot of trouble to pit Pablo against me and distract us. I haven't spoken to him recently, but he's going to be pissed."

"Pissed about what? Who do you think gave me the idea?"

I don't believe him. Or rather, I don't want to believe him. I got past planning how to kill Pablo for hurting Sumiko. I don't want to revisit that. But I will. If he had anything to do with scaring my *malyshka* with the text and calls, then I will end him. She tried to hide how much they bothered her, but I knew. She didn't let them ruin our trip, but I know they took time for her to get past each day.

"You're a lot of things, Finn. But you didn't use to be a liar. Power's going to your head. Dillan, aren't you due to lead next? Donovan, Declan, Dillan. Your family's not that original. How'd Finn wind up making any decisions? Clearly, not a good idea."

Maks looks at Dillan, who watches in silence. We suspect Dillan is actually pulling the strings. That's why seeing Finn in the security video shocked us. But if Dillan is issuing the orders, then Finn is just a foot soldier. One he's willing to sacrifice, even though he's close family. It's stupid because Finn is the second smartest person among the O'Rourkes. Maybe that's why he trusted Finn to not fuck this up. Finn's twin brothers, Sean and Shane, are good at carrying out orders, but they aren't leaders. Finn's cousins, Cormac and Seamus, are the same.

Neither Finn nor Dillan flinch. They give nothing away, which tells us plenty. We keep our expressions blank because we're always hiding shit. Now to figure out what is behind those blank Irish stares.

"What I want to know is how you convinced Carmine to send the money to Ignácio."

I look between Salvatore and Finn, but my attention is on Dillan. His brow furrows for no longer than a blink, but I saw it since he's close enough to Finn to keep him in my line of sight. What is going through his head?

I don't have time to formulate an answer. The front door bursts open, and every man reaches for his gun. I wasn't interested in asking questions when we got here, but the restaurant is empty except for us. Now it's filling with Colombians. Fortunately, there aren't any other customers here.

"Having a sit-down, and no one invited us. Or did it get lost in the mail?"

Enrique saunters in, but I'm looking past him at Pablo. I can see him, but he's not facing inside the restaurant. What's going on?

"Where are your little *pendejo* nephews, Salvatore? They've been causing shit that's bad for business."

"In Italy."

"Funny how my shipment from Brazil to Spain wound up in Italy. Imagine my surprise when I got that call an hour ago. What the fuck, Salvatore?"

"I had nothing to do with that."

"Bullshit, *puta.*"

"*Brutto figlio di puttana bastardo.*" Ugly son of a bitch bastard.

"What do you want, Enrique?"

I watch Maks lower his gun as he speaks. It only makes me raise mine higher. He doesn't put it away, but at least it's not pointing at Enrique. His other nephews, Javier, Joaquin, and Jorge are fucking insane. Like legit not right in the head. And that's saying something coming from me. Pablo is the most likely one to be Enrique's chief enforcer in private, but no one wants to tangle with the *Tres J,* as they like to call themselves. Alejandro's with them, and he's levelheaded, so there's hope yet.

"Pablo."

I call out to him because I want to know why he's at the door. He's usually beside his uncle, so something feels off. I look around and meet gazes with each of my family members. They feel it too.

"*Maks, nam nuzhno idti. Plokhaya ideya byt' zdes' so vsemi. Nas slishkom mnogo v odnom meste.*" Maks, we need to go. This isn't a good idea being here with everyone. There's too many of us in one spot.

"*Ya znayu.*" I know.

"We're done here. Stay away from our women. This is the last time any of us will remind you. From now on, it's war. Salvatore, clean your fucking house. Finn, stop licking Dillan's ass. Either lead or get out of the way. His hand is so far up your ass, you're fucking Pinocchio. Your nose keeps growing every time you lie. Enrique, my cousin's relationship is none of your nephew's business. He sticks his nose in it again, and it's likely to get cut off. Along with his dick."

"You don't decide shit, Maksim."

Dillan finally steps forward.

"Taking the training wheels off finally. I decide whatever the fuck I want. Considering how your family has crossed mine lately, I'd sit all the fuck the way down."

Maks is done, and so am I. We didn't get anywhere, but we can leave the other three syndicates to fight amongst themselves. It weakens them and leaves us in a better position. I stand up, but something catches my eyes through the window. It's a reflection through a window across the street. A small circle flashes as it moves left to right. Then I see it. The red dot on Maks's chest. I glance down. I have one too. I launch myself at Maks as I yell.

"Get down."

I tackle my cousin to the floor as gunfire rips through the restaurant. Everyone is looking around since none of it is coming from inside. Not yet, at least.

"Maks, we need to get out before they turn on each other. Someone had their sights on both of us."

"I know."

He uses the same whistle our moms did when they wanted to round us up at the park when we were little. We had to be where they could see us, and we could hear them. The whistle meant it was time to go. I get off him, but we both stay low to the floor. I look around and spot Anton first. He's covering Sergei's back as Sergei leads them toward the door. Misha and Niko are together, and so are Aleks and Bogdan.

"If we're all here, who the fuck is this?"

Niko has to yell over the sound of bullets and furniture breaking. Now that the windows shattered, men are shooting out of the restaurant. There's more than one marksman aiming at us. I try to tell if anyone's been hit. I can see blood splattered on a few walls, but no one has screamed.

"It's Simms."

Pablo is crouched in the doorway, his gun pointed toward

the window, where I saw the reflection. It's only a pistol. It won't do much good.

"How do you know?"

"I had a feeling this was a shitty idea, but *tío* Enrique insisted on coming. If Simms got you, Pasha, then he's watching carefully. He had to know we were all here."

"Has he gone rogue? If we're all here, and he's trying to kill all of us, who the fuck hired him?"

Pablo twists and fires at someone down the street. He dives back into the restaurant as bullets hit the doorframe he was just leaning against.

"I don't know. But someone wants us all dead."

This is not a good time for my phone to go off, but I know the ring tone. How the hell am I supposed to answer Sumiko's call while I'm trying not to get shot? I ignore it. It stops ringing when voicemail must pick up It starts again. It goes to voicemail three times. On the fourth call, I can't ignore it.

"Maks, it's Sumiko. Something's wrong. She's at the house with the others. I have to know."

I inch my way into the kitchen and huddle behind an island. I notice I missed six texts from her. They all say it's urgent. When it rings a fifth time, I answer.

"What's wrong, *malyshka*?"

"What's that noise, Pasha? Oh my God, are those gunshots? Pasha!"

"I'm here, baby girl. What's wrong? Why'd you call so many times?"

"I think Simms is coming after you. Is that him shooting at you?"

"Probably. Him and his team. He must have hired new people. How do you know?"

"One of Laura's former clients, some Chinese businessman,

called as a courtesy. He said his friend's nephew was missing. The man told her Simms is the kid's dad."

"Fuck. Thank you, *malyshka*."

"There's more. I talked to Pablo."

"What?"

A bullet whizzes too close to my head. I can't keep chatting. Even the kitchen isn't safe.

"*Tio* Ignácio recorded the call from who we thought was Carmine. He sent it to my dad. I sent it to Pablo on a hunch. He said it was Dillan O'Rourke."

"Dillan and Pablo are here. But we have to deal with Simms first."

"Be careful, *fofinho*. I love you."

"I will. I love you, *malyshka*. I have to go."

"Bye."

"Bye."

Holy fucking shit. We have to get out of here first. Then we can deal with this. I creep out of the kitchen. Maks and my family have fallen back. They're closer to me than the front door. I'm quick to explain.

"Maks, it's Simms. This is about his son. That's why you and I were the targets."

Anton speaks over his shoulder as he moves in front of me.

"We go out the back, circle around the block and get the guns. Then we go in. It's the building diagonal from this one."

We all make our way to the fire exit, grateful that it doesn't go off when Misha pushes open the door. We might be in suits today, but our paramilitary training takes over the moment each of us steps outside. We fall into the same formations we've used for years. Anton leads with Sergei covering his back. Maks is across the alley with Aleks at his back. Misha and I follow our brothers, while Bogdan and Niko follow theirs. As we round the corner and our SUVs come into sight, the two lead teams are ready to shoot at anything that moves in the wind. But unlike the others inside, they aren't shooting for the sake of it. They're saving their bullets and looking for targets as Misha, Bogdan, Niko, and I bolt for the SUVs.

Misha and I unlock the vehicles as we run. He and Bogdan grab the rifles from the back of his SUV while Niko and I grab the ones from the vehicle I drove. We grab the bags with the scopes and the extra rounds ammo. Each of us slings one semi-automatic over our back while we carry the other, our eyes and barrels roaming our surroundings until we get back to our brothers.

Then it's something of a blur. Yet, everything is in hyper focus. It's a blur because nothing else matters but getting into the building across the street. But that's the same thing that makes me so focused.

"We go over another block, then around to the back of that building. We go in that way."

Anton issues the orders. When there's no assigned leader because shit's gone sideways, it's Anton or Maks who calls the shots. No matter what, Maks will always be at the leader's side. He won't send anyone into a situation he isn't willing to go into first. We hug the shadows as we leave the alley. We're headed away from the ongoing gunshots, but we're vigilant. Who knows who Simms hired? I glance toward the restaurant and see more than one body on the sidewalk. Each has the same type of high-powered rifle I carry. I spot Pablo as he leans out of the door. He aims toward us, but he doesn't shoot. He shifts his attention to someone directly across the street from him and fires. We enter the target building and go up the stairs to the fire exit.

"It's the fourth unit. I counted the windows."

It's the weekend, so the office building is empty. Anton pulls a flashbang from one of the ammo bags. He pushes open the door and tosses it in. We all fall back and press our ears shut. It explodes, and the sound is deafening. It does its job. We enter the office suite and immediately start working our way through. Simms's team wasn't just on the street. We shoot and won't bother asking questions later. We sweep the office, but there's no Simms. The fucker is already gone, or he was never here to begin with.

"Pasha!"

I glance toward Misha, who's pointing to a wall at the far end of the office.

FIND MY SON

It's spray painted on the wall. Simms knew we would come here. He planned it that way, or he knew it was inevitable. We're not finding shit. James is the least of our problems right now. The only person I want to find is Simms. The fucker has done his last job.

"Do you think he's gone?"

Anton comes to stand with me, so I ask his opinion.

"No. Simms is the type to move to a new hidey-hole, then watch to see who's left."

"Do you think he's in this building or somewhere else?"

"Probably a car. That way he can go before anyone catches him."

"Maks, do we look for him?"

He shakes his head as he wipes sweat from his brow. No more gunshots are coming from outside now that we killed the gunmen and women in here.

"We need to find Pablo, and we need to find Dillan. Sumiko said her uncle sent her the recording from when Carmine allegedly tried to set up the deal. She sent it to Pablo, who analyzed it. He said it's Dillan's voice."

"She still trusts Pablo?"

"On this. I think that's the real reason he and Enrique showed up."

Maks nods, and we make our way back out of the building. Anton's on the phone with our cleaning crew that will come to take care of the mess we left. No one will be the wiser by Monday. There're sirens blaring, so we have no choice but to run to the SUVs. With no glass, it's easy to see into the restaurant. It's empty. I scan the streets, and there aren't any SUVs like ours. The Italians, Irish, and Colombians are already gone. How nice of them to run while we finish the job. Typical.

Once I'm behind the wheel of my vehicle, and Misha's in his, we set off for the Kutsenko Partners' office in Manhattan. It's closer than the warehouse, and we can't go back to Maks's to strategize while Sumiko's family is there. We ride in silence as we catch our breath, each of our minds working through what just happened. No one talks until we're in Maks's office. Then I don't hesitate to call Pablo.

"I talked to Sumiko."

I'm not interested in pleasantries.

"I figured. There's no one else you'd take a call from."

"She said it was Dillan on the recording."

"It was. He's recorded my voice and Carmine's at some point. It's obvious he has the equipment, or someone he knows has the equipment, to match the tone and pitch of our voices and overlay it. They're close enough matches to fool anyone not listening hard."

"So it was Dillan who wanted to set up the trade with Ignácio. He wanted us at each other's throat to disrupt our trade with the Brazilians, assuming trapping Sumiko in the middle would piss off Ignácio. He used Carmine and Gabriele to take the fall in case it didn't work."

"Yeah."

"Except he never imagined a forensic accountant would get

involved. I'm certain he assumed Sumiko would never have access to the software needed to hack the bank systems, even if she had the tracking software at work."

"That's what I assumed. What now? We didn't know the O'Rourkes were going to be there. We came to tell you. Sumiko must have gotten scared and called you to be sure you knew."

"She didn't trust you to tell us."

"Or she thought shit might go sideways, and you'd kill me before I got to talk."

I cock an eyebrow, even though he can't see it. I doubt my girlfriend is that worried about Pablo anymore. He came up as we talked about our future last night. Damn, that feels like days ago. She's in the same place Laura is. She considers their friendship over, but she can be civil. If it comes to us versus them, she said she'd turn her back on Pablo without a second thought.

"Pasha, I promised her I wouldn't call or text again, and I won't. She made her choice, and I don't want to die."

"You're right. I would kill you. I'm choosing to believe you about Dillan and about staying away from Sumiko. But I don't trust you any more now than I did before I met her. I'll put a bullet between your eyes, then go home for dinner with her and not think about you for a moment."

"Keep her safe, and there won't be any need for me to be involved. But all bets are off if she's in danger."

"Do you love her?"

"No."

I believe that. I doubt Pablo is capable of love, or at least, he's not capable of allowing himself to love. We suspect Pablo's been forced into a role no single person should bear. My cousins, my brother, and Sergei and Misha share the burden of dealing with our warehouse guests. The brunt of the coercing doesn't fall on one person's shoulders. We think in the Diaz

Cartel, it all falls to Pablo. None of us are the boys we knew growing up, but there's a darkness to Pablo.

"Fine. Thank you for the intel, but why?"

"I may not love her, but she's a good person. I couldn't give two shits whether you draw your next breath, but she does. She'd be devastated if you died, and she doesn't deserve that. If this helps keep her safe, all the better."

"I can accept that."

"I don't care if you can. It is what it is. What're you doing about O'Rourke? And what's the deal with Simms?"

"Simms is back in the wind. He's not done yet since Maks and I were the targets, and we're still alive."

"How do you know that?"

"I saw the dots on us."

I won't share anything about James. I don't want to make him a target, and I'm not giving Pablo any more info than he needs. He might not come after me, but that doesn't mean another member of his family wouldn't if they think they could get a bounty for me.

"Are you just going to wait until he comes calling again?"

Pablo's questions bring me back to the conversation.

"No. I may have a way to track him. We'll see. Are you dealing with O'Rourke?"

"I figured you'd want to do that. It was your girlfriend he threatened and her family he involved."

"He was willing to pin part of the blame on you."

"He's not worth my time. *Tío* Enrique isn't interested, either."

"I'm sure you'll hear whatever happens."

"I'm sure I will."

I hang up with him and look at my family. The call was on speaker, so they heard all of it. Maks crosses his arms.

"Pasha, he went after your woman. What do you want to do?"

"We've taken out one of the Irish warehouses at the docks and another upstate. We've killed half his family. Unless we take out the members that were there today, they're going to keep coming back. Except we can't take them all out. The Murphys will only take their place, and that's the last thing we need. They aren't ready to run in our circles. They'll fuck up business. We're better with the O'Rourkes. The Devil we know. But this doesn't go unpunished. The Dubliner in Midtown is a free-standing building. It's also their biggest money maker of all their pubs. It's time for a gas leak. They're closed tomorrow since they're such good Catholics and all."

"That's it?"

Niko is appalled. I almost laugh. It's not quite the vigilante justice he got after Ana was taken. But I'm not even close to done.

"Nope. Their connections to gun running from Ireland aren't that strong now that they don't have family involved. We shut them out of that business entirely. It's their ships that go back and forth. Get rid of those, and they can't get the weapons here. But we take them out one at a time. That way we get the last shipments and sell them as our own."

I smile as one last idea pops into my head.

"You know that pony Dillan's paying an insane amount to train? The one that's supposed to win at least one cup next year. It's headed on a slow boat to China. Horse racing is a big deal in Hong Kong. It's our way of smoothing out Wing-hung's ruffled feathers over James. Finding the kid isn't our problem. We'll let him know we set the horse free from Dillan, just like we set James free from Simms."

I think we'll always think of him as Robert Simms. We've

known him as that for too long to associate another name with him. Maks surmises my plan.

"You want to hit their businesses, but you're letting Dillan know this is personal."

"Yes. If we can't kill any more of them because that'll ruin the balance of power among the four syndicates, we make their lives miserable."

I look at the men I've known my entire life. We're not immortal, but as a family, we are invincible. Somehow, we just came out of that shootout unscathed. None of us have even a scratch. I don't know about the other families. The thing about being in the mafia is, you know your rivals, and you'll do what you have to, to remain on top. But if none of you were mafia, you'd probably be best friends. We're all too much alike. And that's where the trouble starts.

Chapter Thirty-Two

Sumiko

I have to pull my shit together. This is what I signed up for. I suppose it's a good thing that I'm seeing what life with Pasha is like before we get married. I know he'd let me leave if that's what I wanted. But it's not. I'm not going into this with my eye closed. I'm getting an introduction that won't soon be forgotten, but I can accept it. However, that doesn't make this any less scary. It's been hours since Pasha left and since I last spoke to him. He sent a text to say he's safe and that he has plans for us. I could only shake my head when he sent a string of eggplant and peach emojis to go with that message. He must be all right.

My uncle called my dad after having time to think. He'd calmed down once he knew my dad was safe, and he remembered he'd recorded the call from the American with the heavy Italian accent. He sent it to my dad, and I listened to it. The accent wasn't nearly as good as the Spanish one they engineered for the call Pablo supposedly made. That's what made me think it wasn't legit. I wasn't hot on the idea of calling Pablo and asking for help, but Laura was right. Without Sergei around, Pablo was the only person we knew who could do it. It didn't seem like something we should wait on.

While I was on the phone with Pablo, Laura got the call from her former client. Who doesn't that woman know? You would never guess the mom of two with a small private practice with one client was once a major corporate attorney with clients in Eastern Europe and Asia, all of whom had dubious business holdings. But her fluency in Russian and Chinese made her invaluable to her firm. Her clients weren't loyal to that firm, but they are loyal to her.

Between what the Wo Shing Wo guy told Laura and knowing the voice on the recording was fake, I knew I had to text Pasha. When he didn't respond, I got scared. When he wouldn't answer, I pictured his phone broken next to his dead body. I won't let myself imagine that again.

"*Malyshka?*"

I nearly jump out of my skin. I'm in the garden by myself. I needed some air. I spin around as Pasha's arms encircle my waist.

"Daddy."

My kiss is frantic as my hands roam over his face and shoulders. He squeezes my ass hard enough to lift me onto my toes. We're near the shed that has the pool supplies. He walks me backwards until we get to the door. I reach behind me and turn the knob, grateful it's unlocked. We stumble into the little building. But it's big enough for what we need. He spins me toward the wall. I push down my jeans and thong, hoping for what comes next.

"You know how I feel about you and panties. You did this on purpose."

"I'm sorry, Daddy."

"No, you're not. But you will be, baby girl."

375

His hand lands against my ass, and it's like everything is right in the world again. We restore the balance in our lives, and we're together how we're supposed to be. Pasha's in control, and I can trust that I'm safe with him.

He only spanks me five times across both cheeks, then my lacy thong is in shreds around my ankles. I spread my feet as wide as my jeans allow. His arm goes around my waist as his other hand pinches my right nipple. Then he's inside me, and we're both sighing.

"Is this what you need, *malyshka*? Do you need to know Daddy's here to protect you and pleasure you?"

"Yes, Daddy. I was scared."

"I know, baby girl. I was too. I was scared I wouldn't get home to you. And I was scared something might happen here if we were all under attack at that restaurant."

"All?"

"Yeah. All four syndicates were there, which is never a good idea unless it's a very public event."

"It was painfully quiet here."

"It won't be for long. I'm going to make you scream."

"Hard, Daddy. I need to feel you, know you're really okay."

"I'm okay now that I'm with you. I just need you in my arms. I need to hear your voice, baby girl. Keep talking."

He's thrusting into me, his chin resting on my shoulder. There's so much strength wrapped around me. It's restrained, but it could snap me in half. But I've never feared Pasha, and I won't. Even at our roughest, he's always aware, always careful with me.

"*Fofinho*, I can't wait until we can have a quiet evening at home, just the two of us. I love our family, but I just want you."

"Our family? Just one?"

"Your family has welcomed me. As far as I'm concerned, you're part of my family. So yes, just one."

He thrusts into me harder. He's sharing emotions he either can't verbalize or doesn't want to. He's vulnerable, and he's not sure how to deal with it. That's why he's taking me from behind. I understand. I reach back and wrap my hand around his head.

"I love you so much, *malyshka*."

"I love you, too."

We fall into silence as we move together until I can't wait.

"Daddy, may I come?"

"Yes, baby girl."

I don't hold back. I clench my hand into his hair, and my nails dig into the hand around my middle. I don't scream, aware that we don't need to draw any of the guards to us, but I release a moan that fills the shed. He grunts once more before he pins me against him.

"Sumiko."

It's a reverent sigh as he comes. This dark and brooding man who does monstrous things has a heart of gold. He loves with all of it, and I'm fortunate to be a recipient.

"Baby girl, you're such a brave and strong woman. I know I can lean on you in a way I never thought I would with a woman. You love me, and I'm better for it. I hate that I cause any fear in your life. Thank you for admitting your feelings. I don't want you to feel like you have to swallow those feelings to be strong. You already are."

He steps back, and neither of us likes that moment when we draw apart. He eases me away from the door and turns me to face him. We gaze into each other's eyes. No words. Nothing physical beyond our embrace. We share so much as our eyes lock. Our silent communication is just as powerful as the words we speak. We move in sync, cupping a cheek and pressing our lips together. We rest our foreheads against each other before I rest my head against his chest. We stand together, in no hurry to do anything but be in the moment.

But we both know we can't hide in here for forever. I look down at my shredded panties. Pasha squats and rips them all the way off. His smile is wolfish as he stands. His pants are back on, and he shoves the remnants of the thong in his pocket. I pull my jeans up and run my fingers through my hair. We return to the house as three other couples quietly rejoin the others. No one says anything, but I feel my cheeks heat as I see my parents. It's obvious what we've all been up to, and I don't love my parents knowing I just had sex. It's embarrassing.

"Did the cops find whoever broke into your businesses?"

Cris looks at Pasha, curiosity and concern are clear in his tone and his expression. Pasha tightens his hold on my hand as we face this together.

"It's all still under investigation."

"I can't believe you had more than one place broken into."

Pasha glances at my parents. We told my brothers and Helena that there was more than one burglary, and some expensive products were taken. Laura, Christina, and Ana corroborated that story. Alina and the other parents reassured everyone that the men were simply busy. Davi asked if they were in danger. I didn't know what to say, but Grigori assured them they had security with them.

"Whoever this is thought they could spread us thin, but we have plenty of resources at our disposal."

Pasha's tone diminishes the gravity of the situation, but my brothers and Helena appear mollified. My parents look less anxious than they did when the men got home. It's not like I want to rush my family back to California, but this turned out to be a super inopportune time for them to visit. But I wonder if there will ever be an opportune one. I think I'll talk to Christina about how she handles keeping Bogdan's life and our family's—

"dealings"—secret from her brothers and their families. I could use some advice.

"Have you set a new date? Do we need to go dress shopping?"

Helena's excitement and abrupt change of subject makes everyone in the know relax. Cris chuckles and kisses his wife's cheek. She beams up at him, and I realize the novelty of so many hot men under one roof has worn off.

"We haven't set a date, but dress shopping sounds, um, fun."

"Daunting is more like it."

Ana laughs, and I know I look guilty since that's what I was really thinking.

"Would all of you ladies like to come with me? You'll all be in the wedding."

With more groomsmen than bridesmaids, the photos might be lopsided. But as I look around the room, my heart fills that I'm joining a family that loves so big and so hard.

"Isn't it bad luck to see the groom before the wedding, *malyshka*?"

"Shh. Or someone is going to hear—oh. Daddy, more. I—"

"What, baby girl? Do you like it when Daddy tastes you?"

Pasha sneaked into the bathroom in the room we've shared at Maks and Laura's. I'm trying to put my makeup on since the wedding starts in half an hour. I turned down the offer for a professional makeup artist, but I got my hair done. If we mess it up, I'll be pissed, and everyone'll know.

Fuck. Pasha's tongue. God damn the things it does to me. I try to press his head to my pussy, but he grasps both of my wrists. He pulls them behind me, crosses them, and holds them in one hand as the other slaps my ass. It pushes my hips forward, and his tongue sinks into me deeper. He'll give me what I want, but on his terms. I love it.

"I'm close, Daddy."

He pulls away. Shit. I should have taken the punishment instead.

"I want to make you come, Daddy."

I drop my robe to the floor. I planned for Pasha not to see my lingerie until tonight, but fuck, I need him. His eyes devour me, and now I worry he's going to tear it off me. He's shredded plenty of my other lingerie. Nighties, two teddies, a bra, and pretty much every pair of panties I've worn since meeting him.

"You are too tempting, *krasivaya*."

"You can't stand before the minister like that."

I look down at his dick, which is pushing against his trousers. There's no hiding his hard on when he's that endowed. I reach for his pants, but he grasps my wrists.

"I'm not ready for you to come, and I won't get off without you."

He reaches into his pocket, and I recognize the little velvet pouch.

"You want me to have those in me during our wedding? How am I supposed to concentrate on our vows? Pasha, I don't want to think about anything but that."

He puts the pouch back in his pocket.

"Fine. But your pussy is mine for the reception."

"My pussy is always yours, Daddy."

"Good girl."

"So about that hard on?"

"Do you think you deserve to come before the wedding?"

"Before and after."

Pasha glances out the window to where chairs are set up in the backyard. No one but guards patrolling the grounds are out there yet. Everyone else is getting ready and guests haven't shown up yet. I invited Sarah to be one of my bridesmaids. We're both disappointed Tiffany can't be with us, but her mom is in hospice. I suspect we'll be flying to California soon. Maks offered the jet on a moment's notice. I've invited some other friends, and I know there will be bratva members here soon.

"We have time. But barely. This is going to be quick."

"And hard."

"I'm always hard around you."

"Daddy."

I pretend to sound exasperated as he slips the silk and lace thong down my legs. He unfastens the bustier and lays it on the counter. He hoists me into the air, and I wrap my legs around him. His fingers dig into my thighs, and I know he loves the feel. He's told me, and he's shown me. I don't dislike them nearly as much as I used to. He's in me with one thrust. I'm dripping for him. Probably not the state a bride should be in when she shows up for her wedding.

"Fuck you're tight, *malyshka*."

"Wait until you get that plug in me tonight."

"You're going to make me come just thinking about that."

He surges into me over and over, his pubic bone rubbing my clit. Our kiss is sloppy and desperate as we hurry. I lean away, breathless.

"Please."

It's a panted whisper.

"Now."

That's all it takes. That and one more thrust. I detonate. It's one of the strongest orgasms I've ever had. Knowing I'm about to marry my soulmate is its own kind of aphrodisiac. I feel him pulse inside me, and his body goes stiff. He turns us, so his back is against the wall, holding him up.

"I don't want to put you down, but I suppose you don't wish to get married with people seeing my cock in your cunt."

"That probably wouldn't be appropriate. Though it's actually kinda romantic. We're joining our lives, so having our bodies joined at the same time is sweet."

"That could probably only happen at a sex club, and that is not where I want our wedding."

"Uh, neither do I. Though they've always intrigued me."

"They have?"

"Yeah."

I shrug. I've heard about them, but I've never been. I like the idea of acting out scenes with stuff we don't have or probably couldn't have at our place. Not unless we had some kind of sex dungeon. I'm not sure what to make of Pasha's speculative look. Who knows what I might come home to? We put a bid on a house yesterday in Queens, near everyone else's. The owners accepted on the spot since it was cash.

"Come on, *malyshka*. We need to hurry before someone comes looking for one of us."

With a grumble, he hands my thong to me. I snatch it and drop a kiss on his cheek.

"I fully expect not to be taking that home with us."

He helps me with the bustier hooks, and I slip my robe on. With one last kiss as he fastens his belt into place, I watch him walk out of the bathroom. I don't hear the door, but I know he's gone. I hurry to finish my makeup. I've just set out my lipstick when someone knocks.

"Come in."

My mom, Alina, Sarah, Ana, Christina, and Laura enter.

"Helena's on her way. She's changing her shoes. She realized stilettos in grass are a bad idea."

My mom loves Helena, but she finds my sister-in-law's fashion choices impractical. They are, but she always looks beautiful. The ladies help me into my gown. My family can't stay much longer, so it was a scramble to get my ring, my dress, and arrange for a reception with two days' notice. But the Kutsenko name and their cash can be very convincing. We agreed on a Methodist minister from the church I attend somewhat regularly. I suggested Russian Orthodox, but Pasha looked super uncomfortable. He explained he felt way too guilty to have one officiate after all that he's done. It broke my heart to realize his faith is still strongly ingrained, but he believes he's too far past redemption. I didn't want to get into that, and I haven't let myself ponder that quandary, but it was still so sad.

"Sweetheart, you look stunning. If I didn't know better, I would think it was custom made for you."

I was worried I wouldn't find a dress that fit well. I'm on the line between regular sizes and plus-size, feeling more comfortable in the latter. Things usually fit one part of me but not another, but this gown is perfect. It was the first and only one I tried on. I knew as soon as I stepped out of the dressing room.

"Thank you. I love it. It's a shame I only get to wear it once."

"I'm putting mine on every anniversary. It's getting more use than one day since it was a small fortune."

Ana laughs, but she's serious. Just like I seem to have naturally leaned toward the heavier side, Ana can eat nearly as much as Aleks, but she's still thin. Maybe she'll fill out with age and if she has kids, but I suspect she'll still be able to fit in her gown in thirty years.

Christina steps in front of me as she adjusts my veil.

"Can you teach me how to do makeup like yours? I think I do all right for day-to-day, but I feel like a clown when I try to do smoky eyes like that."

Christina barely wears any makeup. None of us really do,

but I probably wear the most because I like it. It's art to me. I'm my own canvas, and I enjoy trying out new things. I can't draw for shit or even paint in real life, but somehow I get makeup.

"Of course. I can show you how to bring the smoke show. Just don't let Bogdan see you until you're home. Nobody needs to see him maul you. The man can't stop touching you."

Laura blows out a puff of air.

"They're all like that."

"I wouldn't have Niko any other way. Would you want your man any different?"

"No."

I giggle. It's Alina who answers first. She shrugs. Grigori isn't any better than his son. But I love seeing them together and Svetlana with Radomir. I'm sad that Galina can't have that with Kirill. I asked Pasha while we were in Croatia if Galina would ever remarry. His answer was instantaneous and decisive. She won't. Kirill was her soulmate, and she'll never want anyone else. She misses him too much. They were childhood sweethearts. They'd been inseparable since they were five. I can't imagine that kind of loss. I pray I never do as I look out the window at people gathering on the lawn.

"Are you ready?"

"Almost, Mom. I just need to put on my lipstick. I didn't want to risk getting it on my gown."

I put it on and wonder for a moment if the red is too much. I add a touch of gloss, and I know it's not. I smile conspiratorially to myself in the mirror. I even cock an eyebrow at my reflection.

All I see as I step onto the terrace is a line of massive men next the minister. All eight of them are there. Anton elbows Pasha, and he spins around. I can see his smile from a million miles away. I barely notice my dad as I take his arm. I just want my bridesmaids to run. I want to get to my groom. I'm wearing my veil, and I make sure to turn my head away from Pasha when my dad lifts it high enough to kiss my cheek.

I have never meant anything more than the vows I pledge to Pasha. His voice is deeper than usual, and I hear the emotion in it as much as I see it in his eyes. He's hiding nothing from me right now. He doesn't care who sees it because it's all for me.

"I now pronounce you husband and wife. Mr. Kutsenko, you may kiss your bride."

He lifts back my veil, and his eyes narrow as he sees my lipstick. I knew it would tempt him. He wraps his arms around me, and his embrace is tight.

"Mrs. Kutsenko, I will remind you of this later."

"Do you promise, Daddy?"

"Absolutely."

We share our first kiss as a married couple. There is no one but us. We're in a world that's only made of the two of us.

Epilogue

Pasha

I watch Sumiko as her gaze sweeps over the massive, dark room. She's cautious not to stare at anything or anyone. She's trying to take in everything, and I know it's a lot. I'm not prepared for it, and I'm the one who planned this outing.

"Is this—"

"Yes, *malyshka*. We will satisfy your curiosity tonight."

It's the club Maks belonged to before he met Laura. I knew he did, but I didn't know Laura belonged to one, too. That was a revelation. When I asked him if he could get us guest passes, if there was such a thing, he asked which one I wanted to go to. I didn't know what he meant. That's when he let it slip. He saw my shock and made me swear no one else could know unless it came from Laura. I saw my life flash before my eyes as he stared at me. I haven't agreed to anything he's said that fast since I was a kid, and he was already a teenager.

"I didn't know you belonged to a place like this."

"I don't. I know someone who pulled some strings."

"This isn't what I thought you meant about a surprise when we got back from our honeymoon."

"Two weeks in Croatia was wonderful, but I admit I've been looking forward to this."

"How do we know where to go, Daddy?"

She falls into the role as easily as she always does. I never imagined hearing a woman call me that could be so—I don't even know, so—everything.

"I think that woman's coming to give us a tour. I was told we could have a look around, then decide what we want."

"Are we only doing scenes with the two of us?"

That makes me pause.

"Um. Do you want someone else to join us?"

"Do you?"

"*Malyshka*, do not answer a question with a question. I wish to fulfill your curiosity and your fantasies."

Please don't let her say she wants a threesome. It might kill me, but I would do it if that's what she wants.

"No. But I will if that's what you want."

"You look as miserable as I feel at that idea. I sure as fuck don't want to see you with another man. And the idea of touching another woman makes me ill."

"I feel that way, but in reverse."

I breathe easier, and I think she does too.

"Welcome. I'm one of the DMs, or Dungeon Monitors. I'll give you a tour and get you started. If you have questions, you can ask me or you can stop anyone with an armband like mine. We need you to sign the consent forms and code of conduct."

She points to the band on her right arm with the large letters DM on it before she shows us to a desk where we fill out our paperwork.

"Thank you."

I hold Sumiko's hand as we walk through an expansive

space where people appear to mingle while others act out scenes. We continue past closed doors, sounds filtering through them. We peek into various empty ones, but none suit us. Neither of us is interested in the little girl's room. That's not what Daddy means to us. The doctor's office and the classroom are interesting, but they don't excite us.

"This one, Daddy."

Sumiko whispers to me as we look at a room in dark colors. I'm thinking about suggesting we go back to the classroom, or we play doctor. Anyone who only wants vanilla would probably look at this as a torture chamber. I've never used a whip or flogger on anyone but Sumiko. But the chains and rods, the cuffs attached the wall—that's way too familiar. There's a huge St. Andrew's Cross to the left. The large wooden X has restraints dangling from it. But I swallow my discomfort when I look down at Sumiko. This is what she wants.

"Do you want people to observe?"

"No."

We answer together, and the DM smiles.

"When you are finished, find me or another DM."

"Thanks."

Sumiko returns the woman's smile before the DM closes the door. I assume there's some way the DM makes it obvious this room is taken and not for voyeurism. I don't even know if that's the right word for people who wish to watch if they're at a BDSM club, and it's consensual. I'm definitely not asking Maks.

"This is why you surprised me with the lingerie."

"Yes. Are you all right with being here?"

"Yes, Daddy. This is the perfect way to end our honeymoon."

Shit's still not right with the Irish, and we can't find Simms or his son. But those aren't my problem right now.

"Strip for me, *malyshka*."

There's a speaker that I can connect my phone to. I've already created a playlist for tonight. I turn it on, keeping the volume low. I lean against the wall, my arms crossed, one ankle over the other. She's wearing the same dress she wore in Anguilla when I found her at the club. I suggested it for tonight, even though I worried it might be too chilly now that we're in mid-fall.

My cock aches as she eases the dress down her body. She's in thigh highs, which I didn't know about. Those make my cock twitch. She's in the lacy midnight blue bra and panties I got her. She's wearing a pair of black high heels, and her legs look amazing. All of her does.

"Turn around, *malyshka*."

She does and wiggles her ass. I'm ready to pounce. But I hold myself back.

"Pick what you want me to use."

She glances back at me before she walks to the wall and picks out a riding crop. She looks at the ball gag, but I can guess what she's thinking. She might not mind using a riding crop someone else has, but putting something in her mouth is a different story.

"I know this has touched who knows how many vages, but I can't with the ball gag."

I know my baby girl. She picks out a few more things and walks to the St. Andrew's Cross. There's padding where the beams intersect. There are also cut-outs for the restraints that accommodate various heights. I follow her over, but I still don't touch her.

"Put them on the table and fasten your ankles."

"Yes, Daddy."

She's quick to follow my instructions.

"What's your safe word?"

"Kale."

"You know it's not a failure or a disappointment if you use it, right?"

"Yes, Daddy."

We lose track of time as we work our way around the room. The St. Andrew's Cross entertains us the longest, as I have her face away and to me. She finds the spanking bench a bit awkward, but she loves my bare hand against her ass. But our favorite is the tantra chair. We've already agreed that's the first piece of furniture we're buying for our house. The positions we try are incredibly intimate, and we make love at a BDSM club. That's something I never thought would happen in this lifetime. Only with my *malyshka*.

Don't miss the next installment

Preorder and have it ready when you wake on Dec 13th.

Our worlds couldn't be further apart...

She's light. I'm dark. She's an angel. I'm a devil.

I'll never walk away from my life with the bratva.

My only choice is to bring her in.

She's mine and always will be.

Maybe she doesn't know we're soulmates yet, but I have since we met.

I'll do anything to protect her. No one's foolish enough to stop me.

And if they are...

I'll take her to the limits of what she thinks she can handle, then I'll please her any way she wants.

The Bratva Angel is an interconnecting, standalone Dark Mafia Romance with a HEA and no cliffhanger. It contains extra-steamy scenes that will make your toes curl and your granny blush. This is book five in *The Ivankov Brotherhood*, a six-book series that'll keep you warm at night.

Preorder now for Dec 13th.

Thank you for reading Bratva Beauty

Sabine Barclay, a nom de plume also writing Historical Romance as Celeste Barclay, lives near the Southern California coast with her husband and sons. Growing up in the Midwest, Celeste enjoyed spending as much time in and on the water as she could. Now she lives near the beach. She's an avid swimmer, a hopeful future surfer, and a former rower. She loves writing romances that will make your toes curl and your granny blush.

Subscribe to Sabine's bimonthly newsletter to receive exclusive insider perks.

www.sabinebarclay.com

Join the fun and get exclusive insider giveaways, sneak peeks, and new release announcements in
Sabine Barclay's Facebook Dubious Dames Group

Do you also enjoy steamy Historical Romance? Discover Sabine's books written as Celeste Barclay.

The Ivankov Brotherhood

Bratva Darling

BOOK ONE SNEAK PEEK

LAURA

As I sit across from the four Kutsenko brothers, I press my lips together to keep from drooling. No four men should be so strikingly handsome. Not all from the same family, anyway. I fight a valiant battle against letting my gaze drift toward the eldest, Maksim, whose ice-blue eyes bore into me. After years of negotiating billion-dollar investment contracts while facing countless ruthless businessmen, I've learned to keep my expression studiously blank. But it's a true struggle today. Instead, I focus my attention on the squirrelly lawyer sitting across the conference table. While he's disingenuous with each comment, he's a good negotiator. But I'm better. How cliché am I?

While I feel Maksim watching me, I focus on Dmitry Yakovitch as he continues to argue the merits of the venture capitalist company I represent, RK Capital Group, merging with Kutsenko Partners. What he means is the merits of Kutsenko Partners acquiring RK Capital Group, then stripping it and making it another money-laundering shell corporation. While most people in New York have little awareness of the Russian mafia, I do. The Kutsenko brothers' names appear on no titles or deeds anywhere in New York City, but it wasn't difficult to determine which shell companies likely belong to them. Their assumption that I'm unfamiliar with them is proving beneficial to me as they continue to whisper amongst themselves in Russian. I think they may even believe they're convincing me that they don't speak much English.

The senior partners of RK Capital Group know who I'm negotiating with, though they may not know I'm aware of these Russians' more nefarious operations. They've given me the go-ahead to agree to a merger with an eventual acquisition, but only for the right price. A price to the tune of twenty billion dollars. Considering an investment firm like Goldman Sachs is worth nearly one-hundred-and-twenty billion dollars, my clients' asking price appears reasonable.

"Mr. Yakovitch, I shall stop you now." I raise my left hand, pen caught between my index and middle fingers. When I have his attention, I lean back in my chair and casually twirl the pen over my index finger and thumb. "Fifty billion is my clients' asking price. You know that. Your clients know that. RK doesn't oppose the merger. What they oppose is the insulting offer you've made. It's nearly noon, and I'm hungry, Mr. Yakovitch. I have a delicious ham sandwich waiting for me. I even have three chocolate chip cookies waiting for me. If we aren't going to make any progress, I shall let you go, so I can move onto my eagerly anticipated lunch."

I cant my head just enough for me to appear as though my gaze rests solely on the opposing attorney's face, but I can see each Kutsenko brothers' reaction. My face battles yet again against showing my emotions as I fight not to smirk. Their muted but surprised expressions confirm what I already know.

"Please tell your clients to make a reasonable counteroffer, or I will conclude this meeting and enjoy my ham sandwich and cookies."

Dmitry glares at me before turning to Maksim and his three brothers. In rapid Russian, he doesn't interpret my suggestion. Oh no. There's no need for that. I can't catch every word because his voice is too low. But I catch something along the lines of "The bitch refuses to budge. What now? A fucking ham sandwich. More like a stick up her ass."

Maksim swivels his chair to look at his brothers. In Russian, he says, "Fifty billion is ridiculous. She's not so stupid or naïve not to know that. My guess is they'll settle for twenty billion. We offer fifteen."

"That's barely better than what we already offered," Aleksei, the second-oldest brother, argues. "She'll be eating the fucking sandwich and dipping her cookies in milk before we walk out the door. We need the buildings."

"We offer twenty, Maks," Bogdan, the youngest, insists.

As I watch the brothers discuss, their voices barely lowered, I pull my lunch sack from the black leather satchel by my feet and set it beside my laptop. It's a ridiculously pink floral bag with an embroidered monogram, the L and D overlapping. It's an empty prop, but they don't know that. I watch as five sets of eyes narrow. I offer a smile that would appear innocent in any setting other than this meeting. It's patronizing, and I know it.

Bratva Sweetheart

Bratva Treasure

Bratva Beauty

Bratva Angel (Coming 12.13.22)

Bratva Jewel (Coming 1.24.23)

www.ingramcontent.com/pod-product-compliance
Lightning Source LLC
Chambersburg PA
CBHW020525110726
47899CB00004B/1251